CRUEL SECRETS

by

KERRY BARNES

Dedication

Penny Mcallen, my friend of 47 years.

Class of 81

Dedicated to all the pupils who attended Walsingham school.

Any reference to the school in the book is purely fictional, because sadly the school closed on 31ˢᵗ August 1990.

Acknowledgements

Writing is always regarded as a solitary occupation, but I owe a great debt to my editor Robert Wood who generously gave me so much of his time and invaluable input. Without him this book would probably be unreadable.

Deryl Easton who has supported me and has always been there to lift me up when I lack confidence and feel like giving up.

I would like to thank all the members of the Notrights book club, The Crime book club and my supporters in The Beech Tree pub and The Ocean Inn.

I would also like to thank my brother, Adam, for his input over the summer, whilst landscaping my garden.

Cruel Secrets

CHAPTER ONE

Using all her strength, she gripped her victim's throat, squeezing it as tightly as she could. It proved to be more strenuous than she could ever have imagined. The unsuspecting woman, in her docile state, fought with every ounce of her life, and of course she would have done because she had so much to live for.

The vision of blood on her hands and the gory mess she was about to make of her victim should have shadowed her mind with tremendous guilt, for as long as her heart would beat. She picked up the long carving knife. It would be like gutting a fish. She knew she would feel nothing when she had accomplished the task. But surely the ultimate prize would be worth it, wouldn't it?

Little did she know that the reward would be a few meagre words of insincere gratitude.

....

Kelly looked in the tiny mirror in the bathroom, the only one in the house, and sighed at the state of her boring face, with her long, limp hair just hanging there either side of her face. Not even a fringe or a trim. God forbid she even suggested hair bobbles to her mother. She hated being called Jezebel and hated the elastic bands even more. The first day back at school, after the summer holidays, was going to be another reminder she was a prisoner in her mother's house. She looked again at her face and lowered her eyes; she hated what she saw, not even a golden glow from the sun. Not surprising, since she was kept inside most of the time, but only to study. The truth was, her mother didn't want to lay eyes on her, and so the best thing all round was to remain out of sight in the bare, cold, characterless bedroom. Then she heard her mother's shrill voice screaming up the stairs. "Hurry up, you will miss your bus. If I call you again, it will be with a sharp reminder!"

Knowing exactly what that meant, she hurtled down the stairs, two at a time, snatched her jacket and bag, and was there at the door for a full inspection. Maureen, her mother, looked her up and down through mean, beady eyes and sniffed the air. "I expect you home at 4.15, and this year, I will want to see higher grades, so no slacking. Do I make myself clear?"

Kelly nodded, and left, desperate to get out of the house and away from those burning, hateful stares from her mother. How could she get higher grades? All her subjects were A stars. If she got any higher, she would be teaching the class herself. Yet no academic knowledge she gained from school was going to prepare her for the outside world.

As soon as Kelly stepped off the bus, she sighed, looking down at those wretched long white socks. Her mother was strict and every rule had to be obeyed, including the knee length skirt and childish flat shoes. As the other girls from her estate clambered off, gossiping with excitement, Kelly bit her lip. *If only she could be a part of it all.* She heard them at the back of the bus, talking about the fun they'd had during the summer holidays. Kelly could only imagine what it would be like to go to a party, a barbecue, or even just hang out over at the park with friends. She wasn't included in their little chit-chats; she wasn't like them, and she had her mother to blame for that.

Penny was the last to get off the bus; she was a trendy girl with a seriously confident personality. She skipped past Kelly, almost knocking her out of the way.

"Soz, Churchy," she laughed and ran to meet the popular group of girls. She wasn't sorry because she didn't really give a shit, and yet Kelly still admired her.

Entering the classroom, it was the same old, same old; some sniggered and some nodded. Kelly took her place just behind Penny's chair. Penny, however, was late as usual, even though she got off the bus at the same time. Just as the teacher was about to call the register, the girl walked in as brazen as you like, wearing a short skirt and the tightest white blouse with her tie in a double knot. Kelly watched, smiling to herself. *Were the class about to witness one of Penny's little cameo performances?* she wondered.

With a way-out hairstyle, shaved on the one side and her fringe dyed pink, Penny looked cool with a self-assured edge. Her shoes were well over the three-centimetre rule but she didn't give a toss. The teachers had tried detention and even exclusion, but she just laughed it off. Kelly thought about herself; if she received detention, her mother would beat her with a stick and make her say twenty-five Hail Marys.

The smell from the newly polished parquet flooring filled the classroom. It was a recognisable odour common to many schools. The first day back after the summer holidays was always the same, with the kids clucking like chickens. The new starters were either cocky because they had an older sibling or nervous because they were alone. The fifth and sixth formers breezed past; they had no worries unless they were anxious to start the year with good intentions to do well for their final exams. Walsingham was a large school; back in the seventies, they had merged the boys and girls to form a mixed comprehensive, and so for the new starts it was incredibly daunting.

Johnnie Kent sat next to Penny, eyeing her up and down. He was the best-looking guy in the school and didn't he know it. Penny stuck her middle finger up at him and then blew a huge bubble gum bubble.

"Penny McAllen, throw that disgusting gum in the bin this instant!" screamed Mrs McAvoy.

Dropping her oversized bag onto her seat, she slowly walked to the front, swaying her hips and flicking her fringe. With a cheeky smirk on her face, she leaned over the bin and gobbed, much to the disdain of the new form teacher. Every teacher knew Penny and probably had a good laugh at her antics, but in front of the pupils, they had to be seen to be uncompromising with the rules.

The sound was loud as the gum hit the base of the metal bin. She turned to face the class and grinned. Then the pupils giggled, angering the teacher. It just made them laugh even more. *Who would want to teach this lot?* thought Mrs McAvoy.

Sliding the chair back, which made a screeching sound, Penny sat down heavily and glared at her teacher. Kelly just watched with admiration, as Penny mumbled under her breath, "Miserable ol' bitch."

"*What* did you say?" shouted the teacher.

With a confident sneer plastered across her face, Penny replied, "Oh, nuffin, Miss, you must be hearing things."

The class tittered again.

"I heard you, Penny McAllen!"

Penny laughed, "You're losing it, Miss. I never said nuffin." Glancing around the room at her fan club, she thought, *life doesn't get much better than this. I've only been in the classroom two minutes and I'm already one up on this dozy old bat.* Penny commanded attention and Mrs McAvoy was royally playing into her hands.

"I clearly heard you!" The spiteful expression on Mrs McAvoy's face intensified, as her piercing eyes narrowed.

"If ya heard me, Miss, then why did you ask what I said?"

The teacher was now red in the face and slammed her hands down on the desk. "Do not be so impertinent, young lady!"

"Miss, I don't know what impertinent means, but whatever it is, I ain't done nuffin. Like I said, you must be losing the plot or going deaf in ya old age!" she replied, innocently, looking up at the laser-like glare focused on her.

Kelly so wanted to laugh but she was too afraid of the consequences. God help her, if she got into trouble like this; her mother would have a good reason to beat the life out of her.

There was silence, but inside her head, the teacher was screaming. They both held their gaze for what seemed like ages. Then, Mrs McAvoy sighed and rolled her eyes. "Right, it's the first day back, and I will be going over the revision timetable, so class, please pay attention."

Kelly wished she had the gumption that Penny so obviously had. If only she had the guts to stand up for herself, then maybe she wouldn't be so miserable. Penny always looked happy and she was surrounded by her friends. Her parents let her wear what she wanted at school and have fashionable hairstyles, even make-up. Unlike her though, she wasn't allowed to even move unless her mother said so. In fact, she was so controlled by her mother's obsessions, she was the butt of many a joke. The teasing was so intense it verged on bullying. Kelly was the girl they poked fun at. Every school had one and Kelly stood out. Perhaps she was bullied, but it was nothing in comparison to her mother's brutal words and harsh punishments.

The first day dragged on, as Kelly daydreamed about the day she would leave home and live her own life, instead of being dragged, pushed, and oppressed by her mother. Just to be able to have a hairstyle instead of her straggly, boring locks would be something. She contemplated taking action now, by changing her personality and standing her ground; after all, she could do nothing about the way she looked.

The bus arrived at 4 o'clock and the pupils were gathered en masse, waiting to get on. Of course, they pushed past her, as if she didn't exist. Usually, she waited for the 4.15 bus, to avoid having to wrestle with the crowd, but today was different. She was going to take a leaf out of Penny's book. As the double-decker bus pulled up, the hoards heaved forward. Kelly could feel her heart racing, as if she were on a roller coaster. It was thumping more with nerves though than anything else. She felt sick with fear and her mouth was now dry. The doors opened and the kids tried to shove past each other to pile on. Four girls in the year below her were in front; they'd already had the foresight to ram their way forward.

"Oi, I was before you!" bellowed Kelly. Her heart was in her mouth. That was the first time ever she had raised her voice.

One of the group turned and mocked. "Piss off, Churchy," spat Helen, the younger sister of Jody, a girl in her class. "Go and crawl under a church pew where ya belong, ya fucking weirdo!"

Kelly was seriously angry now; it was all well and good having girls her own age taking the mick but not one younger than herself. With a spike of gumption, which, to be honest, she didn't feel she even had, she pushed the girl aside and glared back, "I fucking said, I was before you!"

She had never sworn before, afraid she may burn in the everlasting fire of hell. That's what her mother had brainwashed her into believing. Helen stood with her mouth open, allowing Kelly to go first.

She managed to get on the bus and secure herself a seat, and yet her heart was still pounding nineteen to the dozen. Helen and her friends walked to the back, whispering about what they had just witnessed. It was outrageous: Kelly Raven swearing at them! This didn't sit well with them at all. Kelly's confidence then subsided, and she looked down at the floor, not wanting anyone to stare at her; really, she felt like crying, but she wouldn't dare, not now and not again. Things had to change, if she was to ever become her own person.

It was no surprise though why she was picked on. Looking down at her starched knee length school skirt and her Clarks baby shoes, it was obvious she was always going to be first in line as an easy target.

The bus drove along the high street and most of the kids hopped off; they were either gathering in McDonald's or wandering around the shopping centre. She wasn't one of them. Her mother insisted on her coming straight home. "Idle time leads to mischief," she would often say.

As the bus stopped outside, Kelly gazed in the clothes shops and sighed with a dull, empty feeling. She could only imagine what she would look like in the latest fashion. Her own clothes were hand-picked by her mother and more often than not from a charity shop. Even her T-shirts were plain; no way would she ever be allowed to wear anything with a designer name or even a logo on. It wasn't that they were poor, either. They lived in a reasonable three bedroomed detached house. It appeared classy from the outside but inside it was another matter altogether. It was sparse and plain, with no photos or pictures on the wall, except the gold framed one of Jesus and the ornate crosses everywhere. Kelly longed to have something of her own, even if it was a tacky seaside ornament, but there was nothing. She had given up crying herself to sleep, as it didn't get her anywhere and only increased the longing to reach the age when she could leave for good and never look back.

Finally, the bus arrived at her stop; she reluctantly got up from her seat and almost dragged her bag off the bus. This was the time of day she hated the most, entering the depressing ambience that seemed to linger in every room, strangling the life out of her. It had all been brought on by her mother.

As she entered the house, she heard voices, even laughter, coming from the living room. Kelly hung up her lightweight jacket on the hallway coat hanger and crept into the room.

"Ahh, here she is, my beautiful daughter!" smiled her mother.

Kelly wanted to laugh out loud. Never had she heard her mother call her *that* – it was usually lazy, or tart, or something even more unpleasant. Kelly glanced at the portly man sitting on the settee and didn't recognise him at all. Her mother never allowed any men inside the house. "The devil's soldiers," she called them, except for the priest, of course: she worshipped the arse off of that old pervert.

"Well, yes, I can see the resemblance, Maureen. She is as you were a few years ago," replied the ruddy-faced fat man.

Maureen blushed and chuckled, taking a sip from her small glass of sherry. She was in her element, hearing all these nice compliments about her daughter, but only because they reflected well on her.

"Kelly, I want you to meet your Uncle Patrick. He is over here on business and will be staying with us for a while."

An uncomfortable feeling came over her, like a chokehold. She had never really spent much time in the presence of a man, aside from Mr Lawrence, her secret karate teacher, and certainly not living in their home.

"Pleased to meet you, Patrick," she said, as she held out her hand to shake his. However, that was clearly a bad move. She was almost screamed at by her mother. "Kelly, mind your manners. He is Uncle Patrick to you!" Then she redeemed her high-pitched squeal with a soft smile and nervously giggled.

"Err… sorry, Uncle Patrick."

Edging himself off the sofa, he stood to greet her with a hug. Kelly froze to the spot. His aftershave was choking her and his harsh bristles grazed her face. He was a huge man, with most of the weight around his middle, and he reeked of cigarettes and whisky. There was no family resemblance at all and Kelly was still none the wiser. Her mother had never spoken of her having any family before.

"Don't just stand there, girl! You have your chores to do. Now run along," admonished her mother.

She left the room, deliberately leaving the door ajar, intrigued as to who this man really was. The kitchen was across the hallway and the washing up was piled high. She assumed her mother had cooked a feast for their guest. She opened the oven to see if there was a plate left for her, but no, there was nothing at all. As she opened the fridge, hoping to find some leftovers, she was clouded with disappointment. There was not even a piece of roast chicken for a sandwich. Kelly washed the dishes, pots, and pans, and then she made herself a cheese sandwich, before creeping back to the hallway to listen. Her mother was still giggling like a schoolgirl; it was a new sound and one that Kelly had never heard before.

Kelly decided to head upstairs to her room and start her homework but instantly paused when she heard Patrick say, "So, Maureen, have you heard about Eddie?"

Holding her breath, she listened.

"No! And I don't want to even hear his bloody name mentioned. The dirty lying paedophile."

Kelly threw her hands to her mouth to stop the gasp from escaping.

"Well, girl, ya best listen. He is out on parole next month, and it's my guess he will be coming for what's his. Mark my words, Mo, he will be on your doorstep. So best you get yourself prepared."

"Patrick, you haven't been around for a few years now, and I have to tell you, things have changed."

Patrick let his eyes wander around the uninviting living room and then at the oversized picture of Christ and said, "Yep, I can see that."

The next morning, Kelly put on her school uniform and headed down the stairs. Patrick was gone and her mother was in the garden pruning the roses. She thought about saying goodbye but then decided it was better just to slip away before her mother asked any questions. She didn't have school today; this was her little secret. She would go and visit her aunt Bet who was her favourite person. If her mother knew, she would have gone spare. So, she hurried off down the road. Her aunt was within walking distance, obviating the need to catch the bus. Instead, she could save the bus fare for a treat. Glancing over her shoulder to make sure no one saw her, she quickly slipped down the side of the house. Her aunt's two-up two-down little cottage was the opposite of hers. She smiled, as she passed the concrete snowman that was still out on the doorstep in September. She pushed aside the big fluffy blooms of pink roses which had grown wildly along the wall. The last time she had been there, a thorn had scratched her face. Still, she liked the smell and no doubt her aunt wouldn't bother pruning. She wasn't like her own mother where everything had to be neat and tidy. She knocked on the back door and then turned the handle.

"Aunt Bet, it's me, Kelly," she called.

"In 'ere, my babe," answered Betty.

Kelly walked past the kitchen and straight into the living room. Her aunt Bet was sitting in her comfortable chair with her leopard print glasses perched on the end of her nose, reading the paper.

"Did ya stick the kettle on?"

Turning on her heels, Kelly headed back to the kitchen. She moved the dirty dishes aside and filled the kettle. The cupboard just above the sink held the mixed assortment of mugs, so she carefully retrieved two and made them both a brew.

"'Ere, Aunt Bet." She handed the mug and sat herself opposite.

"So, what do I owe the pleasure ... and does ya muvver know you're 'ere? I don't want no fucking grief from her right now. Me back's playing up again."

"No, she thinks I'm at school, but the school's got a training day, so I thought I would come and see you."

Betty sat up straight and removed her glasses. She had soft eyes, round and grey, and so different from Kelly's mother, Maureen. Her eyes were vindictive and dark. It was hard to imagine they were sisters. They even spoke with different accents. Chalk and cheese, as they say.

18

Betty looked her up and down. "Jesus, gal, you look like ya go to one of them grammar schools."

Kelly laughed. "Well, yeah, that's mother for you. I mean, I can't even wear tights. I look like a right idiot, you know. But I can't handle the shit I would get if I tried to argue about it."

"Are ya all right, though … I mean, ya don't get bullied or nuffin?"

Kelly bit her lip. "Not exactly, no, but I get the mickey taken out of me. Still, no one hits me, well, not that often, anyway. I just don't have friends, that's all!"

That comment really hit hard. Betty was choked up and Kelly noticed her eyes filling. "But I'm happy enough though, honestly. I'm gonna get me a good job and me own place one day. Away from her."

"One day, aye, gal, one day," smiled Betty. She loved her niece and felt gutted that the poor kid was raised by an evil bitch. She knew that Kelly was so sad inside and the sweet smile was just a front. At every opportunity she could, she would offer her a decent meal; the sight of her niece's skinny body though really sickened her.

The photos, arranged haphazardly along the mantelpiece, were of her and Betty's sons, Ricky and Billy. Anyone else would have thought that Kelly belonged to Betty. One showed the boys and her together on the sofa, and then there was another, with just her in Betty's arms.

"Aunt Bet, who is Uncle Patrick? He was at ours last night."

Betty shot a look of concern at Kelly. "Patrick? That fucking little shit of a man? He ain't your uncle, he is … He is a no-good waste of space." She got herself to her feet. "By Christ, I thought ya muvver had more fucking savvy than to have that wanker knocking about!"

Kelly was wide-eyed and taken aback. "Who is he?"

"He's one of ya mother's brothers, cousin's sister on the decorator's side!"

"What?" asked Kelly, screwing her nose up in complete confusion.

"Aw, Kel, he ain't any fucking relation. That slimy nonce, he used to sniff around ya mother, years ago. He was married to ... oh, never mind."

"You're joking!" emitted Kelly. "My mum and a fella?"

Betty snatched the fag packet from the sideboard and lit up, puffing furiously.

"No, girl, this was the same time as your dad ..." Immediately, she clammed up.

It was Kelly's cue to jump in. "Talking of my dad—" She had no sooner got the words out when Betty was on to her. "Kel, listen, as much as I dislike my sister, you know that I cannot talk about the past." She sat down heavily and flicked the ash into the freestanding 1950s ashtray.

"But ..."

"No buts, my babe. I made an oath to Mo that I would not say a word until you were sixteen. We both had secrets and I made her swear she would keep my little secret silent too." She looked up at the photo of her Billy and shook her head. "Don't s'pose my secret matters anymore, though. My poor Billy is gone, dead and buried, love his heart."

"So, why not tell me then, Aunt Bet?"

Taking another drag, Betty shook her head. "Babe, an oath is an oath, and I may not be a lot of things, but a woman of my word, I am. Please don't ask me again. Ya know I can't ever say no to you."

"Aunt Bet, I heard that Patrick tell mother that Eddie is out in a few months. I know he is me dad, but I just wish I knew more about him. Mother has always said he is a paedophile. I hope I haven't taken on any of his genes. I mean, I think I'm normal, but who knows?"

"Gawd, babe, of course ya normal …" She paused, getting her thoughts together. "So, what else did ya hear?" asked Betty, as she tried to gauge what was said.

"Nuffin. Should we be worried? That Patrick did say that Eddie will be coming for what's his, so what did that mean?"

Betty swallowed hard. "I don't know, babe. Anyway, don't you go worrying that pretty head of yours. You concentrate on getting good grades and getting yaself a decent job." Betty knew that would be a tough ask, as Kelly was so quiet and terribly shy. How could the poor kid even get through an interview?

As Kelly sipped her tea, she relaxed, sinking deeper into the puffy well-worn sofa. She kicked off her shoes and swung her legs around, which was a pleasure she could never have at home. "Sit up straight like a lady," her mother would always demand.

"Aunt Bet, can't I move in with you?"

Looking empathetically at her niece, Betty replied, "Oh, my babe, I would love nothing more than you 'ere wiv me, but ya muvver would burn the fucking house down. When you reach sixteen, you can move in then 'cos you can make ya own decisions, can't ya." Betty swallowed to remove the lump in her throat. She could sense Kelly was begging her, but her niece was a genius at showing little emotion; Maureen had knocked that out of her. Her sister had a lot to answer for, turning a once lively little girl, who would light up a room, into a waif of a kid, with nothing much to say and who walked with the world on her shoulders and her face always tilted to the floor.

Kelly smiled and continued drinking her tea. She had dreamed of living with her aunt. It would have been a different life altogether; there would have been no antibacterial wipes everywhere, no starched school uniform, and all the freedom in the world. She wasn't allowed friends, and she couldn't even mention a boy's name, as her mother would go nuts. She hated going to church, with the constant quotes from the Bible and the never-ending threats of burning in hell. It was too awful to fight against her religion, as the punishments were severe and sometimes cruel. She gazed at her aunt, whose face was glowing with emanated love, and she just wished she could have been her mother. It was hard to imagine they were related. Betty was forty-two, with a curvy, fuller figure and long black wavy hair. She never left the house without a full face of make-up and always kept her nails brightly painted, usually red. She was slower these days, after falling down her stairs and damaging the disc in her spine. Maureen was the opposite; she had thin mousy hair, and she always kept it pulled back in a bun. She never put on make-up and wore clothes more suited to a sixty-year-old, and yet she was only forty, two years younger than Betty, in fact, but no one would have guessed.

"Aunt Bet, will you tell me the truth about the past, when I turn sixteen?"

Betty stubbed her fag out and clasped her hands together. "I made a promise to ya mother all those years ago, when things were different. If I fucking knew then what I know now, I would never have sworn an oath, but I did. Now that promise was to never mention the past until you reached sixteen … Strange, 'cos I can't really remember why. I guess she thought you would be a grown woman, a bit like she was at that age, I s'pose. Anyway, I promised I would tell you when you reach the right age, and like I said, I am a woman of my word."

"Okay, I won't ask again until then," she smiled. "That Patrick reckons I am the image of my mum."

"Nah you ain't, and you look fuck-all like the snotty prune-faced bitch." Betty laughed aloud. "Cor, Jesus, that creep, Patrick, must have shit in his eyes, if he thinks that. Ya muvver might have been a looker twenty years ago, but fuck me, she ain't now. Looks more like a rat on speed."

They both laughed because they could and because it was how they saw her.

"So, I guess I look like my father, then?"

22

Not wanting to say much more, she smiled and concededly nodded. It wasn't a surprise to Kelly, as she had guessed as much. There was only one mirror in the bathroom and the reflection of an olive-skinned, green-eyed girl, staring back, was nothing like the face of her mother. She wondered if her father was foreign; maybe he was Spanish or Italian. His name was Eddie — well, there was nothing exotic about that!

They spent the rest of the day watching a few horror films. It was a special treat, since her mother refused to have the television on unless it was to watch history documentaries, and, of course, any religious films. She must have seen *The Ten Commandments* at least thirty times.

Four o'clock on the dot, Kelly leapt from her seat, slipped her feet back into her flat school shoes, and said her goodbyes. Betty hugged her tightly and kissed her forehead; she felt sorry for Kelly and had a deep-seated hatred for Maureen.

As she watched her niece from the window, walking down the road to the bus stop, her heart felt heavy. Maureen didn't deserve a daughter as sweet as Kelly. More to the point, Kelly didn't deserve to have a mother so cruel. Her niece may look happy on the outside but Betty knew inside Kelly must be suffering. With no friends and no social life, she was missing out on her youth. It was a far cry from when they were young; as teenagers, they were always out, especially Maureen. She was invited to any party going, dressed in the skimpiest of rig-outs and knocking back the vodka like there was no tomorrow. Nothing and no one stopped her. Betty was less outgoing, but she still had the freedom to join in the fun, if she wanted to. She had her boyfriend at the time and therefore a balance. Saturday nights were saved for her mates, and the rest of the week was spent either washing her long hair or going out with him.

By the time they had both left school, Betty had a job in the bakers and Maureen worked in the factory in Cray Avenue. Work was easy to come by, then. The avenue was a long strip with factories on either side. The wages weren't fantastic but decent enough to pay their way and there was also enough over to buy their clothes and have a few good nights out. Back then, that was all they had to worry about. Lucky for them, their parents were not strict at all. Betty thought about her mum and dad; she still missed them. It was such a shame that their mother had died of pneumonia and their father died a few months after of a heart attack. Betty always said it was because of a broken heart. They would turn in their grave now, if they knew what had been going on.

When Kelly arrived home, she heard her mother talking to Patrick. Quickly, she popped her head into the living room and said hello, before she was chastised for being rude. They practically ignored her, with just a grunt and a nod, so Kelly went as usual to the kitchen to wash up. She didn't bother making herself a sandwich, as her aunt had cooked them both a roast, followed by devil's food cake, which, of course, they had both laughed about.

Once Kelly finished her chores, she went to her bedroom. However, on the landing she noticed two suitcases, clearly labelled Patrick Mahoney, and so she assumed he would be staying in the spare room. Jesus, she thought about the bathroom and shuddered. She would keep herself in her bedroom and wait until the coast was clear, if she needed to use the toilet. There was no lock on the bathroom door, but there was a cast-iron doorstop in her room, in the shape of a wolf, and that would have to make do. Her mum had bought it in the charity shop and used it to keep the door open to air the room. For some reason, her mother insisted on having the bedroom window open to ward off evil spirits, or something mad like that. Kelly hated it, especially in the depths of winter. As soon as she was home from school, she would run upstairs to close the window and the door and allow the room to warm up, before she settled down for the night.

She sat on her bed and gazed around the sparse square room with a single bed, cream walls, pink curtains, and a plain pink quilt cover. On the wall by the window was a desk to do her homework, next to that was a bookshelf, and on the opposite side was a wardrobe made of white melamine with a faded plastic handle. Beside it was a chest of drawers with her hairbrush and comb. No pictures, no posters, no colourful knick-knacks – it was all just plain and boring. It was probably like a prison cell without the bars, but, of course, she was free to come and go. Well, not so much free – but at least not locked away.

Carefully, she listened to hear if her mother was still talking but the sounds were indistinct. Taking her time, she slid out the magazine she had bought with the tenner her aunt had given her. She hid the change in the lining of her bag. Her work folder was bigger than the magazine, so she slipped it inside and sat on the bed, propped up by her pillow. Admiring the cover for a while, she stared at the two celebrities with tans and tons of make-up – they looked so beautiful. She then turned to the story with all the make-up hints and tips. She dreamed of the day she could buy lip gloss and try some mascara and wondered if she would look like these young women. She must have dozed off before the magazine slipped away and onto the floor.

Without warning, she woke with her mother screaming at her, pointing to the magazine as if she had just discovered a used condom or something. Maureen was red-faced and foaming at the mouth, causing Kelly to bolt upright, ready for the backlash. The first slap across the face nearly knocked her off the bed. The second one missed her head and caught her neck which angered her mother for missing her target. With that, she backhanded her with a clenched fist and it caught her cheek. Instantly, the stinging and throbbing gripped her, making her eyes water. But rather than retaliate, she sat still, holding her breath, hoping that was the end of it and her mother wouldn't drag her outside to the shed. It was always her worst fear.

Luckily, Maureen had other ideas and turned on her heels and marched away, leaving Kelly alone, with her fresh bruise and raging heartbeat. Holding her throbbing face, she stared down at the magazine and wished she had never bought it. Inside, she was seething; she wanted to fight back, but she was terrified of her mother. Years of slaps and whips had made her afraid, so she had cowered before her into meek submission. Therefore, the teasing from the girls at school really meant nothing in comparison.

It was ten o'clock, so Kelly snatched her nightdress and dressing gown that were hanging up on the back of the bedroom door and quickly hurried into the bathroom. Patrick and her mother were still downstairs. She heard his voice. "You have to keep that girl in check, Mo. Ya don't want a lovely child like that spoiled by these sex-mad teenage boys, now do you?"

Kelly shuddered; *how dare he discuss stuff like that about her!* She quickly got herself washed and slipped into her nightwear. After she cleaned her teeth, she headed back to the bedroom. As she closed the door, she suddenly felt uneasy; maybe it was the tone in Patrick's voice that made her feel ultra cautious, but she decided to push the iron doorstop up against the door to keep it shut, all the same.

That night she didn't sleep too well at all. Her face was still throbbing and she kept thinking about Patrick. *What if he came into her room?* By the morning, she was ready for school, eager to get out of the house. Patrick was in the spare room, snoring, whilst her mother was in the kitchen, making herself tea. Kelly noticed her hair was down, which softened her face, and she was wearing a satin dressing gown. That was new. She didn't speak to her mother except to say goodbye.

"Don't you ever bring pornography into this house again! Understood?"

Eager to get away, Kelly didn't bother to answer, so she left the house and headed for school. By the time she reached the bus stop, the September chill had reached her bones. She wouldn't go back to grab her jacket – it just wasn't worth the grief. Penny jumped on at the next stop; she had dyed her fringe purple and it looked so pretty. She ignored Kelly – pretty much par for the course these days – and sat at the back of the bus with two other girls.

More kids bundled on at the MacDonald's stop, and by the time they reached the school, the bus was packed. Kelly was in her own world. Her face was bruised and she was too, inside that is. She hadn't noticed Jody and her mates standing outside the school, and of course she had completely forgotten about the incident getting on the bus two days ago. Jody, Helen's older sister, was waiting for her. Helen had exaggerated the small conflict from earlier, saying that Kelly had pushed her to the ground to get on the bus and called her a whore.

Walking along with her head down, Kelly headed towards the main gate. So, she didn't see Jody lunge forward at her. The girl grabbed her by the hair and swung her around. The first punch hit Kelly in the stomach, and as she doubled over, one of the other girls swiped her bag, throwing the contents into the air. Jody hit her again, this time in the face. Kelly was still in shock and didn't retaliate. Then Sarah Jones, known as a vicious bitch, kicked her hard in the leg, and she felt the girls rub her hair and laugh. Kelly went down and curled herself into a ball. She could have beaten every one of them but lacked the confidence to do it. An unexpected voice screamed out, "Oi, leave off, Jody!" It was Penny.

"Not your business, Pen, she was bang out of order. She pushed me little sister over, trying to get on the bus!"

"Fuck off, Jody, she never did. Ya sister's a cocky little mouthy prat and is using your name to bully people!" she retaliated.

There was silence, except for the sound of people walking away. Penny grabbed Kelly by the arm and lifted her to her feet. Kelly was in pain, and worse, she felt humiliated. All she wanted to do was run to her aunt's, but she couldn't. The school would inform her mother of her absence and then she would be in for another beating.

"Are you all right, Churchy?" asked Penny.

Kelly shyly nodded and tried to flick her hair out of her eyes but something stopped her hair from moving. She put her hands to her head and then gasped when she felt the thick, sticky chewing gum. She looked up at Penny to thank her but Penny's eyes widened, "Fucking 'ell, you need to go to the doctor or something. The state of your face!"

With her head tilted, she asked, "What's wrong with my face?"

Penny pulled out a mirror. "'Ere, have a butchers!"

Kelly was still shaking when she held the mirror. Her face was black down one side and she had a gash above her eye on the other. But it wasn't her face that hurt, it was her leg. She looked under her skirt to see what was causing so much pain, and then she saw the enormous blue swelling.

"Jesus, that's a nasty bruise. You have to go to the med centre."

As Kelly tried to walk, she almost buckled, as the sharp pain shot up her leg.

Penny put her arm around Kelly's shoulder. "I absolutely hate bullies. I can't stand that bitch Jody, and her shit-leg friends. I 'ave 'alf a mind to give her a good beating meself. Anyway, ya gotta get that poxy chewing gum outta ya hair, before it starts sticking all ya barnet together. Come with me. I'll sort it for ya."

The pupils were already in their first lesson when Penny helped Kelly to the girls' toilets. Kelly could get a better look then, and sure enough, she did look a wreck. Her hair was matted and glued together.

"Right, I've got me hairdressing scissors. Let's see if we can cut that crap out!" Penny was smiling, holding her tools of the trade. Yet, Kelly was nervous and the fear was written all over her face.

A high-pitched chuckle left Penny's mouth. "I ain't about to cut all ya fucking hair off, ya know. I ain't that twisted."

With an anxious smile, Kelly nodded. Penny got to work, easing every glued strand, snipping only the pieces that were stuck together. Slowly, but surely, the blobs of gum were removed and dropped into the sink. She then pulled out her soft brush and began brushing Kelly's hair.

"See, I told ya, I wouldn't scalp ya. You have got gorgeous hair. It needs a good trim though, to put some life into it. I learn about all that stuff in the salon, ya know. They reckon I will be better than Vidal Sassoon, one day."

Kelly was listening, imagining Penny working in a top salon, and admiring the girl. She had obviously secured herself a Saturday job and was working towards being the best hairdresser she could be. No wonder school wasn't important to her because she was already going places.

"It's kind of you, Penny, to help me. Weird, I thought you would be the last person …"

Still brushing Kelly's hair, Penny calmly asked, "Oh yeah, and why's that, then?"

Surprised by Penny's so matter-of-fact expression, she bravely said, "Well, you don't like me much, do you? You normally take the mick."

Penny laughed. "Nah I don't, well, except to call ya Churchy, but we've all got a nickname."

"So, you don't dislike me, then?"

Penny put the brush back inside her bag. "I don't hate ya, but I gotta tell ya, ya just boring. I mean, ya don't talk, and ya wear … well, shit clothes, really, and I ain't ever seen ya with a boy or even with lippy on for that matter. To be honest, behind ya back, they call ya *Carrie*, off that Stephen King film."

Kelly knew the film well – she had seen it twice at aunt Bet's. She laughed. "I'm not surprised, really. I guess I kinda do look like that, what with me mum being a born-again Christian lunatic."

Penny roared with laughter. "Ya know what, Kel, ya all right you are. Now, we better get that cut on ya face cleaned up, or they will all be freaking out, all that blood over ya boat."

After wetting some tissue, Penny started cleaning the cut above Kelly's eye, but then she stopped. "Cor, that Jody hasn't 'arf bruised ya face."

Kelly shook her head. "That was me mum. She did that one."

Shocked, Penny stopped, dropped the tissue in the bin, and stared for a while. "Why did she do that then, Kel?"

Kelly bit her lip and shrugged her shoulders. "She caught me with a celebrity magazine."

Penny frowned. "What was ya doing with it? Shoving it up a cat's arse?"

"No," she laughed. "Just reading it. She hates that sort of thing."

The usual wry expression on Penny's face softened. "Does she clump you a lot, then?"

Kelly shook her head. "No, I try not to give her a reason to. I go straight home from school, do the housework and me homework, then I cook dinner, and go to bed."

Penny leaned against the basins and pulled out a packet of fags. "Want one?"

Kelly smiled. "I would have more than a bruise, if she smelled smoke on me."

"Ya know that's wrong, don't ya? I mean, ya mother treating you like that. Cor, if my mother did that to me, I would have it on me toes."

"Yeah, well, you have more guts than me," smiled Kelly. "I have nowhere to go, and if she found me, I know she would kill me."

The rest of the day was spent sitting through boring lessons but lunchtime was a pleasant surprise. Ignoring the calls from the group of popular girls already seated, Penny made her way over to Kelly. "How's ya boat?" she asked, as she dropped her heavy bag down on the table.

"I'll live," smiled Kelly.

The whole incident and the story Kelly had told her about her mum had bothered Penny. It had literally shaken her to the core. Part of the reason for sitting with Kelly at lunch was morbid curiosity but the other part was almost certainly guilt. She had snubbed her so many times and called her 'Churchy'. At heart, Penny was the kindest and most sensitive girl you could find. But she wouldn't admit that to anyone. She was one cool bitch and needed to keep up appearances.

"So, I was thinking, Kel. Do ya fancy coming back to mine after school? I have a project and I think you would be perfect."

Kelly put her sandwich aside and took a deep breath. "I would love to but I can't. My mum clocks what time I get in, and if I'm late ... well, I'll have another walloping."

Penny sipped her Fruit Shoot. "I've got an idea." She pulled her mobile from her bag. "What's ya mum's number?"

"Why, what are you going to do?" giggled Kelly, now entertained. She hadn't had so much excitement in years.

"Trust me."

She reeled off the landline number.

"Oh, hello, it's Mrs Green here. I am calling to ask if it would be okay with you if Kelly stays behind today ... No, no, she is not in any trouble. We have a speaker arriving to help the class with their English Literature course and we are inviting the top-grade students to stay behind to benefit from the talk." She smiled at Kelly. "Oh, yes, it is indeed a worthwhile talk ... It will finish at eight. Ah, good, thank you. I will tell her she can attend."

Kelly's face lit up. "I didn't know you could put on that posh voice."

"All sorted, so I will meet ya outside the gates at 3.30." With that, she winked and left.

Thrilled, Kelly finally had one over on her mother and was about to break her boring routine.

She waited by the gates, and sure enough, Penny appeared with a big grin on her face. They jumped on the bus. No one this time tried to push in front. Penny was talking for England about fashion, make-up, and her latest boyfriend. Kelly was in awe of her and wished she could be like Penny; life would be so much more exciting.

Much like her own house from the outside, Penny's was the same, but inside, it was warm and homely. There were pictures, photos, and ornaments. Her dad was asleep in the armchair, still wearing his work clothes, whilst her mum, a pretty woman, was cooking in the kitchen.

"Pen, love, fancy some egg and bacon … Oh, I didn't see you had a mate with you. All right, love, fancy a bit too?" She nodded at Kelly.

"Yeah, me and Kel, we'll have some, but chuck in a few chips, I'm fucking starving."

Kelly gasped. Penny had sworn in front of her mum.

"Crinkle or straight cut?" she replied, as if she hadn't batted an eyelid.

"Anything, we will be upstairs. Shout us when it's ready, will ya?"

Frozen to the spot, Kelly awaited the backlash, but there was none. Incredible. *Were other homes like this one?* she wondered enviously. If that had been her mum, she would have had the frying pan wrapped around her head. Instead, her mum had just laughed and carried on as if it was normal, which, of course, it was. *Maybe all this was normal*, thought Kelly. They headed upstairs to Penny's bedroom. It was larger than Kelly's, with a huge flowered quilt cover on the bed, wall-to-wall wardrobes, an enormous dressing table, and boxes upon boxes of hair products and make-up. Kelly was wide-eyed and tried to take it all in. It was beautiful, untidy, but just a dream room.

"Penny, are those wardrobes full of clothes?"

As Penny spun around, she found Kelly gazing with eyes like a child at Christmas, and for a second, she felt sad. "Yeah, but they are not new. Some should be thrown out, really. So, this project of mine ..." She tried to change the subject, for she knew only too well that Kelly never had decent clothes; she had seen her outside school dressed like a little kid with knee-length skirts and old-fashioned tops.

"Yeah, go on," urged Kelly, eager to find out what it was Penny was proposing. This was like heaven to her. A new friend, having tea, and sharing whatever it was in this perfect bedroom, what was there not to like?

"I have to do a makeover for the salon. They said, if I want to get into hair and beauty, I have to start practising, so I thought I could take a before-and-after picture of you. Ya got a pretty face and with make-up you're gonna look like a model. Up for it?" She raised her neatly plucked eyebrow.

Kelly was nodding with excitement. She had never worn make-up and she longed to try it.

Once she had taken a headshot of Kelly, she positioned her in front of the dressing table, with her back to the mirror, and for half an hour she worked away. They laughed and chatted about nonsense, and then, finally, Penny stepped back and grinned. "Cor, blimey, Churchy, if ya went to school like that, you'd 'ave all the boys after ya. I have managed to cover the bruises too."

Kelly chuckled, "If I went to school all made-up, my mum would call me a dead girl walking."

As soon as Penny turned the chair so that Kelly could see herself in the mirror, there was stunned silence, as she just gazed for a while, hardly believing it was her own face staring back. It was as if her face had come alive and she was like the girls at school; she could fit in, if only her mum would let her. Tears welled up and without thinking she leapt from her seat and hugged Penny.

"Yeah, all right, mate, no need for fussing," blurted Penny, who was surprised by the emotional reaction. "It's only a bit o' slap."

Feeling awkward, Kelly let go and smiled with embarrassment. "Oh, sorry."

Unable to believe she could actually look like one of the models in the magazine, Kelly stared again.

"Girls, ya dinner's up!" shouted Penny's mum.

Penny angled Kelly's face in the light and snapped away with her small digital camera. Then they both skipped downstairs for tea. Debra, Penny's mother, raised her eyebrows. "Cor, look at *you*! All ya need is a long dress and you would be ready for the red carpet."

A warm, comfortable feeling swept over her. Penny's home, her mother so charming and funny, the whole atmosphere, it was all incredibly relaxed. To top it all, they didn't correct or criticise Penny, even though her mouth was like a sewer at times. When it was time to go, Penny saw her to the front door. As Kelly stepped down one step and looked back, she whispered, "Thanks, Penny, for being my friend."

Penny frowned. "I wouldn't go that far."

"Well, thanks for being err...Thanks for being kind," replied Kelly, with a sudden lump in her throat. Of course, Penny wouldn't be her mate – no one was.

Just before she walked away, Penny noticed the sadness that crept across Kelly's face and she felt guilty. "'Ere, Kel, I was joking. 'Course you're me mate. See ya on the bus on Monday."

Kelly's face lit up; just hearing those words gave her a huge lift and a spring in her step. Finally, she had a friend she could chat to and have a laugh with, and that's all she had ever wanted — a mate who would understand her. For Penny to be her new-found friend, the most popular girl in the school, was a dream come true. She had no idea that it would be the last time she clapped eyes on Penny for five years.

CHAPTER TWO

Kelly walked back towards her house; there was no need to catch a bus. The short walk was spent dreaming over her own face all made-up. Luckily, Penny had had enough wipes to take it all off. She noticed a car driving at a snail's pace in front of her. Nervously, she looked around and realised the street was quiet with not a soul in sight. The street lamps were on but not fully lit up, so she couldn't see who was in the car but she did notice a plume of smoke billow from the small gap in the window. Maybe they were looking for a house number. She was virtually home when she spotted the vehicle pull over. She hastened her pace, but as soon as she reached her house, the driver stepped out.

"Where have you been, Kelly? Only, ya mother said you were at school, which means you should have got off the bus, but ya didn't, did ya? I saw you walk down the hill." His voice was slow and demeaning.

Kelly stared at Patrick and shivered; he was strange and almost threatening.

She had to think quickly before he told her mum. "I, err ... I missed the stop and jumped off up the road and walked back."

Patrick laughed. "Nah ya never, there was no bus. Anyway, ya mother's gone to the church. She said to make sure you were home by 8.15, and by my watch, it's 8.20. But I'll keep it a secret."

Kelly didn't know whether to run or go inside. He was fast approaching and she was rooted to the spot. He pulled out a key and shoved it in the keyhole. As the door opened, he gave her a devious nod and waited for her to go in first. He was not as pleasant as he had been on their first meeting. Not for love nor money would she wish her mother was at home – until now.

"Right, Kelly, go on upstairs, get yaself bathed and ready for bed," he said, with a firm voice and a sly grin.

His tone uneased Kelly and his inappropriate words made her shiver. Nevertheless, the sanctuary of her bedroom was as good a place as any. She fled up the stairs and into her room, trying to push the metal doorstop quickly up against the door. She slowed her racing heartbeat by taking deep breaths. Then, she heard him climbing the stairs. In a blind panic, her eyes darted around the room, looking for a weapon, anything, to protect herself.

Petrified by his heavy breathing outside her door, she shouted, "Go away!"

Her mother had drummed it into her that all men were after one thing — sex.

The hairs on the back of her neck stood on end and a prickly feeling swept over her scalp. Her hearing senses were on high alert. He was still there, his deep breathing almost in time with her own, and then she saw the door gently being pushed open, the doorstop having little effect. Her eyes widened and her pulse quickened. His chunky, grubby fingers gripped the door and caused her stomach to churn as fear absorbed her. Then, he was there, inside the room, with his belt hanging from his trousers, and a sick, twisted grin spread across his face. Enjoying the look of terror in her eyes, he took another step forward and was now at the foot of her bed.

Kelly wanted to close her eyes and pretend he wasn't there, like a small child afraid of the bogeyman, but this was real.

"I said, take a bath," he said, in a low, creepy tone.

Kelly could feel the vomit rising to the back of her throat. He lunged forward to snatch her arm, but she leapt from the bed and tried frantically to get out of her room. Viciously, he caught her by the hair and rammed her face into the wall. As she stumbled and fell to the floor, he lost his grip. In a split second, he tried to reach down and grab her hair again. In fear and haste, she seized the nearest object, the cast iron wolf doorstopper. Her adrenaline was racing through her veins, giving her the strength to lift it into the air and smash it down hard against his head. She felt the impact, as if she had just hit a brick wall. The clanking sound caused her to cringe, yet, more shockingly, his heavy body was on top of her, jolting and twitching. Kelly tried to catch her breath and hold in the scream. She wriggled until she escaped his dead weight. In an instant, she was on her feet and ready to run. But there was an eerie silence, and she peered down to find Patrick's head at an awkward angle and black blood pooling around him. The gaping hole was horrific and for a moment she thought she was dreaming. Then she saw the twitching end; with his lifeless eyes cold and glaring, she realised right away he was dead.

It was like something out of one of those horror stories she had watched at her aunt's. For a second, she stared – not out of morbid curiosity but to comprehend what had just happened. It then hit her, she had to get away. She dashed down the stairs, snatched her coat and bag from the hallway table, and ran out of the door and along the road. It wasn't until she was approaching the park that she stopped to catch her breath. The cold air and the heavy breathing made her lungs feel like they were on fire. She was gasping but dread made her carry on – she had to get away now. Her mother would kill her. The police would arrest her. She couldn't go to her aunt's; she couldn't face her. In fact, she couldn't face anyone; she was now a murderer. It was all so fast: one minute she was having a makeover, the next she was bludgeoning a man to death. *Keep going, Kelly, keep going.*

Across the park and along the river, she ran as fast as she could. It was hard to know which way to turn; she rarely ventured outside the town, and on those occasions when she did, it was with her mother. The darkness was daunting but the idea of turning back was far, far worse. She had to get away. Eventually, she ended up in the woods; it wasn't a forest but well away from people. There were no lights or street lamps for miles. Without a watch, she had no idea of the time. Further and deeper into the woods she walked, slipping and sliding over the muddy roots.

However, she was away from the town and hopefully far enough away from being caught. Her feet were sore and she was overcome with fatigue, having been running for hours. There, in front, just visible by moonlight, was an old tent still erected but vacant. She looked about and then bent down and crawled inside to find an old sleeping bag rolled in a ball. She was concerned by what she would find inside, but it wasn't as if she had many options. She hoped fervently the police weren't on to her yet.

That night was probably the most terrifying experience of her life. She lay there in fear of her safety, of her freedom, and of anything else that could creep into her tatty tent and scare the living shit out of her. The cold, the damp, and the traumatic event she had suffered, made her shiver relentlessly. Maybe she would burn in the everlasting fires of hell. She laughed, a sign of hysteria. Having been terrified of even swearing up to this point, she had, in the space of an hour, risen quickly up the criminal scales to the point where she had committed the ultimate sin — murder.

Eventually, she drifted off into a light sleep filled with monstrous dreams, with the damp creeping into her bones. The late September sun was bright and highlighted the mouldy sleeping bag, along with a dead rat for company lying next to her. She squeezed out of the tent and stretched herself, feeling every ache and pain in her muscles. She didn't like running and last night was probably the longest ever. Although she was fit, running for hours had taken it out of her.

In the light, she noticed her white socks were covered in blood and she had the presence of mind to immediately chuck them. In the distance, she saw a town and didn't recognise it at all. Inside the torn lining of her bag, she found the change from the magazine. She almost laughed again. Why was she carrying her school bag? She retrieved the change and ditched the bag. Then, she continued to walk until she was on the edge of what looked like a busy high street, and within seconds, a bus pulled up heading for St Pancras. Knowing she was close to London, and away from immediate danger of being caught, it seemed as good a place as any to head for. She hoped it was as hectic as people said it was. Maybe there she could get lost in the crowds and plan her next move because going back to her home was not an option, not now, not ever.

With no idea of where she was, she handed the driver the fare and realised she was off to a place with no money on her to purchase food or clothes. The warm air hit her, as she headed towards the back of the bus; well, she could at least warm up. Even her clothes still felt damp and she was hard-pressed to get rid of the putrid smell of mould and the dead rat. People came and left, but she remained huddled in the corner at the back, half asleep, nursing her aching muscles and keeping her face hidden. Every time she thought of that gaping hole in Patrick's head and his lifeless eyes, she wanted to puke. Eventually, the bus came to a complete halt. The driver opened his door and threw his jacket around his shoulders. She guessed this was where the bus terminated.

After looking around, Kelly got to her feet and set off into the unknown. London was lively and colourful. Everyone was on a mission: there were commuters, businessmen, and tourists everywhere, all too preoccupied with their own lives to give her a second glance. The shopping centre looked inviting, so she decided to have a nose around. Her mother never took her to London. She could hear her telling her, "It's full of pickpockets and prostitutes." Outside, on the streets again, the heavens opened and the rain poured. That was her cue to get inside the train station. She was already cold and becoming more fearful by the minute. Her paranoia of being caught was at its peak, and she was beginning to feel as though everyone was looking at her. As soon as the rain stopped, she left and began to walk the streets of London, unable to take in the surroundings where old meets contemporary. Too afraid to look up, she continued to walk aimlessly, going over and over in her mind what she had done. It was intriguing that no one took any notice of her – after all, wasn't she Kelly the murderer?

The night was drawing in and a place to sleep was a priority – *maybe a job with a room*, she thought. Hours passed and it was dark, and she still had no idea where she was, but she soon realised the buildings were now houses and all of them run-down. She was in the middle of a council estate. It was gloomy and foreboding.

Then she spotted a small kebab shop which still looked busy. She thought that maybe they could tell her where she could find a place for the night; perhaps she could even work off the cost of a room. It hadn't crossed her mind she would be plastered all over the news. Her mother never had the news on, so she grew up not really knowing what was shown. Yet, she was fully aware that the police would be after her. As she opened the door, the heat hit her. The smell of chips made her mouth water and she soon realised how ravenous she was. In her pocket she had two pounds, enough for a hot chocolate.

Three Turkish men stood behind the counter, frying chips, slicing meat, and talking loudly. There were five tables in total, one empty and the others occupied. Whilst ordering the drink, she noticed two of the men winking and nudging each other. One told her to take a seat and the drink would be brought over. She sat down and started to plan her next move; a smart decision was needed or it would be another night in the cold.

As she looked up, one of the Turkish men smiled. He must be the boss, she assumed – he certainly looked older. The cold air blew in, as a group of people left without closing the door. Kelly got up and shut it.

"Thank you, sweetie," acknowledged the older Turkish man. She smiled back; he seemed nice. She needed money and considered asking him for a job.

In the corner sat a black man on his phone; she guessed he was Jamaican, as he had long dreadlocks, a gold tooth, and his accent gave it away. He caught her looking and raised his eyebrows. Quickly, she diverted her gaze.

The older Turkish man came over to her table with the hot chocolate.

"There you go. I have put extra chocolate sprinkles on the top."

He seemed gentle and kind. This was her chance. Normally, she was shy and wouldn't even look at a man, but now things were different, and it was a case of speak up or freeze to death.

"Err, excuse me," she said, as he went to walk away.

He turned around. "Yes?"

"Do you have any work going? Only, I need the money and a room for the night."

She then realised this was not the smartest move; it was two o'clock in the morning, by the clock on the wall. She was in the middle of God knows where, and now she was gripped by fear, and the chill was sucking the life right out of her. *Kelly, get a grip*, she said to herself.

He smiled, as he pulled a chair out and sat opposite her.

Two other groups of people left, leaving only the black guy with the gold tooth.

The Turkish man nodded. "Yes, I have a room upstairs." He pointed upwards with his finger and gave a dirty chuckle. He then ran his big sausage-like fingers over her tiny hand. As he leaned forward, she could see his skin was covered in a layer of grease, his teeth were like rusty railings, and his eyes were so slanted they almost disappeared when he smiled.

Instantly, she pulled her hand away. "No, no, I am looking for my own room." She hoped he would laugh it off and walk away, but he didn't. He looked around to see who was watching. But the only person was the Jamaican, with his phone stuck to his ear.

The Turk grabbed her hand roughly.

"Look, sweetie, you need a room and a job. I have a room and a job. Don't turn down my offer and insult me." His affable voice took on a sinister tone.

She stiffened when the fat, greasy Turk squeezed her hand. Then she tried to pull away, but he was so strong. She glanced around to find there was no point in screaming for help – the only one left was the Jamaican. It was as if she had entered a house of horrors, and she almost wet herself.

"Hey, little one, don't be afraid, I won't hurt you. Come upstairs with me. I will give you a nice bed, warm sheets, and a little job. You can earn fifty quid." His voice was sickly sweet again, which alarmed Kelly even more.

His other hand was now under the table, rubbing her bare knee. She flinched and looked at the two other men, hoping they may help, but they were laughing. The Jamaican was still on the phone. She prayed for someone to walk in but the younger Turkish man from behind the counter was locking up. The backlights, the kebab rotisserie grill, and the lamps inside the open display fridge were now all turned off. She noticed the Jamaican glance at his watch.

Really panicking now, her brain calculating the options, she thought about Penny and what she would do. Her stomach was in knots and her heart was pounding. The fat Turkish man was gripping her hand so tightly it was hurting. Penny would kick him in the shin and run out of the shop, sticking her two fingers up.

She didn't have the guts to do that though, so instead she said, "Please, let me go!"

The young Turkish man was opening the door and the Jamaican had finished his call and was now up from his seat and ready to leave. She glanced at the door and tried to get up but the fat Turk seized her and tried to pull her back. It was now or never. In an even greater panic, she shouted, "Fucking let go of me, you creep!"

With that he did, and she ran out of the café and careered past the Jamaican, almost knocking him out of the way. She was still sprinting, when she heard him call after her. Her fear was so great that even though the icy air was burning her lungs, she kept going. The estate was frightening enough, with only half the street lamps working, but the thought of being raped was worse. In the partially lit street, she didn't see the pile of rubbish and tripped, landing heavily in the road. Her knee hit the concrete so hard she heard it crack and then the pain came a second later. She tried desperately to get to her feet, when there was the Jamaican, grabbing her arm and pulling her up.

"Slow down, shorty."

Out of breath and shaking, she glared into his eyes like a rabbit caught in the headlights. Her fear gradually subsided. Maybe he wasn't the Yardy gangster ready to pimp her out as she first thought. Yet she still felt as though she had been thrown to the wolves without a weapon. The greatest tool to survive was knowledge of the streets. She had no hope. He noticed the look of dread crossing her innocent face. With a comforting chuckle, he said, "Hey, it's okay. If you want a warm drink, there's a café up the road and a woman who runs it."

"Thank you," she replied, still trying to catch her breath.

"I'll walk you there." He ruffled her hair, a gesture that helped calm her fear.

She nodded and shyly looked away, too afraid to make eye contact.

The café was small and a bit grubby but it was warm and the worn seats were a comfort. Her knee was throbbing though. The Jamaican called to the large Irish woman behind the counter. "Mary, me beauty, bring up two hot chocolates and a bowl of chips, please. Me lickle friend here is in need of fattening up."

Mary looked over at Kelly. "Be Jesus, ya look froze to death. Would you like an egg with those chips?" Her voice was coarse but friendly.

Coyly, Kelly nodded and gently smiled back. At the back of the room, she spotted a sign for the toilets. She needed to see what she had done to her knee, as it was still hurting. His phone rang again and Kelly jumped up and headed for the ladies' room. Mary handed her the toilet roll as she passed the counter. Surprisingly, the toilets were cleaner than the rest of the café. As she looked at her reflection in the mirror, Mary was right – she did look frozen, with blue lips and a purple nose, but then she noticed the blood in her hair. Frantically, she ran the hot water, washed her face, and cleaned away the vile remnants of that gruesome murder. A nauseous feeling swept over her as she watched the water turn pink and run away down the plughole. Was this a premonition perhaps? She could see her own life easily being swept away down the drain, just the same. A deep, dreaded sensation clouded her once more and she inhaled a lung full of air to hold back the vomit. As she lifted her skirt, to see the black bruise, which had made an instant appearance, she unexpectedly felt sorry for herself. She crouched down on the floor and silently sobbed until she couldn't cry anymore. But she was still alive, the hunger pangs confirmed that much, and she was still free.

As she warily returned to her seat, he stared, not in a leering manner but just in a strange way. Kelly was too tired and exhausted to care; perhaps she had jumped out of the frying pan into the fire. Then she looked over at Mary and hoped, if there was any funny business, the big Irish woman would jump in.

"So, shorty, what's ya story?" he asked, as he leaned back on the chair. Rudy had seen that lost, desperate look before, and he felt a deep sadness for the girl. She had the biggest round eyes that were lifeless, like she was living life going through the motions but with an insufferable fear and a cute face that had the remnants of nasty bruising. Something inside him connected with her. He, too, was once on the streets many years ago, looking out for his sister, after their mother, who was a first-generation immigrant, turned to drink and then ran off with some random man, leaving them both homeless and living a hand-to-mouth existence. He had worked every hour of every day, doing anything, to earn a place to sleep and a meal for them both. His sister's eyes had held that same expression as the child before him now. For a second, he wanted to hold the girl and tell her everything would be okay, but she was too sweet and nervous to be touched; he sensed that right away. One thing he was sure of, he wouldn't allow her to roam these streets alone; he would help if he could.

She shrugged; what *was* her story? She was brought up by a religious nutcase and her father was a paedophile, serving a long prison sentence, but who, she couldn't remember. She had no friends, except for Penny, and she had just smashed a man's head in and for what? She couldn't even say he had raped her.

The hot chocolates arrived in tall glasses topped with squirty cream. The egg and chips tasted delicious, and as Kelly munched away on the greasy offerings, she realised she was starving and didn't look up until she had finished every morsel.

He was still staring at her. "So, you need a room and a job, then?"

She sighed loudly and said, "I suppose you want a blow job too." Then she realised what had just come out of her mouth and was shocked she could even speak like that. Unlike the kids at school, she never did.

To her surprise, he laughed, but he was so animated, he put her in mind of a puppet with his arms and legs all over the place. Then, he placed a finger over her lips and said, "My man piece wouldn't even fit in your mouth."

She stared, searching for a sign he was genuine, and then he smiled. Kelly lowered her gaze, feeling foolish and yet relieved. He was so different from anyone she had ever met before – he was almost alien.

"Shorty, I ain't no muvver fucking pimp either, so here's the deal."

With the heavy bricks lifted off her shoulders, she was now prepared to listen. His voice somehow commanded attention, so she nodded, feeling a little more grown-up.

Her change of expression didn't go unnoticed and Rudy felt warm inside; she stirred something that made him feel so protective towards her, as if it was his job to look out for her, and so, come what may, he would love this child.

"I have a house down the street with a spare room, just a bed and a blanket, one night only, but I want a favour."

Kelly was holding her breath, hoping it was nothing sexual.

"You can set up a computer, right?"

"Yes," she replied.

He leaned forward and whispered, "I can't read, nor write, ya see, so I need someone to do it. I can't ask me friends 'cos … well, just 'cos."

With enormous relief, she eagerly replied, "I can do that."

Rudy felt a lump in his throat. She had almost brought him to tears with her angelic face so eager to please.

That was a fair deal and Kelly was too afraid and cold to be outside. She would have to take the risk he was telling the truth. With that, he got up to leave.

"Mary, me Irish beauty, put that on me tab!" he called.

"Bye, Rudy, bye sweetheart," she replied.

Kelly smiled to herself. So, his name was Rudy. She would have to make one up for herself.

It was one of those old Victorian houses with a basement and three further floors, but from the outside, it looked small. The net curtains were grey and hanging unevenly, the paint was peeling off the walls, and the large sash windows were rotting away, but Kelly didn't care — she just needed a bed.

They walked up two steps and went inside. She was surprised by the light glaring from the hall and the smell of skunk which hit her as she followed him in. A reggae thumping sound was coming from upstairs and there was laughing to be heard from a room near the back. With rooms to the left and the stairs on the right, she could just make out a kitchen directly in front. She heard voices and then a large black woman, dressed in shorts, a crop top, and a purple weave, came into view, waving a huge spoon.

"So, you finally decided to come home, then?"

Bouncing with her hand on her hip, she sucked her teeth. Kelly felt self-conscious and awkward.

"Ahh, man, what are you doing with that chil'?" she asked, as she rudely pointed to Kelly, who could barely understand her thick Jamaican accent.

Rudy laughed and bounded towards her. He slapped her behind and then turned to face Kelly. "This, here, is me niece." He was now speaking with a Jamaican twang.

Expecting her to argue, Kelly was surprised that the woman just sucked her teeth again and pointed at the chair in the kitchen. "Sit, chil'," she invited pleasantly. Kelly wanted to laugh. How the hell could she be his niece? She was white, with green eyes, and there was no resemblance whatsoever. She guessed it was his way of saying, "Don't ask questions."

She quickly took a seat and gazed around the large kitchen. It wasn't modern or particularly tidy but it was warm. Pots were boiling, pans were frying, and the oven was seeping steam. It must have been three o'clock in the morning but the house was noisy and full of action.

Two big black men joined them and again she struggled to understand their accents. One man, by the name of Pat, leered at her with malicious eyes, and, unexpectedly, he leaned over the table and ran his hands down Kelly's face. He was a huge man with big hands.

Kelly could just make out what he said. "I'll take her home with me."

Oh, sweet Jesus, what have I just gone and done? But before she could try to escape, Rudy was across her with a blade at the big black guy's face. His eyes widened and he backed off.

"Hey, easy, man, just joking, I thought she was——"

Before he could finish, Rudy snapped back, "Well, she ain't."

Deliberately, he tucked the knife at the back of his jeans and nodded at Kelly. "She is me niece. Any of you touch her, I'll fucking cut ya!" The man looked down in shock, as did the lady with the purple shorts. They were just as surprised as Kelly by Rudy's threat.

Kelly was still frozen to the chair, when, all of a sudden, there was a commotion coming from the stairs. It sounded as if someone was tumbling down them. At the same time, she heard screaming. "No, boy! No, boy!"

The two big men, Pat and Phoenix, sitting at the table opposite Kelly, jumped up and flew against the wall, gripping each other for dear life. Rudy was already on his feet and the woman went as white as a black woman could. Then, Kelly saw him bounding towards the kitchen; he was a good fifty kilos of mastiff, snorting and growling. He charged into the room, snarling with gunk falling from his slobbery chops. Kelly could almost taste the fear in the room; even Rudy jumped onto the counter, screaming, "Grab his lead!"

The young guy, who chased the dog downstairs, she later knew as Ditto, went off to fetch the lead. Then there was silence, as the animal stood in a stance staring at Kelly.

"Don't move, baby, don't move an inch." Rudy was trying to keep his voice low, now terrified the dog was going to rip the child to pieces.

She wanted to laugh because she wasn't scared of animals – people yeah, but not this big old dog.

"Sit, fella," she said, in a flat tone.

The dog cocked his head, his snarling stopped, and he slumped his heavy body down. As Kelly put her hand out to tickle him under the chin, he moved closer, nudging her knee.

"I know, boy, it hurts," she whispered.

The tension in the room was so incredibly tight. She leaned down and nuzzled her face against his and kissed his forehead. He gave her his paw.

"There you go, you big softy."

As she looked up, everyone was open-mouthed and Rudy was scratching his head.

"He is a killer devil and will bite any white-skinned man," said one of the men, still pressed against the wall.

The other guy laughed. "She must be Rudy's niece for real, 'cos he can smell the black in her."

"That beast is a dangerous dog, bit more than ten people already. I, for one, am not going near that thing," said the woman, sucking her teeth. "This chil' has special powers. Nobody can touch that dog, except to put his lead on."

Kelly laughed because she felt safe, she laughed because she was happy, and she laughed because this was so far removed from her own life.

The big black guy sat back down at the table, and as he leaned forward to apologise for his previous comment, the dog growled and Kelly laughed again.

"Hey, are you still hungry or do you wanna see ya room?" asked Rudy.

Kelly was tired, and yet, in a peculiar way, she was enjoying the excitement. The smell of the curry mixed with the skunk, the manner in which they spoke and joked, she didn't feel awkward anymore. She knew she could be herself, whatever that was. *But who am I?* she thought. All her life she had been told what to think, what to say, and what to wear. Penny was right, she *was* boring. Before her circumstances had changed, the only thought of her own was that one day she would find a job and run away from her mother, even though she didn't have a clue what she wanted to do for work. Here, though, it was as if she could be someone. They were admiring her because she wasn't afraid of their soppy animal. *Oh, Kelly, you are just dreaming, get a grip.*

The spare room was small, as he had said, but it did have a bed, a clean quilt, and a pillow. The window was dirty and the net curtain had holes in it, but overall, it was just fine.

"Get your nut down, shorty, and come and find me when you get up." With that, he winked, closing the door behind him. But before she had a chance to test the bed, he was back in. "Oh, yeah, the bathroom is on the first floor, first door on the left, and there's a toilet just through the kitchen." He winked again and was gone.

She was relieved to feel safe; the way he had looked at her with affection reminded her of her aunt Bet.

The gentle reggae beat was somewhere in the distance, the muffled voices were comforting, and eventually she nodded off to sleep.

When the morning arrived, the sun streamed in through the window and she was sweating under the thick duvet. She had been too afraid to remove her school uniform. She pushed back the cover and lay there, cooling down, going over yesterday's events. It was like a dream, a fuzzy memory. Then, reality kicked in; she was a murderer, and, somehow, she needed to make a plan because for sure the police would catch up with her soon. After all, they would easily recognise her, as she had the same damned uniform.

The kitchen was buzzing again, and this time there were two young guys, sitting at the table, tucking into a fried egg sandwich. Kelly smiled and took a seat.

"Hey, you Rudy's niece?" asked the younger one, Ditto. She had briefly met him yesterday.

She shyly nodded and said good morning to the woman with the purple weave and dressed in a fluffy dressing gown with some net over her hair.

"You want fried egg toasties, chil'?"

"Yes, please, err …"

"Tulip, but everyone calls me Lippy."

She had to think quickly. What name should she use? Her real name was plain old Kelly Raven.

"An' your name, honey? What's yours?"

She didn't hear Rudy behind her. "This, here, is Blue." He ruffled Kelly's hair. A strange sensation engulfed her. She felt as though she really was his niece and her name actually was Blue. But that was probably because deep down she wanted to belong to someone. She didn't care if he was a dangerous Yardy skunk-smoking gangster, she just wanted to belong. In the time she ate that fried egg toastie, five or six people came and went and the atmosphere was so laid-back. There seemed to be no rules, but if there were, they were unspoken. The only firm statement made was she was Rudy's niece, somehow giving her respect. It seemed odd though how none of the others questioned it.

Once Kelly had finished her meal, Rudy led her to a room at the back of the house; it was like an office, yet it was messy and disorganised. There, on a small desk, was a computer. He pointed to a chair and she sat facing the brand-new machine.

"So, Bluey, how do I turn it on?" he laughed.

It then occurred to her he was talking more like a cockney. She supposed they used their Jamaican accent or patois, as it is called, when talking to each other.

Straight away, she got to work, plugging in the charger, downloading the apps, and setting up Google. Within ten minutes, she had it up and running. Then, it dawned on her, she had done the job, and so she had in fact paid for her room, but she didn't want to leave just yet. *Where would she go?*

"Um, can I do anything else to help … only I'm …" she paused, not sure how to ask if she could stay a little longer.

"You skint, need money, Bluey?"

Kelly looked to the floor and bit her lip, and at that point Rudy sensed not only her embarrassment but her predicament.

"Yeah, I got plenty, only it's our secret, right? Got it?"

Her eyes widened. This was so exciting: no one had ever trusted her with a secret because no one had ever got close enough to ask.

"I want you to teach me to read and write. I wanna be able to use that thing. I wanna make sure none of me men are diddling me out of me dough. Get what I mean?"

Kelly was ecstatic; maybe she could hide out here.

"Another job I have for ya. You can train Legend, that mad dog, and I will pay you well for that."

So, she ended up in Peckham with her so-called uncle Rudy. Kelly learned quickly who everyone was and what was what. Lippy, with her ever-changing hair colour, was a prostitute, but she only worked the weekends. She ran the house like she was everyone's mum. Reggie and Ditto were Rudy's sister's sons. They had been living with their uncle since they were very young, when their mum succumbed to drug abuse. The two big guys, she had met the first night, were Rudy's foot soldiers or so he called them – Pat and Phoenix – although they didn't live there. But there were always people coming and going. The house was the nerve centre for a variety of highly profitable but illegal enterprises.

The next day, she was woken by a tapping on the bedroom door. She jumped into her tartan school skirt, pulled the same jumper over her head, and then called, "Come in."

Rudy popped his head around the corner. "Hey, Bluey, I have to go out, sort out me business. So, take this, buy some clothes. See ya later," he said, as he threw her an envelope and left.

She sat back on the bed and opened it to discover a wad of twenties. She had never seen so much money let alone held it. Perhaps he was testing her to see if she would run off without sticking to her end of the bargain. But she wouldn't have because she liked it here. The excitement made her feel alive. She didn't want to spend all the money but just enough to cover a couple of changes of clothes. Lippy gave her directions into the town centre; it was only a ten-minute walk. Rudy had given her four hundred pounds.

This was a new experience, having money and being allowed to spend it on whatever clothes she liked. She must have looked a right moron, walking around in a school uniform on a Sunday in the cold with no tights or socks. She wandered through the market stalls, feeling the excitement of being able to purchase any one of the outfits and all within her price range. She bought jeans, tops, and underwear. She had never been allowed to wear jeans; her mother would say they were worn by a tart. Then she spotted the coats, some fake and fur-lined, with a fur hood. She wasn't allowed to wear fur either, as her mother said they were slutty accessories. The final items purchased were a pair of fur-lined boots with heels and a pair of slippers. She was surprised that her two huge bags only came to eighty pounds. She didn't want to be greedy, but as she walked back, she saw a range of make-up in the health and pharmacy window. She used the excuse she needed to purchase a toothbrush and toiletries. Aware that Rudy had said to buy clothes, she hoped he wouldn't go mad if she just added a little bit of lipstick and mascara.

As soon as she reached home, she put her clothes in the bedroom and then handed Lippy back the door key before she headed for the bathroom. Placing her own toothbrush and toiletries on the window sill, along with everyone else's, she felt at home. It was a good feeling to have a hot bath, wash her hair, and comb out the knots, and afterwards she pulled on clean white knickers, new jeans, and a sweatshirt. Her best buy, on sale for a pound, was the pair of slippers, into which she slipped her feet, and now she was feeling so much happier about herself and with life in general.

Lippy shouted up to say she was going out to fetch some groceries, and the house was silent, all except for Legend, whining from the upstairs bedroom. She opened Rudy's door without going in and let Legend out. His whole body swayed as he wagged his tail. She took him into the lounge and played games. It was surprising how quick and eager he was to learn new tricks although, of course, a Rich Tea biscuit helped with his motivation. So engrossed in training Legend, she didn't notice Lippy had returned. She marched past the lounge with heavy bags only to be followed by Legend, making a dash into the kitchen, snarling and growling. Lippy dropped one of the bags and stood rigidly to the spot.

"Legend, come here," Kelly commanded, calmly and quietly.

He turned and was instantly by her side. Lippy, a deathly white, was visibly shaking. Normally, the dog was kept upstairs in Rudy's room.

Worried, Kelly picked up the shopping, which had rolled all over the floor, and helped Lippy to take a seat.

56

"Sorry, Lippy, I was training the dog. I didn't hear you come in."

"It's all right, chil'. You 'ave that devil's dog under control. Take no notice of me." She looked beyond Kelly at the dog, whilst Legend stared eagerly at his new mistress.

"Go get your ball, Legend," she instructed, and with that he returned to the lounge.

"I swear you 'ave super powers. That animal likes no one, but if you stop him biting me, then that's just fine."

"Shall I make you a nice cup of tea?" asked Kelly, afraid that the little slip-up could cost her her room.

Lippy raised her eyebrow. "No one ever makes me nothing, sweet chil'. I think I need a tea. I just seen me whole life flash before me."

That was how Kelly and Lippy bonded. Lippy showed her kindness, but she never asked about Kelly's past and Kelly never probed hers. They now had a mutual understanding, and for the first time in her life, she was treated as an equal. She assumed it was the dog thing that intrigued Lippy.

That evening, Lippy cooked an enormous pot of curry and everyone who lived in the house came into the lounge to eat. It was a big room, with three large sofas and an old leather grandad chair that belonged to Rudy – his throne, he called it. It was a relaxed atmosphere and one that Kelly was not used to. She couldn't remember sitting on a sofa to eat dinner; it was always up at a table, with her mother's eyes glaring and tutting if she smacked her lips. Kelly didn't care that she was the only white person or had a plain accent. With a new purpose in life, she hoped she could make this home a permanent one and be a part of this mishmash of a family. Legend was allowed downstairs as long as she was around because the dog did everything she told him to do. It was then she learned how everything functioned. Rudy had everyone working illegally, but for the benefit of the family business, as he called it.

Pat and Phoenix picked up the drugs; they were in the distribution department. Solly, another big black guy, who didn't live there but was always in the house, was the finance man, and he also collected the money. Ditto and Reggie, the two younger men, Rudy's nephews, were in charge of the fake merchandise. To Kelly, it all seemed a well-run business and yet so far removed from her own life. In fact, it was probably the exact opposite, as she thought about her mother and how she would have a fit if she knew how her daughter was living.

"Did ya get some clothes, Blue?" asked Rudy, through mouthfuls of food.

Proud of her new wardrobe, at a fraction of the cost compared to the top-quality shops, she was pleased to tell them she had been down to the market.

Rudy looked up and put his plate on the floor. "What?"

Ditto and Reggie were rolling around laughing, whilst Phoenix nearly choked on his food. Kelly was left dismayed; *what was so funny and shocking about that?* Instantly, she was back at school, with the kids teasing and laughing at her clothes. The sadness crept over her, and she felt as if her new life was just the same as her old one.

"Ditto, take her upstairs and sort her out, will you?" Rudy shook his head, laughing, and returned to his curry.

Oh, my God, what did he mean by 'sort her out'? She felt clammy and sick.

"Come with me. I have your skinny ass size," said Ditto, still laughing.

Relieved he was giving her clothes and not a shag, she followed him upstairs, mentally kicking herself and feeling humiliated for trying to be careful with the money entrusted to her. But perhaps she had completely misread the situation downstairs.

Up to now, she hadn't ventured onto the top floor. It was like a warehouse, with boxes stuffed everywhere, fake watches spilling out of holdalls, tracksuits in laundry bags, and coats, suits, trainers, and bags all over the room. As she passed each section, her eyes widened and Ditto laughed. "My curry's gonna get cold, so you just help yourself." With that he was gone and Kelly was left in wonder. She could hear them laughing downstairs, yet it wasn't the same laughter being directed at her in the way she had been humiliated at school. No, this was different; it wasn't cruel at all.

With a beautiful tailored Chanel suit, a Rolex watch, a Louis Vuitton Bag, and Gucci shoes, she paraded in front of the mirror in the hallway and liked what she saw — in fact, she was over the moon.

Rudy nodded when she returned to the lounge and Phoenix whistled. She had a smile on her face which refused to leave.

"Hey, me niece looks proper grown-up now. That's what ya s'posed to look like," grinned Rudy.

Kelly looked down at her outfit and chuckled. "Thanks Rudy, Ditto." She nodded in his direction.

With a curry-ladened spoon an inch from his mouth, Ditto stared. "I got an idea," he said, placing his spoon back on the plate.

"Now, what have I told you about this thinking lark? You leave that to me," laughed Rudy. His voice and actions were so over the top, it made Kelly laugh. Most men of his age she had ever come across were reserved and controlled. Rudy was different; he would slap his leg and roll around, often with a childish giggle.

"Nah, nah, listen, those Pakis down Commercial Road. Well, we have been trying to get them to buy the gear, yeah?" said Ditto, equally animated.

Rudy nodded.

"Well, they won't have it with us, me nor Reggie, but Bluey may be our answer," suggested Ditto, jumping from his seat. "See, up there for thinking, down there for dancing," he laughed and gave a little two-step dance.

"Oh, my daze, Ditz, ya finally found ya brain." Rudy high-fived him.

Kelly looked from one to the other in astonishment. She had no idea what they were talking about, but whatever it was, she was certainly up for it.

Solly turned the TV on. "Don't mind, Rudes, do ya? I wanna see what's happening in the world."

"The politicians ain't gonna change the price of me ganga, are they?" Rudy sniggered and winked at Kelly. She sat herself down next to Phoenix and lifted her plate from the floor. Observing Pat and Phoenix, Phoenix was definitely the softer-looking, and he always seemed to have a smile on his face and a twinkle in his eye. Pat, though, wore a mean expression and a moody attitude to go with it. She was nervous of Pat because he possessed a sly grin and was so unlike the others, with their open expressions. His size was intimidating too: he was a huge man with dark scarred skin, and his hair was greased back with wet-look curls. She perceived he pushed Phoenix around a bit. That was her gift: she could sense people's feelings and gauge their character, having always been the one on the outside, looking in.

The aroma was mouth-watering and she was eager to get stuck in. The first mouthful was a shock as it was hot and spicy and a taste she had never experienced before, but once the initial burning sensation left, she savoured the aftertaste and scooped up another spoonful.

Then the room went quiet and Kelly felt her head burning, she felt her heart begin to pump madly, and the curry becoming lodged at the back of her throat. There, on the screen, was a head and shoulders shot of herself — a school photo. Sitting rigidly, she listened along with everyone else in the room. Lippy stood in the doorway and could only gasp.

The newsreader was describing her as missing and the body of Patrick Mahoney found dead in her bedroom. "Police are still looking for Kelly Raven and they cannot rule out murder," reported the newscaster.

As if a lion had stepped into the room, Kelly was gripped by terror. She had blocked the whole incident out of her head, but there, as clear as day, was her photo, and the incident being broadcasted to millions. As soon as the subject changed to world news, they all turned to face her.

Right then, Kelly wished she was invisible. Ill at ease and shamefaced, it was a humiliating experience for her. Placing the plate on the floor, she stood up. "Please, please, don't turn me in. I will go. I'm so sorry about this. I would never bring trouble to your door, I swear. I didn't mean—"

"Hey, wait, Bluey, sit yaself back down." Rudy's voice was calm and his tone accommodating. No one else said a word, as they waited for Rudy's decision. Little did she know, they were all criminals and wanted by the police for one thing or another, even Lippy, as she had murdered her husband ten years before and was still on the run.

Life seemed so unfair to her. Reality kicked her in the teeth, and like the fifteen-year-old she was, she cried. With her hands cupping her face, she broke down and sobbed. Phoenix, not used to tears, put his arms around her and cradled her like a baby. Her longing to be a part of this new-found family, and to leave the past behind, she saw it for what it was: it was an illusion, pure and simple, and totally ridiculous. How could she ever really ignore the fatal event? *Christ, she had killed a man, bludgeoned him to death.*

Rudy came and knelt by her feet and removed her hands from her face. "Hey, Bluey, don't cry. We can work this out."

Eventually, Kelly stopped crying and looked up. Solly, Reggie, and Ditto were staring, but there wasn't anger in their eyes: it was more like compassion. Pat, however, was glaring, as he hadn't liked the fact that Rudy had held a knife to his throat over a stranger.

"Are you all the ticket, Rudy? You have to get rid of her. The Ol' Bill will have a party, if they find her here."

Rudy was on his feet so fast and in Pat's face, he didn't have a chance to move. Rudy grabbed him round the throat. "Ya better shut ya mouth, before I shut it for ya. If I say she stays and she is me niece, then she fucking stays, and you, ya rat, will treat her like she's me own flesh and blood." He pushed him aside and turned to face Kelly.

"Please stop it!" she shouted. "I will go! You have all been so kind to me, and I would never want to cause any trouble. Honestly, it's best I go." She got up to leave.

"Nah, wait!" shouted Rudy. "This is my home and I say who stays and who goes, and you, Pat, have fucked me over. I know ya did. I let you off, 'cos I give people chances, but you owe me for that lickle blind eye, and don't get cocky. You know ya place, man, and if ya don't like it, then you can fuck off."

Pat seemed to recoil into the sofa. He knew that Rudy had sussed him out. He had tried to earn a little extra out of a cocaine deal by cutting it with speed and creaming off a bigger profit. It had been only the one time, and he hadn't planned to do it again. Rudy was small but he was fast and reckless and not many men took him on.

"All right, fam, no trouble," he replied. Rudy backed off and approached the frightened Kelly.

"Finish ya curry, Bluey. Don't worry about a thing. Ya safe here, I promise."

Kelly wiped her face and sat back down. She couldn't eat the curry; she felt too sick and she was worried to let that spoon pass her lips.

Rudy walked into the kitchen with Lippy, whilst Phoenix put his arm around Kelly, whispering, "We got ya back, Blue."

They were so kind, she wanted to cry again. There she was, surrounded by black hard-core gangsters, with a plate of curry, and her face plastered all over the news, and somehow, apart from Pat, it was all right, in their books.

Rudy and Lippy returned. "So, me chil', first thing is we is gonna change ya hair. Ya have to have a story too." She laughed. "Being Rudy's niece won't work. Besides, you is white and he is chocolate," chuckled Lippy, happily.

CHAPTER THREE

Lippy took Kelly up to her room. Kelly had not been inside until now and was wide-eyed. It was so colourful. Her huge double bed had a bright pink duvet and red cushions stacked at the head. The fluffy rugs were like a 1970s psychedelic poster and hanging from her wardrobes were slinky, shiny dresses.

"Oh, wow, it's a lovely room, Lippy."

Lippy looked at the wonderment in Kelly's eyes and a sadness crept over her. She looked posh and clean but what lay underneath, in the depths of her past, played on Lippy's mind.

"Oh, me chil', it's just trashy, is all."

Kelly laughed. "Well, then, I like trashy," she remarked, as she sat on the bed.

Not wanting to push the matter too far, Lippy cautiously remarked, "Ya don't have to chat ya know, but I'm all ears, if ya want to."

The thought crossed Kelly's mind that maybe she should be honest, for, after all, what did she have to lose? The truth would come out one day anyway.

"I killed that Patrick. I didn't mean to. I was so frightened that he was going to ..." She stopped, as she didn't want to say the words.

Lippy sat beside her and placed her well-manicured hands on Kelly's knee. "You no need to worry ... I s'pose ya miss ya mum?" she asked, concerned that Kelly was so young and obviously naïve to their ways. Instead, she was met by a cold glare; it sent a chill down her back.

"I hate her. She brought that man into our home. I didn't even know him. She said he was my uncle. But he wasn't, Lippy, he was just some old pervert."

The sudden outburst left Lippy anxious for the child. Instantly, she placed a meaty arm around her shoulder, letting her know she wasn't alone. "Now, don't you go worrying, you safe 'ere with us." She paused, wanting to know more about Kelly's mother because she had been brought up that no matter how strict your mother was, you had to respect her. "Ya mother wicked, was she?"

Staring out of the window, Kelly gave a small thought to her mother. What did she really think about her? *There's no two ways about it*, she thought: she knew she hated her. Maureen didn't love her, had never loved her, but she was determined to control her. All of her life had been spent being totally disciplined and restrained by the one woman who should have let her grow into a person. But she wasn't a person, she was a robot. Never allowed to think for herself, never allowed an opinion, imprisoned in a loveless home, and surrounded by crosses and open windows blowing in cold air, she had been wickedly subjugated into a life that was not hers to live. The never-ending brainwashing, of burning in hell, was relentless. Kelly was thirteen when she stopped believing in Maureen's definition of God. She was eight when her mother had beaten her badly, cruelly scarring her back.

It was just after her eighth birthday. She was drawing a picture on the dining table, minding her own business. Her mother was reading the Bible as usual, and the only sound was the grandfather clock ticking with its rhythmic precision. Other than this sound, the silence seemed to emanate like a loud scream that left a buzzing noise in Kelly's ears. She hated the quiet and wished her mother would just talk to her about anything other than Jesus. So, she decided to start a conversation.

"Mummy, when I grow up, I want to be a dancer …" No sooner had the words left her mouth, than her mother leapt from her seat like a mad woman possessed. She grabbed Kelly by her hair and dragged her off the chair. Only her toes were touching the floor and she squealed as the pain shot around her hairline. "Mummy, let go of me, please!"

Maureen shook her like a rag doll and threw her to the floor. "Dancer, dancer!" she screamed. "You are the devil's spawn and no daughter of mine will dance for the devil, you evil Jezebel!"

Just this one time, Kelly shouted back and would forever regret it. "I ain't the devil's spawn, I ain't evil, but you are!"

Maureen was like an animal, foaming at the mouth, as she dragged Kelly from the floor and marched her out to the garden and into the dark and towards the shed. Inside, the shelves were made of slatted wood. Tossing Kelly to the ground, she retrieved a rope neatly curled in a ball. After tying the rope to the slatted wood, she grabbed Kelly's arms, pulling her up from the floor and facing her to the wall. She then entwined the rope round her wrists so tightly that Kelly felt her fingers go numb. She didn't cry or beg her mother to stop: she was too afraid of the consequences. Once Maureen had Kelly stretched out like Jesus on the cross, she seized the cotton shirt off her back. Kelly was shaking with fear. In her head, she prayed for this God, who was so kind and loving, to help her now. But God didn't answer her prayers. The first whack was wicked. Kelly heard the whipping noise of the cane, before it tore into her skin. The pain was unbearable. She had never felt agony like it. But a scream still couldn't leave her mouth. The second blow made her buckle, so now she was hanging by her wrists. She could feel a trickle down her back, and then, without warning, there was a barrage of blows, as her mother, in her brutality, slashed her bare back to pieces. The suffering was so immense that Kelly blacked out. She eventually came to, still hanging from the ropes, but it was dark and cold. She hated her mother at that point, more than anything. Even in those young years, she knew that the beating was wrong. Eventually, Maureen came into the shed and cut her loose, before marching her into the house and upstairs to the bathroom. Kelly couldn't see the mess of her back, but as she stepped into the bath and was forcibly immersed in the water, the stinging gripped her and the water turned pink. That pain was now edged in her brain; nothing could ever hurt as badly as that.

It took weeks to heal, but in a small child's mind, that must have seemed like forever. It was the summer holidays and so there was no school. Kelly lay on her bed for days with no top on; it was too excruciating to have anything touch her raw skin. Maureen never spoke to her in her time of desperate need, but when she finally did, it was to warn her that any backchat like before would find her back in the shed.

Her thoughts returned to her present predicament. Lowering her gaze, she spoke in a slow, cold tone. "Me muvver's a wicked, cruel woman." Deliberately, she got to her feet, removed her jacket, and then her top, and turned to face the wall. Lippy stared in horror. The scars looked horrendous: there must have been twenty in total. Kelly didn't need to say another word and Lippy would never question her.

A lump lodged in Lippy's throat. She had never had kids of her own – her husband had seen to that, by kicking the baby she was carrying out of her stomach. She would have loved a child, and there before her stood a beautiful girl, with innocent bright eyes and a smile to die for, whose mother only saw fit to torture. What that poor girl had gone through was beyond Lippy's imagination.

"I was only eight years old, Lippy."

With cupped hands, Lippy covered her mouth and bit her lip, fighting the urge to cry. She had seen some things in her time but this was beyond words. She knew then that without a doubt she would look out for this child.

"Okay, me beauty, we have to look at changing your appearance. Now, ya probably gonna hate me, but what if we cut ya hair an' change the colour?"

The tension lifted, as Kelly's smile lit up her face. "Lippy, do whatever ya want. I ain't too fond of me hair. It's boring, like me."

"Ah, me sweetness, you ain't boring, you just haven't found yaself yet. But that's okay now. See, you is still a baby, and you got to give yaself time to grow."

Two hours after cutting, dyeing, and fussing, Kelly emerged into the lounge. Rudy was half-asleep or stoned – Kelly couldn't tell the difference. Ditto and Reggie were playing some game on their Nintendo and Phoenix was texting his girlfriend. She noticed that Pat and Solly had left.

They stopped what they were doing and faced Kelly. Rudy was now wide awake and raised his eyebrows. She turned around to show off her new look.

Phoenix, a man of few words, was the first to speak. "Bluey! Ya all grown-up."

She had never felt that any of them looked at her in any way other than as a child. Phoenix was about thirty-eight years old, the same as Rudy, and Ditto and Reggie were probably about eighteen; it was a comfort that they didn't look at her with sexual intent.

Rudy laughed. "How's I gonna get anything done now with ya strutting around looking like a model?"

Lippy pushed him out of the way. "She's the baby in this house and you mind ya business."

Rudy winked at Kelly and smiled at Lippy. "I know that, but I bet the Ol' Bill won't. She ain't the same lickle shorty. She's a hot woman." He watched Lippy's expression and realised she may have the wrong idea. "I know, Lippy, I know. I ain't looking at her like that."

"Thanks, Lippy." She paused and then let the words trip off her tongue. "I wish I'd had a mum like you."

Kelly realised she had voiced her emotions and quickly laughed it off before heading back to the bathroom to have another look. Lippy had cut her hair into a clean-edged bob, adding plenty of highlights. She had done a first-class job and now she looked ten years older. With eye make-up, her round pools of green were smouldering. She added blusher to her cheeks, accentuating her high chiselled cheekbones. It was a far cry from the plain, insignificant schoolgirl she once was. This was who she was meant to be. She looked tougher, not a wimpy pushover, with a confidence embellished on her face. It was as if another person was staring back from the mirror: she wasn't 'Churchy' Raven anymore, she was Bluey now.

That night, in bed, she knew that Rudy must want more from her than to teach him to read. All this for just a few lessons didn't make any sense.

She was right, although it wasn't planned, it just happened. The fake business was taking off and the penalty was less harsh than for pedalling drugs. The boys could offload some of the gear to the beauty salon and cafés to sell, but Rudy wanted the bigger buyers – the Indians in Commercial Road. He saw his 'niece' as young, but he knew she had a good head on her shoulders and probably the ability to sell. As a trusted white woman, Kelly was expected to try to win over the Indians; she looked more credible than Reggie and Ditto.

Ditto took Kelly out with him. They had their holdalls with samples and he was showing her how it all worked. The girls placed their orders and the runners delivered the goods. Reggie picked up the returns and the money; it was that simple. Commercial Road was another story. Rudy knew the Asians were buying fakes, but they would not entertain the boys because they looked like street dealers. He wanted Kelly to try. With her head held high, she approached the buyer and asked to go to the back of the warehouse to have a more private talk. The buyer was a slim and smartly dressed Indian who brazenly flirted with her. But she didn't fall for the flattery. Instead, she negotiated the sales with ease and precision and would not back down on the price. He offered to sample the goods, starting at a hundred bags. Kelly agreed, on a sale-or-return basis, confident he would easily get rid of that amount. She had cleverly gone into Selfridges and carefully scrutinised the real thing and those fakes were spot on.

So, despite her lack of experience, she was able to call on her assets, all for the benefit of her new family. An abundance of natural self-confidence, good looks – she actually looked much older, thanks to Lippy's make-up skills – business acumen, and her determination to show her 'boys' she was no pushover, she was a winning combination and would have the Indians eating out of her hand. Who would have thought she was actually the girl in the police photos and wanted for murder? It was a joke, really.

At first, Ditto was concerned with the sale-and-return issue, but when she pointed out that the copies were so good they would fly out of the door, he took her word for it.

Ditto was the sweeter one of the two; he had long eyelashes and a light skin. He kept his hair cane rolled; it suited him. Reggie had a longer face and fancied himself as a bit of a hard man, bouncing when he walked and flicking his eyes from side to side, but underneath his cool exterior, he was just a harmless lad earning a crust.

Five weeks had passed. Kelly was in her room fixing up a set of red curtains to match the poppy print bedding. She had purchased a wardrobe and a chest of drawers which was a laugh trying to get them through the door. The delivery men wouldn't go inside the house so Ditto and Reggie had to help. Anyone watching would have thought it was a comedy set with the Chuckle Brothers.

Once the furniture was inside and pushed up against the wall, Kelly started filling them with her own new clothes, courtesy of Rudy. She now had a long full-length mirror glued to the wall. Her mother would never have one. "Vanity is a sin," she would say. Kelly laid out the make-up and hairbrushes. She now owned a curling tong. Life was on the up. She had pushed the Patrick incident to the back of her mind, as her nightmares had lessened and her future looked safe. She had everything she could possibly want. And Legend had taken up residence in her room and refused to go back upstairs. Kelly loved the big dog and often fell asleep with him next to her. She didn't mind him being there and sometimes slobbery down her ear. She wasn't used to hugs; she only received them from her aunt Bet, and other than her, she was never cuddled.

Rudy and Lippy were in the lounge, watching the TV, when suddenly Kelly was on the news channel again. This time it was a different story. Her mother had been found murdered in her own home. Lippy glanced at Rudy with her hands over her mouth. Rudy was wide-eyed, like a bush baby.

"Fuck me! Who would 'ave done that?" exclaimed Rudy.

Lippy stared into space for a while.

"What is it, Lip?"

"I think it may 'ave been Bluey."

Rudy grinned, thinking that Lippy was joking. She shook her head. "Rudy, she hated her mother, I mean truly hated her …" She paused, in deep thought. "Rudy, has she ever told ya what that mother did to her?"

He frowned. "Nah, what she do?"

"She beat that dear chil', scarred her back like a road map. I seen it for meself."

Sitting up straight, he said, "We need to tell her about her mother."

Rudy knocked on Kelly's door. "Enter," she chuckled. Rudy was surprised to find her little room looking so vibrant and fresh – a room fit for a teenager. Then he saw the life in her eyes and the cute grin across her face. She was wearing one of the fake Nike tracksuits, and her face was fresh and glowing, just as a young girl should look. He had come to know Kelly by now, and he was as certain as anyone could be, she hadn't a bad bone in her body to brutally murder her own mother.

"Yo, what's happening?" she laughed, taking off Ditto's words.

"Bluey, babe, come with me into the other room. I need to tell ya something."

Kelly jumped from the bed and left the second curtain hanging. Concerned by the look on Rudy's face, she followed him into the lounge. Lippy looked at her with compassion in her eyes and patted the seat next to her. Kelly now felt uneasy, sensing a tension in the room.

"There's no easy way to say this, so I'm just gonna say it." Lippy took a deep breath. "Ya mother was killed last night. It was on the news."

Unsure how to react, Kelly looked from one to the other. Was she heartless to shrug her shoulders? Or, should she appear to be sad? After all, that would be more normal. She thought for a moment. Should she actually have feelings for her mother or was her reaction – her feeling of indifference – weird? But the fact was, she hated her mother, and faking her reaction or not, the truth was still slapping her in the face. She just didn't give a shit.

"Oh, did they say who killed her?" She was still and calm.

Rudy looked at Lippy and raised his eyebrow.

"Err, they don't know yet, but, sugar, they mentioned that you were still missing," replied Lippy.

Kelly shot an implied glance at Rudy. "Jesus, you don't think I had anything to do with it, do ya?" Her eyes begged to be believed.

Rudy shook his head. "It didn't cross me mind."

With puckered lips, Lippy threw Rudy a cynical smirk.

"Who would have killed her? I mean, I know one day I probably would have, but I didn't, so I wonder who did?" she asked, with a blank face.

Rudy wanted to laugh. It was such a strange reaction from Kelly. He walked over to his grandad chair and slumped himself like a sack of shit. "Beats me, babe."

❧*❧

Eddie Raven was downing a well-deserved pint at the Ocean Inn pub on the south coast. He had been released from prison a week previously, and then he had headed straight for Hythe to his hideaway pad. It wasn't a small, insignificant home either – far from it. But Eddie Raven was one for an all-over flash existence.

He was on a life licence for the murder of two men. Luckily, he hadn't used his shooter that time, so he only served twelve years.

❧*❧

Five years before he was arrested, he had carried out a robbery of rare and valuable diamonds. The idea had come from Patrick Mahoney's sister, suggesting that there were items of extreme value sitting there, waiting for the taking. Eddie was the mastermind behind it and planned the execution to what he had thought was a faultless finish. He had a strong team. Mickey 'no thumbs' O'Toole was his daft sidekick; he had stupidly raised his hands when a rival firm 'heavy' attacked him with a machete – hence the loss of his two thumbs. The explosives expert was Jack McFarlane, otherwise known as Jack 'Black', on account that he was so white: he had white skin, white hair, and grey eyes. He wore thick bottle-end glasses that made his eyes look ten times their size.

The very first big job they did was a travel agency. They got away with £5 million in travellers cheques and all three were living it up in Spain for a year.

Not much more than a kid at that time, Eddie was a cocky lad and clearly going places, so it wasn't long before he and his men came back to England wanting more of the action. The first bank break-in should have been a straightforward stick-up job, although it actually turned out to be fast and reckless; nevertheless, they got away with it. The

74

second one was so carefully planned that they went under the sewers and drilled up through the floor. Although the money they stole greatly exceeded all expectations, it was more about the audacious style of the robbery itself, as it earned these villains serious kudos among the criminal fraternity. So Eddie, Jack, and Mickey, with money and clout behind them, began to call the shots within their patch in South London.

Some of the old-school villains were in with them, and within a few years, Eddie had it all sewn up. He wasn't stupid and listened to the likes of Cyril Reardon and Frank 'the butcher'. They were almost old enough to be his father but wise enough to have him onside. They weren't getting any younger, and the truth was the manor needed a ruthless and young-bloodied villain to run it. Eddie ticked all the right boxes.

It was Cyril who had first taken Eddie under his wing, when he was fifteen. Starting off in small petty crimes, he worked his way up, viciously taking people down who got in his way — all except Cyril and his firm, that is. Instead of trying to take them on, he joined them, along with his mates, Jack and Mickey. Any business to be had in South London was taken by Cyril. Eddie was growing an empire with his protection racket and cocaine deals. But he wanted more and wasn't happy unless he was constantly turning his hand to illegal moneymaking scams. It wasn't long before the older men backed off and allowed Eddie to run the firm. It was easier for them, as they had their money and were living with only one hand in the game.

Eddie's sidekicks, both older than him, were involved in a third job. It was their biggest yet — a safe deposit heist — and Jack and Mickey got seriously greedy, as Eddie saw it.

It was late January 1994 when the heist took place. The gang knew they had a small window of opportunity because the next patrol would take place at 3.15 a.m. All the valuables they wanted — jewellery, watches and gems — were placed in fifteen small holdalls. The most important one was holdall thirteen. This contained a black pouch holding a number of gems of which two, in particular, were highly valuable. The holdalls were filled to the brim, and they counted each one, as they were thrown into the van. A horn sounded. Mickey nodded for Eddie to go and see what the noise was outside. That was when Jack opened holdall thirteen, grabbed the blue gem he wanted, and, for good measure, he and Mickey removed some jewellery and precious stones from some of the other holdalls, placing them in special body pouches made for the occasion and hidden under their clothing.

By the time Eddie returned, they had all the bags loaded, ready to take to the van. And, indeed, they both assumed Eddie was none the wiser. Little did they know though that he had a plan of his own. He had conspired with his source – and part-time lover – to take the largest of the blue gems from the pouch, whilst his men were busy in another room. Eddie had taken this one, as he assumed it was the most valuable in the collection. In fact, its true value was around £1 million. He was unaware, though, that the smaller gem, which Jack stole, was worth considerably more.

In his typical offhand manner, Eddie asked the barmaid for another pint. She looked him up and down. He wasn't from these parts and seemed out of place in his smart tailored suit. Janice craved excitement; she had worked in the pub for twelve years now and wanted to get out of Dymchurch. She had only moved there with her husband because he craved the country life. However, unlike her husband, she missed the bright lights of London and found herself twiddling her thumbs and suffering her loveless marriage.

Eddie was gagging for a decent screw with little affection. He didn't fancy paying for it either. He wasn't the sort for sweet talk. So he leaned across the bar and flicked his head for Janice to come closer.

"What's ya name, gorgeous?" His raspy voice stole her attention.

Janice wasn't looking her best and could have kicked herself. He was just her type. She loved men with a mystery about them. With his dark hair, falling neatly around his ears, and his green smouldering eyes, he was every woman's fantasy. It was hard to judge his age, maybe forty-odd. But it was his smooth smile she liked. It was a half-cocky grin that said I am a real fucker. She summed him up. Yes, he was a bad boy.

"Janice. Why, what's it to you?" she responded in her usual flippant way.

Eddie laughed and walked outside to have a cigarette. Janice was used to men flirting with her. Not a bad-looking woman at thirty-five, she could easily get away with being at least ten years younger. Well, in her own mind, that is. Her long blonde hair was almost down to her waist and her eyes were always heavily made-up – they were certainly her best assets. She kept her figure trim and showed it off, wearing body-contoured dresses and killer heels. Jolting her out of her daydreaming, Old Major slammed his empty pint glass on the counter, mumbling under his breath.

"Major, what d'ya want? Ya usual, love?"

One of the old locals, Old Major nodded and slapped his change down.

Gazing out of the window at the mystery man, Janice pulled Old Major's pint.

Since there was no one else to serve, she popped out of the back door and into the ladies'. There, she reapplied her lipstick and took her hair out of the ponytail, allowing it to fall messily around her face. She knew she looked good like that. *This could be my lucky day,* she thought.

When she returned, there was the mystery man supping his pint.

"I ain't seen you before. Down on ya holidays, are ya?"

Eddie was leaning with one arm on the bar. He didn't answer right away; instead, he just smiled. Then, as he stood up straight, she noticed he didn't have a beer belly – not even a small paunch – and looked in great shape.

"No, I have me own place in Hythe," he smirked cockily.

She smiled, as she thought, *this gets better and better*. "Me name's Janice but you can call me Jan." What she wanted to say was, 'You can call me what the fuck you like, as long as you're on top, shagging the life out of me'.

"Nice to meet you, Jan. You can call me Ed." He grinned and winked. He didn't miss a trick; her loose hair and added lipstick were all telltale signs that this fit-looking bird was as ready as he was for a great time. Unless she was interested in the old sergeant major, there was no one else in the pub.

Janice leaned on the bar close to Eddie. "I gotta say, ya kinda look out of place here. I guess ya from London?"

He nodded and laughed. "You sussed me, then?"

With his smile oozing sex, and his half-closed emerald eyes, he took a loose strand from Janice's hair and twiddled it round his finger.

With a feeble attempt at playing coy, she asked, "'Ere for a while, then?"

"I might be, if I have good reason to be."

Janice raised her well-defined drawn on eyebrow and heaved her small chest over the bar, pleased she had worn her push-up bra.

"Shift work?" he asked.

She laughed. "Yep, I get off in ten minutes." Looking at the clock, she hoped he would whisk her away. Tommy, her husband, was out on a fishing trip, so she could easily kill a few hours.

"Fancy a ride, blow the cobwebs away?" he asked, with sheer menace in his tone.

"Yeah, why not." She tried to act cool, but inside she was screaming with excitement.

The flash car said it all; he was a villain and she was in her element. Her husband had once been into crime too, but when they moved away from London, he stopped any nonsense, got a job in the power station, and settled down to a boring life. Janice only took the barmaid's job in the hope of a bit of excitement. She had found it now!

Ten minutes later, they were pulling into his drive. She looked up at the monster of a house and smiled. He had money all right and bundles of it. He didn't say too much, but he did open the door for her to step out – a proper gentleman, or so he seemed.

They didn't waste time with the small talk; within minutes, they were naked and in the huge bed between top-quality Egyptian cotton sheets. He was gentle at first, and then, when he felt her get excited, he threw her all over the bed. Janice loved it. Her husband was a plain old missionary-position man. She liked the rough, hard shag. Ed was in control; he was strong and held her up against the wall, banging away, until, finally, they both came. They lay there for a while, catching their breath.

Getting up to go to the bathroom, Eddie grabbed her by the arm, "Oi, where do you think you're going?" His voice was now very different, somehow menacing in tone.

Janice's eyes widened, now scared she had bitten off more than she could chew. Naked in this guy's house, a stranger, who blew hot and cold, was not clever. He sensed she was afraid, but many people felt the same; he was used to it. Accordingly, he softened his tone. "Come here and give us a kiss."

She laughed then and fell on top of him. His urge back again, he threw her on her back and pulled her legs apart. She was loving it, as he entered her and bashed away, for far longer this time. But Janice was now sore and hoped he would finish soon. She glanced up at the clock and noticed they had been shagging for two hours solid. Finally, he jerked, it was over, and he flopped down beside her.

"Cor, blimey, Ed, I don't think I'm gonna be able to walk straight."

He didn't say anything this time, as she walked to the bathroom. The full-length mirror lit up, when she turned the light on, and she looked like she had just been fucked within an inch of her life. Her hair was a mess and her lipstick was all around her mouth. She sat on the toilet for a while, thinking about this man and her Tommy. She needed a shower but was careful not to get her hair wet. How would she explain that one: wet hair?

Drying herself off quickly, she combed her hair and returned to the bedroom. He was gone. She climbed back into her tacky tube dress and headed downstairs. Janice hadn't really absorbed her surroundings, when she had entered his house, so intent on getting a good shag. The kitchen was as big as her home, with its marble floors, granite tops, and huge glass doors, which opened out to a well-kept garden. Eddie was in his boxers and the light showed every contour of his body. With his olive skin, making him look younger, and his piercing green eyes, he had all the hallmarks of a good-looking man. She smiled, feeling very self-conscious. She knew she was attractive, but looking at him, she was probably out of his league. He could pull any bird younger and prettier than her. With this realisation was the urge to go home, back to her Tommy. Yes, he was as boring as a slut on her period, but she felt comfortable with him.

"Want a coffee?" he asked her, his expression cold.

"Yeah, if you're having one."

He shot her a glance. "Well, yeah, I am, that's why I offered you one."

The sexy look, the teasing, and the flirting had all gone out of the window. He'd had what he wanted – a shag – nothing more, nothing less. But she felt uneasy.

"D'ya mind dropping me back, in a bit?"

He snidely chuckled, as he made a coffee. "No worries."

Eddie got dressed. He pulled on a pair of Levi's, a white T-shirt, and a black blazer, whilst Janice wandered around the house admiring the décor. When he appeared, she smiled warily; he looked even more handsome than before.

"Where do you need to go, Janice?" He sarcastically drew out her name.

"Back to the pub. I've got another shift." She felt somewhat insignificant.

He nodded and drank his coffee; he hadn't bothered to make her one after all. Grabbing the keys to his Porsche, he walked out of the front door, with Janice following him. Sitting in his car, she looked down at the mottled skin on her legs and tried to move her dress down to hide them. They rode in silence: Eddie had things on his mind.

He drove into the car park and stepped out. He had just made her feel as though she had done something wrong – it was odd.

"Oh, are ya coming in, Eddie?"

With a smug grin, he nodded. "Yeah, why not? I think I fancy a good old malt whisky."

There was something strange about the whole situation and it had her on edge. She didn't know what to say, and so she continued into the pub and out the back. Placing her bag in the kitchen, she headed for the bar. Old Major was still there, along with two other customers, both local men from the builders' yard.

Eddie was leaning against the bar in the corner waiting to be served. Janice grabbed a glass, retrieved the expensive bottle of Scotch whisky from under the counter, and poured a double. She winked at him. She had her confidence back. Maybe that was it; she always felt assertive behind the counter. Here, she had some sort of purpose.

The side door opened and in walked Tommy, Janice's husband. She glanced at Eddie and then at Tommy. Her hands were shaking, as he walked towards her. Clearly oblivious to her nervous expression, he was just pleased that the sea-fishing trip had gone to plan. He had caught four sea bass and ten codlings. The sea wind had reddened his big round face and his mop of silver curls were wild from the breeze.

"I think I deserve a pint of Guinness," he announced proudly. Janice was shaking inside, praying that Eddie wouldn't let on what they had been up to. The last time Tommy had discovered her indiscretion, he had beaten her really badly. She knew she had deserved it and had begged shamelessly for his forgiveness. That was three years ago, and although she was still bored, she was also piss poor and had no place to go.

As she turned her back to take a pint glass from the top shelf, she heard Eddie say, "Well, hello, Tommy, long time no see."

Horrified now, her mouth went as dry as a cream cracker. How the hell did they know each other? Nervously, she turned and placed the glass under the Guinness tap. Biting her lip and holding her breath, she watched the expression on Tommy's face. She had never seen him look so panic-stricken.

"What's up, Tommy? You look like you have something on ya mind." Eddie's tone was cold and his eyes demonic.

Tommy shook his head. "Nah, mate, just surprised to see ya, is all."

With his slightly threatening body language, Eddie stepped forward and whispered in Tommy's ear, "I think me and you need to 'ave a word outside."

Tommy shot a glance at Janice; he turned to leave and was followed by Eddie.

Once they were outside, Tommy began to shake. Eddie opened his jacket slightly, and there, tucked in his trousers, was a gun. It was just a warning, but it served as a powerful reminder that Eddie had clout.

"So, Tommy, moved away, then?" leered Eddie.

Tommy's eyes darted around, looking to see if anyone was around. Surely, Eddie wouldn't shoot him in broad daylight in the pub car park? "Look, Eddie, I don't know what ya want, but I am straight now, mate. I got a job, me own pad, and me missus."

Eddie tilted his head and looked at Tommy's feet. "Yeah, so I see. There is this little matter I need to straighten up. Ya know the one I'm on about, don't ya, *silly boy?*" He gently slapped Tommy's cheek.

"Ya see, I know how you managed to pay for ya little house down by the seaside."

Tommy's mouth was drier than a granny's fanny. He twitched his head and tried to swallow.

"You are lucky, though, Tommy. See, Mickey and Jack, they weren't so lucky, were they?" taunted Eddie, through gritted teeth.

Calmly, he put his hands inside his jacket pocket, keeping his eyes on Tommy, who was now as white as his mop of curls. He pulled out his cigarettes and lighter and carefully took a fag from the packet. He lit the end and blew the smoke in Tommy's face.

"Ya know ya owe me, big time, don't ya?"

Tommy was silent. Eddie stepped forward until he was almost in the other man's face. "Ya know I ain't letting this go, don't ya? So, it's like this. You will pay me back, and I don't mean in poxy diamonds. I mean you are gonna say I was with you last night. All fucking night!"

He stepped back and gave a generous over-the-top smile which only unnerved Tommy even more.

"Ya see, ya thought I didn't recognise who pulled up at that job. The three of ya thought that little distraction would be enough to have me fooled. Well, I have to tell ya, I ain't easily mugged off, see. Ya know what was worse than doing bird over Mickey and that cunt Jack?" He paused and glared. "It was not serving time over all three of ya. No, you got away with it, Tommy, living it up for twelve bloody years, while I was inside, fuming. No, what was worse was I didn't get to fucking torture *you*."

"Look, mate ..." Tommy's voice, usually loud and insolent, was now meek and pathetic.

"Shut it, Tommy, and listen. I will forget ya stole from me, I'll forget that you was in on the diversion with Mickey and Jack, but I was with you last night, got it ... or ..."

Tommy nodded. "No worries, whatever, Eddie. Just tell me where we were and when. No trouble, eh?"

Eddie grinned and gently slapped Tommy's face once more.

"No trouble, as long as you stick to the rules, 'cos, Tommy ..." he threw his fag butt on the floor and casually ground his foot over the top of it, "... no matter if I'm inside or not, you will get the same as Mickey and Jack, those two-faced scumbags. Nah, in fact, Tommy, I don't think I will kill you so quick. Get what I mean?" He shot his head to the side like a mad man and then he winked.

"Now, then, I was with you all night at your house. I was wearing this same outfit. We watched *The Godfather* and chewed the fat. Then I left at four in the morning. Right, Tommy?"

The words formed in Tommy's mind but he wasn't really hearing them. The thought of being killed at Eddie's hands disturbed him more. He nodded, now unable to speak.

Eddie clicked his key fob and his Porsche lit up. The bleep as the doors unlocked made Tommy jump. He was still standing in the same spot, when Eddie tore away.

Craning her neck to see into the car park, Janice snapped the pint glass she was wiping by twisting the tea towel too tightly. She saw out of the window the white Porsche drive away and now she waited anxiously for Tommy to return. *Did Eddie tell Tommy about their shag?*

Tommy felt the urge to have a shit and wondered if he had already filled his pants from Eddie's threats.

After fifteen minutes, Janice couldn't wait any longer. She threw down the tea towel and marched outside. Tommy was returning from the longest crap ever and bumped into her on the way. He looked sick.

"You all right, Tom?" She grabbed his shoulders and turned him to face her.

He shook his head. "Listen to me, Janice, I have to go home. I need to sort a few things out."

Janice searched his eyes for an explanation. "What's going on?"

Instantly, Tommy snapped out of his gaze and took a deep breath. "Nothing, I'll catch ya later."

She let him go, unsure if he was angry with her or not. Something that Eddie had said had shaken him up. She was surprised, though; her Tommy was a monster of a man, six feet four and chunky. She would have called him a meathead, except for the fact he had a thick mop of hair. She fell for him because he was a big hard man with a serious reputation, and she was his little tarty blonde he loved to parade around with. It suited her: all she wanted in life was to be a villain's bird, with furs, diamonds, and status.

When Tommy climbed into his Range Rover, the gratification of a good catch was completely overshadowed by the encounter with

Eddie. He drove away and headed to his home, courtesy of Jack and Mickey. As he stopped, pulled onto his drive, and looked up at the dream house, his stomach turned over. *Was it all worth it?* He thought back to Jack and Mickey. They were merciless men and trusted no one, but they didn't have Eddie's cunning.

Tommy was younger and had dabbled in a number of robberies and served a few years inside for his silly cock-ups. Then, Jack had approached him with an offer he could not refuse. All he had to do was pull up in the side alley of a safe deposit house at bang on 3 a.m. No questions asked. "Pull up and then drive away," he'd said. Tommy didn't ask why; he just thought of the money.

His stomach stirred again, and he leapt from the car, but he didn't make it inside; in fact, he puked all over the Italian white plant pots. The bright pink japonica was now laden with lumps of carrot. He heaved again, holding onto the wall. A sixth sense alerted him, and he saw the white Porsche creeping along the road. It was Eddie again; he lowered his tinted window and pointed his gun. Tommy felt his bowels move of their own accord. As quickly as it appeared, the gun disappeared and the car shot away.

With shaking hands, he struggled to unlock the door, but when it eventually opened, he fell forward and landed flat on his face. He lay there for a few seconds, trying to get himself together. Eddie wasn't joking – he could have shot him in cold blood. He knew where he lived.

His only hope was to go along with the alibi. Once his front door was shut tight, he made for the small bar in the corner of the lounge and poured a large brandy. He sat heavily on the beige suede Chesterfield and his mind wandered back to Jack and Mickey. He'd had no idea about their plan; he just knew he would be paid a right few quid. If he'd known they were doing over Eddie Raven, or Eddie Cako as they called him, he would never have entertained the idea. No one in their right mind would have fucked with Eddie Cako.

Jack and Mickey had gone on the missing list. When the police finally found them, they were bloated and almost unrecognisable.

Fished out of the Thames, with boulders tied to their feet, the worst of it was the fact that their eyes were missing. Tommy felt the burning brandy meet the vomit and instantly he threw up again; it was like a fizz bomb sweet, exploding out of his nose.

By the time the landlady arrived, Janice was a bumbling wreck. She looked Janice up and down. "I know you, Jan, and there is something on ya mind, love. I can take over, if you need to get off home."

Teary eyed and shaking all over, Janice was worried. Her husband, the big bruiser, was frightened or angry, she wasn't sure which, but she needed to know what was going on.

"Thanks, love, I'll make it up tomorrow."

June, the landlady, smiled and watched her hurry out of the door.

The bus pulled up just along from the bus stop and Janice ran after it, cursing her high heels. She could walk in them but running was another matter. She went over on her ankle but managed to straighten herself to catch the bus before it drove away. Her heart rate was probably going through the roof. She must give up the fags. The journey was less than ten minutes. Across the road was the lane, a quiet country lane, with a few decent-sized houses dotted along, opposite a field. She wasn't much for country living but did appreciate the views. It was the silence she couldn't stand though.

Like Tommy, she struggled to get the key in the lock. But Tommy had locked the door from the inside. Out of breath and sweating buckets, she banged hard.

Tommy was now six brandies down and still a nervous wreck. He pulled the blind up, and there, much to his relief, stood his missus.

Unlocking the door, he almost dragged her in.

"Christ, what's going on, Tom?"

She misunderstood his fearful glare for anger.

"Pack ya bags and leave!" he growled. He wanted his wife away from the house, before Eddie had any mad notion of hurting her.

"Tommy! Listen to me, please. It wasn't like that. I love you!" She tried to grab his arm.

Slowly, Tommy turned away from the window to face her. He cocked his head and frowned. "You what?"

"I swear to ya, Tommy, it was just the one time. There ain't nuffin between us."

The penny dropped. He shot a look out of the window and then back at his wife. She had shagged Eddie.

He didn't clump her this time; rather, he sat back on the sofa and poured the large brandy down the back of his throat.

"Well, say something, Tommy!" Her tears were falling now. She hated Eddie and the way he had taken her away for a quick screw. She hated herself more though for doing it and confessing her mistake, when, really, she should have kept her mouth shut. Too late, the cat was out of the bag.

"Get ya gear, slag, and fuck off." He didn't scream or shout. She knew then he meant it.

She guessed the cold, calm tone in his voice wasn't about her and Eddie; no, this was something far worse.

"Who is he, Tommy?"

Tommy looked up and with an empty, almost sorrowful expression, he replied, "My worst nightmare."

Janice was confused. "Ah, come on, Tommy, I know you, ya don't love me that much. It's hardly like he has torn ya world apart, just 'cos he, err ..." she couldn't bring herself to say the words.

Tommy laughed, "You, Janice, for once in your fucking life, are right!" He stood up and placed the glass down on the coaster. "You are one serious slut. Ya always 'ave been a dirty bitch, and ya always will be. So, nah, I couldn't give a flying shit about you and him."

Staunch reality slapped her in the face, and she took a step back. Her world was caving in. If she didn't get out soon, then Tommy would hurt her.

"I loved you, Tommy, still do, I s'pose."

"Janice, I know what you're all about. A little shag here and grope there, ya love the excitement. But ya fucked the wrong guy this time. This one I ain't forgiving, so, like I said, get ya gear and do one."

He didn't push or poke her. She guessed he was done with her, and so she left the room, and stupefied, she packed her bags to leave.

Tommy remained in the lounge. Janice was the least of his worries. He didn't even turn to see her struggling down the stairs with her Louis Vuitton designer suitcase. No amount of cheap mascara tears would affect him now. He heard her snivelling but remained on the sofa, gulping another stiff drink.

With shaky fingers, she dialled the cab office. She had blown it now. She couldn't hang on to his shirt tails and beg him for forgiveness, not this time. Struggling along the drive, she took one last look at the near-on perfect home, albeit in the sticks. The self-pitying tears stopped flowing, as the cab came to an abrupt halt. She made up her mind. If Tommy didn't want her, then maybe Eddie would. He had money and she had fuck all. Without knowing the exact address, she directed the driver to where she thought Eddie lived.

His car was in the drive, along with two other expensive-looking motors. She scrambled through her handbag to find a baby wipe and mirror. Looking at her face, she was a right mess. Still trembling, she cleaned away the black stains and applied her red lippy. Paying the driver, she hopped out, and then, after ringing the doorbell, she stepped back and waited. Janice didn't have to wait long. The door opened, and there stood Eddie, with a cruel sneer on his face. He leaned on the doorframe and glared, without a word, making her feel uncomfortable. After all, what was she really doing here?

"Kicked you out then, has he?"

Janice nodded.

"Wait there." He disappeared inside, and then he returned with a few notes. "Look, I don't usually pay for a fuck, but 'ere ya go, love. Now, hop it!"

Janice was flabbergasted and furious. She snatched the money and spat, "My Tommy's gonna kill ya for this, ya flash wanker!"

In an instant, Eddie grabbed her by her hair and pulled her face to within an inch of his own. "Listen, ya silly little strumpet, words like that may just get ya fucking ol' man killed. Now take the payment. Ya acted like a brass and I'm paying ya like one. Piss off, and don't ever come 'ere again. You ain't invited."

"Eddie, ya phone's ringing, mate!" came a deep gruff voice from somewhere inside the house. Then another voice said something. Janice couldn't quite hear but it was a woman. As he let go of her hair and tapped her cheek, she saw the tall stunning-looking woman appear at the door. Her legs were long and shiny brown and her silky hair was pulled around on one side of her very sophisticated face. Janice stared for a short while to see the young woman place an arm around Eddie's shoulders.

"Come on, Eddie, we have a drink on ice," she said, as she mockingly grinned at Janice, looking her up and down like she was a bit of shit. Eddie laughed and closed the door.

Janice felt foolish and unimportant; her life had turned upside down in less than three hours. She only had herself to blame.

CHAPTER FOUR

Rudy sat in the messy office, staring at the computer screen but oblivious to its contents. Anything which involved reading instructions was a no-no for him. He knew he had it in him, but living on the streets had given him no time for schooling. With Kelly's help, he could at least try now.

"Rudy, the key on the right-hand side is 'enter'. Now, click it, and there ya go. You have just sent ya message up there to the satellite, and now it's landed in my inbox." Kelly giggled like the teenager she was.

He watched her face; it was so alive with life. It was ten months ago, when he had found the terrified child on the streets, but in that short time, she had changed so much. She even talked differently, with a strong South-East London accent now. She had ditched her posh words and her anxious expression for a laid-back, bubbly persona. The boys, Ditto and Reggie, enjoyed having her around; they were like the three musketeers, all for one and one for all. They were on a decent earn, all thanks to Kelly and her put-on lady-of-the-manor act.

Rudy was concerned that Pat had gone AWOL. No one had heard a thing. Not that he missed the man; in fact, the atmosphere was better in the house. He sensed that Phoenix didn't like Pat because he seemed a different person, putting forward ideas to make money. He was never like that before; it was always Pat who called the shots. A bit like a pecking order, Rudy was the main man, then Pat, followed by Phoenix, and last, the two boys, Ditto and Reggie.

"What's up, Rudy?" Kelly had noticed him staring at her. She didn't feel nervous or uncomfortable. She trusted him with her life.

He smiled and kissed her cheek; it was totally out of character. "You have changed so much from the quiet little door mouse you were when I found ya."

Kelly turned to face him. "Oh yeah, I s'pose I have changed a bit."

The loud bang at the door made them both jump.

Kelly got up. "I bet Ditto's forgotten his keys again."

Before Rudy could stop her, she was pulling the door open. "Wait!" he screamed. It was too late; the door was wide open and two huge men, the size of Mike Tyson, one bald the other with dreadlocks, stood either side of Ditto. Kelly couldn't take it all in, at first. Then she saw the state of him. His face now swollen like a balloon, he was unable to stand, so both men had to hold him up. Rudy grabbed her arm to pull her away, as the huge men aggressively threw Ditto down the hallway.

Like a scorpion, she found she had a nasty sting in her tail, and it really surprised her. When 'Dreadlocks' grabbed Rudy and tried to drag him away down the steps, it must have been the look of sheer desperation on his face that caused Kelly to go into a blind fury. She lost it – completely.

"Let him go, you bastard!" she yelled at the top of her voice. 'Baldy' then tried to grab her. But her swift dodge saved her. Without a thought, she lifted her leg, kicked hard, and caught the man right in the solar plexus. He instantly folded in half.

"Legend!" she screamed.

'Dreadlocks' was rag-dolling Rudy, when, out of nowhere, Legend came hurtling down the hallway and threw himself off the step and on top of 'Baldy'. In his frenzy, the dog tore at his ear. The growling was fierce but the attack was worse. Kelly watched as Legend went in for another bite; this time sinking his teeth into his head. The scream was blood-curdling and high-pitched. So much so, that Rudy was flung to the kerb, as 'Dreadlocks' ran for his life. Legend unhinged his teeth from 'Baldy's' head and ran past Rudy, chasing after his accomplice.

Kelly jumped the two steps and helped Rudy to his feet, pushing the bloody victim aside. Rudy was dazed and bewildered but Kelly wasn't. Once he gripped the doorframe and steadied himself, Kelly called Legend back. The bald-headed man, with half his ear hanging off, glared at her. "You're gonna pay, all of ya, when Keffa hears about this." With that, he gripped his loose flesh and staggered in the direction towards his mate.

"Ya can tell Keffa he will get the same, if he tries a stunt like that again!" she screamed after him.

Legend appeared by her side with blood around his mouth, looking pleased with himself. "Good boy." She patted him on the head.

Inside, Ditto was groaning on the floor, with Lippy and Rudy trying to get him to his feet. They managed to drag him into the lounge and to lay him on the sofa. Kelly was raging, as she peered down at her friend's battered face. She wasn't afraid – just angry. It was as if a light had come on, relinquishing her from the dark place she had been all her life. Her mother had never allowed her even to raise her voice. Nevertheless, that rage was there, festering inside. The lid had been lifted, and she was now who she was supposed to be. She was a woman. But she was more than this: she was a woman with real passionate emotions. When push came to shove, she was able to fearlessly stand her ground.

On her knees now, she opened Ditto's shirt to see the extent of his injuries. His ribs were black and blue. Lippy was like a mother hen. She had a first aid kit she kept under the kitchen sink. "Bluey, make some sweet tea. Ditto's in shock, poor chil'."

In a flash, Kelly jumped to her feet, ran into the kitchen, filled a cup with hot water, and threw in the teabag. She scooped two teaspoons of sugar, added a dash of milk, and ran back to the lounge, nearly spilling the drink down her legs. Rudy tried hard to get Ditto to speak but all that left his mouth were incoherent mumblings. He was then helped to sit up enough to sip the tea. The puffiness around his eyes held them tightly shut, so he couldn't see. Lippy wiped his face with the antiseptic and cleared away the blood. "Sweet Jesus, why? Why would they hurt him? He is only a boy."

Racked with guilt, Rudy stood up and moved his wild dreadlocks away from his face. "It's a warning. They wanted me. It should 'ave been me, the no-good sly bastards."

Unexpectedly, Ditto spoke. Through dribble and swollen lips, he muttered, "Pat, it was Pat. He set you up."

Rudy rushed to Ditto's side. "All right, mate, you just rest. We'll get ya better. D'ya need the hospital?"

With his eyes still tightly shut, Ditto shook his head. "Nah, just a joint, Rudy."

Rudy set about rolling the fattest spliff, hoping it would ease his nephew's pain. After gently placing it on Ditto's bottom lip, he held it there, while he took a few deep drags. Within seconds, Ditto was asleep. Rudy finished it off. The whole incident was a shock and unexpected. He wasn't prepared and had been left wide open.

Lippy was still wiping Ditto's face, when Rudy laughed. "Well, our lickle Bluey is a kung fu fighter. Seriously, ya got some kick on you. That soldier was folded like a piece of paper, and Legend, ya trained that dog well." He giggled, shaking his head.

Her sudden confidence allowed her to join in. "Yeah, well, they can go back to that Keffa, or whatever the hell his name is, and give him the message from me."

The reality kicked in and Rudy stopped laughing, his expression turning serious. "Listen to me, Bluey, that Keffa is a bad man, a lethal man. Maybe it's best you leave. Move into me mate's flat. I know that Keffa, and he will stop at nothing to hurt anyone."

"I ain't going anywhere. I'll knife him, if he shows his face." She flared her nostrils in defiance.

"Bluey, he won't come here. I know he is shit-scared of dogs. Nah, that nutter will wait for ya. I can't have it on me conscience."

Lippy was looking from one to the other. "D'ya think you should call the others? Only, I've not seen them all day."

Rudy sprang from his seat and frantically searched for his phone. It was in his back pocket.

He dialled Reggie, and much to his relief, he was with Phoenix. "Get back. Ditto has been hurt badly by Keffa's soldiers."

As the minutes ticked by, Kelly began to realise that it was her fault. Pat had never liked her and was no doubt angry that Rudy had told him to clear off, placing herself higher in the rankings. Her mind was an avalanche of thoughts all running into each other. Finally, she concluded that they would all be safer if she left.

Whilst Lippy was still fussing over Ditto, and Rudy was rounding up the troops, Kelly snuck off to her room. Legend was on her bed, his regular spot now. She gazed around. It was so perfect – more than she could have ever dreamed of. It was safer for all of them, if she just packed up and moved on. Rudy and Lippy, strangely, had become more like her mum and dad; in fact, she loved them more than her mum and she never remembered her father. If Pat was so determined to get back at Rudy, then he would probably call the police and disclose her whereabouts. Her new family would be done for harbouring a criminal. Tears fell aimlessly down her cheeks. She never meant to cause any trouble. It seemed that her life was on a downward spiral, and she would not take down with her those she loved.

On top of the wardrobe was a large fake Prada holdall. She stood on the bed, reached up, and pulled it down. Carefully, she folded her jeans and tops, grabbed her underwear and socks, and placed them inside. A knot in her throat choked her; it was the hardest thing she had ever had to do. On her cabinet lay five hundred pounds which was her cut from the business. She felt uncomfortable taking the money, but she had to have some, and Rudy did say it was hers. *Ah, Rudy, she would miss him, him and his animated laugh and childlike eyes.*

At that moment, she heard the boys coming in through the front door. Her room was right next to it and adjoining the lounge. "Jeez!" hollered Reggie. He must have seen the state of Ditto. Kelly felt sick. Poor Ditto. She listened, and she didn't have to strain either, as their voices were loud when they were excited.

"Why would Keffa do this, Rudy?" asked Phoenix.

"I know what's happened, it's Pat. That sly cunt has sold him shit skunk in my name. I only ever sold Keffa top gear, and I also know that Pat did me over not so long ago. He cut the cocaine and creamed off some profit for himself. Pat has always had it in for me, but, as the saying goes, ya keep ya enemies closer. Now, he's done the off and so that's what has happened. I can bet me life on it."

"But why do this to Ditto? He ain't part of any of it," pointed out Phoenix, with a real sorrowful tone in his voice.

"Keffa is a shrewd man. He used Ditto to hurt me."

"What about Bluey? Is she all right?"

"Our Bluey saved me life. She set Legend on them and sent them packing. She has some guts, threatened them an' all. I swear that child has a fire in her belly."

Kelly heard Phoenix and Reggie laugh. She didn't feel good about it though, not now, and she wished she hadn't made that threat. Besides, it wasn't for her to get involved. Now, she couldn't take it back, and she feared Keffa's men would return and really do some damage. She listened to their conversation once more.

"They'll be back, ya know," warned Rudy.

"Maybe we should pay him a visit. I mean, he is only up the road," fumed Phoenix.

"Is he still at Latchmere? I thought he had moved. Only Pat dealt with him. I can't stand the man. He was good for business, though. He always came up with the money. See, that's how I know this is Pat's doing."

With her ears pricked, Kelly heard everything they said. She left the bag on the bed and crept out of her room. Carefully, she opened the front door and silently closed it. She heard Legend whine but tiptoed quietly and then ran along the street. It was dark now and cold, but dressed in her tracksuit and trainers, she was warm enough. However, the thought that this Keffa would hurt them made her shiver inside; it was a notion she just could not bear to live with.

Latchmere was a twenty-minute walk away. She wasn't so afraid of the streets as she had been ten months ago. And despite never having met the man, she wasn't particularly scared of Keffa either. Perhaps it was her innocence that allowed her to go and do something that could cost her her life.

The block called Latchmere was a new build; it consisted of a classy set of apartments, compared to the others on the estate. Kelly stood at the entrance and watched two older women march past with their heads down. The steel dustbins were foul-smelling and a sudden gust of wind, which had just started, caused loose paper to swirl in circles. A tall, smartly dressed black man went to open the main door.

"S'cuse me, d'ya know which number Keffa lives at?"

The guy looked Kelly up and down. He frowned. "What ya want him for?"

Kelly swallowed hard. This person must be a friend or an associate of Keffa.

She stood with her legs apart and gave him a cold stare. Her anger was rising and the picture of Ditto popped into her head. "Look, mate, ya either know where he lives, or ya don't. My business with 'im is my business."

The stranger narrowed his eyes, and then he flicked his head for her to follow him. She got the impression he was in a rush.

The inside was clean and fresh, unlike the street outside. They walked up one flight of stairs and faced a black door. He stepped inside the apartment and nodded for Kelly to join him. Then, unexpectedly, he slammed the door closed and bolted it with the three heavy metal bolts. At that point, Kelly was nervous: she now had no means of escape. In her mind, she expected the place to be full of skunk smoke with all the heavy reggae drums, a bit like Rudy's, but she was about to have a shock. She realised there were no voices, no music for that matter, and the air was devoid of smoke; in fact, there wasn't any ambience in the spotless property either. He flicked the light switch on, and instantly she felt hot and nauseous and assumed he was some random guy who had locked her inside.

The lounge had a somewhat minimalist look, perhaps reflecting this man's character. She liked the enormous Bang and Olufsen TV and Hi-Fi system in the corner though and was impressed with the leather furniture – very classy.

"Sit!" he ordered, his face now expressionless. He removed his expensive leather jacket and placed it over the back of a chair. Kelly's mouth was dry and her heart was thumping. She followed him with her eyes.

"So, like I said, what do ya want him for?"

She glared, trying to remain calm and in control. "And as *I* said, that's my business."

"Well, ya found him. I am Keffa, so what *is* ya business?"

"Nah, mate, you ain't Keffa, I'm going!" She raised her voice, more out of fear.

Pat was good with his descriptions, so Keffa guessed right away who she was.

"Ya got some front, I'll give ya that. Ya mutt did some damage, by all accounts," he said, but too calmly for Kelly's liking.

"I am going to make some tea, it's been a long day. Would you like one?"

In total bewilderment, Kelly noticed how green his big round eyes were. His skin was a very light caramel colour, like Ditto's, and his hair was clipped close to his head. She was taken aback by his looks, confidence, and overall demeanour. Her perception of him, whilst walking to the address, was another monster of a man, like 'dreadlocks', surrounded by machete-wielding soldiers. This was too surreal. She thought back to what Rudy had said. In fact, he hadn't said too much – simply that Keffa was lethal and shrewd. Also, to her surprise, this man didn't even talk like a Jamaican; he was a well-dressed, attractive black cockney.

He returned with two white cups each with a teabag string hanging over the top. He passed her one and then sat down. She then eyed him over. He was clean-looking, that was evident. Despite the gold Rolex on his wrist and a white designer shirt, the most distinguishable feature about him was a nasty scar across his neck. She couldn't guess his age, maybe thirty-five, but he was fit. Under that white shirt was a muscular, well-defined individual.

"So, you know who I am, then?" she asked, as she took a sip of her green tea.

"I make it my business to know who everyone is." He was sitting back now with his hand holding the cup, totally at ease.

"Well, then, Keffa, if you are that good at knowing who's who, you have to know Rudy ain't done nuffin to you and what you did to Ditto was a proper cunt stunt."

Keffa raised his eyebrows. "Don't swear, it's not ladylike."

"I s'pose setting me dog on your men weren't either."

Keffa laughed. "No, now that was clever."

"Yeah, well ya man didn't think so. He said you were gonna make me pay for it!" She tried to stay confident. She was there on business.

He laughed aloud this time. "Maybe Blade deserved what he got, then, 'cos only I can make those threats, and I don't much appreciate people using my name to make menaces."

Kelly sipped her tea. This was all a bit mad. His manner, she could see now, bore no resemblance to the dark, aggressive men who had attacked Ditto and rag-dolled Rudy. She was curious and in some way drawn in by the confidence and class of the person opposite her, who was sitting so relaxed.

"Look, mate, this is all a bit mental. I don't get it. I came here to sort it out, I mean ..." she paused. Actually, she didn't quite know what she did mean. The only thing that crossed her mind was facing Keffa, and if she got a beating, then so be it. She couldn't handle the pain she had caused Ditto and the fear of the men hurting Rudy. "Look, Keffa, I might be wrong. I ain't used to all this violence and shit. All I know is, it may have something to do with Pat. Did he tell ya that the gear ya got was from Rudy?"

Keffa stood up and walked to the window. "Ya got so much guts. Not many would come to my home and front me out, unless, of course, they had a gun. Ya ain't got one, ya come here unarmed, and for what? Tell me?"

Uncomfortable, Kelly looked at the floor. All she had was what she knew. "I don't know ya, Keffa, and to be honest, I don't know the street life – the who's who of the criminal world and all that shit. Rudy saved me life. He took me off the street and looked after me and for nuffin. Like I said, I don't know about drug deals and stuff, but I do know people, yeah. I know that Ditto didn't deserve what he got and neither did Rudy. He might have his business going all right, but the one thing that man is, he is not a mugger. I do his bookkeeping, so I know a little bit."

Keffa was seated again, fascinated by Kelly. The kid spoke from her heart. He was used to scallies lying through their back teeth to save themselves, and every one wrapped around him was after something, in one way or another.

"What d'ya know?"

"All I know is …" She stopped in her tracks. "Hold on, how the hell do I know you ain't the filth, undercover or something?"

This time, when Keffa laughed, his face glowed, and he gave Kelly a smile that softened his sharp expression and made his eyes light up. "Good girl. Come with me."

Casually, she stood up and followed him to the bedroom, confident he wasn't about to rape her. The room was spacious, immaculately designed, and pristine, with everything in its place. The double bed had mink furs laid neatly across it. He pulled open the door to the oversized mirrored wardrobe and retrieved a box. They walked back to the lounge and sat down again. He smiled. "Take a look at this picture." He handed her a small framed photo.

Kelly was shocked. It was a photo of him graduating years ago and underneath it said Keffa Jackson.

Her mind ran in all directions. Nothing made much sense. This dangerous man, with foot soldiers who could beat anyone half to death, was sitting in a pad that she would associate with a stockbroker and showing her old photos. It was bizarre.

"So, I am Keffa. Happy now?"

Kelly giggled for the first time. Keffa watched the innocence of the girl and felt warmed. Nothing was more refreshing than an honest child who spoke from her heart. However, there was something about her, as if he had met her before; it was a familiar feeling that would plague him until he knew the truth. Those eyes of hers were not so childlike; there was strength and determination there, and she was certainly very much more attractive than how Pat had described her. But then, Pat didn't like her at all.

"So, you were saying." He urged her to go on.

"Yeah, so Rudy, as you know, does sell weed, but he has three grades, and when the parcels go out he has an initial next to them. He uses the last initial of ya first name, so when *you* get sent a parcel it has an A on it. All the top-grade ones have red tape, that's how he grades them, ya see. The best quality has red tape, the medium bog-standard has yellow tape, and the shit that he sells for less has green tape. So that's how I know you always get the best. He wouldn't do you over, he has no reason to. I know Rudy, he ain't a scammer, he likes a peaceful life. And as for Ditto, well, he is a passive bloke. We just sell fake shit, there's no violence, no underhanded dealings, just a plain old sale-or-return arrangement with the Indians down on Commercial Road. So, all I'm saying is, if you had the need to go after Rudy and hurt someone who is innocent, then firstly, that was bang out of order, and secondly, Keffa, someone else is trying to screw you over."

His face turned serious now. He was in deep thought when Kelly spoke again.

"Keffa, Pat don't like me. I've no idea why, but he was always in our house, every day in fact, and now he ain't. He stopped coming months ago. I thought maybe he had something to do with it. I also know that Rudy assumed you had another dealer, 'cos ya initial wasn't put against any parcels."

Keffa leaned forward. "Months ago, ya say?"

Kelly nodded, eager for him to believe her.

"No parcels have been sent to me in over a month from Rudy, is that right? Are you one hundred per cent sure?"

Kelly sensed he was working something out. "Keffa, I can honestly say, with me hand on me heart, Rudy has not sent you a parcel in over a month. In fact, it's more like ten. I know, 'cos I do all the sorting and recording."

Folding his arms, Keffa inclined his head. "I gotta parcel last week and it had green tape on it. Funny, 'cos I spotted it. I haven't taken much notice before."

Kelly was on the edge of her seat. "Who gave ya the parcel?"

"It was Pat. The dirty fool. I had the Yardies on me back over it," he replied, with disgust written across his face. Then he realised the kid had him talking about his business and wondered, like this girl had earlier, if he should be talking in such an open manner.

"I ain't surprised," replied Kelly. "That shit sells for half the price. Usually, it's the heroin addicts who buy a few ounces, here and there."

The girl's obvious openness lightened his mood. He was a cagey character and would normally never discuss business with anyone. He had a team of men on his books – all sinister hard-core men. He never got his own hands dirty and didn't even smoke weed. The early days of dealing were done with aggressive violence and he took no prisoners. After a few years, his reputation preceded him and not many firms would cross him and live to talk about it.

Of course, Kelly had no idea how vicious Keffa could be. He was a wealthy man, with pads all over the city, yet he still returned to

Peckham, where he had grown up. His mother, a big Jamaican woman, had scrubbed toilets for a living and saved hard to put her son through university. She still lived here and wasn't happy to move away. She had her church-going friends, and with her son only around the corner, she felt safe.

He knew the streets and so he used his maths degree to work the supplies like any legitimate business. He could fight too and was not afraid to use a weapon to prove a point. His dear old mum watched him parade around in a business suit driving luxury cars and was proud he had achieved something in his life. Oblivious to the degree of villainy her son was in, she boasted regularly to her gospel friends how handsome and professional he was. When asked, she would say, "In finance."

"Keffa, I love my new family. They are good people, honestly. Rudy would never have done you over, 'cos, well, he is good to us, and he wouldn't bring trouble to the door."

Studying her face carefully, he came to a decision. "Ya know what, kid, I believe you. I'm man enough to say I've been mugged off and big enough to say I'm sorry. Listen to me, you go back to Rudy and tell him I won't hurt him. I have no beef. He will believe you, 'cos I am many things and a man of honour is one of them." His words reminded her of her aunt Bet, and she trusted her aunt.

"Actually, kid, I'm gonna pay Rudy a visit meself." He grabbed his keys and his jacket. "Come on, I'll drive you home. Ya shouldn't be out on ya own this late, it's too dangerous."

Kelly wanted to laugh. He was the most dangerous man in these parts, well, so she was led to believe. In the Peckham area alone he probably was, but in South London there were harder men who were even more violent. It wouldn't be long before she found out this for herself.

His Range Rover was parked around the corner, top spec, no less. Kelly jumped into the front seat and admired all the lights and the suede interior.

"Cor, this is lovely," she said, with excitement.

Keffa smiled to himself. He liked the girl. She wasn't flash, flirty, or sly, but just sweet and innocent, with a good head on her shoulders.

Rudy was looking out of the window, when the well-known Range Rover pulled up outside.

"Fuck, fuck, it's Keffa!" he hollered.

Phoenix and Reggie were weak-kneed and shitting themselves.

"Oh Jesus, Joseph, and Mary, he's gonna kill us all," exclaimed Lippy, who was still kneeling next to Ditto.

"'Ere, wait! It's Bluey, she's with him!" screeched Rudy, still shitting a brick.

Phoenix rushed to the window. "She's talking to him."

They didn't have time to run and hide before the key had turned in the lock and Bluey and Keffa were inside.

"Rudy!" called Kelly, her voice upbeat.

The men looked at each other, dumbstruck.

Suddenly, Keffa was there in the doorway, with his hands up. "All right, guys, I ain't here with menaces." He looked at Ditto and raised his eyebrow. "They did that?"

Kelly was by his side. "Yeah, bad, ain't it?"

Rudy was still in shock and so were the others.

He turned to face Rudy. "Okay, Rudy, it looks as though ya man Pat has mugged me off and let you take the blame. I came meself. I think it's only right and proper to let you know that there is no war between us and to apologise. Ya see, I don't make mistakes, but it appears that Pat took a right liberty and not only put me good name at risk but me life too."

Flabbergasted, Rudy gave a half-smile, unsure if this was some kind of joke. Keffa never said sorry for anything.

Keffa peered down at Ditto. "It seems my men have gone too far this time. They weren't meant to do that much damage. I said one hard clump to leave a mark, as a warning. But, as I see it, Ditto took a right good hiding."

Lippy stood up. "That chil' is eighteen years old and covered in bruises. Him no fighter, dear lickle boy."

There was silence as Keffa nodded and knelt by Ditto's side. He held the boy's wrist, looking at the fake Rolex. Gently, he unclipped the watch and held it up. "Good copy but it ain't the real thing." With that, he took off his own Rolex, an oyster-faced, diamond-edged twenty-grand beauty, placed it round Ditto's wrist, and clipped it shut.

"Right, I am here to personally tell ya that ya won't have a visit from me men, and if ya want to keep up the supply ..." he winked, "... red-taped no less, then I am happy to do business. Oh, and you leave Pat to me."

He ruffled Kelly's hair and left, leaving them flummoxed. Reggie bent down and looked at the watch. "Ahh, Ditz is gonna love that monster, when he wakes up. Always wanted a real one."

Rudy lunged forward and grabbed Kelly by her arms and shook her. "He could have killed you, he would 'ave fucking brutalised you, what the fuck was ya thinking? Sweet Jesus!" He let go of her arms and then hugged her. "Bluey, Bluey, don't ever do anything like that again." As he pulled away, he turned his head to hide his watery eyes.

They spent the rest of the night with a low light around Ditto. Lippy cooked a mega curry and Rudy opened his expensive rum. They talked over the day's events and looked at Kelly with pride. She had guts, she was foolish, but, Christ, she was brave. By the early hours, Ditto was awake; he was sore, yet able to talk. His eyes were still swollen slits, so Reggie and Phoenix described his new Rolex in great detail.

Now, that did please him.

CHAPTER FIVE

Eighteen months later

The months rolled by and the business grew. The Indians were taking in more fakes, and Kelly had negotiated a good price from the northerners. The factories now sent the goods directly to the warehouses in London. Kelly and the boys weren't running around with a few boxes; no, they were unloading crates and had two men distributing them by the thousands. She couldn't believe it: from a few hundred pounds a week, their profits – in percentage terms – were rising faster than a new Rihanna single in the charts, to over ten grand and counting. Reggie taught her how to drive, but she couldn't have anything official because she was still a wanted person.

Late one Saturday afternoon, Kelly came home from a shopping spree. She had found a new boutique that sold clothes for the larger woman. There, hanging in the window, was a red dress with a neckline encrusted with crystals. She had it boxed up and tied with a huge red ribbon. It was classy but still had the bling that Lippy would salivate over.

Lippy was making her own birthday cake; it was a multi-coloured tower of sponge and cream. Saturday and Sunday nights were set aside for her business. She had three punters who were kept for her pocket money. At eight o'clock, she would put on one of her shiny dresses, slap on the make-up, and leave, to return around two o'clock in the morning. This Saturday was her one and only day in the year she kept for herself. The pots and pans were bubbling away, the tantalising aroma filled the house, and the music changed from the usual reggae to 1960s pop. The boys, Ditto, Reggie, and Phoenix were wrapping their gifts in the lounge. Solly, unfortunately, could not make the occasion, having come down with flu. It was almost how Christmas would be.

Kelly arrived and slipped into the lounge and beamed, showing them her tastefully wrapped present. The atmosphere was jolly. Kelly had learned over the months that the hard-man talk and stance was just a front because inside the boys were just that – boys.

She was part of them, she joined in their banter, and she was totally involved in all the business talk. Phoenix was older and more of a friend to Rudy; he looked similar to him with long dreadlocks but his skin was darker. Ditto was the closest to Kelly. He would never forget what she had done for him that night Keffa came to apologise.

Rudy finally came home with a huge grin on his face and four large bottles of rum in his hands.

They piled the presents on the coffee table and waited for Lippy to come in. She finished the last layer of cream and proudly entered the lounge with her masterpiece.

"Happy Birthday!" they shouted.

Lippy blushed with pleasure and placed the cake on the coffee table beside the presents.

The rum was poured and the food served. Kelly loved to see the family enjoying a special moment together. She had never celebrated her own birthday in such style. Her memories were cold. She received no birthday cake, unless she was allowed to visit aunt Bet. The only present was a second-hand coat or a book, but, of course, it was usually a religious one.

She recalled the day she reached her thirteenth birthday. She had never asked for a party or if she could invite friends over for tea, as her mother would have slapped her across the mouth. Instead, she asked if she could go to the pictures. The girls at school were always going and chatting to each other about the big screen. Kelly wanted to see for herself, but her mother went into one of her rages and called her the devil. Kelly tried to explain that she would only be going to see a film like *The Ten Commandments,* which her mother had made her watch when it was shown on the TV, and that it was not devil worshipping but just a film. But, her mother didn't listen; all she heard was Kelly backchatting and for that she dragged her to the shed. Kelly was too big to tie up, so she left her locked inside, along with the mice and beetles all night. By the time she was let out in the morning, she was frozen, and her body was shaking relentlessly. Two days later, she had collapsed on her bed, hardly able to breathe. Maureen tried to pull her from the bed, accusing her of faking being sick. So she tore her nightdress from over her head and pushed her in the bathroom and into the freezing cold shower. Kelly remembered the icy water attacking her body and her head feeling as though it was on fire. Then she was dragged from the bathroom and had her school uniform thrown at her. It was a case of getting dressed and going to school. She had it in her mind though she could go to the sickbay and rest.

That morning, her mother walked her to the bus stop. All Kelly could see were the bright lights of the oncoming traffic with everything else seemingly a blur. The bus eventually arrived, and Kelly had to stand, as there were no seats left. She held on to the bar next to the exit door and watched as the fuzzy outline of her mother walked away. She never made it to school though. Instead, she collapsed on the bus and the driver had to stop and call an ambulance. She woke up in a warm bed with a nurse by her side. The nurse was asking who she was and who to contact to come and visit. Kelly wouldn't answer any of the nurse's questions: she was too poorly and feeling emotionally vulnerable. So she just closed her eyes and hoped she would die. Later on, in the afternoon, the hospital made enquiries with the school. They managed to contact Maureen, and by visiting time, she was there, with her loveless eyes peering down at Kelly.

"You had better not be putting this on, Kelly. If I find out …" She stopped, as the doctor arrived and moved her aside. Kelly remembered his words like it was yesterday.

"Kelly, you are very poorly, you have pneumonia, and we would like to keep you in for a few days."

Maureen tutted and the doctor quickly turned to her. "Are you the mother?" His tone was suspicious and openly critical.

With a snooty expression and pursed lips, she nodded and glared back with her usual pretentious air of authority.

"I find it hard you could not tell your daughter was so sick. She arrived here needing oxygen, so I am certain that she would have been in a poorly state a few hours ago," he said, in a judgemental tone. He stared, as if he was waiting for an excuse or a reasonable explanation, but all he got from Maureen was a roll of the eyes. "Right, when will she be home?"

It was obvious that the doctor was annoyed and did not take too kindly to Maureen's dismissive attitude, so he took a deep breath and replied, "When I feel she is fit enough!"

Maureen glared at him in annoyance. "I will discharge her tomorrow and treat her at home. I am not one for hospitals!" she spat back.

Kelly recalled feeling helpless and frightened. *Please keep me here.*

"I think you have misunderstood the seriousness of your daughter's condition. You will not be able to nurse her at home because you do not have the equipment. And, I will warn you now, if you try to discharge your daughter before she is ready, then I will fast-track a court order that she becomes a ward of the state. I am sure you won't want that, will you?"

He marched past Maureen but stopped in the doorway of his patient's isolated room just long enough to hear Maureen say, "Wait till I get you home, making a fuss over nothing!"

Dr Ranjam had had enough: he swung around and asked her to leave, telling her visiting was over. She didn't argue but swanned off with her nose in the air. Running his hands through his thick mop of black hair, and in utter frustration, he visibly counted to ten. After

112

calming himself, he approached his patient's bed and gently moved the hair away from Kelly's face. "We will talk in the morning, Kelly. You get some rest and I will be back." She closed her eyes but listened to the doctor just outside the room. He was talking to a nurse. "If that mother comes back, make sure she is refused entry. I want Kelly's door closed. Please pay special attention to her. That poor child ... who needs a mother like that."

Switching back to the here and now, Kelly looked around at her new family and smiled. This was what a home should be like: being part of a warm, caring family where there was fun and laughter. Lippy handed her a bowl with her new curry recipe and Rudy gave her a small measure of rum. "Easy, shorty, with me special medicine!" he laughed.

The taste was bitter, as she took a gulp and swallowed. In an instant, her throat was alight. She gasped and made a real fuss, much to the amusement of the others. As a warm feeling hit her stomach, she felt her muscles relax and held out her glass for more. Rudy winked and poured her another drop. "Slowly, this time, ya don't wanna be sick, eh?"

The curry was extra hot, now Kelly was used to spicy food. The cake was eaten – it was extremely sweet but still delicious – and then it was time for Lippy to open her presents. Kelly couldn't wait to see what the boys had bought her. To her surprise, they had gone out on a serious mission and bought special gifts – no crap. Ditto winked at Kelly and then said, "That long box is from all of us."

Lippy was embarrassed, something of a rarity. She opened the carefully wrapped parcel but unhurriedly lifted the lid, her eyes lighting up. "It's lovely." Her eyes watered, as she held up the stunning crystal-covered designer watch, the real thing.

"Read the back," urged Ditto. His eyes were wide and his face held a cheeky grin.

As she turned the watch over, she threw her hand to her mouth and allowed a fat tear to trickle down her face. They'd had the word 'Mum' engraved on the back.

Kelly felt an unexpected tear leave her eye as well, and it was then she realised that Lippy had been a mum to her, in every sense of the word. She fussed over her, fed her, made sure she was never hungry, and hugged her every so often, just to let her know she cared. The other gifts were beautiful too; one was a genuine multi-coloured coach bag, which Lippy paraded up and down perched on her shoulder.

Next, she held Kelly's box, all eyes eagerly awaiting to see the contents, although all were aware that girly gifts were not really their thing. But Lippy was special to them and they wanted only the best for her. Carefully, she pulled open the ribbon and removed the box lid. Her eyes widened, as she held the stunning dress up against herself. Kelly watched Lippy's face almost melt with emotion. There was silence while she admired the free-flowing style, the crystals, and the pure class of the gown. Placing it back in the box, she pulled out her handkerchief to blow her nose. "I am blessed, what more could I ever want?" Kelly then realised that Lippy was overwhelmed. There was no fake over-the-top expression of thanks – she was genuinely moved by it all. Kelly had never been able to give anyone a gift, apart from a school painting she had once presented to her aunt Bet, because she had never had the money. One of the few school assemblies she remembered was at Christmas several years ago. The head had talked to the pupils about the difference between giving and receiving. She knew now what this meant: seeing the pleasure on Lippy's face meant the world to her, and Kelly believed this moment would be remembered by them both for ever.

The evening was fun. They danced and sang. Kelly drank a few more rums and was talking for England. They were amused by her carefree words because she was so pissed. The party came to an end and Kelly staggered back to her room. Legend hopped off the bed, unsure what to make of his mistress, with her slurred speech and wobbly posture. When the morning arrived, she sat on the end of the bed nursing a splitting headache. She eased into her slippers, unaware they were on the wrong feet, and shuffled herself along to the kitchen. Lippy was as normal, in a pair of skin-tight shorts and T-shirt and her hair in a net. The eggs were frying in two inches of fat and the bacon was crispy. Kelly sat heavily on the chair, still holding her head. Then Lippy laughed loudly. "'Ere, chil', drink me special medicine." She handed Kelly a tall glass of what looked like puke.

"Drink, chil', it will do you good."

With her shaky hands clasping the tall glass, Kelly pinched her nose and swallowed the slimy concoction. Immediately, she felt her stomach churn and had an overwhelming urge to be sick. The toilet was just on from the kitchen and she ran to empty her stomach. Here, she met a woman Kelly didn't have time to be polite and say hello to, as she threw her head down the pan that was still going through a mid-flush. With one heave, she was rid of probably a week's worth of food. She slumped next to the toilet trying to catch her breath. The hot, feverish feeling left her and the cool sensation brought her back to the realms of reality. She washed her face and sluiced her mouth in the sink, before returning to the kitchen.

"Okay. Now, Bluey, fancy egg and bacon?" asked Lippy, with her back to Kelly.

She felt almost normal although her head was still giving her gyp. "Yes, please!" she answered.

With a great effort, she smiled at the woman she had passed in the hallway, "Hello. Gawd, you must have thought I was mad, dashing past you like that. Jeez, no more rum for me," she giggled.

The woman was sitting on the chair with her face staring into a hand mirror, applying lipstick. She was attractive, with light skin, like Rudy's, but with a long silky black weave. She gave Kelly a sideways glance and raised her well-defined eyebrow. "Hmm, and you are?" her voice sounded cold and her expression definitely was.

Lippy whirled around, an egg slice in hand, and replied with a hint of annoyance, "That's our Bluey."

Before Kelly tried to start a conversation, Rudy appeared, as lively as ever. He was dressed smartly in jeans around his waist instead of loosely around his arse, a fresh lemon polo shirt, and a black leather jacket. He had tied his dreadlocks back in a wide band. Kelly was going to wolf whistle for a joke but thought better of it. She didn't know who the woman was and got the sense banter probably wasn't her forte. The po-faced lady gracefully got up and swaggered over to Rudy, boldly kissing him on the lips. Lippy stood open-mouthed and jolted when the egg slid off the utensil and splattered on the floor.

Rudy was grinning like a Cheshire cat which was so uncool for him. Then they were gone. As the door closed, Lippy mumbled under her breath, "Gold digger."

Kelly bit into her toasted egg and bacon sandwich. The gooey egg dripped down her fingers, and the taste was so delicious, she continued tucking in, making a mess.

Once it was all gone, Lippy placed a mug of tea beside the plate and shuffled herself under the table with her own mug of special herbal drink.

"Who was that?" asked Kelly.

"That, chil', is Krystal. She's a low life, an' a money-hunting scrubber woman."

Kelly laughed at Lippy's screwed-up face. "Not keen, then?"

Lippy sipped her tea and then pursed her lips. "She is Rudy's pleasure, the fool. Him blinded by her. I can see straight through the girl. Thinks she's som'thing special. She ain't any more than a flea living off Rudy's blood. Ahh, he's a buffoon."

Kelly felt an overwhelming sense of compassion for Rudy, and as a result, her stomach became tight and an angry sensation gripped her. She bit her lip.

"D'ya think she has turned up because she knows Rudy is on his uppers? I mean, he has just bought a new BMW and a Rolex and been seen out and about, splashing cash."

"Ahh, chil', you don't miss a trick, you are smart. Yes, she is back on the scene, teasing the poor boy, sucking him back in, but be warned, chil', she will swallow him up and spit him out, after she has bled him dry."

"Not in front of me, Lippy, she won't. I'll punch her straight in her over-made-up face."

Lippy looked at Kelly's hard expression; she had transformed almost overnight into an older and more grown-up individual.

"Bluey, men are fickle, they go foolish over women, and Krystal is his Achilles' heel."

Kelly bit her lip again, annoyed that Rudy could be sucked into a fake, sly bitch when he had such a level head normally and a keen eye for business. He could see straight through people and was always one step ahead. "I'll tell him," she promised.

Lippy raised her eyebrow and stared into Kelly's innocent big round eyes.

"You 'ave a lot to learn about men. As much as Rudy loves you, he loves to satisfy his screaming donkey more."

With her head tilted and looking perplexed, she asked, "What?" She had no clue what Lippy was on about.

"Rudy is like other men. They go silly over a woman that can hypnotise them in the bed. They are ruled by their man piece and not their brain. It makes them do foolish things. It's best you stay outta it and let the storm pass, 'cos, chil', it will. One day, he will wake up and realise she is using him and that will be the end of it, until another woman comes along. Krystal is a clever whore. She knows black men like him. That girl has never worked a day in her life. They give her things for free, new cars, clothes, everything."

Kelly looked at Lippy and contemplated what she had told her. "Why do you work every Saturday night? Ya know you don't have to. I earn a lot now. What you get paid, I can give you!"

Lippy held her hand up, shaking her head. "Stop, Bluey." Her voice was harsh. Kelly realised she'd said something wrong, and quickly she tried to redeem herself. "Lippy, please, I didn't mean to offend you, I was just …"

"I know, chil', I know, you wouldn't offend me. You are innocent of our ways, ya know. I'll never get cross with you. Okay, let me explain som'thing. There's women like Krystal and women like me an' you. We have pride. I do what I do 'cos I earn me own money. Rudy would look after me 'cos I look after him, in me own way, cooking, cleaning, and being there for everyone. I couldn't take for nothing. I buy the groceries, he pays my rent. Me lickle job ain't so bad, you know. Me lickle old men, well, them me friends, too. I like 'em. It's more like having three men friends. They like a womanly touch and they pay me well."

Kelly had a notion that Lippy was selling herself in a sick, sordid kind of way, and this conversation had opened her eyes.

"So ya see, chil', not everything is how it appears."

"I do understand, Lippy, I really do." She was thinking of herself.

It was Sunday evening and Kelly had been lazing around all day. The hangover had knocked her sideways. The boys were about and they were laughing at Kelly; she was still hung-over, lying on the sofa in her pyjamas, and watching some romance film.

Ditto sat on her back and gripped her head, laughing, "Too much rum, eh?"

"Get off me, Ditz, ya arsehole!" she yelled back. Ditto let go of her head and jumped up.

"Bluey's hanging!" he laughed, as he and Reggie high-fived each other.

Then they were gone, leaving Kelly to get back to her film. Eventually, she fell asleep, only to find herself awake at eight o'clock and starving. No one was at home and the kitchen was immaculate, and so she dare not make a mess. After slipping on her jeans, a T-shirt, and a long leather coat, she pulled on her high boots and left the house. The fried chicken shop was only a short walk. She would have taken Legend, but he lifted his head momentarily, before dropping it back down again, not in the mood for walkies.

It was a pleasant evening and there were a few people hanging around. As she approached the shop, a white Range Rover pulled up alongside her. The tinted window came down. "Hey, Bluey, that shit will fuck up ya insides, jump in!" said Keffa.

Kelly laughed and opened the passenger door. He looked as sharp as ever; his hair had grown, and he had a neat layer of cane rolls. The diamond in his ear sparkled brightly. The smell of new leather hit her along with his expensive aftershave. He had lost the hard-man glare and was smiling with an open face.

"Bluey, fancy an Italian?"

She chuckled, "What, like a younger version of Donnie Brasco?"

"Pomodorra, down the road," he replied, grinning at her.

She nodded. "Yeah, why not, no one's at home and I'm bored!" she said.

"Oh thanks, Blue."

"I didn't mean it like that!"

The restaurant was busy for a Sunday evening, but the waiter made up a table. Kelly sensed their eagerness. The waiters were offering specials and top wines and were falling over each other to serve him.

Keffa had a soft spot for Kelly; ever since the day she had bravely confronted him, he now looked out for her. Every so often, he would stop and give her a lift and share a coffee, but they had little in common. They didn't do business together, as the skunk deals were not her domain. But there was something about her that he liked, and he would quite happily listen to her girly small talk, just to be in her company. She was still so young, but her eyes drew him in, and despite her neat body being in the early throes of womanhood, she walked with grace and poise and turned many a head.

He ordered the special and offered her the same. They shared a bottle of the good wine, yet Kelly only occasionally sipped it, her recent hangover a stark reminder of what alcohol could do.

She laughed and spoke of her funny stories around the fake trade business and Keffa found himself laughing along with her. She had not noticed she was doing all the talking, while he sat admiring her.

"So, girl, what do you want to do when you grow up?"

Kelly teased, with a smile. "In case you ain't noticed, I am grown up, and I am doing what I want to do."

Once they finished, he paid the bill and drove her home.

"Thanks, Keffa, that was lovely. I had a good time. Maybe next time, I will pay."

Keffa looked at her innocent face and smiled. "Yeah, baby, maybe next time."

Rudy was looking out of the window and was relieved to see Bluey. He had arrived home with Krystal to find the house empty and started to worry.

"Oh, thank goodness, I was …" mumbled Rudy.

"Rudy, what is it with this girl? I mean, she ain't ya honey, is she, and she ain't no kid either."

The sharp glare that Rudy shot in her direction was enough to say don't push it. But Krystal was annoyed: no one should come before her.

On his guard, Rudy was anxious. Why was Bluey with Keffa? He felt uneasy and couldn't wait to find out, and so he opened the front door and hopped down the steps.

"Yo, hello," she giggled. Rudy looked at her upbeat expression and then bent down to acknowledge Keffa.

"Go inside, Blue, I want to talk with Keffa." None the wiser, Kelly smiled and left. Rudy opened the car door and got in.

"All right, Rudy?" beamed Keffa.

Rudy felt hot under the collar, as he had just realised he had jumped in uninvited and was stumped for words. Keffa laughed. "Rudy, ya don't think I was …" he pointed up the steps.

"She's a baby, Keffa."

"Rudy, I know. I was just looking out for her." He stared off into space. "I know she's a kid but she's also like a woman, but hey, don't worry, I ain't after fucking her."

Rudy nodded and smiled. "Sorry, Keffa, I just … well, I don't know. I feel I have to look out for her, too. Don't even know why."

Keffa's eyes softened, as he grabbed Rudy's shoulder. "I know exactly what ya mean. Me, I am the same. Fucking mental, eh?"

∽*∾

Kelly was in a jolly mood; she had really enjoyed the evening with Keffa. As she flopped down on the sofa, to untie her long boots, she spotted Krystal sitting at the far end where the lounge was in darkness.

"Oh, hello, I didn't see you there."

Krystal wore a malevolent look on her face. "Well, get used to it because I will be around a lot more."

"Oh yeah, is that supposed to bother me?" replied Kelly, as she sat upright now, itching for a row.

With a snidely glare, Krystal nodded. "I know your game. Ya just white trash, poncing off my man. All this bollocks you're his niece. A name like Bluey, eh? I don't buy it, girl, for one minute."

"If Rudy says I'm his niece, then I am," she confidently answered back.

Krystal stood up to intimidate Kelly, who just rolled her eyes and tutted. *If she wants a row, bring it on, girl*, she thought.

"He may call me his sexy mamma but that don't mean I fucking gave birth to him."

Kelly ignored Krystal and went to her room. She heard Rudy come back and listened. She knew they were unaware she could hear everything in that bedroom. But the sound somehow collected inside her four walls.

"Rudy, why is that girl having it away with Keffa and living under your roof? Maybe she is a plant. I mean, that Keffa is gilded and yet she is here. Rudy, something doesn't make sense. I personally wouldn't trust her in my home."

122

There was silence and Kelly waited to hear Rudy's response. She couldn't go flying in there, confronting Krystal. This was Rudy's call.

"Krystal, me lickle angel, this is me own business, not for you to worry ya pretty lickle head over. Now, ya making me too horny to stand chatting shit. Let's go to me room and let Papa unleash the monster."

Lippy was right: Rudy was under Krystal's spell and ruled by his cock.

The next morning, the house was buzzing: the boys were in the kitchen, Lippy was cooking, and Kelly joined them. They bantered over the girls they'd pulled that night, teasing and pushing each other and laughing in hysterics. Unexpectedly, the room went quiet when Krystal walked in. She had a sour expression as she sat at the table. Lippy turned her back and continued frying. Ditto and Reggie got up to leave but Kelly remained. The tension was looming, but she was determined to stand her ground and not let Krystal push her out of her own home — not now she had finally found happiness and security.

Lippy handed Bluey a plate filled with food and winked and then left the kitchen without a word.

Krystal took a deep breath, annoyed that she wasn't offered any, particularly since her stomach was churning, and she really fancied the idea of tucking into one of Lippy's delicious dishes. One thing she couldn't deny was the fact that the old prostitute could rustle up a feast from nothing.

As Kelly began to eat, Krystal leaned forward, pointing with her long pink-painted fingernails, and in a cold, menacing tone, she whispered, "I know exactly who you are, Kelly Raven!" She held her glare for a second and then got up to leave. Stunned, Kelly placed the fork back on the plate and stared into space, as if she had been slapped in the face with a wet fish.

Dressed in a black suit with an oversized black hat, Lippy stood in the kitchen doorway. Kelly was surprised to see her in anything other than hot pants, a dressing gown, or one of her fancy dresses.

"Right, lickle sweet pea, me off to say goodbye to me matie, Massie, God rest her soul."

"Krystal knows me real name, Lippy," said Kelly, looking to the floor.

Lippy sat on the chair opposite. "Listen, chil', don't you worry. That woman won't say a word, if she knows what's good for her. Rudy will kick her into touch."

But it wasn't so much what Krystal had said — it was how she had said it that rattled Kelly.

CHAPTER SIX

Over the next six months, the tension in the house was noticed by everyone. Kelly tended to hang around in her room, and the boys stayed out later than they normally would. Krystal was making herself right at home and every chance she had she would sneer at Kelly. Rudy was as Lippy had said — blinded by the need to shag Krystal, which, needless to say, was often.

Friday morning, Kelly was up and dressed. Krystal had gone on another shopping spree with Rudy, Ditto and Reggie were visiting their mother, and Phoenix and Solly were on a delivery. She wandered into the kitchen and found the stove cold. Lippy must be out too. She poured the dog biscuits into a bowl and called Legend. He came bounding down the hallway and skidded to a stop to plunge his nose down into his breakfast. Then, there was the sound of heavy banging. Kelly left Legend to finish his food; she hurried along the hallway, assuming Ditto had forgotten his keys, as he often did.

She didn't think to look first, before she pulled open the door. There, in front of her, stood four armed officers. This was serious. She heard Legend bark at the back door and then realised they had surrounded the house. Her stomach did a back flip and her mouth immediately went dry. She looked from one copper to the next. The fourth one, a woman, stepped forward. "Kelly Raven!" She wasn't asking, she was telling.

How could she escape? Kelly was frozen to the spot, her mind in a complete turmoil. She shook her head. "No Kelly lives here!" was all she could say. The female officer snorted and nodded. "Yeah sure, Kelly, you are under arrest."

"Like I said, I ain't Kelly, ya got the wrong person, sorry." She turned to close the door in the WPC's face, but a burly male officer stuck his foot in the door and grabbed her arm.

"Kelly Raven, you are under arrest." They handcuffed her in a matter of seconds. Completely in shock, she didn't hear the rest of the caution. Her heart was pounding against her chest and she swooned. An officer lifted her up and walked her down the concrete steps. He pushed her head down to ease her in the car. The WPO then said, "I am Officer Farmer, and I will be taking you to the station. Do you understand what is going on here, Kelly?" The immediate shock had worn off. It wasn't worth denying who she was. If the police were sure, then they probably had a good reason. She stared ahead, as the car drove through Peckham. For a second, she thought she saw Keffa about to pull out of a junction.

"Kelly, when we get to the station, you can make a call, okay?" Farmer was being motherly.

Jayne Farmer was assigned to the hunt. They were after a kid wanted for a double murder: Patrick Mahoney and her own mother. Jayne tended to be given these domestic cases only because she was good at these and could normally coax people around. But on this occasion, they weren't sure what they were walking into. They had nothing to go on except that Kelly was an exceptional student who lived alone with her mother and occasionally visited her aunt. There was no history of drugs, no alcohol misuse, no ASBOs, and no deviation from conformity.

Her disappearance had had them all flummoxed. They'd assumed that maybe she had killed herself and they would one day find a body. The photo of her face on the news for more than a week had turned up no witnesses either. They were lucky to receive the phone call with the address and description. Assuming Kelly was alive, and she was probably a very troubled kid, two murders within a few weeks of each other would have taken some careful planning. The brutal murder of her mother was particularly nasty: she had received a stab wound to the face and throat.

Kelly remained silent and stared at the road ahead. She didn't move or even acknowledge the officer. Then, everything began to run through her mind. She was part of a family she loved and felt at home with, happy and safe, and now it was all being taken away from her. A tear pricked her eyelid and fell down her cheek. Jayne observed the girl's blank expression and the tear.

The police car pulled into a back entrance to the station. They helped her out but guarded her, as if she was some kind of serial killer. Two officers held her arms and guided her inside the building. She felt as though she was walking into the lion's den. For almost two and a half years now, she had lived in a world where the police were the enemy. She had listened to the boys telling her their stories of how they had been mistreated; they had been thrown over cars, handcuffed, kicked, and punched. Kelly was waiting for the same brutal treatment, assuming this would be the case. Every door was made of chunky metal and each bang, as it closed, made her jump. They marched her along a corridor to the main desk where she was presented to the custody sergeant who seemed cold and expressionless. He looked up, stared at Kelly, and then he returned his eyes to some paperwork. The atmosphere was tense; after all, they had no idea how to treat her. She was fifteen when she had allegedly murdered Patrick, almost sixteen, in fact, and yet she was now a mature-looking woman with a past about which they had no idea. For all they knew, she could have carried out more atrocities.

Jayne went through Kelly's pockets and removed a bunch of keys and two hundred pounds. That was all she had on her, not even her mobile phone. She placed them in the plastic bags. After a few questions, to which Kelly nodded, she was escorted to a holding cell. The thought of being locked up terrified her and she began to shake. She tried to push away, as they opened the door, but the two officers didn't need to struggle with her and pushed her inside. Jayne went in with her.

"Kelly, you have to take off your boots and belt, but you can keep on your jeans and shirt."

Kelly didn't argue, as she sat on the blue plastic mattress; she slowly removed her things and handed them to the officer. The anxiety at being shut in the room was overwhelming, and yet before she could blink, Jayne left and locked the door.

To protect herself, she closed her eyes and covered her face with her hands. She concentrated on her breathing and felt the warmth of the room and the comfort of the bed. It wasn't the shed, it wasn't winter, and she wasn't surrounded by insects. She tried to imagine Lippy's round shiny face with her big expressive eyes and her voice telling her it would be all right. She was strong. *Breathe, Kelly, breathe.*

Jayne looked in through the small glass window. Kelly was sitting in the same spot an hour later, with the paperwork now all in place. They had to follow protocol. "No fuck ups," the Commissioner had told them, and he had been very clear to his officers about this.

DI Maddox had lost it when the girl had slipped off their radar, following a double killing and this fifteen-year-old on the run. She had made them look like complete imbeciles. He was called into the station and was livid. The timing of this arrest was unfortunate, to say the least. He was about to set off on his holiday with his new bit of skirt.

Jayne heard him stomping along the corridor, long before he entered the custody suite. The door was almost thrown open, and there, with an angry expression and cloaked in arrogance, stood DI Maddox. A lump of a man, tall and stocky, wearing a dark-green blazer and black trousers underneath his trench coat, he was a class-one bastard. The outfit was not really to his taste, but Hillary, his new tart, had bought it in the sales and insisted he wore it. He liked his weekend shags and keeping her sweet guaranteed his oats.

"Where is she?" He never spoke quietly and always seemed to talk with such a fierceness in his voice. Maybe that was what Hillary found attractive. Jayne found it odd that he could pull a bird as pretty as she was, when he was so mean-looking with piercing amber eyes. His hair was a thick mop of auburn locks and it flopped in all directions.

128

"All right, Gov, she's in there." Jayne pointed to the first cell. Without a please or thank you, Maddox marched over and glared through the glass at the petite-framed teenager perched on the edge of the bed.

He took a deep breath. "Right, take her into the interview room."

There was no finesse and no warm twinkle in his eyes, yet for some reason everyone respected him. Jayne didn't. She couldn't stand the vain man, but she still acted politely and jumped to attention. It was that niggling doubt that Maddox was as bent as a nine bob note because he drove expensive cars, wore top-of-the-range watches, and holidayed in the Caribbean twice a year. But how could he on the Met's police pay?

She unlocked the door and was surprised that Kelly didn't jump to her feet; she was still hiding her face in her hands.

"Stand up, Kelly!" she commanded in her firm but gentle voice.

Kelly removed her hands from her face and slowly got to her feet.

She was taken to the interview room where DI Maddox was already reading the arrest notes. Kelly was asked to take a seat.

"Kelly Raven!" barked Maddox.

She remained with her head down, not caring what the man said or did. She was going down, that was for sure, and she wanted it over and done with as soon as possible.

"I am Detective Inspector Maddox."

There was no response; Kelly didn't even raise her head or reply.

"Kelly, have you been read your rights?" He knew she had.

The room was brightly lit, and there was just the one table and four chairs, but it had that sterile, almost clinical appearance.

Maddox stood up and opened the door. He called out, "Will someone fetch two teas? I am fucking parched in here!"

Jayne hurried to the drinks machine and fumbled with the thin plastic cups; the hot liquid was burning her hands and she cursed under her breath. "Fucking smug prick." Once she had returned with the two teas, she slid one under Maddox's nose and carefully placed the other in front of Kelly. She gave the young girl a sympathetic smile.

"Listen, Kelly, we can get this over with quickly or drag it out for hours. I will get pretty fucked off and you will have a numb arse. The choice is yours," growled Maddox.

Kelly wanted to laugh, but as she looked up, a sadness flickered across her face. Maddox then saw her innocent eyes; she wasn't a hard-looking teenager, and she didn't have the attitude, like her father. She was just a kid with a soft glow and a pretty face. He mellowed his tone accordingly. "Kelly, you can make a call, let someone know you're here. Do you want representation, a brief, a family member?"

Kelly shook her head. "Mr Maddox, I don't want to call anyone. There's no need, and as for a lawyer, I don't need one of them either."

"What about your father?" No sooner were the words out of his mouth, he gritted his back teeth and wished he had kept quiet. Eddie had told him, if he found the girl, he was to call him, as he wanted to have a word himself.

With a deep frown, Kelly shook her head. She brushed the thought aside, assuming the detective was unaware of her situation regarding not knowing her father, and he wouldn't refer to her mother because she was dead.

Maddox sat back on his chair and stared for a while. He was concerned because she wasn't behaving as a normal person would.

"Kelly, ya know you're in a lot of trouble, right?"

130

"Yeah, I know I am, so what's the point in lawyers and shit. Just get it over with."

Maddox left the table again and called for Jayne. "Call the duty solicitor, will you? She said she don't want a brief."

Jayne frowned. "Well, she needs one, that's for sure."

Maddox rubbed his bristly chin. "Yeah, well, it's her fucking right, I ain't pushing it. She can have the duty brief … but call social services."

Jayne noticed how easily he had dismissed the idea of having her own solicitor. Had she been in his role, she would have explained the importance; after all, Kelly was still a child in the eyes of the law. She was under eighteen and still classed as a minor.

Within half an hour, the duty solicitor and a woman called Nancy, from the social services, arrived. Maddox looked at Nancy, the assigned adult for Kelly, up and down and then rolled his eyes. He was pissed off with these young wet-behind-the-ears do-gooders. "How old are you?" he glowered.

Nancy gave him an unappreciative glare. "Old enough to know my job and old enough to know yours. So, where is the child?"

Grinding his back teeth, Maddox pointed to the interview room. Nancy looked the consummate professional in her high heels and pencil skirt, as she edged around him holding a leather briefcase in her hand. Jayne smiled. *That told him.*

John Kirby was the duty solicitor, eager to work his way up the career ladder, and therefore always on hand. Any overtime to be had, he was all over it, like a rash. Jobsworth Johnnie they called him at the station, behind his back of course.

The three reconvened in the interview room. Nancy introduced herself to Kelly in a soft, gentle voice, whilst John sat the other side, unable to speak until his potential client gave him instructions.

Kelly looked at the three pairs of eyes.

"My name is Nancy Sterring. I have been informed that you do not have a guardian or anyone for that matter to be present."

Maddox stared at Kelly, trying to guess what she was thinking. Nancy was too prim and proper – there was nothing warm about her, and it was his guess that Kelly wouldn't open up to her. He then looked at Johnnie, who looked like an estate agent, with his eager eyes and quick moves.

"John is the duty solicitor. I know you have the right not to have a brief but it's a good idea to. If you want some time alone, I can leave you with these two," stated Maddox.

Kelly shook her head. "Look, Mr Maddox, please can we just get this over with?"

With a raised eyebrow, he nodded for John to leave.

"Kelly, do you know what you have been arrested for?"

She casually nodded.

"Can you please tell me in your own words what you understand you have been arrested for?" asked Maddox in a kinder tone, for the benefit of Nancy.

Without hesitation, Kelly replied, "For killing Patrick what's-his-fucking-name."

There was silence, as Maddox waited to see if she would add the killing of her mother.

He leaned forward. "Did the officer read you your rights and say what you were arrested for?"

She couldn't remember and shrugged her shoulders.

He opened the brown file in front of him and turned the papers around for Nancy to be able to read them.

"I think you need to explain what's going on."

Nancy snatched the papers and read the first paragraph. She reread the arrest sheet and turned to face Kelly.

DI Maddox and John waited outside the interview room to allow the social worker to explain the situation. "That girl in there is one complete nut job. I want her in court first thing and out of this station. The duty officer at the court can take over … For fuck's sake, this is all I need, missing that damn plane."

John wasn't interested in Maddox's moaning; he was adding up the pound signs.

Nancy gave Kelly a fake sympathetic smile, as if to say, 'You poor child, you have no idea that you may go away for a huge chunk of your sad, pathetic life'.

"Kelly, they have arrested you, my dear, for two murders. The first is Patrick Mahoney and also, sweetheart, for the murder of your mother."

Kelly snapped out of her stupor. She frowned and curled her lip. "What? I never killed me mum. I only killed Patrick."

That was a smack in the mouth. Nancy had never expected her to admit she had actually killed anyone. "You know you have the right not to say anything and to let a solicitor advise you, and, sweetie, I think that's really your best option. Now are you okay, pumpkin?"

As if someone had jabbed her in the ribs, Kelly sat up straight, now annoyed. She hated pretentious and condescending people. "I know you mean well, but I ain't no sweetie, or bleedin' pumpkin for that matter. I didn't kill me muvver but I did kill Patrick. Do I understand what's happening? 'Course I bloody do. I ain't a fool you know, and I ain't five either."

Nancy was shocked and put out by the outburst. She stood up and opened the door for Maddox to join them. "She understands fully, so you can carry on." Maddox sensed she'd been given an unsympathetic rejection in there by Kelly. Nancy flicked her perfectly shaped bob and straightened her dark-rimmed glasses. Maddox looked at her neat arse, defined in her slim-fitting skirt, and decided she may be a good shag, and she probably needed one to loosen the starchy look on her face.

Kelly's whole demeanour had changed and she was ready to talk. Her fears were still there but her confidence had now returned.

After two hours of questioning, Maddox had everything he needed to hand the paperwork over to the CPS and secure two charges of first-degree murder. It was a cakewalk.

She was held in the juvenile holding room until the court appearance the next day. Jayne was on duty and in charge of the custody suite. Kelly was moved to another room, much like the cell, yet it was more comfortable. She felt less anxious and lay on her bed trying to sleep. She would miss her family, but she guessed this would have happened one day; she had just hoped that it would not have been so soon.

Concerned, Jayne popped her head inside the room every hour to check on the girl. She bought some food from the canteen and a magazine. Kelly smiled gratefully.

"Are you all right, Kelly? Do you need anything?"

Kelly smiled. "I'm fine. Thank you for being so kind. I thought it would be worse, ya know, locked in a dark room with bars up at the window and a dirty-smelling bed."

Jayne felt sorry for the girl because she knew that's exactly where Kelly would be going when she was put on remand. No doubt, there would be bars up at the window and the comforts a bare minimum.

The next morning, she was taken to the magistrates to be held in custody until her court date arrived. The judge was efficient and it was over in ten minutes. Kelly just went with the flow; there was no point in trying to fathom out the procedure. She was taken by a custody van, in a sweatbox as they called it, to Downview Prison in Surrey. The journey was rough because she barely had room to move, but that was it, she was in the system. No one would know though and that is how she wanted it. But she thought about her aunt Betty. She hadn't seen her for over two years now although at least her aunt knew she was okay. A few weeks after she went on the run, she returned and hand-delivered a letter explaining everything, in the hope that Betty would understand.

As soon as the van arrived inside the gates, she was escorted off in handcuffs and taken to the reception area. With no one else in the van, other than two escorting officers, it felt like the first day at senior school. Yet here, she was accompanied everywhere. The officers were hard and cold. They shoved her in the back to move her forward and manhandled her when she tripped. The reception area was small and the atmosphere distinctly sterile. Officers were there to prepare Kelly for her stay. They took the files, her belongings, and read off a series of rules. However, the information was too much to absorb at once.

Eventually, she was led into a doctors' office with two men in white coats. She soon realised that one was a psychiatrist. He was an odd-looking character himself with a misshaped head and perfect white teeth. He put her in mind of Uncle Fester from the Addams family. The other doctor looked pretty normal and started by taking Kelly's blood pressure and then her temperature. He asked the usual medical questions. "Are you allergic to anything, any major head injuries in the past, any previous history of serious conditions?" He went on and on.

Then the shrink took over. "So, Kelly, are you sexually active?"

Kelly frowned. "Piss off, I'm nearly eighteen years old, not twenty-six."

The psychiatrist twitched. This wasn't normal. He scribbled some notes and looked at her reaction to the next question. "Are you heterosexual, bisexual, or gay?"

Furious with these demeaning questions, she snapped, "I ain't any sexual weirdo."

"Do you like men or women?" he asked, totally unperturbed.

Kelly flared her nostrils. "What sodding difference does it make?"

"Do you find men or women attractive?"

Kelly thought about the question. She had never really fantasised about either. Her mother had removed any such thoughts so far from her mind that she had never actually broached the idea. She could tell if a man or woman was attractive, but as for a relationship, it wasn't something she gave any thought to. She was too busy living, after being so devoid of any kind of life under her mother's roof.

"Look, doctor, I guess you are trying to get inside my head, but let me save you a shed loada trouble. I ain't suicidal, I ain't a nutter, I ain't a lesbian, and I ain't crazy like a shit-house rat."

The psychiatrist nodded and scribbled more notes.

"Kelly, how do you feel about your mother's death?" He didn't look up; instead, he remained with his pen poised.

Leaning back on her chair, Kelly stared at the odd shape of his shiny bald head. At this point, she was wondering if he was either dropped at birth or squashed coming out of his mother's fanny.

"Kelly, I will ask you again. How do you feel about your mother's death?"

She visualised her mother lying there in a pool of blood, but all that popped into her head was her spiteful face and those evil-looking eyes.

"I don't think about it!" she raised her voice. He was irritating her, with his monotonic style of speaking and his silly questions.

"Are you angry right now, Kelly?"

She sighed. "No, I ain't angry. I am just tired and bored with you going on."

As he stood up, she noticed his misshapen back and that one of his legs was shorter than the other and instantly felt sorry for him.

One of the officers was called to take her away. Before she was escorted into another section, Kelly could smell the Dettol. The room had a clinical yet cold, distinct smell and one she didn't like; it was too close for comfort and a stark reminder to her of her mother. When she was asked to strip and stand in the shower, Kelly felt uncomfortable and humiliated. Then it hit her; she had no privacy and was cattle-herded like a lamb to the slaughter.

"Hurry up, Raven, we haven't got all day!" shouted the fat screw. She later knew her as Charlie.

As she peeled off her jeans, removed her shirt, and took off her underwear, she turned to step into the shower. Charlie was used to women and girls of all shapes, sizes, tattoos, and birthmarks. Yet what she saw shocked her to the core. She had never seen a girl with so many cruel scars on her back. She winced, as she stared at the many grooves that marked her otherwise perfectly toned skin. Charlie had been informed of the charges; she now began to wonder if this young woman had killed her own mother because she had whipped her. There lay that doubting question mark, and what about the man she was supposed to have murdered? Either way, the kid had suffered at someone's hands. Who else would have caused those hideous marks?

As Kelly stepped out of the shower, Charlie handed her a towel and turned away, leaving her with some dignity. "Raven, your prison issues are on the bench. Get dressed, and follow me."

Kelly quickly dried herself and lifted the sweatshirt; it was a bit big but it was comfortable. She then held up the sweat pants, which were also too big, but hey ho, she was hardly out to impress anyone. So, these were the prison issues. Not so bad. Charlie had a reputation in the prison as the hard-ass screw. The inmates hated her. She walked Kelly over to the block, still smarting from the girl's scarring. The corridor was long and daunting with doors evenly spread on either side. The cells were the same: there was just a bed, a bookshelf, a toilet, and bars. It wasn't as grubby as she had expected: she had envisaged early Victorian, with water running down the walls and infested with rats. In fact, the room was small, clean, and warm and so unlike that awful shed at home. While she sat on the bed, Charlie read her the rules: these included the times to get up, go to exercise, have meals, and final recreation before lock-up. Kelly nodded and smiled. As Charlie went to lock the door, Kelly said, "Thanks, Officer Bryant."

Charlie, to her surprise, realised the girl was genuine: there was no hint of sarcasm. She nodded and smiled back. It felt very strange, her smiling to an inmate.

Three days had passed and Rudy had the boys out looking for Kelly. Lippy was sick with worry, and they had then begun to assume the worst – that the police had, in fact, nicked her. What they found odd were the deep scratch marks on the front and back door. Legend was stressed when Rudy had arrived home; he was in attack mode, panting heavily and walking in circles. As soon as Ditto had come back with no answers, Rudy made the decision to knock on Keffa's door. Either she was there, or he would know how to find out if she had been nicked.

Krystal had seen the other side of Rudy and realised that calling the police was a huge mistake. She had underestimated the impact it would have when Rudy paced the floor and made all kinds of threats. "If I find

138

who grassed her up, if she *was* grassed, I am gonna rip them apart, limb by limb, with me fucking teeth." He turned and glared at Krystal as if she had an inkling. She tried to take his mind off it. "Rudy, baby, you don't need to threaten me. She is just another needy, passing through. She's woman enough to make up her own mind. Maybe she's gone and got herself a nice man!"

Rudy grabbed her throat and squeezed. "You, Krystal, are just a needy, passing through, not her. She is me family!" His eyes buried themselves so deep into Krystal's, she realised she had fucked-up, big style.

Hacked off, he left Krystal, who was still gawping in the lounge, and then he snatched his keys and was gone. As he tore away, she felt pushed out and insignificant. Now she hated Kelly with a passion. That will teach her to muscle her way into what was supposed to be *her* family. Lippy stood in the doorway. She had seen Rudy attack Krystal; although she hated violence, she was satisfied because Krystal deserved it.

"What are you staring at?"

Lippy smiled. "Krystal, you have a lot to learn about life."

With a face like a smacked arse, she looked Lippy over and scowled. "Well, I don't want any tips from an old brass like you!" she countered.

A sarcastic grin swept across Lippy's face, and she nodded, indicating she was summing up Krystal. Then her words cut through Krystal like a knife. "I may be old, I may sell meself for cash, but I can hold me head up high, see. But you, Krystal, can't. You have no compassion or pride in ya soul. You use people and abuse them. I know your kind, and when I tell you one day you will wake up and feel shame like you 'ave never felt before, then that's God's way of punishing you. Shame and guilt are hard feelings to bear."

"Aw, really, Tulip? You know nothing about me. You have no idea who I am!" she screamed back in anger, still feeling the frustration and humiliation from Rudy's dismissive display.

Lippy was calm. "No, I don't know who you are, but I do know *what* you are. Rudy will see through you very soon, if he hasn't already." With that, she turned to leave.

"You watch. When my Rudy hears what you have just said, he will turf you out on ya fucking ear or rip you a new arsehole."

Fuming, Lippy whirled around. "If you stay here, Rudy won't have to turf me out, I'll 'ave gone, and while we are on the subject of telling Rudy, I think he has already worked out that you are the grass among us. So, think on, Krystal, because *you* will be the one with the new arsehole."

No more was said: Krystal collected her overnight belongings and left.

❧*❦

With his mind all over the place, and fraught with worry, Rudy banged hard on Keffa's door.

It didn't take long. A moment later, Keffa wrenched it open, sensing there was something wrong. He had seen Rudy pull up in his new car and park it haphazardly in the car park.

"All right, Rude, what's up?"

Rudy scanned the hallway and walked into the lounge. "Is Bluey here?"

Keffa narrowed his eyes. "Nah, mate, the last time I saw her was Monday night. I dropped her home after a quick coffee in the high street. Why, what's going on?"

140

Rudy was fidgeting from one foot to the other. "She's gone, Keffa, disappeared. She didn't even take her jacket. Three days now. I thought she might be here. I thought maybe you two ..." his words trailed off.

Keffa's mind went into a spin; he felt his mouth dry up and thoughts of her with another man, or, even worse, nicked, shrouded his mind. Rudy instantly saw the sadness creep over Keffa's face.

"She ain't 'ere, is she?"

Without hesitation, Keffa shook his head in despair. "I wish, Rudy, she was. Is she seeing anyone, I mean like any geezers?"

"No, Keffa, and she ain't like that, she's just a kid."

Keffa turned his head away in shame.

"Oh my God, you like her, don't ya?"

Keffa couldn't deny it. Who was he kidding? "Rude, I know she's only, what, almost eighteen, but I can't help it." He paused and looked at the inquisitive expression on Rudy's face. "I swear I have never touched her, though."

At that point, the dynamics changed. Keffa, the hard man feared by everyone, was now looking at Rudy like he called the shots – as if he was Kelly's father. Perhaps that was how he was viewed now and with that title came respect.

"Have you upset her and that's why she's fucked off?" demanded Rudy. Despite having just raised his voice, his anxiety was far greater than his fear of Keffa's wrath.

"No! Jeez, I would never hurt her, ever! I love ... I mean, I care about her too much."

Rudy saw the anguish on Keffa's face and knew then that the guy had deep feelings for Kelly. He sighed heavily. "I've got a gut instinct she has been nicked. She will be in a state, Keffa. I mean, underneath her bravado is just a frightened child, really. It's odd, 'cos I don't know why, but I love the kid. She is like a daughter to me. We all love her. There is something special about her. I dunno, she seems to light up the room …" He broke off as he felt the tears and blinked them back before Keffa saw him getting emotional, and yet Keffa felt exactly the same. He then realised he'd said too much and Keffa would question why Kelly would have been nicked.

Keffa stepped back and offered Rudy a seat. "Listen to me, Rudy. I know who she is."

Rudy's eyes were like saucers. "What d'ya mean?"

"I ain't stupid. I recognised her on the crime programme. She was on the news for a week. That little innocent face stuck in my head. Jeez, I knew who Patrick Mahoney was, and then there she was, standing in me lounge, bold as brass, trying to protect you." With a half-smile, he looked at Rudy's anxious expression. "That's why I always try to look out for her. That kid has more than a few bricks on her shoulders."

Rudy looked at the floor. "Oh, so ya know, if she's been nicked, what it's for, then?"

Keffa sat opposite him. "There's more, Rudy." His voice was even more serious now.

Rudy looked up and tilted his head. "What?"

"She is Eddie Raven's daughter."

Fraught, Rudy turned ashen. "What, as in Eddie Cako?"

Keffa nodded.

"But Bluey never said. I heard he's outta prison now. D'ya think she's gone to see him?"

Keffa shook his head. "She might not even know that Eddie is her father. He was banged up for twelve years. She must have been three or four at the time. Let me tell ya something. Years ago, I had a bit of business with Eddie, nothing big, just a firearms deal. He's a fucking dangerous man. He keeps his little firm tight, I mean fucking tight. Anyway, he trusted me, and one night, he came over to me pad in North London. We shared a few drinks, and he had a few lines of Charlie. Then he got talking. See, I'm not much of a chatterbox, but on cocaine, he is. That's why he sticks to his own firm, never mixes with anyone other than those he can trust, get what I mean?"

Rudy nodded. "Yeah, go on, mate."

"I'm telling you, Rudy, but it's from me own mouth so ..."

"I'm good for keeping schtum," replied Rudy, eager to hear the story.

Keffa nodded. "Eddie has this thing. He believes what's his is his, no fucking messing. He killed his two sidekicks, Jack McFarlane and Mickey O'Toole over a few diamonds. I mean, the man is minted. He killed them and took out their fucking eyes. He told me he did it. Jeez, Eddie is a sick muvver fucker. But that's not all! He told me that his missus was once a right stunner, loved a bit of sex, and kept him sweet in the bedroom, 'cos Eddie is a sex addict, ya know. He fucking admitted it to me. I swear the man don't give a shit. But, one woman wasn't enough, so he was shagging his way through half of fucking London, even Naomi, Jack McFarlane's nineteen-year-old daughter. When Maureen, his missus, found out, she went all weird on him and turned to God or something. He said to me back then that once he had his villa in Spain renovated, he was doing the off with his daughter, Kelly. She was his and he was taking what belonged to him, whether Maureen liked it or not. But he didn't get far 'cos his missus grassed him up, by all accounts."

Rudy was taking it all in. "D'ya think Eddie killed the muvver?"

Keffa slowly nodded his head. "Yeah, I do, and incidentally, that Patrick, who Kelly is supposed to have killed, was a no-good wanker anyway."

Rudy frowned. "Who was he?"

"Patrick was Eddie's brother-in-law. Married to Toni, Eddie's little sister. So, as you can see, mate, it's all fucking messy. Why d'ya think I have a soft spot for the kid? Poor thing has been dealt a raw hand in life. They are all a bunch of nutters, and she don't even know what she was born in to. To top it all, she is probably going to take the rap for her own father's wrongdoing. 'Cos, it's my guess, he did kill that Maureen."

Rudy looked distraught with the news. It was a lot to take in but still they had no clue if Kelly was inside or had just done a runner.

"I can ask me mate down the Yard. He will know. I am surprised it ain't on the news. Unless, of course, the Old Bill have something up their sleeve."

Keffa clenched his phone and scrolled down to the number logged under 'Pig'. "Mate, did your lot arrest Kelly Raven?" He was short and sweet. The officer on the other end swallowed hard; he was told her arrest was not to be made public, but it was Keffa on the phone. He couldn't fuck with him because he was his cocaine supplier.

"Yeah, she didn't want to make a call or have a brief. She's been taken to Downview on a double murder charge. You didn't hear it from me."

As he slid the phone back inside his pocket, he nodded. "She's in Downview on remand. A double murder. Strange they are keeping it a secret. Fucking filth are more dodgy than any villain I know."

Rudy put his face in his hands in disbelief. "Why didn't she call? I would have been there for her."

Keffa sat beside him, placing an arm around his shoulder. "'Cos, mate, she is a free spirit. She wouldn't want to bring any trouble to your door. Ya know, the day she confronted me about that cunting cock-up, I could have fed her to me men, but there was something kinda real about her. She put herself up for a good kicking for you."

Rudy looked up, as if he'd just had his heart torn apart. "Yeah, I have to admit, I do love the kid. She is real. Ain't many like her about, is there?"

Keffa agreed and then he came back to reality. "Ya know, Eddie will be on her case. If we are seen to get involved, then he may come after us. The man has no sense of reason."

"So, what do we do?"

"Nuffin, let's see what unfolds," replied Keffa.

"But we did no wrong, just helped the kid," Rudy pointed out.

"Let me tell ya, that Eddie won't give a shit. I know him. He will shoot first, and if there's anything left of ya, he will ask questions after."

CHAPTER SEVEN

Kelly slept well, even though it was a strange room and bed. She was overwhelmed by all the rules and procedures but this was it now. She had been caught and would have to face the consequences. The doors opened and the corridor had become a hive of excitement with young women noisily bustling their way through. Kelly walked ahead, as her door was the last on the right and closest to the exit. The screw did a head count and allowed two through at a time. As they were ushered along, she had to wait for some of the girls. She heard them talking and received a few glares but guessed she wouldn't be popular: she hadn't been at school, so why should it change now in prison?

One girl, more woman really, whispered in Kelly's ear, as she slid past, "Muvver murderer."

Those callous words cut her to the core. Another girl, older than Kelly, made another snide remark and blew in her ear. As they passed, Kelly got a closer look. They were tough-looking with cropped hair and each had tattoos on their neck. Kelly shuddered and then moved forward.

"Right, Raven, you're with me, back to the medical." A new officer, with fair hair and more of a motherly face, nodded in her direction. Kelly sighed with relief. The other inmates all passed her, off to their allocated jobs, and Kelly followed the officer back to the medical unit to face the weird psychiatrist again.

He looked the same as yesterday. "How are you this morning, Kelly?"

She shrugged her shoulders. "Okay, I s'pose. How should I be?"

He glanced up again with his blank expression. "Kelly, I have a doctor here who has been brought in specially to talk to you." With that he got up, opened the door at the back of the room, and stepped aside for another doctor to enter, before resuming his seat. Kelly was surprised to see a woman who captured her interest – but this time more for her appearance. She didn't wear a white coat but was dressed in a navy-blue suit and a bright green shirt. Her light auburn hair was neatly trimmed and she wore a heavy layer of make-up. She sat next to the psychiatrist and smiled. Her face lit up and Kelly felt her shoulders relax.

"Kelly, my name is Molly Bedford. I have been assigned to your case. Is that okay with you?"

Kelly, none the wiser, nodded and smiled sweetly.

"I want to get to know you, so could we start by you telling me about yourself?"

"Like what?"

"Whatever you want, Kelly. Maybe we could start with what it was like at school?"

Kelly frowned. "I didn't like school."

Molly waited to see if Kelly would put more meat on the bones but there was nothing.

"Tell me about your relationship with your mother. Was it like a friendship, was she strict, or was she kind?"

"How do I know? I had only one mother, so I had nothing to compare."

Molly asked her last question before she made up her mind about Kelly's personality.

"How do you feel, now that your mother is dead?"

"How should I feel? I mean, I don't bloody know," replied Kelly, with her head inclined and a deep frown forming across her face.

With an overzealous mind, Molly decided that they may be dealing with a psychopath and so they would need to go through the checklist consisting of a series of a hundred questions that may determine this young woman's state of mind. Molly and the other psychiatrist left the room, and they returned again, half an hour later.

They had the files containing the questionnaire. Molly came across a few real certified psychopaths but not many. She supposed Kelly was a possibility, with her detached view of her life. The way she asked, 'How should I feel?' suggested she may have a more serious problem. Yet, they were unaware that the girl had been subjected to cruel abuse.

The questions were monotonous, to which Kelly either shrugged or answered with, "I don't know."

Finally, they decided she might well have psychopathic tendencies. As Kelly was escorted to the door, she turned and frowned at Molly; her eyes darkened and her face changed. "I didn't murder my mother. I wasn't even there."

Molly turned to her colleague and smiled. "It is hard to know whether she is telling the truth because she admits to the murder of Patrick."

As soon as Kelly was back on the wing, she was again in the throes of women who had returned from their jobs to have lunch. Kelly was handed a tray and told she would be better off in her cell until they could allocate her work. Once there, she peeled back the paper bag to find a cheese and tomato sandwich; it tasted like sour milk and cardboard, but she ate it anyway. There was a small carton of orange and a bruised apple to follow. She sat alone on her bed and wondered what was to become of her. Ten, perhaps, or even, God forbid, twenty years? Her thoughts were interrupted when a woman came in — tall

149

and thin with long hair and narrow dark eyes — walking like a man, swinging her arms, and bouncing her hips. "So, you are Kelly Raven, then?" Her manner was cocky and abrasive.

Kelly stood up, and with nothing to lose, she answered back. "Yeah, why, who wants to know?" She remembered Penny saying that, one time.

"Oooh, daring little fucker, ain't ya?"

Kelly glared, narrowing her eyes. She was not going to be intimidated. Then another girl walked in and the tall one stepped aside. She was a nasty butch-looking character, with a scar across her cheek. Kelly guessed she was older than eighteen. She lit up a fag and blew smoke in Kelly's face. Kelly didn't move, too afraid to take her eyes off her.

"Double murder charge, was it? Well, well!"

Kelly said nothing and continued to stare the girl out. Inside, she was nervous but knew she had to keep calm. Running to the officer, or crying like a baby, would do her no good.

"Killed ya own muvver, ya fucking sicko!" The stocky woman was goading Kelly, hoping for a response. Milo was the hardest bird on the wing and the one who called the shots. It was like a pecking order and she was at the top. Once news had reached the inmates that Kelly Raven, the double murderer, was on the wing, Milo had to show who was in charge to maintain her status.

Kelly's heart was racing and the heavy pulse made her head nod in rhythm just slightly. Nervously, she remained silent with her eyes glued on Milo.

"Gonna fucking say somefing, or are ya gonna be rude?"

"Yeah, I am Kelly Raven, the fucking double murderer, so who are you?" she managed to say without faltering, even though she felt sick.

150

"'Ere, you wanna reel ya fucking neck in, little girl."

Kelly was hot under the collar and watched as Milo clenched her fat fists and tightened her square jaw.

Kelly's eyes darted from one woman to the other. She tried desperately to hold the mean expression, hoping it would put them off from starting on her. Once again, she tried to think of what Penny would do. But this was prison: here the rules were different, these inmates were vicious, and she was totally out of her comfort zone.

"When ya get ya money, I want soap and deodorant. It's your payment to me, got it?"

Kelly was about to nod but something about the girl's eyes made her angry. They were like her mother's used to be: piercing, threatening, and venomous. "Nah, mate, it ain't 'appening." No sooner were those words out than Kelly wished she had never said them.

Milo stepped forward, so she was only a few inches away from Kelly's nose. "Don't fuck with me, bitch, or you will fucking wish you had never been born. I will scar that pretty little face of yours and cut off ya fingers."

Kelly didn't falter; she stayed still, her stare transfixed on Milo. Being subservient again was not going to happen – not here, not ever.

"Cut me face, will ya? Yeah, try it, and like you said, I *am* a double murderer. If I can kill me own muvver, killing you will be a fucking breeze." Again, she thought she had overstepped the mark but something inside was goading her on.

Milo stepped back, shocked that the new girl had the balls to answer her back. She was uneased by the situation and yet gripped by the challenge facing her. Kelly didn't look like a fighter; her soft complexion and round innocent eyes though may be hiding a real nutcase. Milo was confident that any newbie would shit themselves and offer her their last dinner. Kelly was different; perhaps it was the blank expression or the lack of fear in her eyes. Whatever it was, Milo sensed danger. She looked at the tall woman. "Come on, Bobby, leave the runt to think it over before she makes a big mistake." Bobby laughed and moved closer to Kelly. "Yeah, ya wanna think on, Raven, if ya know what's good for ya."

Kelly smirked, and in a raised voice, she taunted, "You too!" As soon as they were out of sight, she closed the door and shook all over.

For the next three days, she followed the same routine of going to the canteen for breakfast and then off to Molly to answer more questions. No one had spoken to her, apart from the screws, who called only to tell her where to go and what to do. Milo had stayed away.

On the fifth day, she was allowed to go to recess. She waited for the inmates on her wing to go to work so she could be alone in the shower. She was uncomfortable being naked in front of anyone. The prison issues were adequate enough and the towels were clean. She had soap and shampoo issued when she first arrived. The showers were three in a row and all available. No one was around, apart from a scrawny-looking bird mopping down the walkway. Kelly folded her clothes, piled them neatly next to the showers, stepped on the cold tiles in the cubicle, and closed the door. The shower was freezing at first but it soon warmed up. She massaged the shampoo into her scalp; it was harsh and stung her eyes, but she felt desperate to wash away the prison smell. She hated the pungent odour; it was distinctive and a bit like the school gym odour. Then it happened – without any warning – as the door was flung open and two women, Milo and Bobby, stood there. The first jab landed on the side of Kelly's head, knocking her against the wall so hard a tile cracked. The second blow was to the ribs and she doubled over. But even those punches were not enough to take her out. Milo waited for Kelly to stand up straight, but as Kelly lifted her head, she lifted her leg too, and in one swift move, she caught Milo in the chest and sent her sprawling to the floor. The other girl, Bobby, who looked so much like Milo they could have been sisters, turned to help her friend get to her feet. Kelly was out of the cubicle and snatching the towel, wrapping it around her, before Milo was up in her face. They stood eye to eye, glaring, and then suddenly Kelly felt a dull thump to the ribs. It wasn't a punch, it felt different. The two women walked away and then Kelly saw the blood and felt the pain. She placed her hands over the wound and felt the claret seeping between her fingers. As she grappled with her clothes, trying to pull them on, she was unable to stem the rush of blood from her wound which gushed down her legs and made a real mess of her prison tracksuit bottoms. She started to panic. There was now no one around and she felt her breathing become difficult. The loss of blood was making her feel faint. She looked up and down the corridor but there was still no one in sight. Just as she fell to the floor, a newly appointed PO turned the corner and stopped in her tracks at the horrific sight in front of her. But she was quick to call through on her radio though and within seconds the sirens went off. Kelly was hurried to the medical centre, while everyone was forced to endure another lockdown. Because the wound was life-threatening, a decision was made quickly for an ambulance to be sent. There was no way the staff in sick bay could deal with it.

Hours later, she awoke in the hospital bed. They had managed to stop the bleeding, clean up the damage, and drain the blood in her lungs. She was weak and sick but at least she was alive. With no time wasted, she was bandaged up and sent back to prison.

CHAPTER EIGHT

The number one governor came over to the sick bay, where Kelly remained for another week, after they had released her from hospital. She was questioned about the incident but pretended she saw nothing.

Charlie, the screw who had taken her through reception on the first day, made it her business to look out for the young inmate. She escorted her back to her cell after the stay in hospital. Closing the door behind them, Charlie sat on the bed with Kelly. "Tell me, Raven, who did this, and I will make sure they get moved."

Kelly smiled. "I'm all right. I've been through worse."

Charlie found it hard to swallow; she knew only too well the truth of that statement. This youngster wasn't like most of the other inmates; she was gentle and harmless and not out to cause any conflict.

"Look, if you need me, come and find me. I am your personal officer. You all have one."

Kelly nodded and Charlie left. She lay back on her bed with her arms behind her head and stared up at the ceiling. She thought about her aunt Bet and longed to see her but sending out a visiting order somehow seemed wrong. She had got herself in this mess and so she would go it alone. There was no point in dragging people along with her on this roller coaster of an ordeal. Just as she was dozing off, the door flew open. Kelly was on her feet in seconds; no way was she going to leave herself wide open again.

In the doorway was a tall inmate, but she was way too old to be on the juvenile wing. Kelly stared for a while. There was something

155

familiar about her. She looked to be in her forties with long dark hair and round green eyes. She wasn't foreign but had olive skin much like her own.

"So, *you* are Kelly Raven then, are ya?"

Kelly didn't answer. She wasn't sure if the woman was being friendly or sarcastic. Her tone was menacing and she had an edge about her: hard and confident. She was puffing on a cigarette and leaning against the wall inside Kelly's cell. "What's up, cat gotcha tongue?"

Kelly remained silent. Everyone was an enemy now.

"You ain't gotta fucking Danny who I am, 'ave ya, me little chicken?"

Kelly tilted her head, as she remembered those words 'little chicken', but she still had no idea who the woman was.

"Right, get ya gear. You're coming with me, in my cell, over on B wing."

Kelly frowned. She wasn't going to be pushed around by any other inmate ever again.

"Nah, you're all right. I'm staying 'ere on me own."

"You what? Don't you know who I am?"

Kelly had had enough of the bolshiness of the inmates. "I don't give a fuck who you are, so if ya don't mind, I wanna be left alone." Kelly sat back down on her bed and sighed. She was acting like some tough nut, when really, she just wanted to be nice — but nice didn't get you anywhere in here.

"I'm Toni, Toni Mahoney, formerly Toni Raven."

Kelly looked up and tried to remember if she had seen the woman before, but she had no recollection.

"Look, Toni, I don't mean to be rude, but I don't know ya."

"I'm ya fucking aunt, for fuck's sake!"

The pain in Kelly's side was back again and her tablets were only issued in a morning. "Look, please, I'm not feeling too good. I don't know ya, and as far as I know, I don't have an aunt. We have the same surname, but that's all, so if ya don't mind." With that, she lowered her head and waited for the woman to leave.

"Listen, kid, I know ya got stabbed. It's a fucking nightmare on this wing. They're all a load of nutters. Ya safer with me. Besides, they allow family to share."

Kelly was feeling sick with the pain and her temper was on a short leash. She knew she would lose it at any moment. "Look! I said I don't fucking know ya, I ain't into all that lesbo bollocks, and I am fine on me own!" The angry words seemed to trip over themselves. That was how it was going to be from now on. No longer would she be nice, polite Kelly; she had to leave that part of her outside the prison to survive with this scum.

Toni laughed and moved towards Kelly. "Look, madam, you listen to me. Stop acting like a spoilt brat. Ya mother ain't 'ere to pander to your every whim——"

Kelly was raging now; all the suppressed anger and the agonising pain had sent her over the edge. She jumped to her feet, snatched Toni by the hair, and rammed her into the wall. "I fucking told you to leave me alone. I ain't fucking spoiled, I ain't never been fucking spoiled, and me muvver's never pampered to my every fucking God-damned whim." She let go of Toni's hair and gasped for breath. Toni was startled and then concerned, when her niece turned a deathly white and staggered to get to the bed. Toni ran from the cell and called the PO. "Quick, get here, Kelly's sick!"

Charlie flew down the corridor to find Kelly slumped on the bed, the blood from her wounds oozing out again. The internal stitches had come away and she was bleeding inside.

It took just four minutes to reach Sutton Hospital, and by this time she was dead – in a clinical sense, that is. They rushed the drain into her lung and started resuscitation. Her heart had stopped. The young consultant, on a short-term contract from his main duties at King's College Hospital, was about to call it a day, when he felt an overwhelming sense of dread and decided to fire up the paddles one last time. He waited a second and then saw the heartbeat return. She was alive and he would make sure she stayed that way. She was not to go back to prison until he was satisfied her lungs were healed. The governing governor received the call and instantly agreed; after all, the girl was not even convicted and was still on remand. That messy news would not go down too well with the authorities in London.

Toni was back on her wing and queuing for the phone. Four women stepped aside, allowing Toni to go in front. Hattie, a big black woman, was on the phone, arguing with her ol' man, and when Toni told her to hurry up, she leaned forward and growled. Hattie had her little firm inside with her, all out of Hackney. Toni wasn't worried by anyone; she was the one who held the reins. Her stints inside spanned years, on and off, and her reputation preceded her. She was a bitch on the outside and a raving nutter in here. She had served six months in total down the block for fighting and had two years put on her three-year sentence for serious bodily harm. She knew how to fight, growing up with three big brothers, who never thought twice about smashing a woman if the need arose. If she wanted to get anywhere in their pack, she had to fight for it. Eddie was her closest brother; they were a year apart and shared business and pleasure. She was the only woman he could ever trust, and in a strange way he looked up to her. There weren't many women who could fight like a man and be hard-faced about it. Toni was a looker in her day, too, with a neat figure, long dark hair, and green eyes set against her olive skin. It was her looks and air of confidence that turned many a head when she walked into a room. But she also had a quick tongue and a foul mouth, the very

158

attributes to impress Eddie, which only incited her to impress him even more.

Hattie realised she was glaring at Toni and thought she had better back off rather than face her wrath. The last time she had gone one-to-one with Toni, she had ended up with a table leg wrapped around her head. She had needed to have her hair shaved and stitched. But she was even more angry that her oversized Afro was now gone and would take years to grow back. The short hair didn't match her big frame.

"Hattie, get off the cunting phone!" ordered Toni, through gritted teeth.

Hattie slammed down the receiver and walked away, hoping that Toni might forget the look she had just given her.

Toni dialled the number. "She's 'ere, Eddie."

Eddie was in the bath, planning his next move. He knew the police had him under observation. Tommy had been true to his word and he'd made a statement putting Eddie in the clear for the night that Maureen was murdered.

"They nicked her, then?"

"Yeah, she's in the hospital. Some bitch has plunged her with a blade."

Eddie sat upright, careful not to drop the phone into the water. "Ya fucking what? Is she all right, sis?"

"I think so …"

"Is she my Kelly?" he asked, with concern in his voice.

"Oh yeah, your fucking double, a cocky little cow an' all."

Eddie smiled to himself. "Right, keep her safe and make sure she sends out a VO. I wanna meet her."

"Ed, do ya think it's a good idea?"

"Don't question me, Toni, just do as I say."

After Toni put the phone down, she marched back to her cell to find Hattie hanging around.

"What d'ya want?" spat Toni, in a strident tone.

Hattie was so huge she took up the doorframe. "We all right, Tone?"

Toni's mind was still on Eddie's demands concerning her niece, so she just nodded and sparked up another cigarette. As Hattie went to walk away, Toni called out, "'Ere, Hat, you can do me a favour!"

Before she turned to face Toni, Hattie paused. "What's that then, Tone?"

"Find out who jerked Kelly Raven. Don't you tell anyone and let me know."

Hattie smiled, with relief showing on her face. She was in Toni's good books; well, she would be, if she found out who had harmed Kelly.

Toni had to do something for retribution or her brother would sure enough take a blade to her. By teatime, Hattie was back; she slipped into Toni's cell, closed the door behind her, and faced Toni, who was sitting on the bed with a pillow propped up behind her, reading a book and puffing on a fag.

"Gotta name, then, Hat?" She didn't look up.

"Tone, it's that fat fuck Milo and that long streak of piss Bobby. They are reckless little fuckers, them two. They run the youths down there. Milo's twenty-one next week and gonna be on our wing, by all accounts."

160

"And Bobby?"

"Bobby will come on the wing 'cos they are cousins, so they say," replied Hattie, pleased with herself and Toni's reaction to her.

"Next week, eh?"

"Yep. Anything else, Tone?" She was twitching and in need of tobacco and hoped her little favour would earn her something. Toni held everything: puff, baccy, in fact any powder floating about, and so was a chief in the inmates' eyes.

"Nah," she replied, still with her head in the book.

"Tone, any chance of some baccy? I really am clean out."

Toni looked up at her and took another drag of her fag. "See that packet there on the other bed? Take it, but, Hattie, it's gonna cost ya."

With greedy eyes, Hattie picked up the tobacco, enough for at least ten roll-ups. "How much, Tone?"

"Oh, not money, Hat, I want another favour," she replied, looking up at the woman coldly.

Hattie felt queasy; she hated owing favours, especially to Toni. "What's that, then, Tone?"

Toni winked. "I'll let ya know."

Hattie wanted to put the tobacco back on the bed, but she had it in her hands now and that was as good as accepting the offer. She walked away with a nasty gut feeling.

❧*❧

Dr Thomas, the consultant who had saved Kelly, had left strict instructions with the nurse to call him right away when she came to.

When the call came, he tore down the corridor and on to the ward. Kelly was placed in a private room, still handcuffed to the bed. One of the prison officers was sitting outside the patient's room. Her presence was enough for the consultant's expression to turn sour and for his eyes to stare coldly at the officer. He wasn't reacting like this from a feeling of superiority: far from it, as his brother was in prison and his mother was dead from a drugs overdose. The screw stood up, as he approached the door.

"All right, Doc, any news as to when we can take her back?" asked Kirsty, the officer with a nasty smirk and with an eye for a good-looking doctor. Dr Thomas glared at her. "When I say so, and that's not going to be any time soon, so take yourself off to the canteen or wherever. I don't like clutter on my ward."

Kirsty was surprised at his manner but was too thick-skinned to care so she walked away with food on her mind.

Peter Thomas stood at the end of the bed reading Kelly's chart. The nurse smiled and left. Kelly was awake but a little dopey. He watched her trying to focus. As she attempted to lift her arm, which was cuffed to the side bar of the bed, his heart went out to her. She was barely eighteen; there was no history of drugs or alcohol abuse and she didn't even smoke. Her smooth skin and virtuous eyes melted his heart. He knew she was on a double murder charge and just could not imagine this slight and pretty teenager committing such a crime.

"Hello, Kelly, my name is Dr Peter Thomas. How do you feel?" He walked around to her side and smiled down at her. She smiled back but a tear fell and ran down the side of her face. Perhaps it was his compassionate-sounding voice, setting her off.

"I feel better, Doctor, thank you."

He soaked up her gentle tone; it wasn't the voice of a murderer, surely?

162

"Kelly, I have told the prison that you must remain here until I feel you are well and truly recovered. We don't want another incident like that, do we?"

She liked his face; it was open and honest. His eyes were like pools of ocean blue and his smile was wide, revealing straight white teeth. His blond waves, akin to that of an Australian surfer, framed a face which looked kind and sincere.

"Thank you," she whispered.

"Can I get you anything, magazines, a nice bowl of fruit salad? The food in here is crap," he laughed. Kelly was amused by his words. She giggled but this action brought on instant pain.

"I know what you do need and that's something for the soreness."

His thoughtful gesture brought new tears – he seemed so kind-hearted and genuine.

Peter Thomas left and returned minutes later with tablets and a fruit salad bowl; it was his own that he had brought in that morning for his lunch. As he sat on the edge of the bed, he felt her forehead. Really, he didn't have to, as it was not for any medical reasons, but he just wanted to touch her face. She was young and probably too young for him; he wasn't into little girls, but there was something about her that aroused his emotions.

"Hey, Kelly, I will let you get some rest, and I'll be back this afternoon. In the meantime, think of a list of mags, and I will see what I can do."

She nodded and watched him leave. She remembered the psychiatrist asking if she liked men or women. She thought about Peter, and for a second she would have liked to have felt his lips on hers. Oh, well, none of that mattered now; she was going back to jail and he would be healing the sick and wounded. She dozed in and out of sleep with the drugs he had given her doing the trick.

The next morning, she awoke feeling brighter, the anaesthetic having worn off, enabling her now to focus. Peter was in the room reading her notes again.

"Hello, Doctor." She smiled and watched his face light up.

"Well, Miss Kelly Raven, I like that name. It has a kind of 'wing' to it," he laughed. She chuckled, joining in the joke.

He looked sharp in a crisp white shirt and navy-blue trousers. She noticed his clean hands and immaculate nails. He pulled up a chair and sat beside her. "How do you feel?"

"Much better, thank you. I'm not in pain so much now, thanks, Doctor."

The door opened, and in walked the cocky screw, as brassy as if she had the right. It irritated Peter and angrily he walked up to her. With harsh words, he snapped, "What do you want now?"

She shuffled from foot to foot, uncomfortable with his cold tone. She was used to showing off with her cocky stance and overconfident attitude.

"Gov wants to know how she is and when I can take her back!"

Peter was angry at her smarmy voice. He had a fervent dislike for prison staff, after they had beaten up his brother in prison – his little brother.

"This is a patient's room, not a hotel room. I am in the middle of a confidential conversation—"

Before he could finish, Kirsty interrupted, "Sorry, Doc, but Raven has lost that right, now she is serving at Her Majesty's pleasure." This remark pissed Peter off.

He took a deep breath and launched in, full force. "I don't for one minute think you have a law degree or a medical degree or a damned

A level for that matter. So, I will inform you of the law, and the right that my patient has, and that is patient confidentiality. You are not a judge or another doctor, so you are not allowed to be present when I am talking to my patient regarding her medical condition. She is handcuffed to the goddamn bed and you are to remain outside. She is not a raving lunatic, who is likely to jump up and slit my throat, so I do not need your assistance, and if I did, then I would ask for it. Now, this is my ward, and I will call you when I feel she is ready to go back. One other thing, Miss Raven has not been convicted yet. Since she is a patient in my hospital, I suggest you treat her as innocent until proven guilty!"

Kirsty was gobsmacked; never had she heard a doctor speak with so much venom. He was right though; she had pushed her luck. In the past, she had got away with it but obviously not this time. She left the ward with her tail between her legs. Kelly was shocked that this doctor, who didn't know her from Adam, had stuck up for her.

She laughed. "That told her."

Peter returned to his chair and smiled. "Yeah, well, she is getting on my nerves, sitting outside, making a fucking nuisance of herself."

Kelly laughed again. She had never expected a doctor to swear.

"It's none of my business, and I would get shot if they found out I asked such a question, but, seriously, did you do what they said? Did you kill your mother?"

Kelly tilted her head and looked into his dreamy blue eyes. "No, I never did. They think I did, and I don't have the energy to fight it. I did kill Patrick, but I didn't mean to. I thought he was going to rape me, and I only meant to hit him to get away, but I guess I hit him a bit too hard."

Peter nodded. "Kelly, you're a kid, you have to fight it. What does your solicitor say?"

Embarrassed, she looked away. "I refused to have one."

"What!"

Kelly was surprised and confused. Why would a doctor be so interested in her? "Why do you care?" she asked softly.

He took a deep breath through his nose. "I have a little brother, not much older than you, in the same situation. He killed someone by accident and he suffers every day because of it. There, that's the first time I have told that to a complete stranger. Please don't repeat it. Those nurses are such busybodies. They love a bit of gossip." He tapped her on the nose.

"They think I am mad, you know. I have been seeing a shrink daily. They ask so many questions. I know I'm not insane. Maybe I *should* get a lawyer. It's all so complicated. I have no one to ask, you see."

Peter felt so disconsolate; those sad eyes were just like those of his brother. There was nothing he could do for little Paulie. He visited him on a regular basis. He saw the bruises, the black marks under his eyes, and the grey pallor on his face. It tore him apart. That was probably why he felt a need to help Kelly.

"Hey, I know you're not insane. Let me help you."

She felt a lump in her throat. "Really?"

He nodded. "I will organise a good solicitor. I am a dab hand at it now, you know. I even studied law myself. Before you go back, I will get all the paperwork and you can contact her. She is brilliant. I'll contact her myself, in fact, and so she will be expecting to hear from you."

She looked up at him and her eyes brimmed with tears. He wanted to reach out and hug her but that would be wrong on every level. Instead, he rubbed her arm and winked. As he walked away, he felt sad. She had plucked at his heartstrings and her perfect face was imprinted on his mind.

Reality had come and bitten her on the arse. Since the day she'd fled her mother's house, she had seen the world in a new light. There was good, bad, and damn right ugly. She could use what she had to either fight or talk her way out of trouble. She soon realised that people were either taken in by her innocent, trusting look or threatened by it. Either way, she knew she had weapons to get through life and being thrown to the wolves would make her strong, one way or another.

Peter came to visit her every day, checking she was okay. The morning she was to be·discharged was shocking for him and what he saw deeply disturbed him.

The nurse was retrieving Kelly's prison tracksuit from the bedside cabinet, whilst Kelly was about to step into the shower. Peter walked inside the room to say his goodbyes but stopped dead in his tracks when he saw the scars on Kelly's back. He turned away, as if she wasn't a patient, but the nurse detected his sudden wavering.

"Doctor, what's wrong?" she asked.

Peter bit his lip and turned to face her. "Nothing I was just …err, I mean I was going to sign the discharge form."

The nurse raised her eyebrow and handed him the clipboard. "Poor kid, those marks are dreadful, aren't they?"

Overcome with horror, all he could do was swallow hard and nod. He couldn't hang around and wait for her to step outside the shower. He left her in peace with her dignity but that vision was engraved on his mind. He had to walk away. Kelly was stirring emotions he should never have.

She was taken back to the prison, feeling well and stronger than ever. Charlie was the screw who was responsible for her. She smiled sweetly but it was so out of character. "Come on then, Kelly, I am going to take you over to B wing. You can settle in with Toni. She has a double room. It's much cosier. She has books, magazines, and, well, it's just a homelier feel."

Kelly stopped dead. "I don't want to go over there. I'm all right on me own. I don't know her!" Her voice was cold. Charlie gripped Kelly's shoulder, forcing her to look at her face. "Now, Kelly, listen to me, you are far safer with Toni than anyone. You want to survive in here, then stick with her."

"I don't care. I am fine in me own cell."

Frustrated with Kelly's stubbornness, Charlie was getting annoyed now. "There's no argument, Kelly. You have been assigned to that cell, so if you don't like it, then next week we will have you moved back down here. All right?"

Kelly nodded. "I ain't gotta choice, 'ave I?"

"Nope," replied Charlie.

Most of the inmates were on jobs in the laundry, the kitchen, or the gym. Toni was in her cell though, waiting for Kelly. She had made the room as nice as possible. Eddie would be pissed off, if she didn't keep a look out for her.

Charlie flicked her head at Kelly. "Go on, in you go, that's the room."

Kelly had a canvas bag over her shoulder; it contained her few belongings and paperwork. Nudging the door open, she stepped inside the cell. Toni jumped to her feet and nodded to Charlie to leave. She pulled Kelly the rest of the way in by her arm and wedged the door shut with a piece of rubber. Kelly looked at the doorstop.

"Gotta be done around here or you'll have no privacy," said Toni, seeing the look on Kelly's face.

Grudgingly, Kelly raised her eyebrow. "It don't look like I'm gonna get much of that now I'm in with you."

Toni felt her temper rising. After all, she was doing Kelly a big favour.

"Ya wanna be careful with ya cocky mouth, Kel. It won't do you any good, let me tell you."

As Kelly sat heavily on the bed, she stroked the soft quilt cover. It was nicer than her bedding on C wing. "You gotta understand, Toni, that I don't even know you, so if you expect me to be over the fucking moon that we are banged up cosy together, then you're wrong."

The likeness to Eddie was uncanny. Toni looked at her niece's face, and she realised she was looking at Eddie when he was a kid. He could charm the birds out of the trees with his big soft eyes and nice words, but rub him up the wrong way, and he had a vicious tongue and a violent temper.

"'Ere, hang on a minute, 'ave some respect. I'm ya flaming aunt."

Kelly laughed sarcastically. "Aunt, yeah? Well, I do have an aunt called Bet, and she sure as hell don't look like you. She's the only aunt I can recall. So, like I said, I don't know ya."

"Cor, Kel, let me tell you, you are the image of ya farver. He's a cocky bastard, too."

Kelly flared her nostrils. She had heard enough now. Being told she was like her father was the worst insult ever. Like a cat with a rocket shoved up its arse, Kelly jumped up. Her face looked severe, as her eyes darkened. "Like me dad, eh? Me fucking dad! You tell me I'm cocky, I should respect you, then you say I'm like that fucking paedophile? Jesus, can this day get any bloody worse."

The shock hit Toni so hard that it physically jolted her. "What do you mean, fucking paedophile?"

Kelly took a deep breath and tried to calm herself before she flew at Toni again; there was no telling what she would do this time. Her new-found confidence had come from nowhere, and all that ran through her mind now was to survive and act like everyone else in here.

"Me ol' man's a stinking paedophile. He went to prison for it," she said, as she sat back down again. Her jaw dropped forward and she had a fury about her. To anyone now, Kelly was a fighter and no silly pushover. Perhaps the lesson in being tough had come from her mother; all that repressed frustration and the fear of consequences had had their day. Now she was a woman on a mission: she would fight with every breath in her body, and woe betide anyone who thought she was a soft touch anymore. The only fear all her life, which had ever plagued her, was her mother's wrath – but she was dead.

A fixed frown edged on Toni's face, as she tried to work out where Kelly would have got that from. Her voice soft and low now, she murmured, "Kel, ya dad's not a paedophile. He was inside for murder. He got twelve years. He's no nonce, love."

She stopped to look at the resigned expression on Kelly's face.

"Listen, babe, do you know who your old man is?"

Despairingly, Kelly shook her head. "No, I never knew him. I wasn't allowed to know until I reached sixteen, and then me aunt was supposed to tell me. Some silly promise she had made to me mum."

Toni knew why. It was because her brother should have been released on Kelly's sixteenth birthday, but he had got out a few months earlier. "You will like him, Kel."

"I wouldn't be so sure about that. You don't know me."

Toni was biting her lip; her niece was pushing her luck, and she was not used to anyone slating her brother. They would get a good hiding, or worse, if they tried it. Toni moved along her bed to face Kelly.

"Straight up, Kel, woman to woman, what's your problem?"

Kelly stared at her aunt and took in all the flaws in her otherwise attractive face. She may have crow's feet and a few wrinkles around the mouth from smoking, but her skin was more or less flawless, barring the scars, one above her eye and the other on her chin.

"Okay, Toni, I'll tell ya. I grew up in a house of fucking horrors. I was mentally taunted at school, and up until a couple a years ago, I longed to have someone come and rescue me. I was suffocated, not allowed to live, and too fucking frightened to move, unless I was told to. I wasn't allowed to know about me past, and I was damn fucking sure I was told how to live me future ..." She looked at Toni, half-expecting her to jump in. "Then I had a run-in with this Patrick bloke who tried to ... not sure what he was gonna do, but anyway I killed him and took off. I had no one to run to – no one. So, as you can imagine, I had a fucking lot of growing up to do, see, and by Christ, I did. So, as for family now wanting to play the bloodline thing ... well, it's too little too fucking late."

Shocked by that outburst of feeling, Toni sat on the edge of the bed, taking it all in. "Who looked after you when you did the off, then?" She wasn't being sarcastic; she was genuinely interested.

That was an odd question but Kelly wasn't stupid either; she spotted the subtext. "Oh, just a few friends, here and there. They kinda looked out for me, but no one in particular." Her voice softened for a few seconds and then Kelly returned to reality. "Anyway, you wanted to know why I wasn't running into your open arms and there it is. I don't trust my family anymore. To be honest, I don't need or want them – I'm too old now."

Toni nodded. She felt some shame but Kelly was a grown-up and she was right – there was no family bond.

At that moment, there was a bang on the door and instantly Toni shouted, "Piss off!"

The door banged again. "Tone, it's recreation. Ya coming?" It was Hattie having a nose.

"Nah, fuck off! I'm wiv me niece!"

Kelly was feeling tired. She patted the bed. "I'm on 'ere, then?"

"Yeah, kiddo, go for it. Ya look peaky. D'ya need anything?" She tried to lighten the otherwise tense situation.

"Nah, just me T-shirt. I'm hot in these sweats. Where did Charlie put me stuff?"

Toni pulled a shallow tin box from under the bed. All Kelly's prison issues were neatly folded and stacked on the tray.

"Ta," said Kelly, as she bent over and retrieved the top. With a daring glance, she looked at Toni, waiting for her to turn around.

Rolling her eyes, Toni tutted and looked away, but as her niece stood up to remove her top, Toni covertly glanced back. The gap between the two beds was so small, she was an inch away from Kelly's back. She could see the mass of long scars on her skin. At first, she thought it had been where Kelly had been lying on her uneven top and the creases had made an indent. However, as she looked closely, the T-shirt tumbled down. Toni lifted the back of the shirt up again. Kelly didn't move. She allowed her aunt to have a good gawp; she needed Toni to understand what kind of life she had faced growing up.

There was silence as Kelly sat down on the bed, flung her legs around, placed her arms under her head, and then stared up at the ceiling.

"Who, err ..." Toni was beyond shock.

"Me muvver. *Now* do you get why I like to be on me own?"

Toni nodded. "I wouldn't hurt you, chicken."

"No, maybe not, but you didn't save me, either. I was left to live with a raving God-fearing lunatic. No one came for me. Me dad abandoned me. You could have visited, you could have seen if I was all right, but no one did. I don't know ya, Toni, and I don't need anyone, not anymore."

She closed her eyes and pretended to go to sleep.

Totally blown away, Toni couldn't get those scars off her mind. They looked old. She must have been young. Her visions of a religious nut whipping Kelly as a child were not wrong. She wasn't close to Kelly but she felt something now – perhaps it was guilt coming to the surface.

The last time she had seen Kelly, she was four years old; she had been a sweet child, with the most amazing round green eyes, and she was such a chatterbox. Maureen was a good mother then. She had always dressed the child immaculately, sometimes even matching her own outfits. Maureen was a good-looking woman, and she could see why Eddie fancied her and why her own husband, Patrick, did for that matter. She tried to remember if there was any hint of child abuse, but she couldn't think of any. Their house was big and tastefully decorated. Kelly's bedroom was like a princess's castle, with every toy imaginable and a wardrobe full of designer dresses.

When they were growing up, they'd had very little. There were three older brothers in one room and her in the small makeshift bedroom downstairs. Their parents were in the bigger room upstairs. They lived in a cramped two-up two-down, with a bathroom just off the damp kitchen. They were without two pennies to rub together. It was circumstances which led them into a life of crime. Joseph, their father, was a coalman, who had worked all hours, breaking his back for a few quid only to be crippled over with arthritis. She tried to remember him without his black coal face. Their mother, a little Spanish woman, had been gentle but naïve; she hadn't had a clue how things worked, especially when the boys were making their own way in life. Her two eldest brothers, little Joe, named after her father, and

173

Alex, were both big men. They took after their father with the Irish blue eyes, pale complexion, and dark hair. She and Eddie though had taken after their mother with her olive skin, green eyes, and dark hair. The five-year gap between them and Eddie seemed like a ten-year one. They had all flown the nest early and rented a flat together, just off the East India Dock Road. It wasn't long before their little scams earned them enough to buy a pub, although they were not into serving pints; it was a legal establishment to cover their arms deals.

Until Eddie was fifteen, he was living off their eldest brother's reputation. It worked, as he was seen as a force to be reckoned with. Unlike Joe and Alex, he was sharp, and his quick movements gave him an edge. So Eddie was the brother she most tried to follow. She learned quickly, watching her brother's wild actions and the way he unnerved people with his sly glances, and so she soon copied him. Eddie had loved his mother and father, and that love continued up until they died; but then he changed. He became violent, reckless, and greedy. She couldn't understand why at the time, but as the years passed, she began to realise he hated the world. Then, one night when they had both gone out together and were in among the usual crowd, Eddie's little firm, she understood why.

They had taken their usual corner in the Drovers, a club on the Old Kent Road, which was not a hangout for local firms but frequented by Eddie's crew. At the back of the club was a cocktail bar and Eddie was partial to a piña colada. It was strange because he looked like a brandy man, but he didn't give a shit. If he wanted to drink a bowl of what was a white fluffy concoction, with pineapples and umbrellas, then he would – besides, who was going to tease him? Who'd have the guts? He was wearing his trademark Italian suit; it gave him authority. Also, Eddie liked the respect it gave him. He used it, too, to get what he wanted. That night, they were in high spirits. Eddie had robbed a jeweller and got away with ten Rolex watches and all the diamonds the shop held. It wasn't a messy operation either; he had planned it most carefully. Those were in the days long before CCTV on every corner. He almost took down the side of the building but he got away and left the Ol' Bill scratching their heads. Eddie had taken an interest in architecture and studied building plans. He could have made an honest living out of it, but he didn't like doing anything by the book. "Line the pockets of those snotty-nosed fucking taxmen, no way," he would say.

Just as Blakey, one of Eddie's older sidekicks, placed another bowl of piña colada on the table, Eddie leaned forward and carefully pushed him aside. They all looked to see who Eddie was staring at. In walked Patrick. He was a Face but this wasn't his turf. He was from North London. Toni watched her brother's expression take on a fierce look of anger. "That cocky cunt!"

"Who is he?" she asked. Eddie didn't take his eyes off Patrick. "That there is what I call a silver-spooned villain. That nob is fucking minted, comes from a wealthy family, his father's a fucking Irish lord or something, and here the prick is acting like the Krays, all 'cos he can buy his muscle."

"Ya lost me, Ed."

"Patrick Mahoney has money, was fucking born with money, but wants to be like the big boys. Instead of keeping to his own kind, he fancied himself as a gangster. Probably bored with being hand-fed grapes off a silver platter, he used his lordly money to start up a protection racket. Cor, the prick makes me fucking mad. I would love to take a shooter and blow his brains out. That Irish wanker has taken from the poor to give to the fucking rich."

That was it; those words resonated in Toni's ears. Her brother stole from the rich because he had come from the poor. He hated anyone who had more than him. Watching their parents struggle for every penny and to die with nothing, with not even a weekend break down the coast, had made him an angry man.

Toni stared, along with Eddie, at the big Irishman. He was handsome too, not obviously good-looking, but maybe it was his confident presence that made him attractive.

They watched Patrick order his Irish whiskey and turn to walk towards them. Toni mumbled under her breath, "Ed, he's coming over here."

"Yep, the brazen cunt, but I fucking know what he wants."

Patrick walked up three steps straight to their table. He didn't smile or sneer but just stood there. "Eddie Raven, I believe," he said.

Eddie nodded, acting cool, sitting there with his arms outstretched along the soft-pillowed backrest of the curved sofa.

Patrick looked at the five men, two on either side of Eddie. Toni was sitting on a stool opposite. Eddie raised his eyebrows and smirked.

"Don't push ya luck, Patrick. These ain't me fucking bodyguards. They are me mates and we are having a few drinks."

A sneer crawled along Patrick's lips. "Well, what I want to discuss with you is private, between you and me."

Eddie leaned forward. "This ain't the place for business and you should have booked an appointment first."

Patrick was surprised that Eddie was so arrogant, as he had half-expected him to jump up and be all over him like a rash, getting in on any offerings. His own business was growing fast and he had a name for himself now. His firm in North London was bringing in a fortune. The Italians, these days, were going to him for protection; it had been a big turnaround because for years they had called the shots.

His sneer turned to a smile, as he looked at Toni. "So, is this ya sister, Eddie? She's a good-looking woman."

In a heartbeat, Eddie jumped to his feet. "Don't fucking push it. You leave her alone." He indicated to his friends to leave. Toni stayed seated.

"Right, what do you want, now you've ruined me fucking night?" His eyes were like slits, as he snarled at Patrick.

Patrick eased himself along the curved sofa and placed his drink right next to Eddie's cocktail.

"Now then, this is the situation. You have robbed my mate, a jeweller, and he wants all his gear back. It's that simple!" said Patrick.

For a few seconds there was silence, as Eddie leaned forward and picked up his drink and sipped it through the straw. "This 'ere, Patrick, is a piña colada. It's made of pineapple, rum, and coconut. Ya wouldn't think they could mix, but they do and *voila* ya have a lovely taste."

Patrick wasn't one for gangsters' riddles. "Yeah, but ya see, right now, Eddie, I have a bitter taste in my mouth. So, like I said, you have fucked with the wrong man."

Immediately, Eddie placed his drink back down, grabbed Patrick round the throat, and squeezed. "Oh yeah, 'ave I, you cunt?"

Patrick was on his back, struggling to remove Eddie's fingers, but Eddie was on top of him, not letting up on his grip. Toni hadn't the courage to intervene or her brother would have given her the same. Then, he let go and watched, as Patrick coughed and spluttered. Patrick took a few deep breaths and straightened his clothes, whilst Eddie sat back down and sipped more of his drink. It was as if he had just swatted a wasp.

Patrick stared at the nutter. "You should never have done that, Eddie Raven."

Eddie slammed the glass down hard and whipped from his pocket his blade; he held it under Patrick's chin. "Nah, ya right, you tosser. I should have used this on you. But I am a fair man, see. But try and threaten me, you Irish wanker, and I will slit ya throat."

Patrick sucked in a deep breath and waited until Eddie removed the blade.

"Eddie, you wanna be careful. My mate is under my protection. I can't have the likes of you robbin' from under my nose. I'll have ya dead and buried before I fucking lose face."

Eddie laughed. "Well, here's the thing. See, Patrick, I have already made you look fucking stupid. I mean that business, paying you a shed load of protection money, and little ol' me taking the fucking lot. You look a proper div already. Now, I know you earn a mint from all the jewellers around South London, but, as I see it, this ain't your manor. North London is yours, and I think, correct me if I am wrong, but you have taken a right fucking liberty."

Patrick sat back on his seat and folded his arms in disgust. "You sly bastard, Eddie, ya fucking robbed that business deliberately to get at me. Ya didn't do it for the money, did ya?"

Eddie displayed a full set of perfect white teeth. "Oh, dear me, Patrick, it looks like you have egg on your face." He leaned back and laughed. "Nah, not egg, more like a whole fucking Spanish omelette."

Patrick felt the blood rise to his face. The cocky snigger grated on him, yet Eddie wasn't finished; he was enjoying the wind-up.

"Well, I s'pose the holdall full of shiny diamonds was a bonus. 'Ere, look at me new Rolex. Lovely, ain't it." He shoved the gold watch under Patrick's nose and then he laughed again. "All right, Patrick, you can have it all back."

Patrick smiled. "I knew a smart boy like you would see sense."

"Oh, I saw sense a long time ago. I've had me eye on you, Patrick. I've watched how you work. See, I like to be one step ahead. You bought your reputation, ya threw ya weight around, in the form of paid bully boys. See, that's where me and you are different. I do me own dirty work, whereas you live off your sister Sheila's reputation, which, until now, has been untainted." He paused, deliberately, waiting for some reaction from Patrick. There was none: Patrick was staring in disbelief. He had seriously underestimated Eddie.

"So, this is how we can remedy this little problem, which, I must say, is your little problem, not mine. I am a fair man, Paddy. As I said, you can have the gear back and your protection will sit comfortably in the eyes of your so-called customers. Your reputation will remain intact, but there is this issue of my cut in it all. See, you must know by now if the filth can't catch me, your little mob can't either, get what I mean? I can make you look a right fucking fanny merchant." He smiled and sat back, waiting.

Knowing he was up against a smarter opponent, Patrick nodded. "Looks like you have pulled a right sly one, Eddie, but I like you. You've got guts. I'll give you that. I think me and you could be good for business."

Eddie sneered. "Don't fucking patronise me. The thing is, you don't have much choice whether you like me or not. So, this is how it works. The protection racket in South London is mine and North London is yours. I ain't a greedy man, so I want fifty per cent."

Patrick's eyes widened. "How do you work that out? I mean, what you gonna do to earn that?"

With a crafty smile and a wink Eddie replied, "I will make sure none of your businesses get robbed."

The reality slapped Patrick in the face and he knew then he had no choice.

That had been twenty years ago. Toni saw then exactly what her brother was all about. She admired him, but she also liked Patrick, and their relationship flourished over the following year. Eddie had her on the payroll, by collecting the weekly poke from Patrick. It was Eddie who pushed them into marriage. He had to keep Patrick close, as he did have a lot of clout, and Eddie didn't want to be looking over his shoulder all the time. Toni, however, fell out of affection for Patrick long before the church bells rang.

CHAPTER NINE

True to his word, Peter had spoken with the lawyer, and the legal visit was arranged. Charlie was the screw who had taken Kelly down to the legal visiting room. The prison was on lockdown for two days after they had found Milo with her throat cut and Bobby unconscious with the knife in her hand. Kelly felt an overwhelming sense of dread when it happened though. She guessed right away it was organised by Toni. Now Hattie was number one at Toni's side and proud of it. Kelly felt sorry for Hattie; she was just used and so blinded by securing a reputation, she couldn't see what was happening.

Kelly recalled the aftermath when they went to the canteen. It was as though Toni was the queen, as all the inmates made way for her niece to get to the front of the queue. There was whispering and a couple of the women patted her on the back. Kelly was irritated by the way she was being feted because of her family connection to Toni. They fussed over Kelly, almost fawned all over her, and it was sickening. She knew it was an act; they couldn't give a shit, really, as it was fear that made them behave in that way. Chicken was served to the first twenty people and Toni was always one of them. The screws had to turn a blind eye; they didn't want a ruckus. Charlie ran the wing and allowed Toni her freebies, and in return, Toni kept the wing in order, so as not to cause the officers a hard time.

The day the knifing happened, Kelly was in her room reading *Eclipse*, the third novel in Stephenie Meyer's vampire love saga, which she had found in the library. It was easier to stick her head in the pages than listen to the garbage that came out of her aunt's mouth. Toni was proud of her endless wrongdoings, from petty theft to violent assaults. The news of Milo and her sidekick spread like wild fire and was at Toni's door seconds later. Julie, a white girl, who followed Hattie around like a lost lamb, was full of excitement to be the first to spill the news. Toni sat up straight and Kelly closed her book.

"Tone, Tone, that fat Milo bird, the one that knifed Kelly, is dead. Bobby, her cousin, has killed her. They have taken her away. Ya got any puff for Hattie 'cos we are gonna go on lockdown?" At that moment, the sirens went off. The sound was so loud that Kelly had to put her hands to her ears.

Toni pulled a parcel from under the bed. "'Ere, give her this. Where the fuck is she, anyway?"

Julie laughed. "In the shower. Cor, that's a fucking sight an' a half, her big fat arse squashed against the glass."

Toni laughed along. "Take that to her before we are locked up."

Julie winked and left. Kelly turned to face her aunt, and it was then she knew she was behind it, and Hattie had been the one who had killed Milo. Toni raised her eyebrow. "Oh well, they shouldn't have fucked with me family. Shit happens!"

In total disbelief, Kelly glared. She didn't want this kind of retribution on her behalf. A 'sorry' from the two women would have been sufficient. She had been hurt, yes, but Milo should not have been killed in retaliation. It was the walk through the middle of the inmates in the canteen that made her realise why it had to happen though. If Toni hadn't taken revenge, then her reputation would have gone down the pan. It wasn't for Kelly's benefit that Milo had to die but for Toni's status. She learned a valuable lesson then that a reputation can mean more in life than anything, including money. Greed was not just about possession, it was about status. Prisons were microcosms of society, but most people going about their daily lives outside prison were unaware of this.

Kelly was escorted by Charlie to the legal visit room. As they walked along the landing, the inmates nodded and asked how she was.

Kelly just smiled in return but really she was thinking, *Fuck off – you aren't my friends.*

Charlie then said, "See, I said you would be better off with Toni."

Kelly didn't answer her; she was going with the flow, biding her time, and one day she would be out and away from the tension and the fakeness of it all. The metal banging and the rattling of the key chains were sounds that echoed in her mind and jolted her back to reality. She could be spending a long time inside, if found guilty. The stairs, which went from B wing down to the recreation room and canteen, had a mesh tread so anyone could see through. It made Kelly feel sick. She hated heights, but more disturbing were the nets hanging there to catch any inmate being thrown over. She trembled; it really was an evil place.

Charlie led Kelly through the double-locked doors and buzzed out the next set where the legal visit room was. It was a glass booth with a table and four chairs. Kelly could make out a woman already seated.

"Right, Kelly, in you go. I'll be back in an hour, okay?"

She liked the fact that Charlie, the so-called mean screw, addressed her now by her first name; to all the others, she was known by her surname.

She stepped inside and sat awkwardly. The lawyer had her nose in some papers before she looked up. Kelly noticed how clean she looked. Her blonde hair was pulled back in a neat and perfectly straight ponytail, and her well-manicured hands displayed a small diamond ring and a hint of pink nail varnish. She was wearing a fitted grey suit and a pink cashmere jumper. Around her neck was a string of tiny pearls.

As she looked up, a very gentle smile crept across her face. Kelly liked her already. Her eyes were warm and open and her cheeks had a natural pink glow; there was no make-up – she didn't need it – except for a dusting of mascara and a layer of gloss. She was an attractive woman, probably in her early thirties.

"Hello, Kelly, my name is Sophie Grey. It's lovely to meet you. Peter told me about you and I am so pleased you have enlisted my services."

Kelly felt the tension leave her body.

"No, Sophie, it's my pleasure." She was perfectly comfortable speaking the Queen's English but because she had gone to a school in South-East London where the pupils used over-the-top slang, she could naturally swing from one way of speaking to another, depending on the person she was talking to.

"Peter is a good, kind man. He was the first person who offered to help. Will you thank him for me?" asked Kelly. Her stomach was filled with butterflies but not because she was nervous; if anything, she was more excited that perhaps, at long last, there was some hope.

"Oh yes, he is special."

Kelly blushed. "Oh, I am sorry, I didn't ... I mean, are you two ... err?"

Sophie gave a friendly chuckle. "No, Kelly, I am not with Peter. He is not my type." She stopped and winked. "I am gay."

"Oh ..."

Sophie placed her hand on Kelly's. "But, if I were straight, I guess I probably would fancy him." She giggled, along with Kelly. That was the icebreaker.

"Kelly, why are you wearing prison issues? You should be in your own clothes because you are on remand. You're not convicted."

"I haven't got any of my own clothes, well, only the ones I was arrested in."

"Is there anyone on the outside who could send you some in?"

Kelly smiled sweetly and shook her head.

Sophie looked Kelly over and made a mental note of her size; she would need a suit for court.

"Right, Kelly, I have gathered all the paperwork from the prosecution, and I am really concerned. There are a few things that just don't add up. Please don't jump to conclusions at this point, but the evidence they have is really messy, and I am surprised they have charged you with two murders. It's as if they just want the case closed and are clutching at bent straws. So, Kelly, do you want to tell me your version of the events?"

Kelly closed her eyes for a moment, fathoming out the question. "There was only one event."

"Yes, that's what I thought. Did you confess to murdering your mother?"

Kelly shook her head. "No, I didn't, well, from what I remember, I didn't. I did say I had killed that Patrick, whatever his last name is. But I didn't mean to kill him. I just wanted to get away. He was in my room with his belt undone. He grabbed me, and that's when I fell and reached for the nearest thing, the metal doorstop. I never intended on killing him, just hitting him to get away, that's all."

Intently, Sophie watched the girl relive the event and was convinced she was telling the truth. Not only was Sophie a lawyer, she was a child psychologist and a specialist in juvenile cases.

"Kelly, tell me about your family, your mother, father, and Patrick." She watched for Kelly's reaction. It was easy to read her expressions because she was an open book; her eyes were expressive, and she did nothing to hide her feelings, not in front of Sophie.

"Patrick is not family, as far as I know. He came to stay for a while. My mother said he was my uncle, but how he was really related, I have no idea. You see, my real aunt, my aunt Bet, said he wasn't related. He was only my mother's friend—"

Sophie cut in. "Kelly, you refer to your mother as 'mother' not mum. It suggests to me, you didn't see her in a fond light."

Kelly bit her thumbnail and then took a deep breath. "The truth is I hated my mother. She was nasty to me. But, I didn't kill her. I wouldn't. I wouldn't kill anyone. Patrick, well … that was an accident, I swear."

Gently, Sophie tapped Kelly's hand. "It's okay, you can hate someone, but it doesn't mean you would kill them. It's good to open up to me. I am not judging you at all. Trust me, Kelly, I am on your side."

"Not like the shrinks in here, every bloody day, questioning me."

"What!" screeched Sophie. Kelly noticed that the lawyer's eyes narrowed and her face darkened at this news.

"It makes my blood boil. Just because you haven't engaged a barrister, they think they can do as they please. Oh, I am so going to take them to task." She took a deep breath. "Kelly, you are not to answer their questions anymore. They are only allowed to assess you once you have been convicted. Unless the CPS want a private assessment, then they need to have your consent and mine too now. God, they make me mad."

Kelly was grinning at the difference in Sophie's face when she was angry.

"So, what can you tell me about your father?" She calmed down, after scribbling a few notes.

"I was four when he left. He went to prison, I believe. Weird, 'cos all those years my mother brainwashed me into believing he was a paedophile." She stopped when she saw the expression on Sophie's face.

"What?"

"Kelly, I have looked into your father's record. It's part of the case, you see, and he was most definitely not a paedophile. Do you know anything about him at all?"

"Well, sharing a cell with his nutcase sister, I only know what she boasts about him."

Sophie put her pen down and sat up straight. Her eyes were bulbous, as though she was going to pop a blood vessel. Kelly studied Sophie's facial expression. "What's wrong, Sophie?"

"Toni Raven is in here, is she? Christ, it just gets worse. My goodness, Kelly, I am so glad you have me to take on the case. Your father, Eddie Raven, is a known criminal, a gangster, in fact. He has murdered a number of people, but he has only been convicted for two murders. He was released around the time you ran away. Is it a coincidence that a few weeks later your mother gets murdered? To my mind, it was convenient too because where would the blame lie, if not at your feet?"

Kelly covered her mouth in shock. "So, you think my own father murdered my mother?"

"I can't say that, Kelly, but I don't believe you were responsible. Oh, and another thing. Did you know it was your mother who gave evidence against him, as it was her statement that got him locked up?"

Overwhelmed by it all, Kelly placed her hands over her face and cried. She didn't cry for her mother, or her father, but for herself. She was born to a family of raving lunatics. How could she possibly be sane?

Sophie got up and knelt next to Kelly, rubbing her back. "Hey, listen, sweetie, I have to tell you everything. Kelly, we need to fathom all this out together, so are you with me?" She waited until the soft sobs subsided. Kelly wiped the snot on the back of her sleeve and turned around to face Sophie.

"I was four years old when he disappeared from my life. I pretended he never existed. I was so good at it that up until now I believed what I had been told. But I do remember being four. It was so different then, so different. My memories faded over the years because I just assumed it was all a fantasy. The pretty pink frills, the soft bedclothes, the toys, birthday cakes, balloons – they all melted away like ice cream. My happy life was slowly, day by day, being dragged away, until, finally, I realised that the bare rooms, the strict regime, and the constant harsh words, were my entire world then. I can't remember my mother smiling at me, ever. I recall the beatings, being tied in the shape of a cross in the shed and whipped. I remember the Bible being shoved under my nose every waking hour. The school was a retreat from the numbing silence or the nagging words from the woman that was supposed to love me. Yet, what I remember most of all in that house of hell was being on my knees praying to this so-called Jesus Christ. I desperately wanted my dad to come back and take me away from it all and make things go back the way they were. He never did. I hung from that cross, bleeding and freezing. And yet I still prayed. I begged Jesus to help me. No one did, though. So, I guess I hated my father for leaving me and I hated God, too."

Kelly looked up to see Sophie on the verge of tears.

"Oh, look, I am sorry, Sophie, I didn't mean to ..."

"No, Kelly, it's all right. I just feel sorry for you. It must have been terrifying."

"Yeah, well, if there is a God, he is punishing me now."

The horror had turned Sophie's stomach. Now she had a clearer insight into Kelly's life, it was worse than she could have imagined. Peter had told her about the scars on her back. He had broken all the rules, but his passion to save Kelly was more important. The poor girl had every reason to go insane. But as far as Sophie was concerned, she wasn't mad at all.

"Kelly, has your father tried to contact you?"

"Toni said to send out a VO. He wants to see me."

Sophie grimaced in annoyance. "I am not comfortable with you sharing a cell with Toni. Whose idea was it, yours or hers?"

Kelly snorted. "Hers, I didn't even know her. She is another controlling freak."

"I am sure she is, Kelly, and a devious one too, looking at her record. Look, if you are content to stay there, then carry on, but tell her nothing about our meeting. It is imperative that you keep quiet about our discussions. I have a feeling there is more to all of this. Oh, and by the way, I'm not sure if you already know this, but that Patrick Mahoney was married to Toni."

"Oh, Christ, of course! I remember now seeing his name on his suitcases when he stayed at our house, and Toni mentioned she was Toni Mahoney. I just didn't put two and two together," she blushed.

When the visit came to an end, Sophie stood. Kelly felt awkward; should she shake hands or just wave? Sophie made the decision for her, by holding out her arms, and before Kelly could do anything else, Sophie was hugging her. Kelly hugged her back and whispered, "Thank you for believing in me."

Charlie escorted Kelly to her cell.

Sophie had work to do and the first thing on the list was to go straight to the medical unit's offices. They were just down the corridor. Kirsty, the screw who had taken Kelly to the hospital, was on duty. She looked Sophie up and down. "What exactly do you want?" she asked, in a bullish tone.

Sophie gave her a sarcastic smile. "To see the psychiatrist who has been interrogating my client."

With raised eyebrows, Kirsty rebuffed Sophie. "Well, you will have to make an appointment or e-mail the office."

"Sorry, what is your full name?" countered Sophie.

"Kirsty." This question put her on the back foot and she felt uncomfortable. "Why?"

"So, Kirsty, when I speak with the number one governor this afternoon, I can give her your name."

Kirsty hated confident women who were more powerful than her. "Oh, well, my name's Kirsty Fellows. I am just following orders. No one sees the doctors unless they have an appointment."

"Yes, and I am just following the law, which, in this instance, has been seriously broken, and I would not like to have to go to the governor's deputy and report that I have been obstructed in allowing the matter to be cleared up at the earliest time, which is now."

Kirsty swallowed hard; she felt her mouth dry up and was uncomfortable with the situation. "Okay, I will see if they are in their offices."

"They are, I just saw them walk in," replied Sophie, ensuring she would not be fobbed off.

She followed Kirsty to the door and pushed past her, before Kirsty was able to introduce her. The two doctors stood up instantly. They were always ready to jump to their feet, if the door flew open.

Sophie waved her hand for Kirsty to leave. She then marched over to the desk, plonked her files on top, and announced she would be making a formal complaint.

"I am Kelly Raven's lawyer. It has come to my attention that over the past few weeks you have been conducting an assessment without her prior consent and broken the terms of her stay. Must I remind you that she is on remand? I don't know what your game plan is, but be warned. This will come out in the court case. So, I suggest you give me a copy of the assessment and don't leave any papers out."

Molly was surprised and had no time to think. She had been assigned by the CPS to get a full report. They wanted the girl in court, sentenced, and the whole case wrapped up in short order.

"Well, you will receive the papers before the trial."

Gritting her teeth, she wanted to wipe the smirk off Molly's face. Of course, she knew who the woman was, even though they had not been introduced by the bolshie officer. This woman had a reputation, for all the wrong reasons. Molly was known as the sly psychiatrist who dug deep to find any small deviation from the norm and have that person classified with some medical term attached to their name. 'Psychopathic tendencies' was her favourite one, based on her PhD thesis on the subject. In principle, this was all well and good. But the problem was she had an overzealous approach to her job; it had disastrous consequences for those charged with murder. She would, for example, go to the extreme to have the most normal inmate classed as completely insane. Of course, the Crown Prosecution Service were backing her findings because it was often easier to get an accused certified insane for a double murder than to prove that a completely compos mentis suspect was guilty. In this case, the trial would take forever and attract an enormous amount of media attention. So, to find that the youth had serious mental issues would dampen down the media speculation. Years ago, having suspects on remand for months on end was acceptable. Now, though, those days were gone because the courts were expected to convict or release suspects, especially juveniles, in a matter of weeks.

"Miss Bedford, may I remind you that what you have done is illegal. You have gained information under false pretences, a little trick of yours, but let me advise you of this. I am going to make a full report to the courts on how you coerced my client into allowing the assessment, how you faked your position, and how, with what should have been the full support of the medical unit here, Miss Raven managed to end up fighting for her life in hospital. You failed to have her on watch, and she ended up being stabbed. So, Miss Bedford, I think it is in your best interests that you hand over the files. Otherwise, I will add to the list of cock-ups the fact that you refused to do what is legally right. Have I made myself perfectly clear?"

Sophie was hot under the collar and yet pleased with herself. She despised Molly with a passion, knowing full well, over the years, that Molly had used her position to play God. She had been the psychiatrist instrumental in putting Peter's brother away for longer than was necessary.

Molly flared her nostrils, making her prissy face look like a spoiled child. "I think you will find I have done everything by the book, but I will see to it you receive the requisite paperwork." She sat heavily on the chair.

"Oh, I am not leaving without it, even if I have to go to the number one governor immediately. You can be assured the paperwork will leave with me today."

As Molly opened the back door, she sighed and huffed. She was followed by the other confused prison shrink. To their horror, Sophie followed them. Molly was in no position now to shut the door in the lawyer's face. Almost ripping the drawer out of the stacked metal filing cabinet, Molly flicked through the coloured sleeves and retrieved the brown folder.

"I will make copies." Her voice was flat and resigned.

"No need. I will do it from my office and return the originals. Besides, they are of no use to you, Miss Bedford, since we both know they were taken without consent. If the CPS wish to make their own assessment, then I look forward to hearing from them in the appropriate manner and through the correct procedure."

Molly handed the file to Sophie while staring her out, like a schoolgirl, daring her on. Sophie snatched it and marched away with her head held high and a mile-wide grin across her face. She had longed to do that for years.

As she left the prison, the thought crossed her mind that perhaps the CPS needed to find a plea of insanity to lock up Kelly and close the case. No matter how many visits she attended, she still walked away and sighed with relief that it wasn't her locked inside. This time the experience had been far worse. Once inside her flat, she poured herself a large glass of wine. She couldn't get Kelly off her mind. The clock was flashing four o'clock; it was really far too early. Her rule was wine after five at the earliest. The cold liquid went down so smoothly, she gulped back another mouthful. Something about this whole case did not add up. Kelly was not some psychopathic killer. She stared at the file for a few seconds, took another swig of her drink, and turned the page. She wanted to laugh out loud. There, staring her in the face, was the form with the one hundred questions: the form to determine a psychopath. "Jesus!" she said out loud. She turned to the last few pages: the report by the two psychiatrists. It was not completed but the wording pointed to Kelly being a cold-blooded murderer with a personality depicting psychopathic tendencies. Sophie felt her anger rising and tried to calm herself with another glass of Chardonnay. She didn't want to drink too much – not before she had reread the police reports.

The sudden rap on the door made her jump. She opened it, expecting some mail, as she had ordered new shoes to add to her ever-increasing collection. It was Peter. "Oh, come in, you can join me for a drink." She headed back to the lounge. Peter took off his jacket and hung it on the hook just inside the door. He opened the fridge and pulled out the orange juice. "So, how was she?"

Sophie was sitting back at the table. "You were right. She shouldn't be in there, the poor girl. Oh, I think she has a thing for you." She turned her head to watch his response.

He bowed his head and then turned away to pour the juice.

193

"Peter, you don't …"

"Sophie! Don't be absurd, of course I, err … I am her doctor, she is …"

"Yes, yes, she is nearly eighteen, so fucking what?"

Peter turned to his friend; his hair looked dishevelled, and his eyes were dull. "Soph, I can't seem to get her out of my head, I don't know what it is. One minute I see her as a child that needs my help, then next, I see this woman with big green eyes. Oh, Christ, I need a fucking lobotomy!"

Sophie got up and walked over to him, "Talking of a lobotomy, that Molly Bedford was in the nick, running an assessment on her. The report almost concluded that Kelly is insane."

Peter opened his mouth in shock. "What?"

"I know, it's fucking mental, pardon the pun. Anyway, don't worry, that report cannot be used in court. Kelly was not advised correctly. They did it without her official consent. The bastards have been taking full advantage of her declining a brief. What utter wankers, eh?"

Peter laughed. He found Sophie's choice of words amusing at times. "So, what now?"

Sophie pointed to the police file. "That, there, is my next mission. I am going to spend the weekend going over every word. I will know those statements off by heart. You watch me, Peter. I am damn sure they will not get away with sending that kid down for twenty years, or worse, pack her off to a nuthouse." She watched his face light up.

"Soph, do you think I'm a bit perverted for liking an eighteen-year-old? I mean, it's wrong, and I am not into kids, you know me, but I like her."

Sophie laughed out loud. "Peter, I have to be honest. Kelly is not like an eighteen-year-old. The girl is more woman than many women I know. I could fancy her myself, but you know me. I like big butch birds who can throw me around the bedroom." She winked and chuckled again.

Kelly lay on the bed and the wing was quiet. She savoured the peace while Toni was at work in the kitchen. That was one of the hardest things to deal with – the constant noise when the inmates finished their jobs. Rudy's house was noisy at times but it was different; she could go to her room or take Legend for a walk. A tear pricked her eyelid and she sniffed it back. Prison wasn't a place for tears. Kelly, along with the rest of the inmates, was constantly facing existential threats. And prison magnified these threats to the point where if you showed any weakness, emotion, or vulnerability you were at risk mentally and physically. How long would it be before she could be herself again, free from the tension of acting hard and fearless? Really, she was frightened: every clang of any metal door being locked, every rattle of the chains, rang like chaotic notes in her head.

She tried to concentrate on the letter. It would be stamped once the staff had read it. She held the pen poised but where should she start?

Dear Rudy,

I am so sorry. I never wanted trouble at your door. Please forgive me.

Out of respect for you, it's only right that I tell you what's happened. I was arrested and charged with murdering Patrick Mahoney and my own mother. It looks like I could get a long sentence but I have got a solicitor. She is really nice too.

I won't write again because you have a life to lead and it's better that you all go on without me. Please may I ask that you look after Legend for me? You know I love that dog.

I want you to know that you were my family, even if it was only for a short while. I loved you all so much — I still do — and I am so grateful that you let me be a part of you all — a real family.

Tell Lippy (Mum) that the food in here is okay but I miss her cooking. Say hi for me to Ditto, Reggie, Phoenix and Solly. I love you, guys!

I love you all and I always will.

Bluey x

Hearing a noise outside and the rubber wedge move slightly, she quickly put the letter under the mattress and removed the doorstop. The door flew open, almost knocking Kelly aside. There, in the doorway, was a woman Kelly had never met before. A large woman in her mid-forties with bleached short hair and black roots, a weathered face, and arms covered in odd tattoos, she looked a real scary bitch. Focusing more closely on the tattoos, Kelly saw a huge cross and some random names that had faded to almost a blur over time. The intruder put Kelly in mind of one of those Hells Angels, without the leathers. She wasn't smiling and her eyes glared with hate. She looked Kelly up and down, and when she grinned, showing her row of cockles instead of teeth, her breath reeked of pickled onions. Kelly froze as the woman stepped forward. "Where's that slag Toni?"

"In the kitchen, working." Kelly stayed composed and kept a neutral tone. She didn't want the woman to see she was shitting herself.

"So, you must be family, then?"

Kelly didn't like the sound of her creepy voice, so she didn't answer. She could see the woman was a bit of a nutter; she was gearing herself up for trouble all right. Her jaw was tight and her breathing was fast. The disturbing grin turned to a look of intense anger. Through gritted teeth, she growled, "I'm returning a favour."

She knew then that the woman was ready to launch herself on her. Kelly was quick to take a stance and prepare to defend herself. The first punch was fast but Kelly blocked her; the second punch was faster still,

196

yet Kelly was ready and swiftly moved, using her arm to counter the blow. Her wrist felt the force, but as her adrenaline was pumping, she didn't feel the pain. The third right hook caught Kelly on the cheek, and she wobbled but not enough to break her stance. Hopping back one step, and in a fit of rage, she lifted her leg high and fly-kicked the woman in the chest. Winded, she fell against the doorframe. As her head came down, Kelly kicked again, this time at the woman's face, splitting her nose. Incensed by the pain, she lunged forward to grab at Kelly, but she was no match for the agile youngster. Kelly was solid on her feet, and as she sidestepped, she pulled back her fist. The blow was like a sledgehammer, cracking the inmate on the side of the face. She fell on the bed and turned to see that Kelly was not even out of breath. The older woman couldn't lose face, not now. So, with her final attempt, she jumped up and swung an almighty punch. It was useless; Kelly swerved the clump, and with an anger she had never experienced before, she tore into this lunatic with a succession of clean punches, using her as a punching bag. That was until, finally, she saw the blood spew up the wall and the crumpled bloodied mess of the woman's face.

Kelly flopped on the opposite bed and caught her breath. She peered down at her bruised knuckles and shuddered. Tears began to flow. The state of her opponent's battered face was mortifying. Not knowing what to do next, Kelly pulled her knees up under her chin and rocked. Her adversary was out cold, blood oozing from her nose and ears, and her lower lip was hanging on by a thread. She was disgusted with herself. Was this what her life had come to – being merciless, using physical violence to stay alive? This wasn't what she was really about, but she had had no choice.

The wing was livening up and the inmates were returning from their allocated jobs. Although her attacker was motionless, Kelly knew she wasn't dead. She could hear her mumbling.

Then Toni returned. Kelly heard her voice outside, organising a deal. She was always wheeling and dealing, running one scam or another. As soon as she pushed the door open, she gasped, looking from Kelly to the unconscious form and back again. Hattie was behind her, trying to peer over Toni's shoulder to get a good look. Kelly was still rocking, holding her knees.

"Christ!" choked Toni, her eyes wide in amazement.

Hattie pushed Toni aside, for a closer look. "Christ alive! That's fucking Lou O'Donnell!"

Toni grabbed Hattie's arm. "OK, Hat, don't state the fucking obvious. Get her out, dump her on the landing, away from here."

Hattie looked outside to see where the screws were but the coast was clear. "Help me, Tone," she uttered, trying to lift the dead weight. "She's a fucking lump!" Her voice was strained, in trying to pull the woman off the bed. Toni was like a whippet and on the bed in a second to grab Lou's feet. "Pull, Hat, ya fucking great moose!"

"I *am* fucking pulling. Lift her feet up, Tone!"

Finally, they had Lou dragged away from the cell and out on the landing.

Toni ran back and grabbed some wet tissues to mop up the small blood smears that had appeared as they pulled her along the floor. Two inmates, Treacle and Patty, rushed over. "Fuck, Tone, that's Lou O'Donnell," screeched Treacle, a small druggie, inside for dealing. She was part of Toni's firm. "Ya fucking done her a right good 'n!"

Toni was too concerned with the backlash from the screws to think about who had done it or respond to yet another vacuous remark from one of her crew. She nodded and said. "Ya saw nuffin, got it!"

Treacle and Patty nodded in unison. "No worries. Oh shit, quick, Tone, the SO's coming up the stairs." It was time for them all to disperse in different directions. As soon as the senior officer was on the landing, the alarm was raised. Another lockdown resulted.

Toni rushed back to her cell to find Kelly still in the same position, still rocking herself. She wedged the door shut and whirled around. "Fucking 'ell! What happened?"

The look Kelly shot in Toni's direction was one of sheer contempt.

"What?" frowned Toni.

The still, creepy silence unnerved Toni. "Kel, my babe, what happened?" She tried to soften her approach.

Kelly stopped rocking, sat up straight, and lifted her head, showing the bruise on her cheek.

"Fuck me, Kel, so it was *you* who did that to Lou." In her mind, she had assumed that someone else had attacked Lou, not her niece.

"Yes," was all she could say, still sickened by the whole ordeal.

"How the hell did ya learn to fight like that?" Toni was genuinely dumbfounded.

Lou O'Donnell was Toni's long-term arch enemy. She had attacked Toni with a bar and broken her arm, scarred her chin, and with a final blow, she had hit her at the back of the head, knocking her unconscious. That was five years ago in Holloway Prison all over an ounce of speed. Toni bided her time and then came face-to-face with Shannon O'Donnell, Lou's daughter. This twenty-year-old was as much a Face as her mother but no match for Toni. Lou was released on parole when Shannon arrived. It was payback. Toni was in the kitchen and beckoned Shannon in, calling her mother an overgrown, ugly lesbian. Shannon ignored the first few jibes, but then she turned the instant Toni called her an inbred. Shannon had to save face in front of the others, and so she lunged forward to attack Toni, but she wasn't fast enough. Toni picked up the industrial cooking pot and swung it at Shannon's head. The thump was loud and the other inmates cringed. Shannon was left with marks on her face that were serious enough to give Lou the message.

Lou had been livid and vowed that one day she would pay Toni back, and so when she was nicked for robbery, she smiled to herself.

"I ain't proud, Toni!" Kelly snapped back.

Toni sat herself down on her bed and faced Kelly. "Ya should be, girl. Cor, you have right fucked her face up. A chunk an' all, she is. 'Orrible fat cunt. I hate her."

The words were going around in Kelly's head, irritating her and winding her up, but she tried to keep calm and just ignored her.

"Cor, fuck 'aving a ruck with you! I knew you had more Raven blood running through your veins than ya fucking mother!"

"Shut up! Just shut the fuck up!" screamed Kelly. "I ain't proud of it, I hate meself for it, and it's all your fault." She got off the bed and towered over Toni. "I have listened to your bullshit long enough. If you think by brainwashing me with how to scam this one, how to do over that one, how lucky I am to be a Raven, that I should follow in your footsteps, you are thoroughly mistaken, Toni. Like I keep telling you, ya don't know me. I am only family by blood, nothing else. So, shut up trying to pat me on the back for nearly killing your enemy. I didn't do it for you, I was just protecting meself. Oh, yeah, and she said she was returning a favour. So, Toni, your tough attitude could have got me fucking killed, so it ain't all about me being a chip off the old block, it's about me suffering again at the dirty hands of the poxy Raven family!"

With that, Kelly slumped back on the bed and placed her head in her hands, uninterested in Toni's response.

The cells were locked down early, and Lou was taken to the hospital unit, suffering from a whole range of injuries that included concussion and facial wounds. Her left ribs were cracked as was the sternum, which left her hard of breathing, and she would need rest for at least three weeks. She lay there resigned to the fact she was fairly beaten by a kid and made a decision to turn the fighting in. She had to admit to herself that Kelly had shit the wind up her. Kelly was a seriously lethal fighter; she knew that from the girl's blank expression and effortless blows. She had never met anyone who could fight like that, with absolutely no aggression. She had scared her — perhaps she *was* a double murderer. Lou thought she had been lucky to escape with just a few broken bones.

Toni lay awake, listening to Kelly purring like a kitten. How was she going to tell Eddie that taking her niece under her wing was not going to plan? She wasn't the innocent teenager who was eager to fall into the arms of her aunt and who could be manipulated into working with the family. Eddie would throw a fit, if he knew what had gone on.

She was beginning to despise Kelly.

CHAPTER TEN

As soon as lockdown was over, Kelly headed for the shower; she needed to leave the tension and avoid any more conflict with her aunt. There was a small queue but Hattie and two others stepped aside and allowed Kelly to go first. She guessed word had hit the wing and now her unwanted reputation went before her. She wanted to get away from them and so gladly jumped the queue. She was now used to having no privacy, and so she stripped off in full view, baring her naked back. She couldn't be bothered to hide the scars. After all, they were part of her and always would be. That set the cat among the pigeons with the gossiping tongues. She grinned to herself, washing off the soap. As if they didn't have enough to talk about, now they had Kelly's disfigurement. Her mind returned to Rudy and Lippy and triggered a thought. Remembering the letter she'd just written to them, she went into panic mode. She didn't want Toni or anyone else knowing about her life in Peckham. She was out of the shower quickly, without even drying herself, and then she whipped on her tracksuit, grabbed her prison issue pumps, and ran back to the cell. Unbeknown to her, though, Toni had found the letter tucked under her niece's mattress. She had read every word and memorised the address. Just as Kelly reached the door, Toni was off her bed and about to make her way to the phone. Kelly spotted the letter, left on show. Her eyes darted from the letter and back to Toni. Kelly grabbed her arm to stop her leaving, but Toni tried to shrug her off.

"Why are you reading me letter, Toni? I thought we were family."

Toni stared at Kelly, unable to find any words. Her niece just glared at her.

"Off to the phone are ya, Tone?"

She let go of her arm and turned her back on her. Staring down at the letter, she felt a gut-wrenching sensation. Instantly, she faced her aunt, and before Toni could get away, Kelly grabbed her by the hair, pulling her back in the cell.

"What the fuck are you doing, Kelly? Get off me!"

Kelly released her grip. "I swear on my life, Toni, if any harm comes to them, I will make sure your nightmares are a safe place to be."

Toni plonked herself on the bed. Thinking quickly, she said, "You got me all wrong, babe. I read ya letter 'cos I wanted to know you better. I wanted to understand what ya been through. I ain't making any phone calls … what the fuck for, anyway? Kel, why do you think anyone would want to hurt them? From what I read in that letter, they were good to you." She smiled, showing her kinder side. Kelly nodded.

"They were good to me, Toni. They were there when no one else was."

Toni took that as a dig at her. "I was going to get me parcels. Apparently, you've got one as well." She hoped that would steer Kelly away from the fact that Toni was about to inform her brother of this Rudy.

"D'ya want me to fetch yours, while I'm there?"

Kelly shot her another glare. "Nah, I'll get me own."

They walked along the wing in silence. As they reached the stairs, Charlie bumped into them. She looked around to see who was about. "You're very lucky, Toni, that Lou O'Donnell claims she fell down the stairs. A joke, really, considering she was found *up* the stairs. Anyway, there ain't going to be no further investigation." Toni stood defiantly, with her head inclined and her arms folded. Charlie's eyes wandered down to Kelly's hands. "How did you get those marks, Kelly?"

Toni watched as Kelly stood unfazed, staring straight through the officer. "I punched the wall in me sleep. It's a bad habit of mine."

Charlie nodded and carried on past. Toni was beginning to realise that her niece was in no way a child but smart, quick, and fucking ruthless.

The prison issue reception was buzzing with inmates collecting their goodies. Ruth, a waifish-looking redhead, aged about twenty-five, was in front. Kelly knew her from the wing; she was the orderly who mopped the floors every five minutes. She never smiled and always looked so sad. Her hair was pulled back in a tight ponytail and her clothes hung off her. Kirsty was on the desk, with her smug pig face, handing over the items in a clear plastic bag. She handed Ruth a small bag, and Kelly couldn't help but notice the threadbare clothes inside. Ruth put her head down and scurried away like a church mouse, trying not to be noticed.

Toni snatched her bag from Kirsty and walked away, not waiting for Kelly; it didn't go unnoticed. Then Kelly watched as Kirsty bent down and struggled to lift the next parcel. She heaved it up and over the desk and allowed it to drop on the floor. "'Ere, Raven, sign."

Kelly scribbled her name and grabbed the bag by the cable ties. *Christ, it's heavy*, she thought. But, for the first time, she felt excited.

Toni wasn't in the cell when Kelly opened the door, so she was pleased she could experience the pleasure of opening her gifts without having her aunt there to spoil the mood. She tore away the plastic and carefully pulled out the items. There was no note from the sender, and she had no idea who would have sent her such beautiful clothes. There were designer T-shirts, jeans, jumpers, nightclothes, and trainers, and all her size too. Quickly, she stepped out of her prison tracksuit and pulled on the red T-shirt and dark-blue fitted jeans. The trainers felt like heaven, after wearing the prison pumps. The nightclothes were also tasteful. They could not have been from Rudy. He wouldn't have a clue about what she liked; it would have been fuck-off, in-your-face stuff with big logos, advertising Chanel or Louis Vuitton. No, whoever sent them must have known her taste and that she was still on remand. *Interesting*.

When Toni returned, she looked more at ease and smiled. "They look lovely on ya, Kel. Someone spoilt ya. Who sent them in?"

Kelly shrugged her shoulders. "I don't know."

Toni laughed. "I bet it was ya dad. Talking of him, are ya ready for this afternoon?"

The question couldn't have been worse timed. It was as if she was wearing a dead man's suit; she had an overwhelming urge to peel the clothes off. The excitement of the unknown sender was ruined by the thought it could have been Eddie.

"What's happening this afternoon?"

Hugely excited, Toni clapped her hands together. "Me and you, kiddo, have a double visit with ya dad."

"You what? I never sent a VO out," she bridled, her face changing from a look of apprehension to one of deep resentment.

"No, ya don't have to send a VO because you're on remand. He can see you whenever. Anyway, the double visit's booked, so ain't ya excited ya can meet him? He is," declared Toni, rubbing her hands together.

The thought of meeting Eddie wasn't a pleasurable one; she had formed her own ideas about him and wasn't about to share them with Toni. Yet, she did want to know what his agenda was because she didn't buy into his loving reunion story.

They were called for lunch in the canteen. As usual, Toni headed to the front of the queue, whilst Kelly stayed at the back, behind Ruth. But Treacle, the fiery scag head, could see the line was building up behind Kelly, so she skipped past Ruth and pushed her way in. Being a member of Toni's firm gave her *carte blanche* to lord it over the other inmates, as she was immune to any comeback. Ruth, with her head down, did nothing. *What?* Kelly's heart rate zipped up a few notches, seeing this piss-taker trying it on. Stepping in front of Ruth, who assumed Kelly was doing the same as her aunt and Treacle, Kelly tapped this hanger-on on the shoulder. She turned around to face Kelly with a big smile on her face, "Oh, all right, Kel?"

"You've pushed in!" complained Kelly, coldly.

Treacle was fidgeting as always. "Ah, sorry, Kel, go on, you can go in front of me," she replied.

"Err, nah, you should have joined the queue like everyone else." Kelly's voice wasn't loud but was still heard by the inmates further up the line. Toni took a step away from the queue and glared at Kelly. Treacle looked at Toni, waiting for an order, but she was miffed when Toni looked away, not wanting to get involved.

"What's up, Kel, have I upset ya, or what?"

With a glare that could kill, Kelly retorted, "Yeah, ya have, as a matter of fact. Ya pushed ya way in. I don't like bullies."

Everyone stopped and listened, as they waited for Toni to say something, but she didn't; Toni just carried on piling on her plate the better helpings, leaving the less savoury portions for the end of the line.

Treacle put her head down and walked dejectedly away, back to her cell. Kelly then retraced her steps behind Ruth. There were mumblings, as the inmates viewed the whole situation as a stance over pecking order.

Then, unexpectedly, Kelly took her tray and sat next to Ruth, who was too shit-scared to say a word.

"So, Ruth, after visiting, fancy a game of snooker?"

Too afraid to speak or look up, she kept her head down and whispered urgently, "What are you doing, Kelly? I don't want any trouble."

Kelly sighed. "Look, Ruth, I don't either. I just want to play snooker and not have to listen to their bullshit."

"Oh, I don't know. I think I wanna keep meself to meself. Please don't take offence. I am just ... well, I don't want any agg."

The quiet, fearful voice resonated with Kelly and she hated Toni's brutes – her so-called firm.

After Kelly had swallowed the last of her orange squash, she stood up and left; she didn't wait for Toni or even acknowledge her. Toni was seething. Kelly was playing a dangerous game, and sooner or later, she would put Kelly in her place. But unbeknown to her, her niece was being regarded as the woman you just don't mess with. Lou O'Donnell had sorted out Toni good and proper: the once scary bitch had never lost a fight. She used to run the prison, and so when Toni had tried to take that away from her, she'd retaliated, leaving marks to warn others not to mess with her. Now, years later, Kelly was the one who had battered Lou, and so the dynamics had changed somewhat – it was Kelly who had the rep now.

Reluctantly, Kelly got herself ready for the visit. She had to wear the armband depicting her as a prisoner. It was a harsh reminder all right. She continued hoping Sophie was her way out and she was going to fight for her freedom. This hellhole was turning her into someone she wasn't meant to be.

Toni returned and slammed the door behind her.

"I am fucking warning you, little girl," she spat.

Kelly was on her feet, ready to take her aunt on, if necessary. She had learnt now that prison was not too dissimilar to a jungle: always be alert to danger.

"You are playing a very fucking dangerous game; maybe you are too young to grasp it now, but let me tell ya. You 'ave it easy, 'cos ya me niece. If ya try to go against me in front of the others, then there's gonna be a fucking change between us, and trust me, Kelly, there will be trouble like you won't believe. These scummy inmates will be choosing whose side to take. They will use every trick in the book to turn you and me against each other."

Kelly grinned. "And that really fucking worries you, don't it, Toni!"

"Jesus, Kelly, if you weren't me niece I'd 'ave ripped your 'ead off ya shoulders and shit down ya fucking neck by now. You really don't get it, do ya? Well, let me explain something to ya. 'Aving a fight ain't all ya need, to keep ya on top in 'ere. You don't think they kiss me feet just 'cos I can wipe the floor with 'alf of them, do ya? I run this wing 'cos they need their little bit of gear, tobacco, puff, whatever, and, Kelly, I have the means to it all, and you don't. *Now*, do you get me?"

Kelly was sick of her aunt's hard and domineering attitude as if she ruled the world. "Yeah, Tone, I get ya, but I don't want to run fuck all. I am me own person, not part of any gang. I hate fucking tormentors and I don't owe you anything. In fact, Toni, your past antics nearly got me a good hiding off Lou, if I'm not mistaken. I ain't over that yet. I'm not like you—"

"Don't I fucking know it!" Toni said quickly, interrupting Kelly.

"And, Toni, I don't *want* to be like you. The others may look up to ya, but I don't, and if that pisses you off, well, tough."

"Okay, I get it, Kel, ya wanna be a rebel. You had it a bit difficult growing up and now ya wanna hate everyone. But you ain't gotta hate me. I'm on your side."

Kelly folded her nightclothes and placed them at the end of the bed; she didn't say another word. There was no point: Toni was never going to understand, and she was too tired to argue. Besides, right now, she needed to mentally prepare for meeting Eddie Raven — her so-called father.

❧ * ❧

Eddie Raven waited in the main reception, before he was allowed to enter the visiting room. A few of the visitors recognised him and nodded out of respect. He didn't sit down like the others. Dressed in his jeans, red pullover, and designer jacket, and leaning against the wall, he stood out like a sore thumb. It wasn't what he wore, which captured the attention of other people, but his whole comportment. Of course, he was a good-looking man, with a seriously mysterious expression and eyes holding many secrets. Women were drawn to him and he knew it. He had learned to use all he had to get what he wanted, including fulfilling his sexual appetite. With one wink, he would have a woman eating out of his hands or sucking on his dick, preferably the latter.

The surnames were called in alphabetical order. The visitors stood up, grabbed their kids, and hurried into the visiting room. Eddie watched as the holding room dwindled down to just him. "Raven!"

Eddie pushed himself away from the wall, nodded at the screw, and swaggered past. Kirsty raised her eyebrow. He was cocky, like his sister; she could have picked him out right away, with his olive skin, those striking green eyes, and chiselled features.

The visiting room was a hive of activity, with families eager to get seated, ready to face their loved ones. The queue at the tuck shop was increasing. He would have bought a few goodies but didn't as queuing wasn't in his DNA. Instead, he settled himself on the yellow plastic chair and watched the end door from where the prisoners appeared. Unexpectedly, a little girl, no older than three, skipped over to him, placed her chocolate covered fingers on the table, and stood smiling. He returned her smile and watched her huge round brown eyes light up. She was like a dolly. Kelly was not much older, when he had said goodbye; he wondered what she looked like now.

"Come here, Rosie. Ahh sorry, Eddie, she's a nosy little madam," said the huge meathead, in a low, gravel voice.

"All right, Connor?" nodded Eddie.

"Yeah, mate, not bad, me missus is in 'ere. She got caught shoplifting again, and the filth also found some drugs on her. A double whammy, eh." He rolled his eyes and bent down to pick up his daughter.

Eddie nodded again and the man walked away feeling awkward; that was the last thing he needed – to have his kid cover Eddie Cako Raven in a Cadbury Creme Egg. He shuddered at the thought.

Finally, the door opened and there, at the front of the queue, stood Toni, closely followed by Kelly. He knew straightaway she was a Raven. As they walked towards him, he felt odd; should he greet her with open arms or remain seated? Toni was beaming and had her arms outstretched. That was how it had been for a few years, her visiting him and now him reciprocating.

He got up and hugged her.

She seemed excited to introduce his daughter. "'Ere she is, Eddie." She turned to face Kelly. "Your fucking double, ain't she?"

Eddie and Kelly were both eyeing each other over. He hoped for a smile at least, but he sensed she wasn't about to fall into his arms and cry with happiness. His heart was beating fast and he felt something, although for the life of him, he wasn't sure what it was.

"So, Kel, ya gonna give ya ol' man a hug?"

Something stirred inside her, yet it wasn't overwhelming love, that was for sure. She saw how confident he was and how young he appeared. It had been too long ago for her to have any recollection of what he looked like, but Toni's description fitted him perfectly: he was your typical East End bruiser, being handsome, flash, and, yes, arrogant!

She remained stone-faced but walked towards his open arms. As he pulled her close, she vaguely recalled a time long ago when her dad was in her life – that same expensive aftershave and the feel of his cheek against hers. It was a warm sensation. She was four then and of course she had loved him. Who wouldn't? He was kind and gentle with her. Flashbacks were returning now, with her giggling and him chasing her and tickling her in their lounge. Why had things turned out so wrong?

"Look at you!" He held her away, still clutching her arms. "You are a looker, that's for sure."

They sat down opposite to each other, Kelly aware of his fixed grin. Obviously, his desire to meet his daughter was greater than hers. *Well, that wouldn't be difficult*, she thought.

It was embarrassing, listening to Toni tripping over herself to impress him with all her hard-girl misdoings whilst massaging her own ego at the same time. Kelly observed Eddie's face convey pride and pleasure.

"So, Kelly, me sister tells me that you had it rough when I got sent down." He tried to make it sound like it wasn't his fault he wasn't around for her. He cocked his head, in a sympathetic gesture.

She thought carefully about her answer; should she pile it on, and let him know how hard it really was, and make him feel guilty? Then, she considered his attitude and decided he probably wouldn't care anyway.

"Yeah, she was a bit strict but I'm still here, ain't I?" she glared defiantly.

Sensing some of the euphoria, which had been building up prior to meeting his baby girl for the past twelve years, was not being returned,

Eddie just nodded his head. Looking from one to the other, Kelly was determined he wasn't getting off lightly for abandoning her.

Leaning across, he grabbed her hand. "I would have had you taken away from her, Kelly, if I had known what a cunt she was——"

Before he could continue, Kelly interrupted him with her sharp tongue. "I never said she was a cunt. I said she was strict."

He let go of her hand and tapped his hands on the table. An uncomfortable silence descended over them. Toni knew that look of menace in her brother's eyes.

"Kelly, I'm sorry I weren't there for ya, but as you know, I got nicked, spent twelve years inside. I couldn't do much, now could I?" His tone was firmer.

"Nah, Eddie, s'pose not." replied Kelly, extending the animosity by staring coldly at him.

The antagonistic reply made Toni's eyes open wide with horror; no one had ever dared speak to her brother like that. She waited for the backlash but was surprised to find him laughing.

"Oh, Kel, you are a fucking chip off the old block. You've got spunk and I like it."

A screech, coming from the corner of the visiting room, distracted everyone. Ruth was being scarfed up by her ponytail by a man twice her size. Kelly felt her heart beating fast again and the anger rising. Poor Ruth was a tiny, quiet, and inoffensive woman. Three little children, with red hair like their mother's, stood holding each other's hands, their eyes fixed to the floor and trembling with fright. It was apparent he was her husband or other half. The look on the woman's face was pitiful, as this giant, with shovel hands and a threatening look on his face, stuck his nose in her ear, growling obscenities and gripping her hair tightly. Then the tension in the room lifted, as he let her go, and her head tilted down. Kelly wanted to jump from her seat and rescue Ruth. Eddie was looking for an expression on his daughter's face and saw there wasn't one: she was not a soppy teenager he could easily manipulate but an independent woman. She didn't give a shit about him or what he stood for. He would have to suck her in, get her onside, and soon.

Toni changed the subject. "Nice clobber ya got for Kelly." Eddie frowned, confirming what Kelly had thought all along. She smiled, feeling relieved she owed him nothing.

"Oh, I thought ..." said Toni.

Eddie was quick. "I wanted to meet our Kelly first and find out what she likes. It's no good buying shit. So, Kel, what do you need? You can have whatever ya want."

Flash bastard, she thought again. *What I need is for you to fuck off and leave me alone*, but she didn't say it aloud, of course. Instead, she said nothing and just shook her head.

Eddie was finding the visit hard work. Normally, people would fall over themselves to get in his good books. This was the other way around. He didn't like it; never before in his life had he felt so unsure of himself.

"Look, Kel, I know it must have been hard for ya, growing up with fuck all, so I am just saying it's gonna be easier now, know what I mean?"

In her own world now, Kelly had a plan to find out if Eddie was there when her mother was murdered.

"Who said I had fuck all?"

Ill at ease, Eddie shot a sharp glance at Toni. "Err, Tone said ya mother ... um, I mean, she was cruel to ya." He was fumbling over his words.

Toni froze; she had never said that Kelly was denied material things. Her eyes met Eddie's, astonished by his clumsy responses to anything Kelly was saying.

"I never said I had nothing. Where Toni got that from, I don't know. All I said, and I've said it three times now, was she was strict!"

Kelly knew then that the only way Eddie could have known about her was if he had been to the hellhole house. He would have seen the sparse rooms devoid of comforts.

"Sorry, babe, I just assumed."

A sly smile adorned her face, as if to say, 'You don't fool me'.

Casting a sideways glance towards the tuck shop, he noticed the queue had gone down. "I am going to get some tea. Fancy some chocolate, Kel, crisps, sweets?"

Kelly thought it best to soften; keeping him onside was important, as well as establishing the truth, one way or another. "Yeah, I'll have whatever, please."

With a wry smile, Kelly nodded and watched, as he walked away to join the queue. Then she looked at Toni who sat there with a cob on.

"Kelly, you should respect that man. He is ya father and what's all this business calling him Eddie?"

"Respect is earned. Just 'cos he shagged me muvver and I was the end result don't mean I have to respect him. Tell me, Tone, what has he done to earn my respect, eh?"

"Just don't push it. Ya really don't wanna get on the wrong side of him," snarled Toni.

Endeavouring to act unconcerned, Kelly tutted and rolled her eyes.

Eddie returned with a tray of chocolate bars, crisps, and three teas. "There ya go," he winked at Kelly.

"I got ya white chocolate. You used to love it when you was a toddler. A bar of that and then you would crawl onto my lap and sleep. Purred like a kitten, ya did."

Kelly was listening, trying to recollect it.

"You used to have this bunny. Ya never let it out of ya sight. I used to prise it off ya, to get it washed. D'ya remember?" His face held a false grin.

"Yeah, I remember the bunny. I carried it everywhere." Kelly smiled sweetly, this time thinking of her comfort toy. She had kept it hidden from her mother, or it would have been binned, along with all her toys. The bunny was special; she had held on to it, as if it were her lifeline.

"I had one as a kid, an old teddy, still got it. Funny, there are just some things ya can never throw away," he craftily mentioned, hoping she would continue with a planned trip down memory lane.

Kelly laughed then. "I know what you mean. I have a favourite pair of socks. I sometimes still wear 'em, holes an' all."

As he looked at the clock, he realised he only had five minutes left. "I tell ya what, Kel. I'll fetch ya socks and ya bunny. I can hand them in on me next visit."

She had followed his gaze, observed it was near the end of the visit, and summed her father up in those two hours. "Don't worry about fetching anything. Kind of ya, but I've got everything I need."

Sucking up the disappointment, Eddie bit his tongue. He didn't want to push her too far, not on the first visit. He needed to work on his daughter, to gain her trust again. Giving her space was probably the best option.

216

"So ,where ya staying, Ed?" asked Toni.

"Down at the holiday pad in Hythe."

Toni nodded. "Well, make me room up. I've got a parole hearing. Ya never know, I could get out on good behaviour."

"You? Good, ya little fucker. You've no chance, but I wish ya luck, sis."

The visit was over. He hugged his sister and then held out his arms to hug Kelly. She smirked and then put her arms around him. "Bye, dad," she whispered, dragging out the word 'dad'. He pulled away, feeling uneasy; her tone gave him the creeps.

Kelly left the visit with much to ponder over. It was obvious that Toni had a close bond with her brother; she looked up to him and he had affection for her. She found it cringing that Toni, the hard woman in prison, was like an eager puppy in front of him. Her showing off was childish and yet Eddie went along with it, even though he came across as a hard-ass charmer.

Despite all the talking in those two hours, he had never even mentioned her court case or how he would help her get out of prison. No one had even acknowledged the fact she had murdered Toni's husband. It was as if she was already convicted of the two murders and the sentence was a foregone conclusion. She went over every word he'd said, and not once did he ask if she killed them.

She decided she would go along with their game, whatever it was, and find out the truth. She had her suspicions and hoped she was wise enough to be one step ahead.

Her aunt had left earlier, still unimpressed with Kelly, which suited her just fine, of course. As Kelly reached the stairs, she noticed Ruth, hurrying back to her cell. A wave of sorrow gripped Kelly, seeing poor Ruth stuck in here and with three little children out there.

She followed her, and as the cell door closed, she knocked out of politeness. Ruth didn't ask who it was. "Come in."

Inside, Ruth was sitting on the bed and clutching a teddy; it was a small, worn, and scruffy toy, reflecting the appearance of this woman.

"How ya doing, Ruth?"

She kept her head down, staring at the toy. "Kelly, I am sorry but I can't talk to you. I really don't want any trouble."

Kelly rolled her eyes; this was ridiculous. She sat down next to Ruth and put an arm around her shoulders. "What's up, mate?" she asked, in a sympathetic voice.

Through gentle snivels, Ruth whispered, "Me ol' man told me to keep away from you, 'cos I have a habit of saying the wrong thing. He reckons if I upset you, then your dad will come for him. So, it's best I don't have anything to do with ya."

Anger clouded Kelly. She didn't want to be associated with him or any of the Raven family.

"Ruth, listen to me. First, you couldn't say the wrong thing to me, and second, I ain't some nutter like Toni."

Ruth wiped her nose on her sleeve. "You are nice, Kelly, but your family are dangerous people. I don't say much but I do listen. There is so much shit-stirring in here that someone else might cause trouble for me, and if it lands on Toni's ears, then, well ... blood's thicker than water, ain't it?"

"Not in my case, mate," laughed Kelly. "I never knew Toni, and my father... well, I don't class him as my dad. I was just unlucky to be born into a family who put their reputation above everything else. When I get out of here, I won't ever have anything to do with them. I have a family, Ruth, and they certainly don't have my blood running through their veins." She laughed again. "They're black, you see."

218

Ruth looked at Kelly, bemused by her soft words and clearer diction. It was as if someone else was sitting beside her.

"Kelly, you aren't like them at all, are you? You are well-spoken and polite, underneath the front."

Kelly nodded. "Ruth, I have learned to be a chameleon, so I adjust to my surroundings. At school, I was surrounded by kids, all with that South-East London twang and the slang words, but my mother, though, would slap me if I slipped my h's. So you could say I am a bit of a con artist, depending on my audience. Anyway, as you can see, Ruth, I am not bad. I hate bullies."

Ruth stopped the snivels and smiled. To Kelly's surprise, her face changed, and she looked quite beautiful.

"I have to ask, Kelly, but you're only small compared to Lou O'Donnell—" Before she could finish, Kelly was laughing. "I know, you're wondering what everyone else is. I'll tell you but keep it a secret, eh."

With huge childlike eyes, Ruth smiled and nodded.

"My mother was a control freak, so I wasn't allowed any after-school activities. I had to be home dead on quarter past four, no excuses. I never had pocket money, only money for school dinners she gave me on a Monday morning. Anyway, there was a martial arts class just opposite the school, and they ran a session at a lunchtime, for adults, not the school kids. When I was eleven, and just starting secondary school, I got bashed up, getting off the bus. Not bad stuff, just teasing me, or so I assumed. Anyway, this man stopped the fight, picked up my bag, and walked me to the school gates. He was a huge man called Terry. He volunteered to teach me to defend myself. I told him the situation with my mum, and so he offered to teach me at lunchtimes. He was such a kind man, you know. He soon realised I was paying with my school dinner money and suggested he train me for free. He even gave me a second-hand karate gi, that's the loose white outfit. I kept this at the centre, and before long I was working my way up to a black belt. I was his prodigy, he said. He soon had me up against the biggest men in the group, and I won more than I lost, so there you have it."

Ruth was sitting with her mouth wide open. "Oh, wow, perhaps I should take up something like that to stop me ol' man from backhanding me," she said.

Remembering the incident in the visiting room, Kelly's face turned serious. "He beats you, but you're so small, and he's massive, Ruth."

She nodded. "I made me bed, I have to lie in it now. Can't do much else. I've got three babies with him." She paused and gave a heavy sigh. "And the last two weren't consensual either … not that I would change them for the world, but … Well, anyway, I have three, and I'm stuck with him."

Kelly jumped up. "Right, Ruth, stand up now an' watch my stance. Come on, copy me. I'll teach you how to handle your ol' man, if he tries to clump you again."

Ruth giggled. "What, Kelly? I can't fight."

"No, but now you are going to learn. I am going to teach you, so get up." She grabbed Ruth's arm and pulled her to her feet. "It's going to be our secret, right?"

Ruth nodded with excitement. "Cor, I bet you was tough at school." She liked Kelly, the real Kelly, with clear words and a kind heart.

"No, I was bullied, to be honest. I knew I could fight, but I just didn't have the confidence. It's different in here, though. I aint got a lot of choice, have I?"

CHAPTER ELEVEN

The mood in the house was solemn. The letter arrived and Lippy read the words on the envelope. It lay on the kitchen side, awaiting the arrival of the boys. Lippy knew where it was from. The envelope had the prison stamp on it. Her heart ached for Kelly. She may have only been a part of their lives for the past two years, but it was as if she had always been there. Her fresh face and infectious giggle were the very essence as to who she really was. She had brought them joy and a sense of purity. And she had moved them all, especially Rudy; he loved her, not in a sexual way, but like a sibling. Lippy heard Rudy cry once in his office, when he thought no one was around. She covertly crept back to the kitchen and allowed him his private moment. And Ditto was turning into an angry man; it was his way of dealing with it.

She had picked up the letter, probably ten times, eager to open it, but it was addressed to Rudy, and she would be doing wrong. Eventually, they arrived home and all were hungry. Lippy asked them to take their curry into the lounge. No one questioned her, as they sat and waited.

She stood by the fireplace and held up the letter. She had always known Rudy couldn't read. Rudy jumped from his seat, lively as always. "Is it from Bluey?"

Lippy nodded. "Shall I read it, Rudy?"

He nodded impatiently. "Yeah, go on."

Everyone was silent and listened, hanging on to every word. Lippy had to swallow hard to stop her voice from trembling. Ditto put his head in his hands and Rudy became tearful. Kelly's letter was heartbreaking.

"She ain't gonna be alone, the soppy cow. I'm gonna visit her, make sure she's all right. If she thinks she can get rid of us that easily, she can think again. Who does she think she is? Wait till I see her. She's gonna get both barrels from me!" Rudy was turning his deep sorrow to annoyance, as if Kelly was in trouble. Lippy lifted her head and grinned.

"Lippy, get a pen and paper. I am gonna write to her right now and tell her what I think," stated Rudy, anxious to get the ball rolling.

Lippy hurried to the office and snatched the pad and pen from the side. She sat on the grandad chair, her pen to the ready.

"Dear Bluey, you stupid little girl … no forget that. Dear Bluey, don't think you can ignore us … no, forget that. Dear Bluey …" Rudy was lost for words.

Ditto cleared the choke in his voice. Dear Bluey, you cannot get rid of us that easily, we are family, remember. We all miss you and love you, so send a VO, or we are gonna break down the prison to get you out. Besides, business is shit without you."

Their sudden laughter lightened the mood.

"Leave it to me!" volunteered Lippy. They all nodded in unison.

It was around nine o'clock, when they were all relaxed and seated, watching a film, that Rudy's phone rang, making them jolt out of their stoned state.

"Yo, Keffa, how's it hanging, mate?"

Instantly, Rudy jumped to his feet. "What, yeah, mate, cheers." He placed the phone back in his pocket.

"Fuck me, Eddie Raven's parked up the road. Keffa's just passed him. Something's going down. Boys, go upstairs, Lippy, you too."

Lippy stood with her hands on her hips. "Leave him to me, Rudy."

The sudden bang at the door hastened their plan. The boys ran up the stairs, and Rudy nodded for Lippy to answer it, whilst he remained in the lounge.

As Lippy opened the door, Eddie leaned against the door frame. He looked her up and down with a menacing grin. "Where's Rudy?" he asked in a flat tone.

"Who wants to know?"

Eddie burst out laughing. There, standing in the doorway was a black woman, the size of a walrus, in skin-tight shorts, with her fat thighs straining at the sides. She was wearing a vest that showed every lump and bump and her appearance was finished off with a hairnet.

"Just get him!" He stopped laughing instantly and his face was like thunder.

Rudy heard the way Eddie had spoken to Lippy and decided she was safer out of the way. He hurried to the door. "I'm Rudy. What can I do for ya, mate?" He tried to sound inoffensive; he didn't want any trouble, not after everything Keffa had said about him. He was Bluey's father all right; the resemblance was uncanny. Yet, he didn't have her soft expression.

"You ain't me mate." In an instant, he grabbed Rudy by the throat, with neither Rudy nor Lippy seeing it coming. Lippy tried to intervene, but Eddie, from nowhere, pulled a gun and held it up at Rudy's face.

"Get inside!" he growled. Lippy backed off, afraid of Rudy taking a bullet; this man was not messing. He threw Rudy backwards and pointed with the gun to go in. With his foot, he flicked the door back, slamming it shut, and sauntered into the house.

Rudy walked backwards, not wanting to take his eyes off the barrel. Lippy followed, too afraid to do much more. Once they were in the lounge, Eddie told them to sit down.

"Right, tell me what you wanted with my kid, 'cos, it seems to me, ya wanted her for something."

Although the gun was still pointing at his face, Rudy didn't like Eddie's tone and wasn't going to have him making sick suggestions.

"I don't fucking know you, but I am guessing you're Kelly's father." His anger was now getting the better of him and he stood defiantly. "I found Kelly walking the streets of this shithole, alone and fucking terrified. We took her in, 'cos, unlike some people, we ain't all fucking bad."

"Sit down, you black bastard. What did you want from her, 'cos no one does anything for nothing? I ain't an idiot, so don't mug me off!" spat Eddie, in his deep, raspy voice.

Rudy remained standing. "Yeah, she did pay me back for a bed and food!"

Before he could finish, Eddie, launched himself at Rudy and shoved the gun under his chin. "Ya fucking dirty no-good cunt, slipping your black cock into my little girl!"

Sickened by his comment, and without thinking, Rudy palmed the gun away with accomplished ease. "Don't fucking judge me by ya own standards. I never touched her!" he growled.

Eddie stepped back in amazement, still holding the gun. No one would try that stunt, risking a bullet through the head. "Oh yeah, so how did she pay you back?" With a menacing expression, he inclined his head.

Rudy turned to Lippy and smiled a resigned expression. "She taught me to read and write."

Totally flummoxed, Eddie hadn't expected *that* as an answer at all. Unbelievable. He looked at Lippy and then back at Rudy.

"Yeah, Eddie, like I said, we ain't all after a piece of fanny. Some of us have standards. I don't touch kids. I never laid me hands on her," asserted Rudy.

Lippy felt the confidence in Rudy mounting and sensed it wouldn't end up in his favour. "Look, Mr Raven, our lickle Kelly is a good chil'. She helps around the house, runs a few errands, and that sort of thing. We did her no harm, so, please, leave us alone."

Eddie knew they were telling the truth, but he was angry with the thought that his own daughter had more respect for this home and its oddball tenants than him, her own father.

"I ain't having my daughter wrapped around you bunch of idiots. Where's her room?"

Lippy was insulted and stepped forward. "Us idiots, loved that chil', when she had no one!"

Eddie felt his rage hit the danger threshold; in a sudden move, he backhanded Lippy across the mouth. Rudy lunged forward to grapple with him, but Eddie was strong on his feet. He cracked Rudy on the side of the head. "Next time, it won't be a smack, it will be a bullet. Now, show me her fucking room!"

The clump caught Rudy off guard and made his eyes water. He knew then that Eddie wasn't fucking about, and if they pushed him too far, one of them would get shot.

"All right, we don't want any trouble." Rudy was glaring at Lippy not to say another word.

Rudy hoped that when Eddie followed him into the adjoining room, the dog would attack the stranger. But Legend was sulking. Since his best friend and mistress had left home, he just moped about, despite their attempts to fuss over him. He lifted his head to see who was there but only to find Rudy and another man, not his owner, Kelly. He flopped his head down, uninterested.

"Does that mutt bite?" asked Eddie, staring at the lump of a dog.

"He's Kelly's dog. He would attack someone, if she told him to," replied Rudy.

Rudy watched as Eddie pulled open the drawers, sifting through her girly belongings. He was not careful either, smashing her neatly placed make-up and trinkets.

Rudy was perplexed. "What ya looking for?"

Eddie stopped what he was doing and glared. "Kelly wants some of her old gear back. You keep ya mouth shut, got it! It ain't none of your business. This is family stuff." He was bent over the chest of drawers, moving her underwear with his gun.

"She had an old bunny and a pair of socks with holes in," said Eddie, looking up.

Rudy shrugged his shoulders. "She had nothing when she moved in, just a school uniform, not even a bag, no money, fuck all."

Eddie stepped closer. "Where's her school uniform, her jacket?"

Rudy guessed right away he was up to something. He was going to play his game.

"Eddie, look, I want to help, in any way I can. Kelly meant a lot to us all, and if she wants her stuff to make her feel better inside, then I can get some boxes, help ya pack it up."

Eddie sniffed the air. "No! She wants the bunny and her old socks. Where's the uniform? She might have them in the pockets. She never went anywhere without them."

Rudy sensed the desperation in his voice. "She burned the uniform in the fire, afraid of getting caught with it, I s'pose. As for a jacket, she didn't have one. She was frozen when I bumped into her. She ran with all she had on her after the—"

"Bollocks!" Eddie interjected, as he pulled open the wardrobe door. He sifted through the jackets and coats that Kelly had neatly lined up. He went through every pocket, whilst keeping an eye on Rudy. Then, gripping the corner of the mattress, he lifted it away from the bed in one fell swoop, tipping Legend onto the floor. Under the bed, it was clear there was no soft toy. He returned to the wardrobe and rummaged through the dresses.

"She bought them after she came."

"With what fucking money?" yelled Eddie.

Rudy put his hands up. "Hey, all right, mate, calm down. She used to sell fake bags up Commercial Road. Earned her own money, she did."

With a cruel, calculated grin, Eddie stopped what he was doing and looked at him quizzically. "Oh yeah, and who fucking told her to do that, eh?"

Lippy, hearing everything, was now in the doorway. "No one did. That chil' had a keen eye for business. She made her own money."

With an evil eye, Eddie looked from one to the other. "You make sure if the filth come sniffing around, you tell 'em that Kelly only rented a room here. You know nothing about her, or her comings and goings, got it?" he spat, wielding his gun.

They both nodded in unison.

Without another word, he pushed past them both, opened the front door, and was gone.

Eventually, Rudy's shoulders relaxed. Lippy rubbed his back. "Poor Bluey, a father like that, eh."

Lippy wandered off to the kitchen to make a saucepan of milky cocoa for everyone. Rudy then looked at the row of coats hanging on the six-hook rack on the hallway wall. He smiled to himself. The rack

227

was ready to fall off the wall, with old coats from years gone by, dusty, and out of fashion. He lifted the two heavy coats belonging to Ditto, and there, underneath, was the thin school jacket of Bluey's. Placing the heavy coats back on top, he walked away, with a satisfied grin on his face.

The others joined them for the hot cocoa, discussing the event. Lippy kept shaking her head.

"That chil' don't fit with that man. She's too sweet," she declared.

Ditto and Phoenix offered to tidy Kelly's room. Lippy shook her head. "There's girly things in there. I'll make sure she has it all spick and span, when she comes home."

It then hit them that it could be a long time before they ever saw her again, unless she agreed to send a VO.

❦ * ❧

Keffa was pacing the floor, waiting to hear from Rudy. Suddenly, there was a bang at the door. He froze, thinking it was Eddie. He moved away from the letterbox, in case whoever was the other side peered in. The next bang was louder, followed by Rudy shouting, "It's me, Keffa, open the door!"

It was 2 a.m. and Rudy needed to speak to someone. Keffa flung the door open. "I was waiting for you to call me. What happened?"

Rudy marched past and sat heavily on the sofa. "That Eddie Cako is crackers. I dunno, I've faced some men in my time, but he had a look, mate, that sent shivers up me spine. Came in with a fucking shooter up me hooter. He ransacked Bluey's room, looking for a toy bunny and a pair of socks. The man's a real fruit and nut … Oh, and he fucking backhanded our Lippy. I mean, who hits an innocent ol' bird, eh?" His chest was heaving in and out with fury.

Keffa was in his loose tracksuit, but Rudy noticed the sweat marks under his armpits. "Been jogging?"

"Rude, what's he really after? I mean, a fucking bunny and socks. What's that all about?"

"She never went anywhere without them. He wants to get on her good side and take the two things to her she carried everywhere. To make her feel better, I s'pose," replied Rudy, none the wiser.

Throwing his head back, Keffa laughed. "No way. Let me tell ya. He is after something." He sat down on the chair opposite. "I haven't told you everything, Rudy. I didn't want you to worry, but Eddie is a sly cunt. He is out for his own ends. Trust me, man, I know him."

He peeled the sweatshirt away from his neck, revealing the length of the scar.

Rudy's eyes widened like two saucers. "Fuck me, no way! Did he do that?"

Keffa nodded. "Fifteen years ago, after he acted like a friend, taking me into his confidence, he then turned on me. We were in a pub, five of us, all sat around this table. A dirty old pub, but then, who was I to moan? He was high on cocaine and acting twitchy. Then he turned. Out of the blue, he pulled a knife and cut me throat. Fuck, I was petrified, I really thought I was a gonna. But I must be thick-skinned or something 'cos he missed me artery. I don't know if he meant to kill me or not. But I was in shock, clutching me throat. The others jumped up when they saw the blood and three of them ran from the pub. Eddie just sneered, folded his knife in half, and said, 'You should have kept ya mouth shut. My business is my business'. They left me there, bleeding to death. Luckily, I survived and kept away from him. He never paid me what he owed. Then, I realised he didn't do it because he thought I had let me mouth run, 'cos I never did. He did it to show his new wingman just how ruthless he was. I tell ya, Rudy, he ain't looking out for his girl. I reckon he is after something else. That psychopath always has another agenda."

Rudy agreed and told Keffa the full conversation with Eddie. No sooner had he finished, when Keffa jumped from his seat. "Jesus wept! That cunning rat, what's he up to? Why, Rudy, would he want you to say that she was just a tenant and you don't know her comings and goings?" Exasperated, he whirled around with spite on his face. "He don't want Kelly to have an alibi for the night of her mother's murder. Jeez, that arsehole killed her mother and he's gonna let the poor kid take the blame."

Rudy was looking at Keffa and seeing another side to him. Usually, he was cool and reserved, but not now though. He was hopping about, like himself.

"The police have already been to the house. They took a statement from me about three weeks after she was arrested."

Keffa frowned. "That's weird because they should have taken a statement as soon as they had her nicked. Rudy, there is something fishy going on and I don't like it. Poor Bluey, she's a kid for fuck's sake. Anyway, what did you tell them?"

"The truth. She moved in, lived with us as a family, and the following weeks after Patrick's murder, she hardly ever left the house."

"So, Rude, you are her alibi. Don't, for fuck's sake, let Eddie know," cautioned Keffa.

"I don't intend to. I am gonna write to Bluey and let her know what's going on, 'cos the poor lickle thing might be sitting in a cell, shitting herself, thinking she has no one helping her."

CHAPTER TWELVE

Kelly spent that night tossing and turning. She couldn't sleep: there was too much on her mind, what with Eddie and Toni in her face with their agenda and her mother and Patrick harbouring secrets from the grave.

Toni was treading on eggshells and so decided to keep quiet. Eddie had made it clear she was to keep his daughter sweet. By the morning, Kelly had made a decision and resolved to inform Toni right away about something she had arrived at the previous night. She perched herself on the side of the narrow bed and smoothed back her messy hair. Toni was already dressed and ready to go to the kitchen. Even her cocky body language irritated Kelly. There was nothing very feminine about Toni's present appearance; she would have been pretty except for the harsh sneer she carried around all day long.

"Toni, I need to talk to you," voiced Kelly, in a resigned tone.

With her cocky stance, Toni leaned on the doorframe and rolled her eyes. "Look, Kel, I dunno what the fuck your problem is, but I 'ave done nuffin but try and make your life easier. Unless ya gonna say sorry, then I ain't interested."

With the tension rising, Kelly sighed heavily. "Yeah, I am sorry, Tone, for not being someone you expected me to be."

Toni frowned. It took a second before she realised the full meaning.

"I'm not like you, and I can't pretend to be either. Your little crew, sidekicks or whatever they are – well, they are your friends that get you. I never grew up with the Ravens. I was dragged up by me mother, and believe it or not, I'm not like her either. I think it's best that I go back to me original cell. Before you say anything, I ain't stupid. I know you don't like me and you're probably just pretending for Eddie's sake." She lowered her gaze, having said all she needed to say.

Toni took a deep breath and sat back on her own bed opposite Kelly. If Eddie knew she was out of her aunt's sight, he would knock her into next week. "'Course I like ya, Kel, you're me own flesh and blood. Truth be known, if I had a girl, I would want her to be just like you."

"I wanna be alone, Toni, and please don't arrange any more visits with Eddie. I don't wanna see him again."

Those words were like a tornado whirling through Toni's head. Mixed with anger and fear, Toni jumped up. Her eyes narrowed and her chin protruded. "You wanna fucking watch ya mouth, ya selfish little bitch. Cor, I've a mind to smash your head up the wall. Eddie is your farver and you need to learn respect. You're his daughter, and sooner or later, you're gonna have to deal with that fact. He brought ya into the world, and sure as hell, he can take you out again. You are fucking clueless, and the sooner you wise up, the better!"

Kelly was pacing her breathing, trying to keep a lid on her temper. If anyone could make her lose it, then it was Toni.

"My lawyer reckons it's best if I stay away, ya know, 'cos of the trial." Kelly knew she was stirring up a reaction but that was her intention.

"You what? What lawyer and what did they say?" The words were pouring out in a panic.

Kelly guessed there was more of a need for her aunt to cosy up to her. She studied her face closely. "Surely, Toni, you didn't think I would go to court on a double murder charge without a brief? Now, that *would* be stupid."

"But I thought … you said earlier you didn't have a brief." Her words tailed off as her mouth dried up.

"I never told you I wasn't represented, so I don't know where you got that from."

Toni was glowing red and her eyes looked wild, as if she had just been caught for murder herself. She swallowed hard. "So why is it not a good idea to be around me? What's it got to do with me?"

Kelly got up from her bed and came nose to nose with Toni. "Well, Tone, I don't know. Why don't you tell me?"

In a fit of rage, Toni grabbed Kelly's arms and shook her. "What the fuck have you been saying?"

With a half-smile she replied, "Nothing, except it wasn't me that murdered me mother."

Instantly, Toni let go, as if she were holding hot coals.

Kelly eased past and left the room with a confident skip in her step and confirmation to her questioning thoughts.

By the afternoon, Kelly had collected her belongings and got the okay from the number one governor to return to C wing. Her original cell was empty, so there was no reason not to return there.

Sophie returned to the prison, armed with folders, and ready to hear and record Kelly's account of the incidents. She was determined to make sure that this young woman didn't go down for a murder she didn't commit. Sophie was nicknamed the secret squirrel because, unlike other barristers, she was into digging up evidence herself and playing the detective.

Kelly was looking forward to the legal visit. She, too, was eager now to fight for her rights and taking the rap for her mother's murder wasn't one of them. She may have hated her mother, and for good reason, but she never killed her. No one had the right to do that: in her book, only she did.

As soon as Kelly entered the room, Sophie smiled and she quickly noticed the girl's new-found demeanour and confidence on her face. In fact, this was obviously the new Kelly, who was now eager and livelier.

"Well, Kelly, you look great. How do you feel?"

Kelly sat down, admiring Sophie's pink wool bouclé suit that shouted Chanel. "I am good. I guess I can say, I'm very clear-headed."

"Right, here's what's happening. Next week, we will have the trial date. They are moving this on fast for two reasons. First, it's high profile, and second, you're a juvenile, so we don't have a lot of time. It also means they will hand over their evidence for me to look at. I need to be a step ahead. I can assume most of the content, but you must tell me everything and I mean *everything*. I am on your side, so even if you think what you tell me will damage the case, trust me, it won't, okay, because the information you tell me, they will almost certainly know, so I have to be prepared and also prepare you."

Kelly agreed. "Yes, Sophie, I will tell you everything."

Studying Kelly's face, Sophie smiled. "I have to say, I like the way you talk, and in court make sure you keep it up. The slang is not cool, not in front of the jury."

"Yes, Sophie, I know, it's just easier in here. Somehow, it's my mask. It gives me an edge. It may be abnormal because I don't really know which way I feel more comfortable. Anyway, it's court talk from now on."

"So, let's start from the beginning, as far back as you can remember."

Kelly put her hand up, as if she were in school. "I know who killed my mum. It was Eddie Raven."

Sophie didn't come across as shocked as Kelly thought she would; the lawyer merely studied her notes. "Yes, Kelly, I am sure he probably did. But, hey, listen, we can't win this case by throwing that in. We can only get you off by proving it wasn't you. That's how it works. The courts either decide the accused is innocent or guilty, that's all. Eddie is not on trial, so we are preparing the case that shows you could not have killed your mother because you weren't there."

Kelly grabbed the table and leaned forward. "You don't sound surprised, Sophie. Why?"

"Because, my sweetheart, I agree with you, and now we are on the subject, please, Kelly, stay away from him. I know he is your father and he can visit but——"

Holding her hand up again, Kelly stopped her. "No worries, Sophie, I have met him, and I have no intention of meeting him again."

Sophie twirled her pen around her fingers. Kelly watched and admired once more her perfectly manicured nails.

"I have moved out of Toni's cell. I don't know for sure, but I think she and Eddie are up to something. As you know, Patrick was her husband, but she never mentioned him. Also, she never asked for the details, and my father didn't either. It was weird. He didn't talk about the murders, the trial date, nothing like that."

Sophie nodded. "Yes, Kelly, just stay away from them and concentrate on getting out of here. Understood?"

"I will do whatever it takes, Sophie."

"Good girl. Right, you need an alibi. Where were you on Monday 3rd October, the day your mother was murdered?"

Kelly looked aghast. "I can't say. I don't want them involved. They were so good to me."

Sophie slammed the pen down. "Kelly, you must not be so naïve about this. The police found you at an address. You don't think they just carted you away and that was that, do you? Let me explain to you: this is a double murder. They will leave no stone unturned—"

Kelly decided quickly and jumped in. "His name is Rudy, and he took me in. I was walking the streets and it was cold. He couldn't read or write. It was a deal we had. I could stay there if I taught him. I was with him and Ditto, all day, going over some accounts. It was Rudy's birthday, so we were up until quite late, celebrating. The next night, we all saw it on the news." Kelly's account was obviously off the top of her head but it was extraordinarily well detailed.

Sophie was scribbling away. "Great, I will go over there tonight and take a statement. I bet the police already have, but I need him and Ditto – that's an odd name – on the stand, as they are your alibi."

As the interview continued, Sophie felt more confident about the case. The charges against her client for killing Patrick would be difficult to refute, but she would do her damndest to secure only a conviction of manslaughter, and hopefully Kelly would get off with a five stretch.

It was time to wrap up the interview. "Kelly, when you are up in the witness stand, I want you to be a typical eighteen-year-old because now, looking at you, all I see is a highly articulate woman. In the eyes of the jury, you could be perceived as a very culpable murderer. No offence, of course."

Kelly sighed. "It's hard, you see. My mother kept me a child, but every day in my head, I fought against it. It was as if I was imprisoned in a body unable to set my mind free. It's difficult to explain, but in my mind, I was living another life. Then, when I ran away, and moved in

236

with Rudy, I was free, free to be a woman. I learned how to adapt to my surroundings. Even in here, I am learning that it's no holds barred. I will try to be that innocent child, when I'm in court. Christ, I should go into acting."

Sophie smiled, leaned forward, and stroked Kelly's arm. "You will be fine, Kelly. We will get through this together. Oh, by the way, were the clothes okay?"

Kelly's eyes lit up. "Oh, it was *you*, and yes, yes they are perfect. Thank you so much."

"Oh, don't thank me. I didn't get them," she winked, putting her finger over her lip.

It must have been Peter. The thought had Kelly's heart racing with excitement.

Kelly returned to her cell with a lot on her mind. She had to fight for freedom; she had too much on the outside to look forward to. To her surprise, there on her cabinet was the mail. Carefully, she removed the letters and cards. Her heart melted. They were from Rudy, Lippy, the boys, and her dear aunt Betty. Each one had sent their own special message. Yet, they all ended with the same words, 'I miss you, love you, and here for you'.

The tears trickled down her face, as she reread them all, slowly imagining their faces, as they'd put pen to paper.

CHAPTER THIRTEEN

Betty was sitting in her favourite armchair near the window, looking through the TV magazine and planning her programmes. She could do little else until she had the back operation that would hopefully give her some of the quality of life she had been missing these past few years. The stress and tension had not made life any easier and most days she was confined to the chair. The back door was permanently unlocked, as getting to her feet was a feat in itself. Luckily, the neighbours would call in and do a bit of shopping. Her son was working away but helped as much as he could, when he was around, that was. Deep in contemplation, she didn't hear the footsteps from the side of the house or the opening of the back door.

And then there he was, unashamedly standing in her lounge. Betty looked for the expression on his face and yet was surprised to see him smile. Just as he was years ago, he was still a very handsome man, marred only by a few grey wisps peppering the sides of his hair. There were also a couple of wrinkles around the corners of his eyes, but other than that, his body still looked fit and lean. He didn't have to speak; he oozed charm. He sat on the sofa, and leaned forward with his hands clasped together. "So, how ya been, Bets? Ya look good, girl." His distinctive voice was still there, although to those who knew him well that tone alone emanated fear.

Betty removed her glasses. A few years ago, she would have been shitting herself, but not now. She was in a world overtaken by grief: her son was dead, her sister had been murdered, and now her niece was in prison. She had begged the police to let her know if they ever found Kelly, and luckily for her a young WPC gave her news that she was on remand at Downview.

She glared at him. "What ya doing, Eddie? We have nothing to talk about."

"Come on, Bets. Me and you——"

"There was no me and you, Eddie. Ya fucking concocted that little notion. Ya really think ya something special!"

Eddie shook his head sarcastically, laughing. "Ya didn't say that back then."

"We both know what happened. One sister just weren't enough for ya, was she? I didn't like you, Eddie. I know what ya did. You couldn't have me, so ya got me trashed and fucking helped yaself."

❧ * ❧

It seemed a very long time ago. She stared at his sly green eyes – they were the same ones that kept watching her all night at the party. Maureen was the looker back then – by, she turned heads. Betty was pretty but didn't flash herself to all and sundry. But Maureen was the party animal, long before she even knew Eddie. It was her bubbly personality and daring nature which people adored. If Maureen was around, no matter where, then there was a party. In the street, in a disused lock-up garage, or on the beach at Brighton, she would be there, attracted to the music, the drink, and dancing in all its shapes and forms. Eddie was drawn to her devilish ways and her neatly shaped figure, of course. Inevitably, she fell for him. Betty remembered her sister's first date. She came home around two in the morning with her dress all crumpled and her hair a right mess. There was not a hint of lipstick. Betty waited up to hear all the gossip, which, of course, Maureen was only too keen to boast about.

"Cor, Bets, he has his own pad, and a right fucking nice one an' all. It has its own well-stocked bar, a power shower, and this bed that could sleep ten people. I swear, Bets, I am gonna be walking up the aisle with him. After tonight, he's gonna be begging for more. He won't get a

240

better blow job than from me. I gotta tell ya, though, the boy has stamina. Luckily, I have too," she laughed shamelessly.

Betty never forgot how her sister won him over. It sickened her at the time but that was Maureen; she had no pride whatsoever. They were married quickly, before she realised he had a wandering eye, and perhaps it had affected Maureen more than Betty had thought. They bought a huge house within a gated estate in Farnborough Park. She loved the finer things and turned that house into a palace, with gold-edged chairs, expensive drapes, and designer sofas. It was over the top, but they had come from nothing, and so she overdid the ornate finishes. Eddie liked his parties, the barbecues, and having the firm over for business meetings, whilst Maureen enjoyed the attention. Her Eddie was a Face and she was his wife. But then the wheels came off: Betty watched from a distance as her fun-loving sister, with the feisty attitude, gradually became quiet, moody, and withdrawn. Then the baby arrived; it was a shock to everyone that Maureen had kept it such a secret. Her excuse was she never knew. Betty found it hard to swallow though; she knew her sister only too well and would have expected Maureen to be out shopping for the best baby gear money could buy. Eddie, showing off his wealth and status, arranged a huge party to celebrate. Betty was married herself by now to a local lad; there was nothing fancy about him, although he was hard-working. Eddie tried to get him on the firm, but he just wasn't made that way.

It was Kelly's first birthday and another party was arranged. Her own son was almost one year old, so she spent more time with Maureen, talking babies. She noticed then that Maureen's interest in Kelly was diminishing. Betty felt sadness for the girl and offered to look after her so that Maureen could shop or visit the hairdresser. It crossed her mind that Maureen was suffering from postnatal depression, but then she discovered that there was more to it.

When Eddie was around, he seemed dismissive of Maureen; perhaps it was because she was like a puppy, constantly following him and trying desperately to engage his attention, but it was obvious he'd lost interest and was shagging all and sundry. Then, the night of Kelly's first birthday, Maureen was in a drunken stupor before all the guests had arrived. Eddie was livid. He grabbed her arms and whispered in her ear. Betty was watching. When Eddie took his wife upstairs, that was the last she saw of her that evening. Dave, Betty's husband, had an emergency call-out to some school's boiler which had blown up. He said he wouldn't be long and would be back to take her home. Once the party was in full swing, Eddie started plying her with more and more wine. The first few glasses, she sipped slowly, and then, as the music played and the guests were dancing, she joined in with vigour. The French windows, which opened up to the vast garden, were lit up with fairy lights, as was a long table covered with sandwiches, an enormous variety of meat platters and cheeses, and several tempting desserts. Finally, Eddie removed his tie and made a toast to his beautiful daughter and switched the lights on to illuminate the swimming pool. That was it; it was the start of a raucous evening, with everyone in high spirits. Cocaine was spread on the table, the champagne flowed, and the guests took to the pool. Some decided to strip off down to the buff.

Eddie gave Betty a pill. "Here, girl, get that down ya neck."

Betty wasn't one for dabbling in drugs, but she was tipsy, the party was lively, and her little boy was asleep in the cot with Kelly. She washed the tablet down with the wine and joined in the fun. By now, everyone was in the pool, completely stripped off, including Eddie. She didn't think about her husband or the fact she had taken drugs and was now completely exposed in front of her sister's husband.

As she larked around in the pool, one of the guests called out, "Betty, it's ya ol' man on the phone. He said you'll have to stay the night. He's on another call-out."

Betty was laughing and keen to really let her hair down. That's when she caught Eddie staring at her with a bottle of champagne in one hand and a glass in the other. There was no doubt about it; he did look handsome, with his hair styled slightly longer and his olive skin set against the blue pool. Yet that was all it was; after all, as far as she was concerned, he was her brother-in-law. He poured her another drink and now she felt well and truly inebriated and decided to get out of the pool. But the problem was she couldn't: she was as pissed as a newt and struggled to climb the steps and then walk into the house. So, at the time, she'd no recollection that Eddie was behind her, holding her up, whilst she, concerned with keeping her balance, forgot she was naked. She remembered him whispering to her that he would help her to the spare room, and she recalled thanking him, as, with one hand on her waist, he guided her up the stairs. The spare room was as big as her lounge. He closed the door behind them and led her over to the bed. It was then, as she lay on her back, she realised she was naked and so was he. Her arms were like dead weights, as she tried to pull the sheets over her, whilst those green eyes of his just stared at her, looking her over. She felt so uncomfortable she asked him to leave but was met with a sneer and a childish giggle. She knew her own strength and right at that point was aware that she was as helpless as a kitten. Whatever was in that pill or drink had left her unable to move. That was when he began touching her breasts. She tried to talk, to scream, but nothing would come out. The room blurred and she felt as if she were floating into another world until reality returned. At this point, he was sucking and biting her nipples; she felt the pain but it was somewhere in the distance. His hands ran up and down the insides of her legs, pushing them further and further apart. Then she started to lose consciousness again until a sharp sensation inside her jolted her awake. He was inserting his finger and licking her. For a second, she felt pleasure but then she felt sick; it was totally wrong, as she'd not intended this at all. She tried to raise her legs to push him away, but he grabbed her ankles, dragged her to the edge of the bed, and pushed her knees up, almost to her face. That was the moment she felt him thrust his tool deep inside as he banged away. Her mind seemed to be in another place, until she found herself back in the present with him towering over her, his face red and his sweat dripping onto her. There was no point now in screaming; he'd already done what he wanted to do, so she gave in, willing him to get this sordid act over and done with as quickly as possible. She closed her eyes and tried to enjoy it but that was impossible; the thrusting back and forth wasn't loving but hard and fast, like he was beating her. She then felt the pain, the soreness, and realised he must have been banging away for ages. Still she lay there, waiting for him to finish, and finally, as he fell on top of her, the ordeal was over.

It was shortly afterwards that Betty found herself expecting baby number two, and she prayed it was Dave's. Little Billy was the image of her Ricky and she comfortably assumed he was her husband's. The first year was a blessing, as she had the three of them most days. Anyone would have thought Kelly was hers. Then, after one of the hottest summers on record, when the three babies became well weather-beaten, not only did Billy's skin turn darker, similar to Kelly's, but his eyes were the brightest green, just like hers as well. Dave commented on how much they looked alike and would give Betty a sideways glare. It was then clearly apparent he knew and something she'd suspected for a while. So, it wasn't long afterwards when Dave did the off with the barmaid from the local. Betty never begged to have him back, as she knew the real reason he'd scarpered, and really, she couldn't blame him. It broke her heart and she hated Eddie even more. When Kelly was a little older than three, there was gossip that Eddie had gone on the run. She never knew all the facts, but she did know her sister had something to do with it. Then, after Eddie was picked up and arrested for the murders of Jack and Mickey, Maureen moved. The huge house was sold to pay off the debts that Maureen had racked up. But as for Eddie's other assets, she was kept in the dark, unaware of the other houses he owned. His business was his business and not for his wife to know about. She bought a modest house in the same town as Betty and allowed her still to babysit. But things changed; Maureen became hateful and malicious. One afternoon, she arrived to collect Kelly after being at church all day. She didn't stay long but it was long enough to vent her anger.

"I know that Billy is Eddie's son. A proper sly move, Betty, but never mind, you weren't the only one. He was shagging a kid as well, the fucking paedophile. Anyway, he's locked up with the rest of the earth's scumbags. So, Betty, I am assuming you don't want him to know about Billy, and I don't want my Kelly to know anything about Eddie. You don't ever breathe a word, not until she's sixteen, then … well, she will be old enough to know, and besides, that evil sod will no doubt be on the scene again. So, do we have a shared oath?"

Betty had to agree, although she felt sick at the thought of her Billy being wrapped around the likes of Eddie Raven.

The bad goings-on and infidelities must have been what had turned Maureen from a fun-loving girl to a religious hard-faced bitch.

She stopped reliving the past.

⊷*⊶

Eddie looked up and smirked, "Well, it was a long time ago now."

"What the fuck do you want, Eddie?" She didn't care how she spoke to him; those days of fearing him were over.

Curiously, Eddie looked up and gazed at one of the photos. "Is that my Kelly?" He stood and approached the fireplace. Betty just watched him.

"Ahh, little Billy. Sorry to hear about him, Bets. He was a baby when I got locked up." He snatched the one of the three children, roughly nine years old, and slowly he turned and faced Betty with a frown and his head tilted. "He looks like Kelly, Bets. Anything I should know?"

Betty struggled to get to her feet. "Ya have a fucking lot to answer for, Eddie Raven. You destroyed our lives. I loved my Dave but he buggered off because of you. Me sister, God rest her, turned into a raving nutcase, and little Kelly was left with a mother that needed to be institutionalised, all down to you and your lot."

Eddie leaned forward, trying to browbeat Betty. "What d'ya mean, 'my lot'?"

She folded her arms under her breasts. "Your bleedin' sicko sister. Just like Mo, following you around, as if she was tied by a piece of string. That Toni is a cruel bitch. The night after you raped me, yes, fucking raped me, Eddie, she came to see me, with a knife at my face. She threatened me if I told anyone, she would slice me face up."

Eddie sneered, showing just the tips of his teeth. "Well, like it or not, Bets, me sister's inside with me daughter, banged up together, nice and fucking cosy."

Betty was taken aback and had to sit down again.

"And, for your information, I've been to see me girl, and she wants me back in her life. So that's why I'm here."

Hot tears pricking her eyes, the thought of Kelly in Eddie's clutches made her shudder. "Surprises me, your sister being shacked up with the kid that killed her ol' man. I mean that is fucked up. But then I suppose the whole Patrick thing is."

Eddie glared. "You what?"

Betty knew she had his attention now, and the anger inside her resulted in her saying everything she'd never dared say before. "Well, it was weird. I mean, Patrick suddenly being your best friend. He used to be Mo's boyfriend before she met you." She paused, waiting for a reaction.

Eddie looked as if his confidence was melting. "She dated him before me?"

Betty laughed, "Oh ya didn't know that, eh? Well, let me tell ya this for fucking nothing. The truth is, he married your shit stain of a sister to either get close to Mo or to you. I mean, didn't you find it odd that Patrick, with all his money and clout, was arse-licking you all the time? I watched how he looked at you. Fucking in love with ya, he was. Anyway, none of it matters now he's dead and so is me sister. So, what do you want with Kelly? She ain't cut from the same cloth as you."

Eddie regained his posture and laughed. "Don't delude yourself, Bets. My girl is just like me and she is gonna follow in my footsteps."

Betty took a deep breath; if she'd had the energy and the strength, she would have stabbed him in the chest and killed him herself than have him anywhere near her niece.

"So, that's why I am here. I wanna make things right. I wanna be a good father."

Betty laughed. "You, a good father … don't make me die! Your fucking heart swings like a lead brick."

"Kelly asked me to take her toy bunny, the one she kept for comfort, into the prison on the next visit. I don't know why. She should be more like a teenager not a baby. Anyway, that's what I'm here for." He softened his belligerent attitude, hoping to appeal to her caring nature.

Betty frowned; this was fishy. Kelly would ask for a girly magazine or perhaps a hairbrush but not a toy; she was no baby. "Oh, that old thing."

She watched as Eddie smiled, but the grin was an eager one. Too eager, in fact.

"Yeah, I remember it. She carried it everywhere with her."

He was nodding too enthusiastically and she established then that something didn't sit right. "Well, her mother threw that old thing in the bin, years ago. It broke Kelly's heart, but she got over it."

Eddie's face dropped; he was visibly white. "Are you fucking sure?"

Betty began to fear that deranged look in his eye. "Yeah, I was there. The evil cow snatched it and threw it in the bin, just before the bin men came. I swear, poor Kelly was inconsolable."

She watched his odd reaction, as he ran his hands through his hair. With a deep sigh, he carefully replaced the photo and left, without another word.

Still shaking, she forced herself out of the chair to lock the back door.

That was a first, locking the back door.

CHAPTER FOURTEEN

Six weeks later

The morning of the court case arrived and it was greeted by Kelly with a mixture of excitement and trepidation, in equal proportions. As far as she was concerned, she wanted the day over with as soon as possible. Not knowing her fate was worse than serving time.

In so far as it was possible, in a prison with over three hundred inmates, she preferred her own company. And since that confrontation with Toni, when she told her she was leaving her cell for good, she had stayed out of her aunt's way, although Toni had tried on many occasions to grab her attention. The only inmate Kelly spent time with was Ruth.

Sophie had sent in a suit, tights, and decent black shoes, all appropriate for court. "Don't wear make-up and keep your hair neatly clipped back. You have to look like a well-groomed schoolgirl."

Kelly did everything as Sophie instructed. She wasn't able to see herself, except her face, for there were no full-length mirrors. She'd had to pack all her belongings, in the event she would be released. And Sophie had also prepared her for the worst, as there was a strong possibility she may not return to the same prison. Under her bed, she had a box filled with letters from Rudy, Lippy, and the boys. She also had pretty cards from her aunt Betty. When she'd received the first one, she had cried relentlessly, as her aunt had blamed herself, and it had floored Kelly to think of her ever feeling that way. Straightaway, she had responded with a letter, letting her aunt know she was still held dear in her heart.

Charlie had arrived; Kelly heard her marching down the landing. She stood in the doorway, beaming. "Ya ready, Kelly?"

Kelly nodded and stood up. Charlie noticed how young and innocent she looked; even her expression was childlike. "Ya look smart, Kelly, perfect really. I want to wish you luck, love, and don't take this the wrong way, but I never want to see you again." She smiled and patted Kelly on the arm.

"I can't promise it, Charlie, but ..."

Charlie laughed. "I know, love, I also know you aren't meant to be here. You will do well in life, that I *can* promise."

"Thank you, Charlie, I do intend to."

She escorted Kelly to the prison van. Again, she was accompanied by two officers; she knew Kirsty but not the other one. As they arrived at the court, Kelly was shocked to see the amount of people outside. Cameras were flashing. "It's all right, Raven, they are the reporters. Looks like your case is a high profile one. Didn't expect that many, though. Keep ya head down."

The van swerved inside the back entrance of the courts, away from the public gaze. They hurried Kelly into the building. She was led down the stairs and into a holding room; it was nothing grand and consisted of just a table and chairs. Before she could sit down, in came Sophie, who looked immaculate but flustered.

"Right, have you had coffee, tea, anything, do you want a drink ...?"

Kelly was surprised by how the usually cool Sophie was tripping over her words.

"I'm fine, Sophie, but are you?"

Sophie flopped on the chair and took a deep breath. "I am okay, Kelly. It's a bad habit of mine to panic just before we enter the courtroom. Take no notice of me. I am on the ball in the courtroom, where it matters."

Kelly observed Sophie's calm composure return. She appeared very sharp in her magpie suit, with the wig neatly placed on her head.

"Now then, we have been over everything, and when Weirs, the other barrister, starts questioning you, remember this: he will try to make you angry, a habit of the old git. Don't rise to it, remain composed at all times, shed a tear if need be, but *don't* lose your temper. That jury will be watching you, like a hawk."

Kelly smiled. "I know, Sophie, we have been over everything, like you said. I am word perfect."

"Yes, good, good. Now, it's going to be nerve-racking but just take deep breaths——"

Sophie was interrupted by a knock on the door. She jumped up and quickly pulled in the visitor, after a furtive look up and down the corridor. Kelly's heart pounded and she felt her cheeks redden. There was Peter, looking anxiously at her.

"I just wanted to see you, to make sure you're okay."

Kelly was shaking inside. The man she visualised every night, before she went to sleep, was there in the room with her, looking more handsome than ever. He was wearing a slim-fit white shirt to go with his pinstriped charcoal grey suit. His hair had grown almost to his shoulders; he put her in mind of an angel, with golden waves and eyes that shone. His half-smile made him appear even sexier. She wanted to run to him and throw her arms around him, but she stood still, too embarrassed to move.

Sophie grabbed the files from the table. "Right, I need to hand these over to the junior. I won't be long, and remember, Peter, you are here as her doctor." She winked at him.

The door closed behind them and Peter moved towards her. "Are you okay, Kelly?" He put out his arms and she fell into them, feeling a lump in her throat and trying to hold back the tears. It was awkward; was he hugging her as a child or as a woman? She hoped the latter.

"Thank you, Doctor, err ... Peter, for the clothes and ..." She wanted to say for giving me hope that one day they could be together.

"I want to give you more, Kelly. I know you're young and this is wrong ... oh, Christ, what am I doing? Look, I care about you perhaps more than I should. I had to come." He ran his hands through his hair and began to pace the floor. "Kelly, I don't know what to say. I can't tell you how I feel, it's not right. But I can tell you, I am here for you. I'll be around, if you need me ..." He stopped pacing and looked at her face. Her eyes were wide and filled with tears, ready to tumble. He couldn't hold back. He grabbed her in his arms and held her tight, gently kissing her cheek. Perhaps his lips lingered longer than was necessary, but she didn't mind that at all. Kelly was silent, absorbing the depth of feeling he clearly found difficulty in holding back.

The bang on the door caused the sudden separation. It was Sophie; she looked at the pair of them and smiled. "It's time, Kelly."

At that precise moment, her heart felt as though it had stopped. The sensation that gripped her was as if she were about to go to the gallows and they were saying their last goodbyes. Sophie nodded to Peter and observed his look of deep sadness. Holding Kelly's hand like a child, and gripping it tightly, he whispered, "I'll always be there for you, Kelly."

The court officers took her to the stairs that led up to the dock. Kelly could feel her heart racing. This was it – probably the most important moment in her life. She wasn't crying for herself but for the family that may be seated in the gallery and who would feel the pain of seeing her in the dock. Hesitantly, she climbed the stairs, and as she reached the courtroom, all its finery was in view. The grandness was unnerving. She looked from left to right, absorbing her surroundings. Her eyes fixed on the gallery, and to her surprise, her aunt Bet was there. She had aged and appeared frightened to death. Kelly smiled in her direction and Betty waved, mouthing the words, "I love you." Then she saw Ditto, Reggie, Phoenix, and Solly dressed in suits. They were nudging each other and giving her the thumbs up. And there was Lippy, who was edging herself along the seats, moving people out of the way, and not in a subtle way. In her attempt to dress for court, she looked more like she was dressed for a wedding. Her hat, with its huge rim, matched her cerise pink satin dress and it was finished off with a navy-blue short linen jacket. For sure, she was a sight for sore eyes and stuck out among the black and blue suits. Then, Lippy saw Kelly, and with absolutely no decorum whatsoever, she started blowing kisses and then blew her nose. She watched her aunt, like a magnet, sliding her way closer to Lippy and whisper something to her, resulting in Lippy clutching Betty's hand, as they cosily huddled together. Keffa was sitting at the back, with a blank expression; she couldn't work out if he was angry or nervous. Then, her heart began to beat faster still when she saw Eddie, standing at the back, blanketed with contempt. *What a shame*, she thought: *all her loved ones were there, and then there was Eddie, with just the sight of him ruining her otherwise perfect family picture.*

Kelly was then led to the seat next to Sophie. The jury, like Sophie, were watching her every move. Sophie was confident her client, dressed in a modest suit like a schoolgirl, would appear lost among the formal accoutrements of the judge, barristers, and clerks, which was what she had intended. She wanted the jury to feel compassion for her client. With the judge, in his wig, sitting dauntingly high up on the bench, controlling events, Sophie felt her client would indeed be given some level of sympathy by those who would shortly be deciding her immediate future.

The first witness was called. DI Maddox was asked to take the stand. Kelly remembered him from her arrest. He looked dishevelled and less confident than she recalled. His hair had grown and his tie was skew-whiff. Weirs, barrister for the prosecution, asked him to give an account of the findings at the murder scenes; the jury were then handed the shocking photos. The prosecution were playing a dangerous game by producing photos of both murdered victims, as if these had happened on the same night – almost dismissing the fact that the crimes were weeks apart. Sophie was annoyed and she didn't care much for

Weirs either; he was a brute in the courtroom. Maddox looked uneasy and Kelly noticed him shoot a glance in Eddie's direction.

"So, there was no forced entry? In your opinion, would that suggest the perpetrator may have had a key or be known to the victims?"

Maddox nodded. "Yes."

"What can you tell us about the condition of the rooms inside the property?" It was a loaded question to which Weirs already knew the answer.

Maddox looked at the jury and replied, "There was no damage except in the accused's bedroom. The wardrobe and chest of drawers were pulled out, as if they had been ransacked. Clothes were strewn around the room and there were contents of the drawers on the floor."

"So, no other room was touched, would you say, except Miss Raven's bedroom?"

Maddox nodded again. "Yes, correct."

"Detective, would you describe to the Court the inside of the property, and in particular, in relation to what you would expect of a home where a teenage girl would live?"

Sophie looked at Kelly and frowned, but Kelly guessed what he was getting at.

She watched as the jury's faces became more engaged at this point. It was such an odd question to an observer, but not to Kelly.

"The house was particularly sparse. There were no pictures, photos, or ornaments, but there were religious icons and crosses on the wall. The bathroom had no toiletries that you normally find in a house with two women. The accused's bedroom contained four items of furniture. There was a bed with a plain sheet and blanket, a wardrobe which contained unfashionable clothes, a chest which held the usual underwear, T-shirts and so on, and under all the clothes there was a copy of the Bible; and, finally, there was a desk with schoolbooks and pens. All the contents from the furniture were strewn across the floor. The room had been ransacked, as I said."

"So, there were no items that you would usually find in a teenager's bedroom, no magazines, books, make-up, childhood toys, an old favourite teddy, CDs, music centre, or radio?"

"No, not even a mirror," replied Maddox.

Sophie and Kelly knew where this was going. Sophie had been given the prosecution's evidence, as soon as the court date was known. She knew who they would call and why. But Sophie and Kelly were prepared.

Sophie didn't cross-examine Maddox, as there was no need. Kelly had turned eighteen and could take the stand herself. The prosecution had really gone to town with their homework, digging up Kelly's past. They were going for a premeditated murder, using Maureen's abuse as the motive.

Kelly detected Maddox glance one more time at Eddie, before he left the stand. Her blood was boiling and she was beginning to despise her father.

The next witness called was Doctor Ranjam. He was sworn in and stood erect, waiting for the questions.

Weirs rose and smiled. "Doctor Ranjam, you placed a report to social services when the accused was under your care. Please would you tell the members of the jury why?"

He nodded and cleared his throat. "Miss Raven arrived at the hospital with pneumonia. She was very sick and hard of breathing. I examined my patient and found her to be so sick that without oxygen she might have died. On my examination, I noticed deep scars across her back. They looked like whip marks. Old scarring. When her mother arrived, she was less than sympathetic and gave me grave cause for concern. So, I called social services and made a report," he replied.

Weirs, in his pompous accent, asked, "Do you believe that Miss Raven was abused by her mother?"

Sophie jumped up, "Objection, Your Honour, Doctor Ranjam is not qualified to answer that question."

The judge nodded and turned to the witness. "You may not answer that question."

Sophie smiled. Radcliff was a fair judge.

"Did you have reason to believe abuse, though, thereby contacting social services?" Weirs asked, revising the question.

"Yes, correct, we cannot confirm abuse, but if we feel there is a concern, it is our duty to contact social services."

Sophie allowed the prosecution to build a story of Kelly being neglected and abused to give the jury a reason to believe she had a motive. She would, at the right time, flip the story on its head. She declined to cross-examine this witness.

When Sophie stood up to call her own witness, her voice was polished and Kelly noticed the jury soften both in their facial expressions and in their body language.

"I call Rudy Jameson to the stand."

Kelly trembled. It would be the first time in months she had seen Rudy. As much as they begged to visit her, she felt it was wrong, as she had to stay focused. As he appeared in the dock, Kelly's eyes began to water. He glanced over at her and gave her a compassionate smile; even his eyes looked glassy. She had never seen him dressed so smartly, with a pinstriped light grey suit and a white shirt with a subtle pink tie. His dreads were neatly tied in a band. His usual bouncy, animated self was absent, and he looked somewhat nervous and lost among the proceedings.

"Mr Jameson, please tell the members of the jury how, where, and when you first met Miss Raven."

Rudy inclined his head and warmly smiled at Kelly, and it was clear to an onlooker that the jury were noting the affection.

"It was the 10th September 2011, at two in the morning. I was in a café, a short walk from my home, when I first saw Kelly. She was alone in a school uniform and looking out of place."

Sophie interjected, "Explain what you mean by 'out of place'?"

"It was late, and the streets of Peckham are not safe for a fifteen-year-old to be on her own in a school uniform. She was not streetwise and looked lost, vulnerable, I suppose. The kids where I live are cocky, they dress different, some even look intimidating. Kelly looked scared to death. I remember it was really cold that night and her lickle face was blue. She was shivering."

The jury could see he was reliving that moment, when his eyes glazed over and his expression turned to sorrow.

"So, Mr Jameson, what did you do?"

He looked around the courtroom at Lippy and then at Ditto. "Well, she was being propositioned at the time by a man in the café, and before I knew it, she was running away. I was afraid for her. I mean, she shouldn't have been out there alone in the dark like that. Anyway, I chased after her and offered to help. She was afraid of me. I could see the fear in her eyes. So, I took her to another café. A woman runs it, so I knew she would be safe there. She was quiet at first, but once she trusted me, I said she could stay at my house, just for the night, until she sorted herself out."

"Thank you, Mr Jameson, and when you found her how did she look – physically, I mean?"

"She looked like a kid who had been through something traumatic. Her hair was a mess, her hands and face were dirty, and her bare legs were blue from the cold."

"But you allowed her to stay at your house for longer than the one night. Why?"

Rudy moved from one leg to the other, visibly uncomfortable. "I couldn't read nor write, ya see. We had a deal. She could have the spare room, if she helped me learn to read." He lowered his gaze in embarrassment. Then he looked over at Ditto and Reggie. They were not laughing but smiling, encouraging him to go on. Keffa held his head high, proud that Rudy was man enough to admit he had been illiterate for Kelly's sake.

"But, Mr Jameson, she stayed in your home for over two years. Surely, you had learnt to read and write by then? So why did she stay?"

"We love Kelly. She is a good kid, and somehow, she just fitted in. I had the spare room, she had no place to go, and that was it really." He gave Kelly a gentle grin. There was silence as the jury watched the unspoken interaction.

It was then Weirs's turn to cross-examine.

He stood up, holding his lapels. "So, I just want to establish the facts. Firstly, you found a child roaming the streets, clearly of school age, lost and frightened, and you didn't think to call the police. Secondly, you took a minor to your home and used her to teach you to read and write, when she should have been attending school herself. Why was that, Mr Jameson?"

Rudy had been primed by Sophie and was ready. He was to give Weirs a lesson in the ways of the streets. "Where I come from, we see street kids. They have reasons why the streets are better than their own home. I know of kids that have run away from foster care. I also know women that have turned to prostitution to survive because they cannot go back home. These kids are running away from something. I didn't want to see Kelly on the street, but what I saw in her eyes that night was fear. Yeah, I could have called the police, but let's be honest, the police were driving around all night. I was watching them from the café, and they didn't pick her up. A kid out alone, they didn't even stop to see if she was okay. Anyway, she had her reasons to run, and I was just doing the decent thing."

Weirs smirked and gave a fake laugh. "Well, that's for the jury to decide, and we have to be honest in this matter. You do not have a track record for doing the right thing, with a previous record of imprisonment yourself."

"Objection, Your Honour, the witness is not on trial!" But Rudy wasn't put off by the question, and before the judge could intervene, he gave Weirs short shrift.

"You're right, I do have a record, and like I said before, I have seen kids go down the wrong road, left on the streets, like I was at her age. So, I wanted to help."

Sophie smiled. She had underestimated Rudy. He may be many things, but he spoke from the heart, and she knew the jury would like that little nugget. Weirs was desperately trying to establish his lack of credibility as a witness, but his efforts, so far, had backfired – spectacularly.

"Mr Jameson, did you ever question Miss Raven as to why she was on the streets or what she was running from?"

He shook his head. "No, I didn't. I gave her space and time, a roof over her head, and food on the table. She was safe in my home, and if she wanted to talk, then I was all ears. But she never did."

Kelly had her eyes tilted down, shamefaced.

"Mr Jameson, one last question. On the night of the 3rd of October 2011, where was Miss Raven?" asked Weirs.

"She was at home with me, Reginald, Demetrious, Tulip, Solomon, and Phoenix."

Kelly was baffled: she hadn't heard two of those names before. Then it dawned on her: he was referring to Ditto and Solly.

"How can you be so sure of that? It was a while ago. In fact, it was over two years ago," stated Weirs. Sophie, of course, already knew the answer.

"It was my birthday, and every year on that day Tulip cooks her best curry and no one misses that."

"Can you be certain that Miss Raven was in the house with you all night?"

He nodded. "Yes, we were up celebrating until two in the morning. Ya see, I can't sleep well, so I never go to bed before two."

Weirs scratched his chin. "It amazes me, and I am somewhat miffed. You say these other people were in the house with you and Miss Raven, yet only you gave a statement. Why is that? Surely, when you discovered that the accused was arrested for murder, you would have been straight down to the police station? Considering you paint such a warm, homely picture of where you live, surely the other residents would be falling over themselves to give evidence?"

Maddox was sweating; he had been careless. He knew he'd needed to get a statement from Rudy, or the case would have looked neglectful. His mind went back to that period. His new bird was up in arms that they'd delayed the holiday and he had cut corners, leaving the statement until after they'd returned home from Dubai. Rudy was Kelly's alibi, but Maddox assumed, with his track record, the prosecution would wipe the floor with him, deeming him not a credible witness. He'd forgotten to mention in his report the others in the house – it was almost certainly a stupid mistake.

Rudy looked at the gallery and smiled. "I told them at the station, when I was pulled in, a few weeks later, following Kelly's arrest, that the others were at home, but that man there, Detective Maddox ..." he pointed to Maddox, "he said my statement was all they needed."

As Weirs flared his nostrils, Sophie watched Maddox squirm.

The court adjourned to reconvene after lunch. Kelly was ushered back to the holding room and allowed to have the handcuffs removed. Sophie followed her, her face alive. "Well, so far, it's looking good, but, Kelly, don't get too confident and let your guard down. You will be on the witness stand and Weirs will do his damndest to make you lose your temper and have you fumbling for words."

Kelly nodded. "I am okay, Sophie, honestly. All I have to do is to tell the truth."

Sophie shot her a sideways glance, uncomfortable with the smirk that spread across Kelly's face. She looked so different; she was not the sweet child she was before the trial.

As soon as the court was back in session, Weirs didn't put Kelly on the stand but instead called a psychiatrist. It was not Molly though, as she had been taken off the case for mishandling procedures the first time around. By the time Kelly was examined, she had already been coached by Sophie and was saying all the right things. Dr Nigel Stamford, a world-renowned doctor, was called. Weirs managed to extract from him that there were concerns over her mental state.

"In your professional opinion, would you describe to us the frame of mind of Miss Raven, under your examination?"

At the time, Kelly hadn't liked his pretentious attitude at all; standing there in his suit and his nose in the air, he irritated her even more.

"Yes, I established Miss Raven to be very mature for her years, and what I found disconcerting was her answers were almost premeditated, unusual for a person of her years. When I broached the question of her relationship with her mother, she barely said much at all, and she certainly showed no emotion. I also found her reluctant to talk about any of her relationships. In my opinion, she'd detached herself from her family with no feelings whatsoever. This can be viewed as disturbing and may manifest into a mental condition in the future, if it hasn't already."

Weirs jumped on his words. "Disturbing you say? Do you think Miss Raven capable of committing murder?"

"Yes, possibly. I cannot say for sure because in my opinion she wasn't being honest with her emotions and who she really was."

A confused expression crossed Weirs's face. "Is a child capable of faking her character?"

Stamford, in his hoity-toity voice replied, "It's unusual, and as I said, they would need to premeditate very cleverly their actions, but yes, it's possible."

Sophie was fuming. The doctor's presumptions and throwing in the word 'premeditated' could make it difficult for her client, if the jury were taken in by him. For Kelly's sake, she would have to turn that around quickly.

It was her turn to cross-examine the witness. "You say, Dr Stamford, that it's unusual for a child to show no emotion when being questioned about the murder of a loved one. Yet, when we look at the effects of shock, and I have no need to tell you the list is endless, does it not include separation from the incident itself? I mean, many children who have witnessed violent crimes, or who have lost a parent, will temporarily block out that emotion."

She didn't wait for an answer and launched into him again.

262

"Rather than use the word 'premeditated', which members of the jury may associate with murder, it would perhaps have been better to use the term 'thoughtful' instead. For, as you said, you believe Miss Raven to be mature, and so that being the case, perhaps she was trying to answer your questions in a more adult fashion, by giving thought to the question, instead of blurting out any answer just to satisfy you."

She hoped she had done enough to establish seeds of doubt about the doctor's opinion, as there was no evidence forthcoming from him.

Sophie looked at him slightly nervously, and she glanced towards Judge Radcliff, feeling lucky he hadn't pulled her up for not actually letting the witness respond to what she'd said. She'd deliberately put her points across without asking him a specific question at the end of her cross-examination. She placed her notes down and smiled. "That's all, Your Honour."

But Dr Stamford didn't appear at all happy. He looked at the judge, hoping for a chance to refute the defence barrister's line of questioning, only to be told he may leave the witness stand. His sneer in Sophie's direction was observed by the jury. He was angry: the barrister had marginalised him, using a clever defence tactic, and he'd been shown up, in his opinion, by a less intelligent person. Not only was he a well-known and respected psychiatrist, but he had junior doctors hanging on to his every word.

Kelly remained with her head tilted down; she didn't want to look around anymore. Her nerves were getting the better of her.

Finally, she was called to the stand. The court officer took her hand and led her into the dock. She was sworn in and smiled sweetly to the judge. Sophie was pleased that he turned his chair sideways to face her.

"Miss Raven, you know what you have been accused of, don't you?"

Kelly nodded and shied away.

263

"You will have to give an audible answer from now on. Do you understand?"

Her face upturned, she replied, "Yes."

"Please, Miss Raven, tell us and members of the jury about the events on 9th of September 2011, but beginning when you first met Patrick Mahoney," asked Sophie, in a firm voice.

Kelly took a deep breath and in a calm and controlled way she went over meeting Patrick on that first occasion and the incident itself. As soon as she had to recall bludgeoning him, she began to stutter and shake. Tears filled her eyes, and she appeared visibly traumatised.

Sophie stopped her. "Okay, Miss Raven, it's fine. Do you need a break?"

Kelly shook her head. The judge watched as the officer handed Kelly a tissue. She blew her nose and wiped her eyes.

When it was Weirs's turn to question her, he was like a rat up a drainpipe. He didn't play the sensitive questioner; on the contrary, he was hard and harsh, speaking with sarcasm in his tone, as he attempted to influence the jury by making her look like she was putting on an act.

"It seems to me that you were jealous of Patrick, having a home to yourself, then suddenly this man arrives, and you felt betrayed. Your mother wasn't nice to you, and yet she was entertaining a man, drinking and laughing with him. And who would blame you, Miss Raven, with your years of abuse and then to see him showered with affection. I am sure that must have stirred some emotion: rejection, anger, hate, even jealousy. Did it?"

Weirs had thrown down the gauntlet and he stood back, waiting for the fury, but he was met instead with an angelic tear-stained face.

"You must have felt something, Miss Raven, surely?" he asserted, his voice getting louder.

Kelly shook her head and calmly she replied, "No, I didn't think about it. I didn't know him. I had no reason to hate him."

"Oh, come on now, Miss Raven, you would feel something? Your mother, years of abuse at her hands, and then to see her showing affection to him, while you were shoved aside, a mere irritant."

"I never said my mother abused me. I never said she shoved me aside."

Weirs stood there looking flummoxed. He had clear evidence she had been abused and now she was denying it.

"You were abused, Miss Raven. We have the social services' report, the doctor's report."

Kelly shook her head. "I was never abused by my mother."

Weirs was knocked sideways by this remark; it was obvious she was implying she was abused by someone else. He bit his lip and then scratched his chin. The jury sensed the pause was longer than it need be.

Even Sophie froze. She wasn't supposed to say that; she was to say she was too young to remember.

Weirs cleared his throat. "Miss Raven, I have heard the reports of your abuse, and noted the scars on your back, and you want me to believe that was not abuse?"

Kelly lowered her gaze, appearing shy and deflated. "No, I didn't say I wasn't abused. I said I wasn't abused by my mother …"

"No further questions, Your Honour."

The jury were on a cliff-hanger, the gallery was whispering, and the judge wanted further answers.

"Miss Raven, please inform the Court who you believe abused you."

Kelly raised her head and faced the jury. She swallowed hard, as if it grieved her to say, "My father abused me, not my mother."

Weirs dropped his papers on the desk; his case for murder was over.

Kelly slowly turned to face the gallery, catching her father's eye. She couldn't smile or sneer, as the jury were watching; she gave no hint whatsoever to her thoughts. She felt him cringe though; she watched his cocky face crumble. The jury guessed right away who the smart, handsome man in the gallery was. The olive skin and distinctive eyes were identical to the young woman in the dock. His reaction was noted too.

Sophie was gripping her seat. Her client had just turned the case upside down, in the blink of an eye. She bit her lip and then looked into Kelly's eyes. What she saw was someone else — it was not a lost child but an astute woman.

The judge was fair in his summing up and the case against her for the murder of her mother was unfounded. The charge for the attack on Patrick was reduced to manslaughter and the judge then passed sentence.

Kelly stood in the dock — awaiting her fate. She gazed at the people sitting in the gallery and smiled. She so wanted to put on a brave face, to show she was all right. Lippy and Betty were still seated together, gripping each other's hands and tearful. Rudy was in the gallery with the boys and Keffa; they were putting their thumbs up and making heart shapes with their hands. She felt a great comfort in them being there, and Eddie could see it. She never smiled his way. He admired her strength and her tenacity. He even thought she was clever, using him as her get-out clause. Did she use him for that purpose or was she having a dig? Either way, she had secured a not-guilty-of-murder verdict because she had no motive. Yet, he was now concerned that the unsolved murder of Maureen would land on his shoulders.

Weirs's summing up had been short and sloppy; Kelly had swung a real curve ball that left him looking an idiot, and in the eyes of the jury, she was innocent. Sophie was like a queen on her pedestal, finding fault in all the evidence regarding her client's supposed mental state and perceived motives to kill her mother.

The judge passed sentence – three years in prison for the manslaughter of Patrick Mahoney.

She was swiftly taken away.

CHAPTER FIFTEEN

After the court case, she was of age to go back to C wing, but instead she went to a cell at the end of the landing, away from Toni on B wing. It didn't stop Toni from pestering her though, trying to get her onside. Kelly had, in no uncertain terms, told her to fuck off and leave her alone.

She kept herself to herself but the one person she had time for was Ruth. One afternoon, while she was in the gym, there was a commotion back on the wing. One of the quieter inmates, an older woman by the name of Sylvia, a motherly sort, ran into the gym. She was discomposed and out of breath.

"Kelly, love, young Ruth is up there with Toni. They have shut her inside the cell. I think they are gonna hurt her!"

Kelly jumped off the treadmill and sprinted from the gym and up the metal staircase. A few inmates were wandering around, not making a scene. The officers were nowhere in sight. *Typical*, she thought. Kelly pushed past Treacle, who was obviously keeping watch, leaning against the wall, puffing on a roll-up. Kelly tried to open the cell door, but Toni had it wedged with the folded rubber. "Open up, Toni!" Treacle grabbed Kelly's arm. "Do one, Kelly. This ain't your business. Ruth's taken a liberty."

As Kelly heard the muffled screams coming from inside the cell, her heart pounded with anger, and her temper got the better of her. She grabbed Treacle by the throat and squeezed. "Get away from me, you scrawny cunt!" she yelled. Treacle dropped her roll-up and backed off.

"Open up, Toni, or I'll fucking smash your head in, I fucking mean it!" screamed Kelly, through the gap in the cell. Immediately, the door opened and there stood Hattie, taking up the doorway. She moved sideways and Kelly could see Toni standing there, out of breath, with poor Ruth still curled in a ball. Kelly pushed Hattie so hard, she lost her balance and fell into the locker. Kneeling beside Ruth, Kelly carefully lifted her face to find the bloodied nose and bruises across her cheeks. Kelly hated Toni at that moment for the job she had done on her friend. Her aunt knew her actions had gone too far this time. There would be ructions and Toni felt afraid.

Ruth murmured and tried to sit up, but the pain in her ribs made her wince. Kelly lifted Ruth's top to see the marks along the bony ribs. She helped Ruth to her feet and put her shoulder under her arm. "Come on, mate, let's get you down to sick bay."

Toni grabbed Kelly's arm. "Kel, she stole from me. Ya gonna grass?"

Kelly ignored her and carried on. As she helped the battered Ruth along the landing, one of the officers came running towards them. Placing her arm under Ruth's waist, she pressed the alarm.

"Leave her to me, Raven. Get back to your wing. Who did this, Ruth?" She glared at Kelly.

"I fell down the stairs," whispered Ruth.

The officer raised her eyebrow at Kelly. "Well?"

Kelly shook her head. "It's her call, Gov."

"All right, Raven, go back to your cell."

Two other officers arrived in seconds to help Ruth to the hospital wing. One of them peered over her shoulder and watched Kelly shoot into Toni's cell but decided to do nothing about it.

Hattie stood in the way to try to stop Kelly. It was a pointless act. With one swift movement, she hit Hattie's collarbone, knocking her to the floor. "Don't fuck with me, ya fat cunt! Now get out of here. I have business with me so-called aunt. Family business!"

Hattie struggled to her feet and without looking at Toni she left. Kelly was now face-to-face with Toni. The dynamics were all very different now with the young kid on the block taking on the adult – the top bitch on B wing – who looked fearsome and had a reputation herself to maintain. This didn't perturb Kelly though.

"Kelly, ya outta line. That piece of shit nicked off me. I ain't 'aving it!"

"Nicked off ya, yeah, what, baccy was it, puff was it, your stash of smack was it?" She was inching forward.

Toni was nodding. "Yeah, she nicked me baccy."

Like a weird demon, Kelly laughed. "S'pose ya found the pouch in her cell, half-gone, and let me guess, Hattie sussed it, yeah?"

Toni stopped nodding and inclined her head. "How did you know? Was you in on it?"

"Cor, Tone, I thought you had more brains than that. Ya fucking stupid tramp. Hattie used that poor cow as a scapegoat. Ruth don't even smoke. Hattie chored ya fucking tobacco. You are nothing but a fucking bully, an 'orrible excuse for a woman!" screamed Kelly.

Toni was angry. A small crowd was gathering outside and her reputation was slipping from under her. "Shut your mouth, bitch. Family or not, I'm gonna mop the fucking floor with ya." Launching herself at Kelly, she grabbed her hair and punched her in the face. The blow stung but it was the pain Kelly needed to fight back. The karate self-defence and composed blows went out of the window. Like an animal, she grabbed Toni's hair and pulled her face down towards her knee and smashed her nose. The shock caused Toni to let go of her grip, allowing Kelly, who was still holding her aunt's hair, to run her face this time into the corner of the metal bed. Toni was poleaxed; she fell to the floor, clutching her nose, which by now was bleeding profusely. But this didn't stop her niece. Kelly kept up the momentum. She kicked and kicked until Hattie and Treacle came in. Kelly then turned and launched at Hattie, headbutting her in the face. Treacle jumped on Kelly's back but with no effect. Kelly simply reached over her shoulder, clawing at Treacle's face until she caught her hair, and then she pulled her over her shoulder, like a gorilla, and threw her at Hattie. Angrily, Kelly pushed past them both and headed for the door, but before she walked away, she turned to the three of them; they were in a bad state, nursing their wounds.

"Pull a stunt like that again, and I'll not stop next time!" she hissed.

It wasn't long after when the whole dynamics changed. Toni wasn't running the prison anymore and all she had wrapped around her were a few pathetic scag heads. Kelly had seen the devastation Toni had caused, ruling through fear and coercion.

After Ruth was out of the hospital, she began to act strangely. It was a Sunday, and she was handing out her belongings and saying goodbye to a few of the inmates.

Sylvia passed Kelly on the landing. "Kel, love, Ruth's going home today. Good news, eh?"

"What d'ya mean, Sylv?"

Sylvia held up a book. "Yep, she gave me this, and she handed her shoes to Tilly and her cup and saucer to Karen, bless her heart."

"Nah, Sylv, she ain't going home, it's Sunday. No one goes home on a Sunday and she ain't due out yet." With that, she ran off towards Ruth's cell, leaving Sylvia bewildered.

Ruth was neatly packing her transit boxes stored under her bed.

"Hello, Kel, look, you can have this." She held up a pretty landscape drawing. "I drew it for you. I'm going home today!"

272

Kelly felt the heart-wrenching pain and the lump in her throat. She sat on Ruth's bed. "Come and sit with me, Ruth."

Ruth had a huge smile on her face as she sat with her friend. "Are you going to miss me, Kelly? I can come and visit."

She grabbed Ruth's hand. "Listen to me, Ruth, you ain't going home today. It's Sunday. No one leaves on a Sunday."

"Yeah, I am. I'm going home. I can't wait to see me babies. They are all waiting for me. S'pect they are gonna have a party. A homecoming one. My Connor will keep it a surprise. He's like that, but I gotta hurry, 'cos he is outside, waiting for me."

Kelly felt a sudden anguish; her best friend had totally lost the plot.

"I'm just going to see the PO, Ruth. I'll be back in a minute."

Kelly stepped outside the cell to find Sylvia and a couple of others waiting. "What's going on, Kel? She is going home today, ain't she? Only, the poor cow's given all her stuff away."

With a sad shake of her head, Kelly replied, "No, she ain't, but, Sylv, do us a favour, get all her gear back. Ruth ain't going anywhere. She has longer to serve than I do. I'm gonna get the number one governor. Ruth ain't well."

Sylvia went off to collect the items that Ruth had given away, now understanding the situation. Everything was handed back without a fuss, and some had given her their own special gifts: a few books, magazines, and even chocolates treats.

The PO, Charlie, frowned when Kelly told her. "Ah, no, we get this, Kelly. I've seen it before. Never mind, I'll see she's all right. We'll get her over to the hospital wing. I tell ya, that beating she got. I know who did it, and she has a lot to answer for. The poor cow has been handed a raw deal. Her ol' man let her take the rap for the drugs they found on him, so that's why she was given such a long sentence."

Kelly nodded. "Can I come over and visit Ruth? She's me mate."

Charlie hesitated but then nodded. "Yeah, I'll see to it. You've been a good friend. Leave it to me."

Ruth remained on the hospital wing for weeks, and it was then that Kelly saw the consequences of bullying. Although the attack on her friend saddened her, she herself gained inner strength from this experience, and, furthermore, she knew she was perfectly capable of exacting retribution when necessary. Indeed, she would continue to hold true to her core values — loyalty to friends and 'family'. When she left this shithole, she would tackle life not only with renewed vigour but also with a strong sense of purpose.

She couldn't wait.

CHAPTER SIXTEEN

Three years later

The gates were opened and Kelly stepped outside to feel the fresh air on her face. The sun was out and the view was new. She had told no one of her release date. She was a free woman to go and do as she pleased. Half of her belongings she left to Ruth; the rest she packed in a holdall, sufficient for her present needs. Dressed in a pair of dark tight jeans and a loose T-shirt, she waited for the taxi. She could have asked any one of them to pick her up – Rudy, Keffa, her aunt – but she wanted to travel alone. It wasn't to get her thoughts together – she'd had three years for that – it was to feel independent, with no one telling her what to do and where to go. At twenty-one, she was more woman than most at her age. Her figure had changed too, with well-developed hips and bust but in good proportion. Her hair had grown down to her waist now and her cheekbones were more defined. Her job inside had been gym orderly; this afforded the opportunity to work out every day as well as to teach Ruth martial arts and watch her become strong in mind and body.

The taxi pulled up and she hopped in the back. She saw the driver's sneaky look at her and rolled her eyes in amusement. "Nearest pub is it, love?" he laughed.

She sighed. "I don't drink. Peckham, please."

Gazing out of the window, she watched as the countryside became a village and the village became a town until eventually there she was on the busy streets of outer London. Nothing had changed much: the pub next to King's College Hospital still had the same winos outside with their cans of Tennent's Super, the traffic congestion was as bad as ever, and the smell from the fried chicken shops still pervaded the main road.

"'Ere, mate, just here will do," she told him.

She handed the driver a fifty and walked away. He watched as she approached the run-down Victorian house, ogling her neat arse and the way her hair bounced off her back. The sound of a horn from behind made the driver snap out of his gaze and drive on. Standing at the bottom of the steps, she took a deep breath: *my new life begins*, she thought. With the exception of Lippy and Betty, it had been three years since she'd seen anyone from the outside. She'd made the decision not to have their lives disrupted; this was her doing and her price to pay, not theirs.

Inside the house, Lippy was mopping the floor, and Rudy was in discussions with Keffa about their new venture, when Legend leapt from the sofa like a puppy and began howling and scratching at the door. Lippy dropped the mop and both Rudy and Keffa ran to the door.

"It must be her!" squealed Lippy.

Before Kelly had a chance to knock on the door, Lippy had it open and almost pounced on her. "Oh, my goodness, come here, give me a hug. Oh, look at you! Oh, Rudy, look at her, all grown-up." She hugged Kelly, almost crushing her. Kelly wasn't used to affection, not in the last three years anyway, but in an instant, she was a child again, as the gentle hint of *Chloé Fleur de Parfum*, overpowered by the smell of curry, made her feel at home.

Rudy wasn't shy either, grabbing Kelly and swinging her around. She was heavy to lift now. Keffa watched from the doorway, with a full ear-to-ear smile on his face. "Ya grown up all right, Bluey."

Then Legend howled; he had waited patiently for the others to get out of the way before he could make a fuss. Kelly dropped to her knees and rolled around the floor, with him jumping all over her, licking her face and yelping. "Aw, Legend, I thought you would hate me for leaving you."

"Come in, Bluey, ya room's just as ya left it. Lippy's seen to it. It's clean and fresh ..." He stopped. "You *are* moving back in, ain't ya, Blue?" asked Rudy.

She smiled. "It's me home, ain't it?"

"Yeah, 'course it is." He looked at her face and felt embarrassed: she wasn't a kid anymore, she was a woman and a very good-looking one. She had sex appeal and self-confidence, a very attractive combination. Keffa sensed it too and was hard-pressed to find anything to say. *How would it be now?* he wondered.

Lippy didn't care. She was off, ready to make a meal fit for a queen. "I'll make tea and then we can celebrate. Rudy, call the boys."

Kelly took a seat in the lounge. She noticed how tired the place actually was but it was home and she felt safe. There was an awkward silence, as both men stared at her.

"Don't look at me like that. I'm still me under these tits," she giggled.

Rudy nearly fell off the chair; he was still so animated when he laughed. Keffa slapped his own knee and joined in.

The laughter died down and Rudy took on a serious tone. "What d'ya wanna do now, Blue?"

She sat back on the sofa, gave a cheeky smile, and tapped the side of her nose. "When I've got the plan sorted, I'll let ya know."

With a different expression on his face, Keffa changed the subject. "Have you seen Eddie?"

Kelly grimaced. "He has tried to contact me, sending me letters, asking me to send out a VO. I ignored him. He ain't my family—"

"Be careful, Bluey, he's …"

With a hard glare, she nodded. "Yeah, a psychopath, so everyone keeps telling me. Well, just so ya know, he don't bother me." She paused and stared into space. "In fact, if he shows his face around here, I will kill him."

Shocked by her harsh words, Keffa raised his eyebrow. "Why d'ya hate him so much, Blue? I mean, I know about the abuse, what ya said in court, but is there another reason?"

"He never abused me. I said that so it didn't look like I had a motive to kill my mother, that's all. I hate thugs and that man is the epitome of one. Anyway, let's not talk about him. How's Ditto, Reggie, Phoenix and Solly?" But she changed the subject too quickly and Keffa sensed there was more to this Eddie story. Still, he was pleased to see Kelly home, although he felt a little awkward. It was hard not to feel attracted to her, with her womanly appearance.

It wasn't long before the boys arrived. They hadn't changed at all; they were still fun-loving and full of banter. It was an evening to enjoy and remember and everyone toasted Kelly's return to the fold.

As the darkness fell, Kelly felt the need to be alone. She excused herself and headed to the quiet of her own room. Lippy had kept it fresh and clean and had even added new items, with a fancy dreamcatcher above her bed and a photo she'd had blown up of Kelly with Legend. Kelly stood staring at the photo – at herself, three years ago. So much had changed: her appearance, her thoughts, and her views. But this was her haven – where she felt at home – here in this scruffy and neglected Victorian house, with the madness of people coming and going, the endless cooking, and soft drums from the reggae music. It would take a while to truly fit back in. She was so used to the four blank walls of her cell, the quiet as the lights went out, and the long solitude of hours for thinking. As she lay on her bed staring up at the ceiling, with the familiar cracks and the peeling paint, and with Legend beside her, resting his head on her chest, it felt just like old times. There was nothing she would miss about prison, with the exception of her friend Ruth. Hopefully, she would be okay alone there, now that Toni had been released.

Legend nestled his head under her chin and Kelly listened to him purring like a kitten. She drifted off to the best night's sleep she'd had in over three years.

As the morning arrived, Kelly was rudely awoken by Lippy, clanging the pots and pans; for a second, those familiar-sounding noises made Kelly think she was back in her cell. Sitting on the edge of the bed, she stretched as the sun beamed in through the new curtains and lit up the soft pink-painted walls. The smell was homely at last and egg and bacon wafted into her room. She popped her feet into her red slippers and wrapped herself in the new satin red dressing gown, both gifts from Lippy. Kelly chuckled. Legend, now very much awake and at last glued to her side, followed her happily down the hallway into the kitchen.

"Good morning, me lickle beauty!" beamed Lippy.

As she watched Lippy with the frying pan in one hand, tilted to show her offerings, and the egg slice in the other, Kelly felt years younger. It was just how it used to be, with Lippy still in her skin-tight T-shirts, frying up goodies for anyone who cared to eat.

"Mmm, looks good. I missed your cooking, Lippy."

"Aw, me chil', was the food that bad?"

Kelly laughed. "Like eating me old school pumps!"

"'Ere, you eat that and I will make us a nice cuppa tea."

Kelly was soaking up the fuss from her friend with both really enjoying this first precious moment together, after such a long time apart.

Rudy appeared looking bedraggled, though this was not unusual, if he'd had a late one. He rubbed his eyes and raised his eyebrows. "Don't let the boys see ya like that, or they'll be dribbling all over their Weetabix," he laughed, as he sat on the chair opposite.

Kelly rolled her eyes. "They are gonna have to get used to it. I can't help that I grew these babies." She pointed to her breasts.

He laughed. "Yeah, but you wanna make sure they don't escape from that thingy you're wearing," pointing to her satin wrap.

Lippy slapped his shoulder. "Leave the chil' alone."

"That's the point. Me thinks she's no child and neither will the boys." He was giggling like a schoolboy.

Once Lippy left the kitchen, Rudy turned to Kelly. "Listen, you will stay away from Eddie, won't ya?"

Kelly nodded. "You look concerned, Rudy. Why?"

"He came here, ya know. Turned ya bedroom over, looking for a bunny or something to——"

Before he could continue, Kelly interrupted, "He didn't hurt any of you, did he?"

Rudy lowered his eyes. "Not seriously, but he is fucking mad. He had a gun in me face. He asked where your school clothes were. I said ya burned them. He then asked for ya jacket. I said you didn't have one." He stood up and walked to the hallway and Kelly followed. The two heavy overcoats were still there, gathering more dust. He removed them, showing the thin raincoat.

"I guess he knew you had that bunny hidden in there, but he left with nothing."

Kelly smiled and spontaneously hugged Rudy. She knew then that, no matter what, he was the one person she could trust with her life. She realised he hadn't even looked in her pockets because the bunny wasn't there anyway, and yet he obviously assumed it was.

She growled, "As God is my witness, I will hurt that man. You watch me."

Rudy shook his head. "Stay away, Bluey, the man's reckless, he cut—" His mouth was running away with him.

"Who, Rudy, who did he cut?" She grabbed his arm.

He paused. "Keffa, although it was years ago. But he cut his throat and left him for dead. Don't say anything."

Kelly shook her head. "I won't, Rudy, I promise." She left him there and returned to her room in contemplation.

She went through the clothes in her wardrobe only to find nothing fitted at all; she had grown taller and her shape had changed. Pulling on some jeans and a top from her holdall, she quickly got dressed. Rudy knocked and then poked his head around the door. "Bluey, if ya need money, here you are. Ya money was kept in the drawer, your share."

She took the envelope and winked. "Soon, Rudy, we will all be millionaires. Thanks for this. I just need to buy a few bits. It seems I can't fit into teenage clothes anymore."

He laughed. "I wonder why! Just you make sure those babylons are held in, whatever you wear. Don't want no car crashes."

Her voice took on a serious tone. "Thanks, Rudy. I mean, thanks for everything. You are my true friend and uncle."

Rudy shuffled from foot to foot. "Yeah, man, fam."

She nodded. "Yeah … Fam." They high-fived.

With the money in her purse, she called a cab and headed for central London. Those three years she had spent in prison were long enough to find the business of London's roads almost alarming. Oxford Street was her favourite place to shop, but there were so many shoppers; somehow, she felt out of place, almost like an alien. The officers had warned her that adapting once more to civvy life would feel strange at first. Three years inside was one thing as an adult, but locked up as a child and coming out as a woman, it was an entirely new experience. She found that out for herself. People treated her differently. Men looked at her with wanting eyes. It was exciting and yet somewhat unsettling.

Selfridges hadn't altered much; although fashions had changed, the store was still laid out as she remembered it. She wandered from one counter to the next, eyeing up the products. She spent quite some time going over the costume jewellery and appraised the fake blue diamonds encased in silver which were ideal for a formal occasion. One caught her eye: it was a necklace. It looked a bit ritzy but the blue gem was almost perfect; turning it over, she then held it against the light, where it shone in all directions. She smiled to herself. If it were real, it would be worth a fortune. Amiee, the shop assistant, was watching her, admiring her slim figure and long hair. Unlike the woman holding the ugly necklace, she was heavily made-up, and she wished she had the customer's perfect skin. Amiee approached Kelly with a huge grin.

"Can I help you, Madam?"

Turning to the assistant, Kelly smiled at her. "Oh yes, do you have any other pieces of jewellery like this one, but with a large blue stone?"

Amiee returned behind the counter and pulled open a drawer where there were others going on sale that afternoon. She placed the tray on top of the counter. "These are similar, Madam. Are you looking for a necklace for a special occasion?"

Kelly smiled. "Yes, very special. How much is that one?" She pointed to an oval-shaped blue stone clasped at the top with a dainty clip and a long thick silver chain to hold the weight. Amiee frowned; the necklace was too tacky and wouldn't suit such an attractive woman.

"Oh, that one is in the sale, fifteen pounds now, but we have some stunning pieces—"

"It's perfect. I'll take it."

Amiee would have persuaded her customer to part with more money to purchase a finer piece – she was good at sales – but sensed she couldn't this time. She wrapped it in tissue paper and handed it to Kelly. "I hope you enjoy your special occasion." Kelly smiled again. "Thank you, I am sure I will."

As she walked away, Amiee watched her, dreaming of having a tight figure like hers and hair that tumbled down her back in natural waves. Not many women were so innately pretty. Amiee sighed and returned to her fake jewellery.

Kelly wandered around the concessions, trying to decide what would suit her now; all she had worn, once she had been sentenced, were the prison issues. She had jeans and sweat tops but she wanted to change her image. She tried on some dresses and was surprised to see how different she looked. The constant training in the gym had given her long legs definition and a flat stomach.

Standing in front of the full-length mirror, she smoothed down the black figure-hugging dress and grinned to herself. Her mother would be turning in her grave. After adding a pair of high-heeled black shoes and a short black leather jacket, she nodded; this was her, this was the person she was meant to be. Lippy had once told her she would grow into herself one day, but Kelly had never really understood what she had meant – until now. She paid for all the outfits and returned to the changing room, placing her jeans in one of the bags. Her new clothes gave her added confidence, and so she headed for the make-up department. The attractive young assistant was falling over herself to assist Kelly, even offering a free makeover. Kelly was enjoying the fuss and agreed. The final result was far better than Kelly could ever have envisaged. She wasn't excessively made-up, but the smoky eyes defined her facial features and she had to admit to herself she looked pretty good. With the transformation almost complete, Kelly decided to have her hair trimmed. She'd been so used to prison life, where it didn't matter what she looked like, she was feeling on a high, with so much self-indulgence.

The hair salon was on the third floor. Kelly wandered up, hoping they would be able to slot her in. The salon was not only trendy but it took Kelly's breath away. Huge life-sized photographs of men and women, with the trendiest of hair styles she'd ever seen, adorned the walls. The sight took Kelly back to the time when Debra had looked at her in astonishment at seeing the effects of her daughter's makeover on her. It seemed such a long time ago now.

The man at the desk, dressed in a black T-shirt, with the salon's logo clearly shown on the front, and black skinny jeans, looked up and his eyes widened. "Oh, hello, how can I help you?"

"I was hoping you could squeeze me in, just a trim, nothing more."

The man was eyeing her up and down. "Err … yes, err, maybe, let me see." He looked at the screen. "Ahh, yes, if you are ready now, can I take your name?"

"Yes, it's Bluey Raven."

He led her to a seat and helped her with the gown. "Penny will be with you shortly."

Kelly sat staring at her own reflection; it was like looking at a complete stranger. She felt an overwhelming sense of excitement. Always the ugly duckling at school, she was a new woman: in name, substance, and style. Then she thought of Peter. Would he like her look; would he be interested in the woman she was now, or was it the innocence in her face he had found attractive?

Shortly, a young woman with a long blonde fringe appeared, wearing bright red lipstick, black jeans, and a black work shirt with hairclips hanging from the sleeve. She was chewing gum and looking down at a clipboard, and so she hadn't even noticed Kelly.

"Just gonna take a few details, right? Ya just wanna cut and blow dry?" Her voice was flat, clearly bored. Well, it had been a slow day.

Kelly grinned to herself. "Nah, Penny, I wanna trim."

Penny looked up, stared at Kelly's reflection, and gasped; she tilted her head, *it couldn't be*, and felt goosebumps over her skin.

"Churchy?" she whispered, truly astonished at what she was seeing.

"It's Bluey, now, Penny," she smiled.

Penny looked around furtively to see who was about. "Fuck me, gal, I thought you was on the run, or dead or something? Does anyone know you're 'ere? I mean ..."

Kelly swung around in the swivel chair. "It's all right, Penny, no one's after me, not now. I've done me time. I'm a free woman."

With her mouth open, Penny was shocked for many reasons. Straightaway, she felt awkward. Churchy was now a confident, stunning-looking woman. Did she murder that man and her mother? How dangerous was she?

"Penny, it's okay, I don't bite."

"I'm just ... well, you look so different. Fuck me, Kelly, I mean, Bluey. What's with the name anyway?"

"Ditched me old life and created a new one."

"So, ya served time in prison? Blimey, how did ya cope?" asked Penny, eager to know the details.

"Truth is, you helped me, when I was on the run, and inside, I would think, 'What would Penny do'."

Penny nudged her shoulder. "Oh, go on with ya!" she laughed.

Kelly's eyes widened. "No, seriously!"

"Did they beat you up or hurt ya in there? Cor, fuck me, I would have died in prison. How did ya manage?"

Kelly gave Penny a loaded look that suggested no one fucks with me. "It's all about your rep in there, and funnily enough I earned one, and so, no, it was okay. Like living with a load of pussies, really!"

Penny swallowed hard; she remembered the gossip and the grim details of Maureen's murder. It was the talk of the town and the school for many months. Kelly Raven, the serial killer, turned to Kelly Raven, the wandering ghost, had caused hysteria at school, with pupils swearing blind they had seen her spirit roaming around the streets.

After an hour of interrogation, which had not been particularly diplomatic, Kelly concluded that Penny hadn't changed one bit. Penny was so open: there was nothing fake or hidden. So, Kelly was only too pleased to divulge the truth behind her time in prison — not that she was proud, but describing the antics put an eager smile on Penny's face. It was certainly the best gossip ever to be heard in a hairdresser's salon. Penny finished with Kelly's hair and showed her the back. Her friend had done a great job.

As Kelly stood up to leave, she hugged her friend. "You were good to me at school. I always admired you."

Penny returned the hug. "We're mates, then, Kel?"

Kelly nodded. "Yeah, 'course we are, but only if you call me Bluey!"

They exchanged numbers, and as Kelly walked away, Penny watched her, still tingling from the shock and blown away by the transformation.

So not such a boring day after all!

Eddie Raven was surrounded by his little firm; his reputation still commanded attention. He had to keep his nose clean, as DI Maddox had tipped him off that the police were still keeping him under observation. They swallowed his alibi, but the Commissioner insisted he wasn't to go off the radar.

"Tommy, I want you to follow Kelly. I wanna know every fucking move she makes, got it?" ordered Eddie. Tommy nodded; he didn't have much choice, as the debt he owed was like a fucking mortgage. His life wasn't his own now. The alibi the night of Maureen's murder was not enough; Eddie wanted blood, his blood.

"Why's that, Eddie?" he asked.

Sitting comfortably in his oversized chair, Eddie now leapt up, like a jack-in-the-box, and towered over Tommy. "Who are you to ask me why? Just do as I fucking say."

Tommy sank deeper into the pillowed sofa, nodding like his head would fall off. "Sorry, Eddie." He sounded pathetic but that was how Eddie liked it.

Eddie was staying in his North London house, a big place, in a street surrounded by doctors and stockbrokers. He called a meeting, every Monday, to get the low-down on how his businesses were doing. The days of robbery were over; he was now back into protection money, along with the proceeds from his nightclub and two pubs. Driven by greed and bullying tactics, he was muscling in on places he should have left alone, yet he was so brazen and reckless that the owners of the two pubs handed over the deeds — well, they'd had no choice. Tommy still remembered those events; how could he ever forget them?

It was after twelve years inside when his protection racket had died a death, and by the time he'd come out, there wasn't much left. Two brothers, the Bristols, had taken over and much of it had been sewn up. They were young, in their early thirties, but, like Eddie, they were also ruthless. Eddie was angry that two kids, as he saw them, had the balls to step on his toes, and he was even more livid when they had shot his right-hand man, Vinnie, in the face, taking his eye out. He had survived but looked a mess. After being out for only two months, and keeping low, Eddie rounded up his firm and went to meet the Bristols, Freddie and Frankie. Eddie had told his men to follow them, noting all their movements.

On a Saturday night, the two brothers would call into the Venue, a trendy pub, which was raking it in. They would stay on the premises, drinking and partying with all the toffs, wait until lock-up, and then collect the money. Normally, they used their firm to do this for collecting the protection money from the other joints on the manor, but at this pub they did their own dirty work. It was too easy; the owner was a stockbroker who had an interest in the pub world but didn't have the clout to keep the wolves from the door. He was making a mint and settled for the brothers to take fifty per cent of whatever they took on a Saturday. They kept their end of the bargain and even acted like bouncers, throwing customers out who got too mouthy.

Eddie took Tommy and Cyril along, just to check out the place. It was full to the rafters and he could see why. The pub was more like a club and the clientele had money – lots of it. He spotted the Bristols, from where he was sitting in the corner, and appraised them critically. They were brash and loud, wearing flash suits, but were they as cold-blooded as him? He didn't think so. Freddie was the younger one with a shaved head and massive hands. Frankie, however, was smaller; not such a meathead, he was livelier, and his neatly groomed hair gave him the edge. It was Frankie who called the shots – he had sussed that out. As the night wore on, the pub was crammed with people. Eddie walked to the toilets and brushed past Frankie, feeling his waist for a gun. Frankie took no notice because it was so packed. Eddie walked back from the men's room and did the same to Freddie and concluded neither had a weapon.

The next Saturday, Eddie returned, this time with five of his firm; they plotted in pairs around the pub. As the night came to an end, they gathered in the ladies' toilets and waited for the doors to lock. Once the pub was quiet, all six of them appeared, each with their back to the bar, as they lined up like six smartly dressed bouncers, much to the horror of the Bristol brothers.

They were aware of Eddie Raven but never knew what he looked like. Gareth Caulstone, the owner, was behind the bar, counting the money. Next to him was the new barmaid. She grinned at Eddie and flicked her long black hair. Gareth stopped what he was doing, his mouth open, trying to fathom the dynamics of the situation. Stealthily, he moved his hand underneath the counter to press the panic button – a direct link to the police – but the barmaid grabbed his hand. "No ya don't, mate," she said. He looked at her and then at Eddie; they could have been twins. Then the penny dropped: they were related.

"So, boys, it seems to me, and correct me if I am wrong, that you two have taken a right fucking liberty. I mean, a man goes away inside and you little rats feel it's all right to take over his business, and to make matters worse, you did so without his okay!" goaded Eddie, as he stepped forward.

Frankie and Freddie looked at each other and then back at Eddie. Frankie was the first to speak. "And you are?"

With a sneaky smirk, Eddie laughed. He looked down at his new black patent shoes. "Who am I? Well, boys, I think you know damn well who I am, so cut the bollocks. You see, I am all for making a few quid, that's why they call me Eddie Cako, but to take from a man that's locked up in the system, well, that's like taking candy from a baby. In my book, that's breaking all the cunting rules."

Eddie took another step closer. Frankie had a cockiness about him and raised his eyebrows. "A bit past it, ol' man, for making any fucking rules, ain't ya? Go home and put ya feet up. This ain't your business. Ya had your day." He expected Eddie to run at him in a temper, and then he would give him a fight and mangle him. The cocaine he had been snorting all night gave him the gumption to say and do as he pleased.

Eddie ignored him and looked at the terrified expression on Gareth's face. He laughed. "So, tell me, Gareth, are these two idiots taking fifty per cent of your earnings for protection? 'Cos, that's another fucking liberty. See, when I ran the insurance scheme, I was fair, weren't I, boys?" He cast a backward glance, indicating to his men behind him.

"See, Gareth, I made sure no one fucked with my businesses, but I took ten per cent. Now that's a huge difference and I just don't get it. I mean, Gareth, these two clowns ain't done a good job here, have they? Look around you. I'm here. I could quite easily blow your brains out, if I wanted to. Ya can't really call that protection, now can ya?"

Freddie laughed out loud. "Really, ol' man, listen. Do yaself a favour, take ya old cronies with ya and leave, before I take ya fucking face off."

Instantly, there was a loud popping sound. Cyril, the oldest in the firm, had taken offence to the words 'old cronies'. Pulling his gun from his waistband, he shot Freddie in the ankle. It caused him to holler and sit heavily on the floor and grip the gaping hole.

Eddie slowly turned and rolled his eyes at Cyril.

"Oh dear, I think you have pissed me mate off! Cyril, no more shooting until I say so." He didn't shout; his voice remained calm and collected.

Frankie stood stiffly, afraid now that the next bullet would have his name on it.

"All right, what do you want?"

Slowly and deliberately, Eddie walked to within an inch of Frankie, staring with his evil green eyes. Swiftly, he pulled out his own gun and shoved it under Frankie's nose. "It's not a case of what do I want, cocky cunt, it's more a case of what is mine." He looked around the pub and back at Frankie, who was now sweating. Eddie grinned; he liked to see a man encased in fear.

"I think it's fair to say that Gareth will be doing business with me from now on. Ain't that right, Gareth?" He glanced at the publican, who nodded back. "Yeah, see, so the question really is what do *you* want?"

He removed his gun and tapped Frankie's cheek.

"Well, I suppose we could make a deal," replied Frankie.

"Yeah, my thoughts exactly. Right, you give your brother a hand and we will take our business outside. I think Gareth over there wants to get off home," stated Eddie.

Naïvely, the brothers agreed to talk outside. Freddie was white, having lost a lot of blood, and he was now in need of urgent medical attention. And Frankie was terrified, if they didn't do as they were told, he would get shot himself. Freddie struggled to get to his feet, his ankle now smashed to pieces. But Cyril helped him – it was only fair.

Toni stayed behind, ensuring Gareth didn't do anything stupid.

"They were taking the piss, though, Gareth. I mean fifty per cent. What was you thinking, babe?" she said, as she stroked his cheek.

A sucker for pretty women, Gareth had taken Toni on as barmaid; despite a few dainty scars, she ticked all the boxes in the looks department, with a neat arse and a sexy smile. He liked a confident woman and Toni was that all right. He hadn't asked for a curriculum vitae or a reference, and so he was totally unaware she was straight out of prison.

"Yeah, I guess they were. So that Eddie guy is your brother, I assume?"

Toni smiled. "Yeah, he will look after the pub and do a better job, trust me. He ain't greedy, either. He will only want ten per cent. Ya need people like him on your side."

For a man who never drank, he poured himself a double brandy. It was still a shock. He had never seen anyone get shot before.

"Now then, Gareth, I am going to clean up that mess and then me and you can have a little quiet time on our own," she winked.

Gareth blushed and turned away, trying to hide the bulge from his aroused cock inside his light grey trousers, to the amusement of Toni.

Outside, the men bundled the two brothers into the back of two separate cars. The brothers knew then they were not going to discuss business – they were effectively dead men walking.

Cyril had a brother called Howie. Howie 'the pig' he was called, on account that he had a pig farm. The beasts were huge, thirty in total, but they were always hungry. He usually fed them twice a day, and if they missed a feed, they would turn on each other. Howie hadn't fed them for two days, so now they were vicious and would eat anything, bones and all.

Eagerly, and out of fascination, Eddie went along to make sure everything went to plan. The long lane leading to the farm was difficult to see in the pitch-black night but Cyril led the way. He knew the roads like the back of his hand. There were no lights following them so they were safe.

Frankie pleaded for his life, but Freddie was out cold; the bullet wound had almost caused him to bleed out. The firm though had foreseen the likely results of their work tonight. They had decided to use stolen cars which would be burnt out after they had completed their task, leaving no evidence for the filth.

With his pitchfork and a nasty sneer across his face, Howie appeared. Eddie wanted to laugh out loud. Howie was nothing like

Cyril; he was dressed in old combat trousers and a holey top and his face was red and rugged. He was chewing a stick, and when he grinned, Eddie could see his teeth were black. He shuddered: Howie was like a character from a horror movie.

"Me pigs are starving. I've put them in the metal pig pen. The way they are carrying on, they would break through me wooden one. I hope those men 'ave got some meat on 'em."

Eddie swallowed hard; perhaps he wouldn't watch after all. Shooting a man dead and seeing his eyes removed was one thing but watching him get eaten alive was quite another.

Wasting no time, Eddie belted Frankie around the head, knocking him clean out, and then he removed his and his brother's clothes and wristwatches. With a few swings, they threw the unconscious brothers up and over, into the pen. Eddie looked away; the smell from the pigs, and the thought of what they would do to these villains, made him sick. Cyril and Howie, however, just leaned over the gate and laughed; they were veterans in the disposal business. Then they heard a few screams, but the snorting and grunting drowned out the dying brothers' cries.

Back in business now, Eddie had the protection racket under his wing, just as he had done twelve years before. He should have been content, as the money was rolling in, and he was on top again. Maddox was still on his payroll, and so Eddie was given a wide birth, most of the time.

❧*❧

"So, Tommy, you don't let her out of your sight. I wanna know everything. That means where she goes, even who she is fucking. Got it?"

Tommy nodded. He had been present that night, and even though the incident was three years ago, he still couldn't get the images out of his head of the Bristol brothers being gnawed at by those brick-teethed pigs. He knew Eddie was evil, but what he had witnessed was something on a whole other level of brutality. "No worries, Eddie," he replied. He sincerely meant that: he didn't want to be the main course for Howie's pigs.

❧*❧

Kelly hopped out of the black taxi and walked around to the side to pay the driver. Just behind the vehicle was a blue Mercedes; she only noticed it because she had a keen eye for a good car. The taxi driver watched her walk across the road; he was admiring her figure, as was the man in the blue Mercedes.

As she put the key in the door, she held her breath in excitement; her new look would shock them, as it had done her. She heard talking coming from the lounge and instantly recognised the voice; her aunt Bet had arrived. She dropped her bags in the hallway and rushed in to greet her. Betty was sitting with Lippy and enjoying tea and a slice of her friend's towered cream cake. Both women were astonished at the sight of Kelly and it left them speechless.

Kelly turned a full circle. "Well, do you like my new look?"

Betty shuffled to get up; her back was better but she still struggled. With her arms outstretched, she held on to Kelly, kissing her cheek. "Oh, my babe, just look at yer, a proper stunner, ain't she, Lippy?"

Lippy was emotional and her eyes were moist. "Ahh, chil', ya look like a princess."

After the trial, Lippy and Betty had become close friends and would often meet up for a coffee and a chat. They would go and visit Kelly once a month together. Betty had learned about Kelly's life on the run and felt guilty that her niece had not gone to her for help. In fact, she felt guilty for so many reasons and particularly holding back the truth until the girl was sixteen. She could have fulfilled her promise to tell Kelly, but prison visits were not the right place.

It was time now though.

294

CHAPTER SEVENTEEN

The truth

Lippy knew that Betty and Kelly needed time alone and made her excuses to go out. Kelly looked at her aunt and gave her an empathetic smile.

"So, Aunt Bet, it's time you stopped feeling guilty. I told you that if it wasn't for you, all those years looking out for me, the best way you could, I would have probably taken me own life. I know you took an oath. So, it doesn't matter anymore. I know who Eddie is and what he did, so ..." She stopped when she saw the tears in her aunt's eyes.

"What, Aunt Bet, what's the matter?"

Betty turned to Kelly and cupped her face. "My babe, there's a lot more you don't know, and I think it's about time you knew the truth. It's only fair and right."

Kelly felt cold shivers up her spine. She searched her aunt's face for answers and watched as her cheerful look turned to one of deep sadness. Betty looked as though she was in pain and had in a New York minute aged twenty years.

"Aunt Bet, what is it? Tell me, nothing is that bad."

"Ahh, my girl, I think you're gonna hate me."

Kelly put her arm around Betty's shoulders and said, "I could never hate you, never."

As Betty looked at the floor, and lowered her eyes, it was hard to reveal the truth after so long, knowing that the secret was a cruel one. "Are you ready to hear this, Kel?"

With wide eyes and a deliberate nod, Kelly said, "Yes, go on."

✌*☞

Betty took a deep breath and then proceeded to tell the story.

When Maureen married Eddie, they were in love, deeply in love. Eddie was proud of Maureen and enjoyed her company. She was a good-looking woman and he was handsome, there was no denying it. The big houses and flash holidays were a lifestyle they both relished. Maureen knew that, as time went on, she wasn't enough in the bedroom to satisfy his appetite. She also knew he was getting his oats elsewhere; it was nothing serious, just the odd soppy tart who put it out. She could handle that, as long as he still came home to her. Somehow, she managed to put those notions to the back of her mind and closed her ears to the gossip. Then, she hit him with the idea of a family. At first, he wasn't keen, but after she persisted, he agreed. That's when the trouble started. Maureen had tried for six months to become pregnant until the doctors told her she was infertile.

At about this time, Eddie was nosing around Naomi, Jack Macfarlane's daughter. He had thought nothing of fucking the nineteen-year-old; it would be his sick way of revenge before he eventually killed her father.

Naomi was infatuated with Eddie and ergo an easy target. She followed him around, pleading to spend any spare time she had with him. She was a good-looking kid too. But that was just it, she was a kid. Eddie enjoyed the sex and spent a lot of time renting hotel rooms. Then Maureen dropped the bombshell she was barren. He seemed okay about this at first, but strangely, and no one knew why, he flipped. He suddenly wanted a child and made it clear to Maureen that by hook or by crook he would have a baby. Maureen was in a right state; she thought he was going to leave her and find himself another woman. No one knew at the time though he had just found out that Naomi was pregnant. He never told Maureen about the kid or who she was; he just told her that some old tart was going to have their baby, like a surrogate mother. Maureen was told to shut her mouth and not to ask too many questions. She agreed – what other option did she have?

Then, one day, he came home with this baby, new born, barely a day old. He placed the baby in Maureen's arms and told her to love the child like her own. It wasn't long after when the police fished Jack and Mickey out of the Thames.

At first, Maureen was over the moon and went out purchasing all the pretty things; she treated the child like a dolly. Then she got depressed: the child had been forced upon her and furthermore they weren't a content family where Eddie would be happy at home, relaxing with his feet up in front of the telly or playing with the baby. And she wasn't maternal at all but kept up the pretence in front of Eddie. Well, she had to.

Almost four years passed and Maureen found out who the mother was, when Eddie got drunk; she was so hurt. It wasn't any old whore, it was Naomi, and Maureen knew her. She was often over at Jack's house. Eddie had known the girl from the age of five years old. No one would have ever dreamed he would have been messing with her – his so-called best friend's daughter.

Eddie's hatred for Jack's so-called treachery led to payback, and so even though it was a year after the diamond heist, he planned their death and carried it out with precision. He had even cut out their eyes – a sick, evil deed. Maureen went insane when she discovered the truth about the mother of the baby, and so she grassed him to the police for the murders. She never mentioned the child though. So, Eddie then went away for twelve years. She'd had the last laugh because she had something that ultimately belonged to him.

Kelly's face was drained; her skin was pale and her eyes looked grey. *What? This was sick.* She stared into space for a few seconds, her mind rapidly processing the chain of events. Betty waited for her to say something. She had always known this news would be a shock.

"I am so sorry, Kelly, really I am. I wish I'd told you years ago, but I couldn't. I daren't because my Billy was Eddie's baby too and I never wanted him to know. I didn't want Eddie to get his filthy hands on him." Her words were like firing bullets.

"What! Billy was my brother?"

Betty looked afraid. She had just opened the biggest can of worms.

"Did you have an affair with Eddie too?" Her voice was harsh.

Betty shook her head defiantly; she wasn't ashamed. "No, babe, he got me paralytic and fucking helped himself."

Kelly threw her hands to her mouth and put her arms out to hug Betty. They held on to each other, rocking to and fro, with tears streaming, each distraught for the other. Betty was racked with guilt, knowing that Kelly would be hurting. The sordid secrets were now out and she would have to find a way to help this admirable young woman get over it. Kelly sniffed back the tears and then stroked Betty's face.

"Did he hurt you, Aunt Bet?" Her voice was full of compassion. Betty looked into Kelly's eyes and wondered what on earth she was thinking – the sweetness of the child. But Kelly was more concerned about her aunt's feelings than her own, despite hearing such earth-shattering news.

"No, not for that reason, but in every other way he hurt me. He destroyed your mother and she hated you for it. So, Kelly, I detest that man more than I hate anyone."

"Yeah, he is one nasty bastard … do you know what happened to me real mum?"

Betty shook her head. "Nah, babe, I don't. She disappeared off the face of the earth. Do you want to find her then, Kel?"

"No. She is obviously another victim of Eddie Raven. Seeing my face will probably haunt her, poor woman."

There was a long silence, as Kelly went over again what she had just heard. It was as if Betty was talking about someone else. Yet it was her; *she* was the baby handed to a nutcase to bring up. *She* was the child who was brought up for selfish reasons. No one really wanted her, except Betty.

∽*∾

That night brought with it the day's tribulations: it was predictable as it was unwelcome. Kelly tossed and turned, going over vivid images of her life: the beatings by her own mother, a lost teenager handing over a baby, her aunt being raped, and, of course, Eddie, the cruel, sadistic monster. She thought of Billy; she had loved him like a brother too. They were close as youngsters, but he was taken too soon by a childhood heart defect, after he had collapsed on the football pitch. She remembered her aunt being beside herself with grief, and she herself feeling so helpless. Then she considered Betty and her heartache; it was extraordinary because actually she wasn't even her real aunt. The only person who was real was Eddie, her fucking father.

Drenched in sorrow and guilt, she rested against the headboard. There was no point in upsetting herself; she was who she was and that was that. Her future would be down to her own doing from now on. She turned on the light and peeled back the carpet to reveal the floorboards. The short board closest to the wall was loose. She lifted it up and pulled from the hole the bunny: it was her comforter as a child.

She recalled vividly the day Maureen tried to take it away and her father's words then. They never made sense until now. She had dropped the bunny on the floor where it landed in some ice cream she had just spilled. Maureen picked up the toy and held it with her finger and thumb. She had ignored her cries, heading towards the bin. Maureen placed her foot on the pedal and the lid popped up. Just as she was about to drop the toy inside, Eddie hollered, "Don't you fucking dare! It's her comfort toy, from her mother. Never, ever, fucking throw that away! Do you understand me?"

That look of hate and jealousy on Maureen's face as her father snatched the bunny away now evoked powerful memories and emotions. He had wiped the toy over and handed it back and said, "There you go, my baby, you look after that, always."

Kelly did: she never let it out of her sight.

She held the bunny and stroked its head; her poor mother had given her that toy and it was the only one she had really cherished. She wondered what her mother would look like. Was she clever, or talented … was she even alive?

She sat on the edge of her bed and allowed the tears to flow. Legend knocked her hand, as he sensed she was hurting. Just then, there was a tap on her bedroom door. She wiped her tear-stained face and said, "Come in."

The door opened, and there, in a pink fluffy dressing gown, stood Ditto.

"What the fuck, Ditz," she unexpectedly chuckled.

He looked down. "Ahh, yeah, it's Lippy's." He didn't care though. His hard-man charisma was for the outside.

"I heard ya crying, Bluey. Everything okay?" He came into the room and sat beside her, placing a meaty arm around her shoulder.

She leaned into him. "I've just learned from Betty some terrible news. Me mother ain't me mother and I didn't even get to know me real mum."

"Ahh, man, that shit's fucked-up. It's like Rudy. His dad fucked off when he was a baby, left them in the shit, and then his ma died. He was living in a car at twelve and looking out for me mum, his sister. Washing windows, sweeping lawns, and robbing shops. Yo, the bro's brave. Look at him now. You'd never know, eh?"

Kelly smiled. "Yeah, actually ya would. Look at us lot. We are all misfits."

Ditto squeezed her knee tight. "Nah, man, I ain't no misfit … well, maybe … Yeah, I guess I am. He looked out for me and Reggie, 'cos me ma was not all the ticket. She couldn't get over the past, took too many drugs. That's why Rudy took us in, I guess."

"He is a good man. I am gonna have to get me own place. I don't trust that Eddie, and I don't want trouble brought to this door. Not after what Rudy and you guys have done for me."

Ditto gave her his raised eyebrow, he glared, and then he sucked his teeth. "Nah, man, you are part of our family. Misfits maybe, but you belong here. *We* will fight that Eddie *together,* if it comes to it, Blue."

He lay down on the bed and pulled her down with him. He stroked her hair gently, telling her to go back to sleep. She did, her earlier demons disappearing as quickly as they appeared. His arms cradled her and she slept like a baby.

By the morning, she was refreshed. Ditto was still next to her on the bed, dressed in the pink fluffy dressing gown. Kelly looked at his peaceful face and a warm, heartfelt feeling engulfed her.

"Ditz."

He stirred and then realised he was lying on her bed in a pink dressing gown. "Oh, shit, I crashed!"

"It's fine. Listen, Ditto. I have just looked out of the window and there's a blue Merc. I've got a feeling someone is following me. Do me a favour, keep an eye."

He laughed. "I'll do more than that. I'm gonna block them in. Me an' Reggie can fuck them up."

"Good, 'cos I need to go out, and I don't want anyone following me. I mean, I could be mistaken but best be careful."

After a long soak in the bath, Kelly applied her make-up, just as the beautician had instructed. She pulled on her jeans, and with her new jacket over her oyster-embroidered swing top, she was ready to go. Ditto grinned at her, as soon as she arrived in the kitchen. He had ditched the pink fluffy gown and was in his jeans and a fake designer top.

"What ya grinning at, Ditz?"

He slapped his knee and pointed out of the window, giggling like a child. "Reggie's parked so close to the blue Merc, and me in front, that the guy got out to have a go. I skipped off and Reggie …" He had to stop because he was laughing too much to speak. "He pretended he couldn't speak English. Ahh, the man thinks he can only speak French."

Kelly laughed. She had missed their comical antics.

"Where's the bloke now?"

"Stuck in the car. He can't move unless he hits our motors. And, well, they ain't like his flash tool, are they," roared Reggie, walking up behind them.

"Who is he, Bluey?" asked Ditto.

She shrugged her shoulders. "Dunno, maybe someone to do with Eddie. Anyway, he can't go anywhere, so I'll be off. See ya later."

"Ya got the phone I gave ya?" asked Reggie, looking out for her safety, as they had always done before. "Yeah," she replied.

As soon as she was gone, Ditto turned to Reggie. "If that Eddie hurts her, I'll kill him ya know!"

As Kelly skipped down the steps, she noticed the cracks were in need of repair, along with the rest of the house. With a surreptitious glance through her mirrored sunglasses, she saw that the man was still there in the blue Merc. She grinned to herself. Ditto and Reggie really had blocked him in.

King's College Hospital was a short walk from her house, so she decided to take a stroll and soak up the warm air. The main road was busy as usual with commuters. As soon as she turned off into the hospital entrance, the nerves kicked in. Her throat was dry. What if he had moved on? What if he didn't fancy her anymore? There were too many what ifs. She paused at the canteen and thought about waiting a while to get her thoughts in order and prepare for what she was going to say. The coffee counter had a queue of around ten people – a good fifteen minutes before she would be served – so she continued past into the hub of the building. The new Jubilee Wing was a far cry from the old one. The huge glass windows gave an air of sophistication. It even smelled differently. She knew where to go; he worked on the top floor on the paediatric wing, where he had secured a permanent position. The lift filled with people and Kelly swallowed hard. Anxious times, indeed. The doors opened and half the people spilled out. Kelly spotted the patient care sign and then followed the directions to Peter's department. It was quiet, as visiting time was later. As she pressed the buzzer, a nurse answered. She said she was there to see Peter and the door opened.

He had not been expecting her, but in fairness, he had said she could call on him at work at any time.

The centre desk was a hive of activity; nurses and doctors were gathered, sharing notes and doing a handover. Then she saw him, surrounded by junior doctors. For a second, she froze; maybe this was a bad idea. He looked so important and busy. He hadn't aged at all and the vision she held on to, before she would sleep, was his face. Then, as if he sensed her there, he looked up from his paperwork and stared straight at her. It was as if he didn't recognise her at first but then a huge smile spread across his face. He handed the notes to one of the juniors and headed her way. She wanted to put her arms out but this wasn't the right time or place. Instantly, he grabbed her arm and took her into a side room where there was a small kitchen used by staff. He

303

closed the door behind him and just stared, with a permanent grin on his face. Then, he cupped her face. "My gosh, Kelly, you are ... I mean, you're a ..." He was staring intensely into her eyes.

"A woman?" she replied graciously.

He nodded. "Stunning!"

"Peter, I came to say thank you, thank you for everything you did for me."

His smile faded then and he sighed heavily. "Oh, I see."

She grabbed his arm. "You kept me going in there."

He was still staring intently, wanting to kiss her lips and hold her in his arms.

"It's been three years, Peter. I know we wrote to each other, spoke every so often, but ..."

"I know, Kelly, you need time and space and ..."

"No! No, I thought maybe *you* had moved on. I mean, it was all a something and then nothing. I wasn't sure what I really meant to you. I know I was a kid but I'm not anymore." Her eyes were moist and she swallowed hard.

He said no more and held her close; running his hand gently down her cheek, he grabbed her chin and kissed her with passion. As she slowly pulled away to look at his face, he had his eyes closed. When they opened, she smiled and murmured, "Oh my God, I have waited years for us to do that!"

"Kelly, I get off soon. Please wait for me. We can go out to lunch, catch a movie, do whatever you like." He was so excited, he was almost breathless. She nodded. "Maybe we could just go back to your place, where it's quiet, and just talk, or ..." She raised her eyebrow and gently swung her hips.

"Wait in the coffee shop. I will be as quick as I can," he said, as he hurried away. Kelly stood for a few seconds; her heart was bursting with excitement. He did still want her – he hadn't moved on. She went over his expression and the way he looked at her. He no longer saw her as a child.

His apartment was nearer central London. He pulled around to the front of the hospital in his Maserati convertible. Kelly looked at it with admiration. She hopped in and he tore away. The roof was folded down and her long hair blew in the wind.

Kelly was impressed with everything about Peter: his flash car, his clothes, and now his apartment. It was sleek and sophisticated. She thought maybe it would be a tad untidy, considering he lived on his own. Her mother had always painted a dull picture of men: they were selfish, lazy, and only after one thing. So far, Peter was the opposite.

"Let me take your jacket." He was still beaming, excited to be in her company. Her new outfit outlined her very tidy figure. He couldn't help but notice her breasts had ballooned and her waist was pinched in. He was attracted to her in every way.

He was going to offer to make her a drink, but he was too captivated and wanted to kiss her again and run his hands over her sculptured body. Kelly was just as besotted with him and was drawn to his lips like a magnet. They kissed and paused. "Oh, Kelly, you are so beautiful."

She nudged her nose against his with her arms wrapped around his neck. "Peter, I missed you," she whispered. Their kissing was passionate and breathtaking. He stopped to take stock, not wanting to push her too fast.

"What's the matter?" she asked.

"Nothing, I am just so turned on. We have to think about this, so perhaps we should talk."

Kelly tilted her head. "Oh, I see." Maybe she had misread the signs. What would she know anyway? She'd never had a boyfriend; she was still a virgin for that matter.

"Come and sit with me in the kitchen. I'll make us a drink."

Kelly followed him into the room next to the lounge. It was a spacious state-of-the-art kitchen with floor-to-ceiling windows, capturing London's view at its best. The table in the centre had four bar stools placed around it. Everything was tidy; in fact, there wasn't anything on show. The acrylic cabinets, with their high-gloss finish, stretched across one wall and shone like glass. She watched as he retrieved two white cups from one of the cupboards, and when he opened one of the drawers, she noticed the cutlery neatly lined up. It was a home so different from anything she was used to. Rudy's kitchen was a mishmash of things: all different colours, shapes, and sizes, and the furniture in the lounge was much the same with nothing matching at all. And then there was her mother's home, which she remembered as being bare and old-fashioned, with cheap laminate cupboards (the ones with long metal strips as handles) and a kettle that actually went on the stove and whistled.

Peter poured the coffee from a fancy espresso machine and returned to the table. He was still smiling and it melted her heart. He may be older than her, but he was still the good-looking man she remembered in the hospital all those years ago.

Then, it hit her; she felt self-conscious and it dawned on her he was out of her league. How could she fit into this, these perfect surroundings, with everything in its place? Her heart began to sink. Although he was all she wanted, she just wasn't cut from the same cloth. The phone rang and disturbed her thoughts. "Excuse me," he said. Even that politeness was alien to her. She listened to him speaking. "Okay, sweetheart, tomorrow's fine, you just take it easy."

He turned to face Kelly. "My cleaner, she's got the flu."

She tried to console herself with the fact that the flat was so clean due to hired help – not that he had an obsessive cleaning disorder. He reached across the table and stroked her hand. "I know, when we first met, you were my patient and a teenager, so my feelings were wrong, so wrong that I tried hard to reason with myself. How could I be so fond and attracted to an eighteen-year-old? But I was and I simply could not get you out of my head. And now it's different. You are so grown up …" he laughed, "… and it's only fair that you decide if it's what you want. You were young and in need back then and now … well, now, you don't need me or anyone."

Kelly nodded, as she sipped her coffee. "Peter, I longed for your letters. They gave me a reason to go on. I read them repeatedly. I couldn't wait for the phone cards, just to hear your voice. Yes, I was needy, and you were there for me. I have never had a boyfriend, never even had sex. Yet, that doesn't mean I want to go out experimenting, I am not like that …" She paused, her mind on her to-do list. "There are some things I have to deal with first. I know you said you have waited for me, and to be honest, I don't care if you have filled your time with other women. I didn't expect any less."

She watched his eyes lower and guessed he'd had a fling with someone. "Once I have sorted out my stuff, and if you are still free, then perhaps we could date, and do it the right way."

He nodded but felt gutted. She was beautiful and he was in love. She had got it wrong. He wasn't interested in sex *per se*. It had only been a stupid, drunken one-night stand, but other than that, he was too busy working his way up the medical ladder.

He offered to give Kelly a ride home but she declined. It wasn't where she was living, which was the problem, but it would be too overwhelming for Peter to meet her family just now. Kelly left, after a long drawn-out kiss at the entrance to his block. "Please come back to me, Kelly."

Her voice trembled with emotion. "I will, I promise. I just need time to sort myself out and then we can try and make a go of it."

He kissed her again and watched her cross the road to hail a taxi. Further along, another taxi was idling at the kerb with a heavyset passenger; he was studying the young woman closely.

It was by chance that Tommy had seen her. Knowing that the black youngsters had fucked him over, he had been fortunate to follow her in a taxi and sighted her jumping into the Maserati.

When Kelly arrived home, she saw the blue Merc parked up but there was no driver. Perhaps she had been imagining the guy was some spy sent by her father.

Eddie was eagerly awaiting news from Tommy, as he was intrigued to know what Kelly would be up to. She was his daughter all right; she had an edge to her and his fascination was increasing. He had thought about Kelly, on and off over the years, but assumed she would have turned into a conceited bitch. The rumours about Maureen walking around with her nose in the air and regularly visiting the church had landed on his ears. Twelve years inside had given him time to think, and he knew he had made a big mistake with Maureen and Kelly. A four-year-old child could easily be manipulated, so, at the time, he had thought his little girl would always love him and do anything for him. His mistake was in being so narcissistic, believing he would be the one who Kelly would run to when he came home.

"What ya thinking about, Eddie?" asked Toni.

Annoyed she was prying into his thoughts, Eddie glared at her. "What the fuck is it with you? Ain't you got ya own home to go to?"

Toni felt gutted; she had only been out a year and wanted nothing more than to get in on the action with her brother, like old times. She enjoyed the wild weekends, the partying, and the ruthless means of earning money. She savoured the fact she was Eddie Cako's sister, and if anyone so much as looked at her sideways, he would leave them with a nasty mark across their face, or, worse, paralysed from the waist down. He had her back and she had his; it had always been the case. Her two older brothers had gone their own ways, leaving just her and Eddie. She had hated him having to serve time. It made her feel lost and anything she tried on her own would usually end up a failure; it was precisely why she'd found herself in stir.

All of a sudden, she felt afraid. Eddie had never asked her to leave before; he'd always kept her by his side.

"What's up, Eddie? You ain't usually so quiet. 'Ave I pissed you off or what?"

Instantaneously, Eddie was on his feet, throwing the tumbler of brandy across the room and watching it smash into thousands of pieces, as it hit the new high-end fireplace. The glass front was totally destroyed and the fragments embedded themselves in his real fur rug.

"Shut the fuck up will you! I hate fucking whining women. You're irritating me, following me everywhere. What is it with you? Shouldn't you be married by now, with kids of ya own? Go on, do one!"

Toni was shocked to the core. Eddie had a foul temper and could be unpredictable but not with her, never. She guessed it was to do with Kelly, who had probably plunged into deep waters without a life jacket. "You need to give up on ya kid of yours. She's nothing but a cocky cunt that needs a right backhander, and if I set me eyes on her, I'll fucking floor her!" No sooner had the words left her mouth, he had his hands round her throat, throwing her to the floor. She went down with a bang, hitting her head on the marble hearth. She gasped for breath, the shock having winded her. Eddie towered over her. "You stupid fucking whore, ya cunting useless! I have had you wrapped around me 'cos you had no one else, but look at you, ya can't get nothing right. I told you to keep Kelly sweet, to do only one fucking thing, and that was to find out what happened to the toy bunny. But you even messed that up!" He stepped back and flopped onto the sofa, taking a deep breath and sighing.

Toni felt a huge hole, as if someone close had just died. The bruise, now swelling from her head, was nothing compared to the sadness escalating in her heart. She had to claw her way back into his affections. He was all she knew and she could not bear to be shunned by him.

"But, Eddie, she isn't what you think she is. Trust me, she is a bitch, she has no loyalties to you, not like me. I know you thought she would be like us, but she ain't. You got me wrong, Eddie, I fucking tried, believe me, I tried, but ..." she cried, stumbling to her feet.

"Shut up and get out. She was a fucking kid. If you couldn't prise one small bit of info from a fucking child, then you ain't no fucking use to me. In fact, Toni, you are a right pain in the arse. My Kelly has more front than you, and I know if I gave her a little job to do, she would have it done."

Toni was angry and humiliated now, gutted he had turned on her and absolutely fuming he favoured his daughter, the no-good bitch from hell, and he was calling her 'my Kelly'. Until now it had always been 'my Toni'.

"I'll go, Eddie, but please remember, Kelly is trouble, and she hates you! Oh, by the way, you should never have laid your hands on me, you bastard. I won't forget that."

As Eddie looked and met her eyes, he laughed. "Good, you make sure you don't forget either, 'cos you might wanna stay away now, unless you want another one ... go on, fuck off!"

She stared for a second, waiting for him to calm down and apologise, but he didn't; he simply stared off into space. She knew then he had never really cared about her, not truly cared anyway. She didn't hate him though; she hated Kelly. Her niece had ruined her rep in prison, going against her at every opportunity. The truth was she hated Kelly because she was afraid of her. That fight had knocked her sideways and she'd never felt the same afterwards. Now, Kelly was the one who would be by his side, if Eddie had it his way. She would be the one given respect. There would be no Eddie's sister, Toni; it would be Eddie's daughter, Kelly.

As she slammed the door behind her, her eyes filled with burning tears, and a fierce anger raged in her heart. She would get that fucking bunny if it killed her and show Eddie she was his real sidekick, not cocky Kelly.

The pub down the end of the road was Eddie's local. He and Toni were well known in there. The punters liked him, he paid for the Christmas decorations, and he lent the landlord money when the rent was due. That was it about Eddie; he didn't like to shit on his own doorstep.

Toni sat heavily on the bar stool and was instantly served by Clifford the landlord.

"A double brandy, Cliff."

"No Eddie today, girl?"

"He ain't me keeper!" she replied, with spite in her eyes.

Clifford sensed the tension and wouldn't push it. He did not want to upset Eddie. He had seen his handiwork at first-hand.

He poured the drink. "On the house, love."

Without a thank you or a smile, she downed the drink and slammed the glass down for another. Clifford pulled out the bottle and placed it on the bar. "'Ere ya go, girl, help yaself." He shuffled away, leaving her to it.

As she slowly got herself pissed, a young lad in his late twenties observed her. She was hanging on to the counter and her face looked like a rat chewing a Ritz biscuit. He watched her naked leg slip off the rail along the bar. Her head bobbed up and down, as she scanned the room. Stevie was bored. He had lost his job a year ago, and now he spent his time down the pub, splashing his dole money. His girlfriend had scarpered because she was too upper class for him. There, on the stool, was a good-looking woman and easy pickings for a free fuck. He got up from the chair in the corner and swanned over to her.

"Hello, darling, it seems to me that you and I both 'ave something to drink over. 'Ere, fancy another?"

Toni looked up and through her blurred vision she saw a handsome man with striking eyes and a fit body. But what she couldn't see were the rotten teeth and greasy complexion.

"Yeah, mate, why not, mine's a double brandy," she slurred.

"Why don't me and you 'ave ourselves a right good time, a party back at mine? I got a bottle of drink!"

Toni's head was still nodding, and as she tried to get off the stool, she felt her legs go to jelly. He managed to catch her before she fell and walked with her outside the pub.

"Come on, darling, let's get you somewhere safe. Me flat's just up there."

Toni was oblivious to her surroundings and too out of it to care. She allowed the stranger to almost carry her down to his dark and gloomy basement flat, courtesy of the council. The damp concrete steps were stinking of piss. She didn't notice how scruffy it was. Once inside, he helped her onto the sofa. The carpets were rotten and had never seen the hoover and the damp mould was growing up the walls. The tap in the kitchen was constantly dripping and the basin leaked water over the floor. The property would have been condemned but the landlord was happy to continue taking the maximum rent supplied by the housing benefit. Stevie didn't care; he spent all his time in the pub or at the park. A rat scurried across the floor. Stevie threw a boot and watched it scarper away. He stared down at Toni; her mini skirt had ridden up and he made out her black lace frills peeping out and her shirt buttons bulging from her ample breasts. He acted quickly before she came to and saw the mess and smelled the stench. The two-seater sofa was not big enough for him to climb onto. He nudged her face, to see if she responded – nothing.

He then decided to turn her over and pull her legs down off the couch. She was unconscious and floppy. Now, she was on her knees, with the sofa holding her body weight. Stevie licked his lips and removed his jacket. Like a mannequin, he pulled down her knickers and positioned her legs. After he rode her skirt up, he sat back on his knees and stared. It had been a long time since he had seen that sight.

Toni stirred, grumbling, so he had no time to lose. He undid his trousers and carefully engaged himself. It had been a while since he had wet his helmet. As he entered her, she mumbled under her breath and forced herself back on him. She groaned, and as he inserted again, she was like a rabbit, moving back and forth. Stevie was surprised and began stroking her back. She was writhing in ecstasy, moaning and groaning with pleasure. He gripped her hips and maintained his momentum, watching her body thrashing up and down. Once he had shot his load, he dropped her like a sack of potatoes and jumped up. She lay there with her underwear around one ankle and her arse still in the air.

Stevie was uncomfortable now and decided the best move would be to go back to the pub and leave her here.

As the evening drew in, Toni came to. She opened her eyes and tried to focus. Her head was pounding and her mouth felt as if she had been eating talcum powder. As she tried to turn around, she realised she was laid out half-naked. She put her hands down below and felt the remains of sex. She tried to swallow hard but her mouth was so dry. Gingerly, she tidied herself up, her mind all over the place; she had no idea where she was until the dread came over her. Was she locked up in this stinking hellhole? She searched for the door and almost tripped over the mouldy pizza boxes and cans of beer. The smell was vile, as if someone had died. She panicked and grabbed at the handle, relieved that it opened instantly. The street light beamed down the stairwell. Her heart was pumping fast. She had to get away. Maybe her assailant was going to return and keep her captive? She ran up the steps and on to the street. Here, the busy commuters were on their way home from the buzz of London and incognizant to the state of Toni. She soon realised where she was; it was only a few streets away from Eddie. She would go there and tell him what had happened. Then her memory came back, slapping her in the face. Like a light bulb moment, she thought if Eddie knew she had been raped, then he would go mad, threaten to kill the man, and go arm in arm with her, ready to hunt down the rapist. They would be back to how it was before: it would be him and her versus the rest of the world.

She hurried past the rush-hour public back to Eddie's, looking a mess, out of breath, and with black make-up spread across her face and her hair in need of a brush.

After banging on the door three or four times, Eddie appeared. He looked her up and down, seeing her breathing hard.

"What the fuck do you want?"

"Eddie, Eddie, I've been raped ... I woke up in this rotten flat ... I think he was gonna lock me up ... the cunt's raped me ..."

Eddie raised his eyebrow. "Oh, yeah, who is he?"

"I dunno. I woke up in his flat, a right crappy place, with me drawers around me feet ..."

"What the fucking 'ell are you doing knocking at my door when ya went and got hammered and fucked some guy and can't even remember it? See, I told ya, you are no fucking use to me, now fuck off!"

"But, Eddie, I can take you there. I bet he's back now." She was pleading with him but the look of indifference baffled her. A few years ago, he would have burned the flat out, with the bloke in it.

"Unless ya want another clump, fuck off. You are pathetic, Toni. If you wanna get off ya fucking face, you do it, but don't you dare come

314

to me wanting me to kill some bloke 'cos you were too fucked to say no. Now, I won't tell ya again, fuck off!" He slammed the door shut, leaving Toni speechless on the doorstep. *Kelly had a lot to answer for.*

᧞*᧞

Tommy was heading back from Peckham, having finally been given sufficient room to do so, and eager to give Eddie the low-down on what he'd seen, which wasn't much really, but he'd had enough of a numb bum, sitting in a car, staring at closed doors. When he pulled up outside Eddie's house, he was annoyed because nearly all the spaces were taken in the street and his boss had three cars parked in his drive. At the end of the road, he saw a woman jump into her car, and so he waited for her to pull away. Then, he managed to ease his car into the tight gap. As soon as he banged on the door, Eddie was there, looking pissed off.

"Get in. I waited for you to call. I thought you'd fucked off."

Tommy stepped inside and waited for a nod from Eddie to be seated.

"Well, what's the kid been up to?"

Tommy had a sinking feeling. "She ain't no kid, Eddie, she's all woman, mate. She's got herself a fella. I followed him and found out he is some top doctor. Anyway, that's all, really."

Eddie slowly nodded. "And she ain't been to any banks or anywhere else? Just with this doctor, yeah?"

Like a school kid, Tommy nodded.

"You best get ya arse back over there. I wanna know where she goes. I wanna know everything. Oh, make sure she don't know you're following her, 'cos that would be stupid, now, wouldn't it?"

He suspected he had been rumbled when the two black guys blocked him in. "No, she ain't got a clue, Eddie. So, shall I go back in the morning?"

Eddie laughed. "Wait there, sunshine."

He left and went upstairs. Tommy could hear voices coming from the kitchen. Cyril had a distinctive squeaky sound and Frank had a deep rasp to his tone. Tommy felt insignificant; if he was to be a part of the firm now, then he should be in there, sitting around the table. Eddie returned with a quilt and pillow. "'Ere ya go, Tommy, ya can sleep in the car now." He placed the heavy bundle into Tommy's arms and patted him on the shoulder.

"Oh, yeah, and *phone* me, Tommy. Don't come here." He saw Tommy to the door and mumbled, "Prick," under his breath.

The summer evening was now drawing to a close. Kelly had finished her dinner, along with a couple of rums, and was enjoying the banter with the boys. Rudy was sitting in his grandad chair half-asleep and Legend lay across Kelly's lap.

"So, Bluey, are we on for tomorrow? I got samples coming first thing and they are supposed to be the mustard. The latest Chanel and Coach bags are proper good gear," said Phoenix, eager to get back to business.

"Of course. Someone needs to get back in with the Indians. I mean, you three just don't have the tits for it."

Phoenix looked down embarrassed but Ditto and Reggie were rolling around laughing; they only saw Bluey as one of them. But Phoenix was attracted and found it more difficult to be the same as he was before. Kelly had changed into one stunning lady.

She eased Legend off her lap and went to fetch his lead. "Come on, boy, let's have a walk."

Legend wagged his tail and sat, awaiting the lead to be attached. She pulled open the door, and there, just down the road, was the blue Mercedes. *Sod this, it's time to identify the owner*, she thought. Legend didn't pull but happily walked alongside her. Approaching the car, she noticed the driver had nodded off; he was squashed up in the front seat, his head leaning on a pillow. She stood watching him for a while before she decided to tap on the window. Tommy almost jumped high enough to hit his head on the roof lining. Blinking a few times, he tried to focus. Kelly laughed sarcastically.

Tommy felt awkward now. What should he do? He couldn't just ignore her, so he lowered the window. "Yes, what do you want?"

"Nah, mate, more like, what the hell do *you* want?"

Legend was growling and lifting his top lip, showing his teeth.

"Look, love, I don't know who you are."

Kelly laughed. "Okay, just tell Eddie that if he wants to know what I am up to, then he should be man enough to knock on my door and ask."

Tommy couldn't hide the shock and fear creeping over his face. "I, err ..."

Straightaway, she knew. "Don't give me any ol' fanny. I am one step ahead of you and that numbnuts father of mine. Jesus, you lot are pathetic."

Surprised by her words, he responded without thinking. "He ain't ..." he stopped dead in mid-sentence. He knew he had blown it. How the hell was he going to tell Eddie?

"In fact, I think I'll call him meself and let him know what I think of his spy holed up outside my house."

With a red face, Tommy was shitting himself. That would be curtains for him. He would be the next one to be thrown to the pigs or in the Thames. "Wait, no don't do that!"

Kelly sensed the panic in his voice and read the dread in his eyes. "Tell me what he wants and I won't call him. I hate the dickhead. There, just so you know."

With a genuine look of puzzlement, he replied. "I honestly dunno, love. He just asked me to keep an eye on your every move. Look, if he knows I have been sussed, he will have me shot, believe me. Listen, love, I don't know you, and you seem like a nice woman, but your dad is ..."

"Yeah, I know, one dangerous fucker. Well, he don't frighten me. In fact, I would love him to come knocking, 'cos I would shoot him meself and do time over it."

Tommy straightened himself up and opened the door. Kelly pulled Legend back before he went for him.

He pulled out a packet of fags and lit one up. "Want one?"

Kelly shook her head. "Known me father long, 'ave ya?"

Tommy didn't care anymore; he had been living on his nerves for three years. The constant death threats, if he didn't do what Eddie asked, were getting him down. He either wanted to be free or dead. "I've known Eddie for years now. Everyone in my world knows him. But, listen to me, if he even suspected that I have spoken with you, seriously, he will kill me. I know nothing about you and I am trusting you literally with me own life."

"I ain't me ol' man. I hate him, for what he stands for, and I can assure you I am a woman of my word. So, tell me, what does he want from me, really? I have nothing." She pointed to the house. "All I have is a room in that house. I don't even own a car."

Tommy shook his head; he sounded so deflated. "Kelly, can I call you Kelly?" She nodded. "If you have something he wanted and it was of value, then he wouldn't tell anyone. He is a distrusting man. Whatever it is you have, we would never know. Not even his sister would know."

"That old trollop! I really detest her."

Tommy laughed. "Be careful of her too, Kelly. She is a nasty piece of work."

"I ain't scared of that bitch and she knows it. She still has the scar across her nose, when I beat the crap out of her."

"It's not how hard she is, it's the shit she stirs."

"Hey, it's late. Do you want a hot drink or something to eat? I think we need to talk," suggested Kelly, with a comforting smile on her face.

He shook his head. "I think I have said too much already." He lit up another fag and Kelly noticed his hands were shaking.

"I won't ask your name, but trust me when I say I won't grass you up. I just have to know a few things. What's Eddie's address? And Toni's?"

After Tommy looked up and down the road, he leaned forward. "Kelly, I am warning you, if you know what he wants, give it to him. He will torture you to get it. Don't go to his house. He is never alone and God knows what he would do to you."

"What makes you so sure I have something he wants?"

"I know Eddie, and something is distracting him, and for Christ's sake, he has me following you, noting your every move. He would only do that if you have something he wants, unless of course …" he paused as though he was thinking, "… unless it's information you have. He wanted to know if you have been to the bank."

Kelly laughed. "What! I don't even have a bank account. Maybe he is trying to be the doting parent, looking out for me," she suggested sarcastically.

She watched as Tommy shook his head. "I am afraid there is only one person Eddie loves and that's himself."

"Yep, you got that right. So, look, you can watch me. I won't say a word. I don't think there's much to report back, though."

"Your boyfriend. He knows about him."

Kelly's face changed and the look of anger in her eyes moved Tommy.

"You tell Eddie I have been meeting another fella, a big black man. I met him tonight and had dinner in the Italian, and tomorrow, you'll see me in the park with him, and then tell him you saw me fucking him in the back of a car, but make sure he knows nothing about the doctor."

With a sad smile, Tommy nodded. "Yeah, all right, kiddo, I will. One day, I'll end up shot in a ditch somewhere because of him, but maybe I will get to save someone else, eh?"

"Take my number, save under another name, but call me if you know anything. Please!" she asked, and Tommy instantly pulled out his phone and tapped in her number.

He got back in the car and watched as Kelly walked away. She didn't deserve a father like Eddie, and he didn't deserve all the shit he was getting. In his own way, he was getting revenge. He was going to die anyway, wasn't he?

As soon as she was back inside, the boys were on to her. "What did he say? We were watching him, making sure everything was okay."

Kelly laughed. "His wife has kicked him out and he has to sleep in the car. I got him wrong, poor bloke."

CHAPTER EIGHTEEN

Three days later

Tired of looking at the four blank walls of her flat in North London, Toni was pacing the floor. She would rather have been inside with her prison mates than all alone with no one to talk to. She missed her brother and hated Kelly, in equal proportions. Finding the toy bunny would enable her to be back in Eddie's good books. It had been as important as Kelly's right arm as a child, never leaving her side. Remembering when she had taken it from her, Kelly had almost clawed her aunt's face to get it back. Toni never bothered again.

She knew where Kelly lived; she had seen the address on the letter. If Kelly still had the bunny, then it would be in that house. She would have to get inside and search; it was the only way. Without a decent plan in place, she left her flat and drove over to Peckham. She found the house quickly and parked up the street but still in view of the front door. It was mid-morning and the mad rush hour had died down. She stared intently, only for a short while, and then the door opened and out walked a black woman, with purple hair, followed by a tall Jamaican with long dreadlocks and a lively spring in his step. He opened the car door for the woman and then jumped into the driver's side. No sooner had they gone when the door opened again; Kelly was there with four men, and they were helping her carry boxes to a van and loading the back. Three got into the van, and Kelly, with the fourth man, climbed into a car. That was it; if she remembered rightly, that was all the occupants. Now she had to find a way in. She assumed the front room, which had a partially opened sash window with the pink curtains and new nets, was her niece's. She must have left her bedroom light on. Without giving any further thought to her objective, she stepped out of her car and hurried along the road, looking around, ensuring no one was watching. At that time of day, most people were at work. She knocked on the door, first to make sure no one was in, and then she leaned across the side of the steps and used her long arms to push up the broken sash frame. A last look about. No one was in the street. She had carried out many break-ins in her time and this was too easy. Almost diving in through the window, she slithered like a snake, landing on the floor, before jumping to her feet, and surveying the room. Little did she know that someone was eyeballing her every move.

She guessed the bedroom was Kelly's. It was basic and spotlessly clean – with minimal furniture. There, on the cabinet, was a brush and comb, a few bits of make-up, and odd fake pieces of jewellery. The bed was made and neatly turned down. She had no time to waste. After opening the top drawer, she found prison letters, a few coins, and more cosmetics, including perfume and nail clippers. There was no evidence of any bunny.

Tommy was sitting upright, watching the house; he looked at his phone and quickly dialled the number. Kelly was stuck at the end of the street, behind cars waiting to edge out onto the main road, when her phone buzzed. "Hello?"

"Kelly, it's me, your daily stalker. Ya need to go back home. Toni has just climbed through your window." Pleased with himself, he stared at the house to watch for her to reappear.

Ditto didn't have enough room to turn around in the street, so he reversed up, stopping just before the house. Kelly dashed out of the car, ran up the steps, and entered the house.

Toni froze. Decisions – her only hope was that whoever had just returned to the house would leave again shortly without discovering her. Getting out of the house without what she had come for was pointless.

Kelly was ready, with a knife down the back of her jeans. She thought it safer to carry one, since Eddie was so dead set on something and she was now at risk. Legend was lazing in the lounge and didn't hear Toni in the bedroom, but he heard Kelly and was always ready to greet her. He jumped off the sofa, trotted down the hallway, and leapt up. But Kelly was onto him, getting him to calm down, without saying a word.

She opened her bedroom door — *where is the bitch?* — to find no-one. Then she laughed out loud: there, hiding under the bed was her aunt. She did look a prat!

"Seize, Legend, seize!" she commanded. Legend jumped on the bed and began sniffing and growling. Then, in a flash, he jumped off and crouched down, trying to get at whatever was underneath.

"Here, boy!" she said firmly. "Get out, before I set my dog on ya!"

Toni was trembling; she hated dogs and all she could see was the animal's huge head and teeth. She shuffled from her position and backed herself up to the wall. Kelly laughed once more at her aunt. Toni, however, looked totally dishevelled and very embarrassed.

"What are you doing here in me room?"

Toni was wide-eyed and stared at Legend. He was going crazy, lifting his lip and snarling.

"I said, what are you doing in me room?"

Toni was immobilized with fear, unable to speak, or take her eyes off the dog.

"Legend, sit!" instructed Kelly. "Well?" glared Kelly.

Relieved that the dog was not going to pounce on her, but still wary, Toni said, "I have come for something that you have and me brother wants."

Kelly stood with her hands on her hips, looking Toni up and down. "What would that be then, Tone?"

"You know what it is," replied her aunt, who was now wound up firstly for being caught and secondly for being interrogated by Kelly.

"Actually, Toni, I have no idea, but whatever it is, it must be important. Only ya brother's turned me bedroom over once already, and now you, ya sly scumbag, are doing the same." She took a step closer and watched as Toni recoiled.

"What's up, Tone, scared of something?"

Toni was really livid now: this was such a piss take, by her niece of all people. "You think you're something special, but you ain't. You're nothing without Eddie, nothing."

Stepping closer still, Kelly sarcastically said, "Oh, is that so? Well, Toni, tell me what it is that me father wants and ya never know. If I have it, you can take it, because I want nothing to do with you or your brother!" At that moment, Kelly jumped over the bed and was toe to toe with Toni, with a knife to her throat. Toni swallowed hard but kept eye contact.

"So, spit it out, Toni. What the fuck is it you want?"

Toni could feel Kelly's breath on her face and the cold blade against her neck.

"The bunny," she croaked.

Kelly removed the blade and stepped back. "What? That dirty old comfort toy, I carried around?"

Toni nodded.

Kelly walked around the bed and opened the bottom drawer. "What this?" she questioned, holding up the grey and worn-out beanbag toy.

Toni's eyes lit up but nervously she glanced from the bunny to Kelly.

"Catch," laughed Kelly, as she threw the toy to her aunt.

With a deft movement, Toni caught the bunny in mid-air. It was heavier than it looked; the tiny grains of rice weighed it down.

"Ya got what ya came for, now piss off. If you ever come near here again, I will slit ya throat and let me dog eat ya." She stepped aside, leaving room for Toni to leave. Toni needed no further encouragement.

As Kelly watched her aunt run up the road, she smiled. She then looked over at Tommy and put her thumb up.

Tommy watched the expression on Toni's face; it was full of anxiety and panic. He then looked back at Kelly and observed the cool, calm expression. She was telling him the truth; she really wasn't afraid of Toni. Tommy took comfort in being on Kelly's side; she wasn't some daft kid, she was bright and fearless, and – no question – a match for Eddie's bitch of a sister.

Ditto was standing at the bottom of the steps, waiting and listening, knowing full well that Bluey was in control. He had heard her harsh voice and was surprised because it didn't sound like her at all. Then he too observed the frightened look on the woman's face, as she fled the house, and the smug expression on Bluey's. A strange feeling gripped his stomach: Bluey was not the same kid who went to prison. She was assured and intense, as if nothing could faze her. He wondered about her past. *Was she really an innocent woman, or was she just a good actress?* They walked back to the car in silence, with Ditto having a lot to think about.

Casually, she asked, "What's up, Ditz?"

"Nothing, but I think you need to be careful. Your father is a serious gangster," replied Ditto, in a resigned tone.

"Sorry you had to hear that, only she is a nasty piece of work. She could have asked for the toy. I would have given it to her. There was no need to break into my bedroom and go rooting around. I spent time inside with her and watched her bully her way through the system. I hate her, and I certainly hate Eddie poxy Raven."

Ditto decided that Bluey was acting that way because she had been browbeaten by Toni and had probably taken all she could. He still couldn't get her voice out of his head though – she sounded like a totally different person, very switched on and calculating, and it sent chills up his spine.

Commercial Road seemed busier than Kelly remembered. Hasan, the main buyer, was just the same and eager to do business as usual. He held his arms out when he saw Kelly. "Ahh, look at you! Living in Spain has done you good. You look well."

Kelly hugged him and winked at Ditto.

"So, what do you have for me?" Hasan asked, eager to do business. He had made a fortune when Kelly was around and they had built up a good working relationship. But his money had seriously dropped when he'd heard she went off to Spain.

Reggie and Phoenix unloaded the boxes and carefully removed the tissue-covered bags. Kelly removed the outer covering and held up an elegant white Channel clutch bag edged in gold, a stunning piece. "These are in Selfridges at £900. There is no difference. Look, see, the chain clasp has the Chanel logo indented. Perfect copies. There are others floating about but check them yourself. They don't have the stamps in the right place."

Hasan opened the bag and scrutinised the product. "It's good, and these are the latest design?"

Kelly nodded. "These are the summer line, and over there are the winter ones, not even on the shelf yet. But look in *Vogue*. They are there ready for the October changeover." Phoenix opened the next box and she smiled. "Take a look at these beauties."

Hasan was excited, like a child at Christmas. "It's good to have you back in business. I will take the lot."

Kelly laughed, "On a sale-or-return basis?"

Hasan shook his head. "No point; everything you supplied before flew off the shelf."

Reggie unloaded the boxes, whilst Kelly collected the money. They contained their excitement until they were out of sight. Then, they all high-fived each other.

"Ditz, I am going to pop over to Selfridges and have a good look. We need to up our game. He wanted everything we had, and I think he is selling them on, which is fine by me. We make our money, and really, he is taking the risk."

Ditto was nodding. "Cor, Blue, we are going to clean up."

She laughed and high-fived him again. Then she looked at the tatty van.

"Ditz, I think our first investment is a new van. That one will get us pulled by the filth. We don't want to take any chances, not now we are going to make a mint."

Ditto agreed, and that afternoon he went with Reggie to check out the van showroom, leaving Kelly to go off alone.

Hatton Garden, the home to the invention of the machine gun, is the focal point for London's jewellery trade. Kelly had made an appointment with a man called Phillip Armstrong at Hammonds, a rare gem specialist.

She arrived outside and pressed the buzzer. The shop front was unusual: there was just one section of glass, perhaps a foot high, which displayed a few pieces of jewellery; otherwise, everything behind the window was hidden from view by a black velvet screen.

The door was opened by a security guard who reminded her of Frank Bruno.

"Hi, I have an appointment with Mr Armstrong," she smiled.

The guard looked her over. "Your name, Madam, please?"

"Toni Raven," she replied.

The guard led her up a flight of stairs to a short corridor with four doors on either side. Kelly was impressed with the appearance, all glass and chrome, with not a speck of dust. As the door opened, she stepped inside to be greeted by a young man, in his late twenties, dressed in a royal blue twill business suit and a bow tie. His hair was long and tied back in a ponytail. Kelly grinned; he wasn't what she had expected, not after hearing his posh voice on the phone.

"Come in, Miss Raven, please take a seat."

Kelly gracefully sat in the armchair and surveyed her surroundings. They exuded class and self-consciously she felt scruffy in her jeans and jacket. Perhaps she should have worn her Chanel suit or her black dress after all.

Phillip didn't seem bothered at all: he was eager to see the gem.

"So, this blue gem you have. You said it's been passed down through the family?"

Kelly nodded. "Yes, I believe it's Persian. It has been in my family for generations since before Persia changed its name to Iran."

Phillip had no reason to doubt her; she obviously had some foreign blood in her, judging by her olive skin.

"So, do you have it with you?"

Kelly pulled from her pocket a small suede pouch and handed it to him. She watched his whole face light up, as he removed the gem from the pouch and held it up to the light. He turned it over and then switched on the desk lamp and surveyed it again.

Turning towards Kelly, he looked up, seeing her in a different light from when she entered his office five minutes ago. Nevertheless, there was still something somewhat incongruous about discussing serious business in a room holding gems having a collective value well north of £50 million with such a very casually dressed young woman.

Was she the genuine article? "I need to run this through some tests, but it looks authentic."

"Okay, how long does that take?"

Phillip stood up. "It will probably take our gemologist up to an hour. I'll get it done right now. In the meantime, would you like some refreshments while you wait?"

"That would be great, thank you."

"I have to say, Miss Raven, I am very excited. It's been a while since I held a blue diamond and never one this size and cut." Kelly could see he was trying to be cool but was overcome with elation.

As she waited patiently in the office, she checked her iPhone for messages, but there weren't any. Gazing across the room, she was impressed by the evenly placed gold-framed pictures which showed gems magnified many times so the customers could appreciate the intricacies of the stones.

The authenticity and valuation checks took slightly less time than Phillip anticipated. The relieved and excited young man was back with a huge smile on his face.

"Well, Miss Raven, it is certainly authentic and a real exquisite piece. Now, I am assuming you want to know its value?"

Kelly leaned forward. "Mr Armstrong, I am afraid I do not have children and I won't be able to have them. I cannot pass this on, so I have decided to sell it."

Phillip's eyes widened and his chest pillowed. "Really? Do you have any idea how much it's worth?"

Kelly nodded. "I believe I do, but I am sure you are going to tell me anyway."

"Oh yes, quite, quite ... well, taking into account the 4Cs, colour, clarity, cut, and carat, the current value is £1.25 million."

Kelly remained composed although inside her heart was pounding.

"I have a buyer, if you are serious about selling it," he informed her, clasping his hands in front of him.

Kelly paused for a second. "Who?"

"Well, we don't give out that information. However, in this instance, I can tell you. It's me. I have wanted a blue diamond for my father's collection for years and this one is ideal, so I will offer you £1 million."

With a casual nod, she agreed. "I will accept your offer, if it's in cash."

Phillip gasped. "Cash? But do you know how much that is? I mean, I can give you cash, of course, but it's a lot of money to carry around. Are you sure? I can easily transfer it into your bank account."

Kelly shook her head. "No, the tax man will swallow that up."

Phillip nodded, so eager to get his hands on the gem. He knew it was easily worth £1.5 million. He could make a huge profit, with a buyer already lined up.

"Okay, not a problem. I will get it for you. Give me a few minutes."

Kelly smiled, trying to contain her excitement. An hour later, she was still waiting.

Eventually, he returned with the guard, who stood impassively at the back of the room. The notes were neatly stacked in a massive case, which was a cross between a brief case and a suitcase. Kelly's eyes nearly popped out from the shock.

"Shall we count them?"

Kelly shook her head but reached in, pulling out a wad of fifties. Flicking through, she nodded. "I'm happy."

Hastily, Phillip pulled from the drawer a form, before she had a chance to change her mind. "I need you to fill out the details. I can then send a bill of sale in the post."

Kelly looked at the declaration and began entering what was required. She gave Toni's name and Eddie's address. Scribbling an illegible signature, she passed the form back to Phillip.

Eager to get this over with quickly, as he had a buyer to call, there was one remaining formality. "Oh yes, did you bring any paperwork pertaining to the gem? Also, I need some ID."

Kelly stood and searched her pockets. "Oh, damn, I have left my passport back at home, and when the gem was passed down to me, there was no accompanying paperwork."

Too excited to care, he decided to waive the obligation. "Never mind. Gus, here, will see you into a taxi, unless you have a car?"

Holding the overlarge briefcase, she left the office and stepped into a black cab. "Primark in Oxford Street, please."

The driver looked her over and frowned. "Primark, Miss?"

"Yes, I need some bits and pieces."

He looked at the case. "You might look out of place," he laughed.

"Oh, yeah, it's me dad's old paperwork he left behind when he retired. He sent me on a mission, just 'cos I said I was going to London."

The driver smiled and drove smoothly away into the busy traffic, heading for Oxford Street.

Arriving at Primark, Kelly wasted no time grabbing some large items of clothing. She filled two big bags and handed these to the shop assistant, who carried them over to the cash desk. But there was a problem. She couldn't carry everything, and she needed the ladies' room urgently. The middle-aged woman at the desk could see her predicament. "We don't have customer facilities, but Robyn, here, will take you to the staff toilets, on this occasion." It was a lifesaver. She had never envisaged, when leaving Hammonds, that £1 million in £50 notes would involve such a large case, and the problem was compounded with the extra items she had needed to purchase at this store. Robyn carried all the shopping bags to the restrooms and left her to it. Once inside the stall, Kelly got to work. She took out most of the bought items and left them in situ. No doubt, they would be of use to someone. Then, she carefully emptied all the notes from the oversized brief case, placed them in the two Primark bags, and covered them with some of the items of clothing. The expensive leather case was left in the stall; it would be a great eBay item for a cash-strapped shop assistant. She just hoped she wasn't singled out for one of the company's random security checks on her way out of the store. How was she going to explain all of this cash? *Christ, this has been hard work,* she thought.

She struck lucky leaving the store, as no one gave her the time of day. But what she was carrying nearly sent her into a cold sweat. She had come a long way, since leaving Downview Prison.

She hailed a London taxi cab and went straight home. The blue Merc was still there. She took her time to pay the driver and pretended to struggle with the shopping bags, as she walked up the steps to the house.

Out of the corner of her eye, she noticed Tommy was taking her picture. She smiled to herself. Eddie had evidently asked him to up his game – now he wanted photos.

Once she was inside her bedroom, she lifted the loose floorboard, stacked the money, and covered it back over with the carpet. Sitting heavily on the bed, she gave some thought to her present situation. She could help those who had helped her.

Then her thoughts turned to Toni and Eddie – stupid mugs. As if she wouldn't know what was in her favourite toy. It may well have been her comforter, but, as the years crept by, the worn-out toy felt odd, as the texture had changed. She had been thirteen at the time of discovering the comforter's contents, but it was old enough to know that the hidden gem was possibly of value and would one day see her okay.

When she had left prison, she needed reassurance that the gem in the comforter was still there, just as she had seen it for the first time all those years ago. And it was, exactly as she remembered it. Her little find in Selfridges – the blue Swarovski crystal – turned out to be almost identical and a perfect swap. Once she had switched the gem and the crystal over, she had restitched the back and then rubbed a teabag over it, ageing the cotton, to hide the fact it had been tampered with.

The heads-up from Rudy that Eddie had been searching around her room had been enough warning to get the gem quickly replaced with the crystal. She wondered how long it would take Eddie to realise the 'gem' was a fake. Then she contemplated Toni's gain in all of this. If Tommy was right, then Toni had some kind of fixation on Eddie. Perhaps being his sister, she felt her reputation would only be enhanced. Whatever it was, Kelly hated the pair of them. When the bill of sale arrived at Eddie's, and he saw the name on it, would he really think Toni had double-crossed him? Kelly didn't care either way. She had the money, and they could fight it out between them.

The smell of Lippy's cooking made Kelly realise she was hungry. Before popping in to the kitchen, she peeped out of the window and saw the man in the blue Merc dozing with his head against the pillow.

Lippy was stirring a huge pot with some kind of stew bubbling away. "Ahh, me Bluey chil', dinner's ready. The rice is in the pot there. You help yaself. I need to lie down. Me head's hurting."

Kelly rubbed her back. "Are ya all right, Lippy? Do you want some tablets?"

"Me getting old, is all it is."

Kelly retrieved one of the big bowls from the cabinet and smiled at the oddly assorted stack of plates. It warmed her heart. She used the oversized ladle to scoop the steaming rice into the bowl and then covered it with the mouth-watering stew. She pulled a spoon from the drawer, grabbed some kitchen roll, and headed out of the front door. Tommy was half-asleep when she tapped on the window, but he soon perked up when he noticed the piping hot offerings. He lowered the window. "Hey, Kelly, what's this?"

She winked. "The best food you're ever likely to eat this side of the Thames."

He reached out and took the bowl. "Cor, smells good."

"Any news?"

"Well, Eddie wants photos now, the sick muvver fucker." He was relieved he could speak freely.

"Thanks, mate, for the heads-up on Toni, the sly bitch, eh?"

Tommy nodded. "Yeah, I won't tell Eddie I saw her, 'cos I was too busy following you around Primark," he laughed.

"Yeah, that's right. I must have spent all day shopping."

"No worries, Kelly. Thanks for this. I'm starving."

With that, she left and returned to the kitchen to fill her own ravenous belly.

CHAPTER NINETEEN

Toni was on a high. Her brother would be pleased she had the bunny, she would be back on the firm, and everything would return to normal. Hopefully, he would get his daughter out of his head. There was no room for her anyway. She was the only woman they needed, not some mouthy kid. The traffic was hectic crossing London. Her new Mini, courtesy of Eddie, was nippy, but it still didn't gain any time in the busy streets of London. She stopped at the traffic lights and gazed down at the manky old toy sitting upright on the seat next to her. The lights turned green and the car behind beeped its horn, but Toni couldn't move, as if she had been hit with a brick. The car hooted again, forcing her to return to reality. That awful feeling of guilt grabbed her – only momentarily, but it was still a bolt out of the blue. The bunny stirred visions of the past, disturbing images she had chosen to block out for twenty-one years. She pulled over to the side of the road and rested her head on the steering wheel. Her heart was working overtime, and her blood was like a torrent of hot needles, whirling around her body. The hairs on the back of her neck stood on end and she unexpectedly had the urge to vomit. She opened her car door and threw up on the road. A car full of teenagers hollered at her, "Pisshead."

She heaved again, and then, when the contents of her stomach were empty, she closed the door and sat shaking, trying to get her breath. Eddie's house was at the end of the road and just visible where she had pulled over. She stared for a while, wondering what it was that made her go running whenever he called and do whatever he asked, even the unthinkable. What exactly had she missed in the years he was locked away? Was it the parties, the thrills, the violence, or being part of a gangster's firm perhaps? Her heart was beating fast again, and a dark feeling of dread washed over her. She must have thought she was nothing without him, afraid of being left behind alone. Was that what had pushed her to do the most disgusting things he'd demanded? Every bad act was praised by him; it was a mark of honour in front of the firm. Eddie's boasts that she was harder than any of them had spurred her on. But her flat, the car, and the clothes, all bought for her, really just meant he owned her.

Then there was Kelly; she was sick with jealousy when Eddie had called her 'my Kelly'. She wanted the admiration, not anyone else. *She* was his only family, and they stuck together through thick and thin. That's how she had perceived it, yet maybe it wasn't that way at all. Perhaps she had stuck to him like glue, and really, he had just used her. Even her marriage to Patrick was set up by Eddie for his own gains. As the getaway driver for all his robberies, she didn't even get a cut; it all went to her brother, although she had been content with the pat on the back and the glory. He had the three huge houses, the cars, the pubs, and the nightclub. What did she have? A small flat and a Mini were hardly worthwhile rewards. She looked at the grand house, which stood out from the rest in the street, and noticed his car in the drive along with his sidekicks' motors – his heavies.

Unexpectedly, she had an urge to drive at full speed and ram her Mini into the front of his posh pad. She cackled in a high-pitched voice – that would make a statement. Her nerves got the better of her though. She wasn't that hard; in fact, she wasn't strong at all. Maybe she'd been without fear in the atrocities she'd committed. But tough? Probably not. However, Kelly was, she knew that. Kelly was the one who had been through a rough time and had the scars to prove it. She was the only person who wasn't afraid of the Ravens. She looked at the bunny again and then it dawned on her; she had been so intent on getting the damned thing, that she'd never even asked what was so special about it. But Eddie was obviously obsessed with the toy. Why? She decided to pick it up and then turn it around, but all she could see was the stained and worn fabric brought about by years of comfort.

It was all Kelly had for contentment and now she'd ripped it from her. Her throat was so tight with grief that she felt as though she was being strangled. She wasn't used to crying; if she was upset, she would down a bottle of brandy or smoke a joint. But she didn't want either of those: the tears had to flow to release the pain and the pent-up guilt.

After an hour or so, she stopped blubbering and tried to pull herself together. Her eyes were swollen and stinging. She lit up a cigarette and watched as the traffic was slowing down, now the evening rush hour was under way. She must have sat there for hours. After she started the car, she realised her legs were numb from not moving. The lights in Eddie's house all popped on, presumably on a timer. She drove past his property and headed for her own. There was no point in going to him — the excitement of having the bunny in her hands had receded. The realisation of what that bunny represented had hit her hard. The only way to cope was by taking some sleeping tablets, and maybe then, she would be free of the sickening thoughts.

But her state of mind was making her ill again: her head was hot and she felt herself beginning to vomit. She opened the door, but as hard as she heaved, nothing would come up. Those ghastly images again plagued her mind, sending her on an intense trip to when she was that impetuous, egotistic person. All those years ago, she'd never even given the evil reality a second thought. But now it was screaming in her face. If only Naomi had agreed to let Eddie adopt the baby. She'd already moved into his basement flat, one of his old dwellings, believing that he would leave his wife and play happy families with her, but she couldn't have been more wrong. Eddie had no intention of leaving his wife and all his worldly goods behind — at least not until he could transfer everything they shared, bit by bit, into his name. Naomi saying no to Eddie was a red rag to a bull.

The plan had been devised by Eddie and left for her to execute. Without a second thought, she had dived in, agreeing to his sick idea, with no conscience of the vile and hideous crime she was about to commit. She'd just wanted to please Eddie and be his number one. At that time, she would have done whatever it took to maintain that position.

Her mouth filled with water and her stomach ached from retching. That vision was there haunting her, taking her back to the past, to Eddie's flat twenty-one years ago. There she was with Naomi.

She put the overdose of sleeping tablets in the hot chocolate, while Naomi was sitting on the sofa, chatting away about the baby clothes. The kitchen was open-plan and faced the lounge. Naomi, oblivious to what was going on, couldn't see what she was doing. Naomi drank the chocolate and within ten minutes she was unconscious. Feeling as though she was being programmed like a robot, she dragged Naomi's heavy body to the kitchen, the floor covered in plastic sheets, and there, by gripping her smooth neck, she committed an unforgiveable sin – the strangulation of a once beautiful young woman. But, unexpectedly, Naomi's eyes opened and she could see them fill with terror, as the unspoken words begged her to stop. But she didn't – she needed to kill her and do so quickly. The pressure it took to squeeze the life out of Naomi left her out of breath, but she did it and felt relief as Naomi's body went limp and her eyes rolled to the back of her head. She knew she had little time to get the baby out. With all that blood and her panicking because she didn't have a clue what the hell she was doing, she realised time was against her. The baby needed to come out alive. The kitchen carving knife was not really sharp enough to make a clean cut, but despite this, she sliced at the flesh, sweating and shaking, to remove the newborn before it died. Layers of flesh lay open before she saw the tiny body. Without gloves, she plunged her hands into the warm, slimy, sticky flesh and eased it out. Her heart, now like a pneumatic drill, she prayed the baby wasn't dead. Eddie would go insane, if she failed. Then, with palpable relief, she saw the little thing scream. She clamped the cord with a peg and washed her in the kitchen sink. Still on the sofa were bags of baby clothes bought for the new arrival. She held the baby now dressed in her new clothes and clutched the bunny that Naomi had bought. She couldn't turn and face the dead woman. The sight was too gruesome, and yet she inflicted it. She killed Naomi, that pretty teenager with a sweet smile and a belly full of arms and legs.

Kelly waited for Rudy to arrive home, concerned about Lippy, who hadn't been the same. The life looked drained from her eyes. Initially, when she'd first come out of prison, she thought that none of them had aged, but now, looking closely, she could see Lippy was tired and her face was drawn. She made a cup of camomile tea, popped two tablets on the saucer, and carefully climbed the stairs, not wanting to spill it. Lippy was lying on her back, just staring at the ceiling. Kelly nudged the door open, noticing how untidy Lippy's bedroom was. It wasn't like her at all. She gently placed the cup of tea on the bedside cabinet and eased herself on the bed.

"Oh, me darling, thank you," stuttered Lippy, through a faint whisper.

"It's camomile tea and I thought you might want some tablets."

Lippy patted Kelly's hand. "Ahh, chil', you is a good girl."

"What's wrong, Lippy?"

"Me just have a touch of the flu."

Kelly didn't buy it at all and without another word got off the bed. A pile of washing was left in the corner of the room and dust had gathered on the sides. When Kelly looked closely at the bed sheets, she noticed they were grubby.

"I'm gonna do some washing. I'll chuck these in, shall I?" She held up a bundle of Lippy's clothes.

Lippy could hardly move; she just nodded and closed her eyes. Eager to help, Kelly went and retrieved a wash basket from the bathroom and went around Lippy's bedroom, picking up all the clothes strewn everywhere. She then realised that the floor hadn't been vacuumed. She ran down the stairs and sorted the washing into piles. Some of the tops had terrible stains on where Lippy had been sick. She threw them in the washer-dryer, added Dettol, and then washed her hands. This wasn't right at all. Lippy was too proud to leave such a mess in her room. Then it dawned on her that if Lippy was too poorly to do all the housework, it would be her room she would leave until last to clean. A lump wedged in her throat. She dragged the vacuum cleaner up the stairs and into Lippy's bedroom.

"Lippy, are you awake? I was gonna vacuum around!" There was silence: Lippy was snoring gently. Kelly switched the machine on and waited to see if it woke Lippy up. As she got to work cleaning the floor, she took hold of a bottle that rolled from under the bed. It was a bottle of sleeping tablets. This was awful – Lippy taking tablets to sleep and her room in such a stinking mess. Within an hour, Kelly had the floors vacuumed, the flat surfaces dusted, and the windows open to remove the stale, musky smell. Lippy remained out of it. Kelly returned to their makeshift utility room just past the kitchen and emptied the first load from the washer-dryer, carefully folding the clothes and stacking them neatly, before she put the next load in. She held the warm pile close to her face and smelled the fresh scent of linen. Just as she was about to go back up to the room, Rudy appeared. He looked drained.

"Hey, Rudy, I need to talk to you about Lippy."

With a sad, resigned expression on his face, he replied, "She's not well, Bluey."

Kelly inclined her head. "How sick is she, Rude?"

"Very sick. I didn't want to tell you, not just yet."

The one woman she loved apart from her aunt Bet was Lippy. She felt sick and cradled the warm bundle of clothes, as if she were hugging Lippy herself.

Rudy shook his head, his usual animated self now gone. He walked slowly to the kitchen and sat heavily with his head drooped. Kelly followed.

"It breaks my heart, Blue, she is so ill, and there's nothing I can do. I can't even fucking help her to go back to Jamaica, to be with her sisters."

Kelly could tell he was gripped by grief.

"Why not?"

He took a deep breath. "Bluey, she is wanted by the police for killing her husband. She is stuck here."

"No way. Can't we get her a passport, a fake one?" she urged.

Rudy rubbed his face. "If it was that easy, I would have done it by now. It's different these days. They are chipped and all sorts."

Then an idea came to her and she placed the clothes on the table. "I have to go out, Rudy. I'll be back."

It was late, so she wrapped her jacket around her shoulders and skipped down the steps. Peter could help; he could have her looked at. If expensive treatment were needed, she would pay for it. She walked towards the main road to hail a taxi. Quickening her pace, thoughts of Peter flooded her mind – he was a good guy. So how would he deal with a dying woman on the run from the police? Although his brother may have got into trouble, he was a top doctor going places, not a criminal. He didn't belong in her world.

With a resigned change of heart, she stopped at the crossroads, turned right, and hoped that Keffa was at home. She pressed the intercom and waited, tapping her foot.

"Yeah!" came the voice.

"Keffa, it's me, Bluey." She heard the buzzer and the sound of the door being released. After tugging it open, she ran up the stairs, taking two at a time.

In an open shirt and with a smile on his face, Keffa stood in the doorway ready to greet her. "Yo, Blue, what's up?" Then he noticed the anguish written on her face.

"I need your help ... it's Lippy." She paused to catch her breath. "I love that woman, ya know, and she is sick."

Keffa watched her walk past him, as she made herself at home, and put the kettle on to make them both a cup of tea. He couldn't help but admire her fantastic bone structure and lithe body, with everything so beautifully proportioned. In different circumstances, she could easily have joined Kate Moss on the model circuit.

"How can I help? I'm no doctor, Blue."

She poured the boiling water over the two teabags, and with her back to him, she said, "D'ya take sugar?"

Keffa laughed, amused by her actions. "No."

She went to the fridge and pulled out a carton of milk before she carefully added some in the cups. "No, it's not a doctor I need, it's a fucking passport."

"Bluey, I've told you before. Don't swear, it's not ladylike."

She turned to face him and lowered her gaze. "Sorry, I am just anxious, that's all. I love her, Keffa, and I can't do anything to help. All she needs now is to fly back home and rest with her sisters."

Keffa took the cup from her and they strolled into the lounge. She kicked her shoes off and curled up on the comfortable sofa. He liked the fact she was so at home in his flat: she was herself, no pomp, no act, just her.

"Look, Blue, I know why Lippy can't fly. I know who she really is. Remember when I came home with you after that terrible cock-up and Ditto getting bashed?"

Kelly nodded.

"Well, as soon as I met Lippy, I was taken aback. She looked so much like me dear ol' mum. Lippy talks like her, too, the old patois. It's kinda nice and homely. I took a shine to her."

Kelly nodded again.

"Anyway, a while after me and Rudy started up a business together, ya know I only have peeps round me that I can trust, well, one told me who she was, bless her. I have to admit, I admire the woman. So, yeah, I know ya problem."

"Keffa, is there any way we can get a passport? I don't know how long she has left. It's gonna break my heart, ya know. What's worse, I feel so helpless."

Keffa told Kelly all the pitfalls of getting a fake passport. " … and besides all that, it takes too long."

Kelly felt the tears filling up and it didn't go unnoticed by Keffa. He put his cup down on the coffee table and moved across to sit beside her. She looked up at his concerned expression and then laid her head on his chest. Naturally, he put his arm around her shoulders.

"Oh, Keffa, there must be some way."

Keffa felt her warm body against his and had an urge to kiss her. He had always loved her, and yet she'd had no idea. She was young, maybe too young, though. It was the day she'd stood in his lounge, as bold as brass and honest as a child, when he had probably fallen in love.

Then, from nowhere, he had a mad thought, but it was too early to mention it, just in case it didn't work. He removed his arm and jumped up from the sofa. "Sorry, Blue, wait there. I need to check something."

Kelly nodded and sipped her tea. She liked Keffa; he was always there, somewhere silently in the background.

Opening the bedside cabinet, he retrieved his mother's passport. It was only a year old. He had sorted it out for her so he could take her back to Jamaica to visit her family. He remembered the pleasure it had brought her, sitting on that wooden porch with her sisters around laughing and talking. He opened the passport to the last page and scrutinised the photo. He smiled and ran back to the lounge.

"Here, Blue, look at this picture! What do you think? Maybe without that mad purple hair and hot pants, she could look like my mum. You could dye her hair grey."

Kelly clasped her hands over her mouth and stared at the photo. She could see a real likeness. Leaping up from the couch, she flung her arms around Keffa's neck. "Oh my God, Keffa, I could kiss you."

He looked at her with a serious expression. "Maybe you should." It wasn't the right time or the right place, but there, he had said it.

Kelly stared for a second. His face was always somewhere in her mind, as if he was meant to be there. Without another thought, she cupped his face and very gently she brushed his mouth with her lips. Neither moved, their eyes closed. She didn't feel awkward, or uncomfortable, it felt right. Then he kissed her and she kissed him back again, holding on to the intense feeling. Slowly, she pulled away from him. He ran a finger down her cheek. "It's okay, Bluey, you go and do what you have to. I am always here if you need me."

"I know, Keffa, I know you are. You always have been."

She wasted no time in heading back to give Rudy the news and book flights; she would have stayed at Keffa's but Lippy needed her — perhaps one day, when the time felt right.

Rudy appeared in the office. "Where ya been?"

She smiled. "To get what we need to fly Lippy home. Here, look, Rudy, this is Keffa's mother's passport."

Rudy laughed. "Fucking 'ell, my daze, you did it. They look like sisters."

Kelly was nodding with excitement. "Look, Rude, flights to Jamaica, Friday evening. We've got two days to get organised. Have you got a passport?"

"Yeah, but I can't go. I've got shit here to do."

"Rudy, I can handle your shit. I need you to be with her, a strong man. She's too sick to go alone, and I don't have a passport. Probation and all that bollocks won't allow it yet."

Rudy looked uncomfortable. "But she needs a woman to go with her. I mean, she is sick, and well, I'm not good with all that stuff."

"I know! Me aunt Bet, she's good friends with Lippy now. She's just the person," she replied excitedly.

Rudy nodded. "Well, looks like you've got it all planned out."

"Rudy, I want to help Lippy. She is good to me, like a mum I would have always wanted."

Rudy kissed her forehead. "Okay, Bluey, you call Betty. I'll get me jobs sorted and I s'pose I best get packing. Are ya gonna be all right, 'ere on ya own?"

Kelly laughed. "I won't be. I've got Ditto, Reggie, Phoenix, and Solly to keep me company or wind me up, one of the two ..." She looked at Rudy and smiled. "I'm all right, ya know."

"Yeah, make sure you stay that way."

❧*❧

Toni lay on her bed, alone in her flat. She closed her eyes. She could remember the smell of the blood and the recollection of feeling the sticky insides of Naomi's womb. Four sleeping pills had relaxed her tense muscles but not her mind. She gripped her shoulders, willing herself to sleep. Her adrenaline levels, however, were still very high and she was constantly thrown into a state of panic. That event happened all those years ago; she needed to leave those images dead and buried. She hadn't worried about it back then, Eddie had seen to that. He'd arrived as soon as she'd called and told her it was the right thing to do; he'd said he was proud of her, in fact. She'd clung to that notion: that being held in high esteem was worth the grizzly act she'd just committed. She remembered the look on his face when the baby was handed to him; not once did he gaze down in wonderment; he just nodded with satisfaction.

He passed her back the baby and with ease he wrapped the body, taped it up, and washed his hands. "Come on, Tone, let's get the baby over to Maureen. That will shut the whinging bitch up. I'll get rid of the rubbish tomorrow." He had no fear or repulsion in his eyes, just gratification. Toni joined in Eddie's upbeat mood. She closed the door behind them and that was the last time she saw the body. A week or so later, when they were sitting together in the pub, waiting for the others in his firm to arrive, she asked Eddie what he'd done with Naomi's corpse. He laughed. "She's still there, well, under the floor anyway." He poured a whisky down his throat and stood up to greet Cyril. It was business as usual.

Toni came out of her thoughts and sat up, reaching for the sleeping tablets; one more should do the trick. She threw it to the back of her throat and swallowed hard. As soon as she lay back down, the room began to close in and she fell into a nightmare-filled sleep. The tablets should have knocked her out for eight hours — instead she lay there for two days. The banging on the door pulled her from a deep slumber.

"Open up, Toni!" shouted Eddie.

Still docile, Toni got up from the bed and unlocked the door. Eddie almost knocked her over with his impatience to get in. She yawned. "What the fuck." Unable to focus properly, she was unaware of his angry look.

"So, where's the fucking money, Toni?"

Toni frowned. "What money?"

Eddie waved the opened envelope under her nose. "This money!" he shouted.

She leaned back, pushing herself into the sofa, trying to get her mind together before she looked at the writing. Snatching the letter, she held it in front of her. "What's this?"

"Ya fucking know what it is, you underhanded slut!"

Toni took the letter from its envelope and read the words 'Bill of Sale', Miss Toni Raven, £1,000,000. She looked at Eddie and frowned. "Is this some kinda joke? Is it one of those con letters?"

Furious, he grabbed her hair and pulled her to him. Her back was contorted and she gripped his hand. "Aw, get off me, Eddie. I don't know what that fucking letter is."

He shook her. "You skank, ya fucking sold the diamond, didn't ya?"

Toni looked totally confused, and Eddie could see by the look in her eyes, she was telling the truth. He let her go and sat down, rubbing his hands through his hair. Finally, he said, "That little slapper's gone and sold me fucking diamond. That's the bloody receipt. She knew what was in that bunny all along ... I could fucking annihilate her."

So that's why he wanted the bunny; of course, it had to be something of value, she thought. Eddie wasn't sentimental, he only cared about himself. Not once in her life had she ever felt this, but now, as she eyed him over, she felt disgusted by him. There he was, in his new black leather jacket, his designer jeans, and his gold Rolex. He had everyone rallying around him, pampering to his every whim, including her, all because of his vicious reputation. Never had her brother earned people's respect – it had been given through fear of the man. She stared at his expression, his cocky presence, and despised him.

"What are you fucking gawping at?" he shouted, but Toni said nothing and stared into space. He meant nothing to her now. In a moment of pure clarity, she saw him for who he really was: the arch manipulator.

"Right, Toni, get over to her place and get me money back. If I get hold of her, I will kill her!"

He looked in Toni's direction. "Are you listening to me?"

Toni nodded, slowly and deliberately.

"What the fuck is the matter with you? Are you on crack or what?"

She sensed he was unnerved by her lack of eagerness to help. "Eddie, you didn't tell me about the diamond, ya kept that one a secret. And you led us all to believe that Jack and Mickey double-crossed you. Fuck me, Eddie, you killed them over it."

"Aw, shut up, Toni, there were two fucking diamonds, and they did nick the other one, so they deserved what they got."

"Did they, Eddie, did they really? You lied to me. So, do you expect me to help ya now?"

"You fucking what! You had better go and sort her out, or I'll ..."

"Yes, Eddie, you will do what?" she asked sarcastically.

He squinted his eyes and gripped the arms of the chair. "If you had just got the fucking bunny off the prat, like I told ya to, you would be half a million richer. So, I will make a serious suggestion, and that is this. You get yaself cleaned up, get over there, and do whatever it takes to get me my money back!"

Toni was used to those words 'do whatever it takes,' and in the past, she had done exactly that. Not anymore, though. She looked down at her chipped fingernails and began scraping back the pink nail polish. She would have been shaking at one time, if he'd shouted at her like this, but not now.

"Right, I'm gonna find that prick Tommy. He was supposed to be watching the prat."

Toni still remained seated, picking at the nail varnish. Eddie walked to the door and looked back at his sister, who was behaving peculiarly. He put it down to perhaps a hangover – she liked a good drink.

Eddie slipped the phone from his back pocket and dialled Tommy's number. He leaned up against Toni's car. "Tommy, get yaself back at mine. I wanna see the photos." He kept his voice calm. As soon as his gaze focused on what was inside the car, he saw the familiar bunny sitting on the passenger seat of his sister's car. He shot a glance back at the flat, and then he tried to open the car door. It was locked. Fuming now, he rushed back and shouted, "Toni, open up, it's me!" His sister had lied to him and he was going to shove the bunny down her throat.

Toni was still preoccupied with her nails. She didn't jump to rush to let him in. Instead, she walked to the kitchen to put the kettle on.

"Fucking open up!" he hollered.

Her head was banging, as she shuffled her feet towards the door. Releasing the latch, she stepped aside.

"Where's ya car keys?" he shouted, while he scanned the room.

"On the table," she replied, in a flat tone.

Eddie gave her a sideways glance, confused by her indifference to him. He snatched the keys and hurried back to the car and grabbed the bunny. He rushed back to the flat and slammed the door behind him so hard that a picture fell off the living room wall.

351

Holding the bunny in the air, he noticed the stitching was intact and it was heavy, so perhaps the letter had been a wind-up. "Toni, where did you get this?"

She poured herself a coffee and slowly turned to face him. "Kelly gave it to me, the other day."

This was all too strange; there he was, holding the bunny, his sister away with the fairies, and a letter suggesting that Toni had been paid a million pounds. Wasting no time in finding out the truth, he pushed his sister aside and opened the knife drawer to retrieve the smallest yet sharpest knife. In an instant, he sliced the front of the soft toy. The rice poured out and onto Toni's tiled kitchen floor. He dug inside with his forefinger — there it was, the blue diamond. He scooped it out, held it up to the light, and admired the bright reflections, which twinkled as a diamond would.

Immediately, he was overwhelmed with euphoria. His diamond was in his hands. "Well done, girl!" he laughed, "ya fucking did it!" So ecstatic about holding the gem, Eddie never gave the letter another thought.

Calmly sipping her coffee, she watched him act like the spoilt child and arrogant piece of shit he really was.

"So, Eddie, it was all about that diamond then, was it?"

Eddie was still laughing with excitement when he spun around and noticed the blank expression on Toni's face. "Hey, sis, look, this little beauty is worth over a fucking million." He shoved it under her nose. "Jesus, I was an idiot for trusting her with this."

He was on too much of a high to be bothered by his sister's sulky expression. Placing what he thought was a very valuable gem in his pocket, he left.

Toni looked at the bunny left on the floor with its insides spewing out. The image couldn't have come at a worse time, with those gruesome visions of Naomi's plight very much alive in her head. She bent down and picked up the toy, carefully scooping up the rice to refill the saggy bunny. In her hand was the very object that symbolised her actions all those years ago. The limp, soft toy with the guts ripped from it represented Naomi's lifeless body and the gaping hole where once a baby had been.

There, in the lounge, in the sideboard drawer, lay her mother's green tapestry sewing box. She thought about her mother, such a gentle, kind woman. Her sweet Spanish accent could soothe the hardest of men to sleep. But she would be turning in her grave, if only she knew what she had given birth to. Opening the lid, she stared down at the neatly arranged cottons and the pretty pincushion her mother had made herself. She sat at the table with the sewing box and the bunny and threaded a needle. The smell from inside the box reminded her so much of her mother's scent that a tear escaped her eye and trickled down her nose. She should have been like her, tender and compassionate, but, unfortunately, she was the antithesis of her mother's kind nature. It was too late now to put things right; she could never bring back Naomi or repay all those cruel wrongs she had committed. After stuffing the rice back, she started to sew it all together but then had a thought and stopped.

A notebook was there on the table, ready when needed. It must have been ten years old and never used. Not until now. With chaotic thoughts going around in her head, she wrote a short letter to Kelly.

Folding the paper and inserting it inside the comforter, she finished by sewing it up. She held it away from her – ironically the seam was right across the belly of the bunny. After placing the toy in a Jiffy bag and addressing it, she sighed. Another tear fell.

Eddie was ecstatic: he had his blue gem and he had won. It was time to sell up everything he owned and live a life like a king in Spain. He was going straight. No more scams, no more robberies, he was going to spend his days sunning it, fucking any bird he fancied, and enjoying his hard-earned cash.

Tommy arrived, complying with his master's orders, and praying Eddie was going to call it quits and forget the debt now. Parking in the drive and holding the camera, he timidly knocked on the door.

Eddie answered with a smile on his face; he had forgotten about Tommy.

"All right, Tommy? Listen, ya can come off the watch now. I got what I wanted." He went to close the door.

"Here's ya camera, Eddie. So, what was it ya wanted?" asked Tommy.

Eddie was twitching; he frowned and then looked at the man as if looks would kill. "You fucking what, Tommy?"

Nervously, Tommy stepped back and smiled. "Sorry, Eddie, I am tired. Anyway, here's the camera. I'll be off."

Without a please or thank you, Eddie snatched the camera and slammed the door shut. He wasn't in the mood for this low life, as he saw him. High on his success, he was already planning his next leap to Spain. All his assets including the gem were locked in the safe under the stairs now. He rubbed his hands together and turned on the computer to check out mansions for sale in Spain. There were a few old cronies living in Marbella, drinking buddies, who would be more than happy to chew over the fat. As he scrolled down, his excitement escalated. The multimillion-pound mansions were out of this world. He would be a king in his castle, surrounded by staff, beautiful women, and ... He paused his thoughts. He should have included his family but did he want to? Slowly, he got up from his chair and picked up the camera. The digital screen at the back of the camera showed all the photos Tommy had been busy photographing. Once he had pulled the connection cable from the drawer and transferred the pictures to his computer, his euphoria quickly diminished. There, staring back at him, stood a beautiful woman: his daughter. His emotions were so mixed up. One photo particularly grabbed his attention. She was standing by the door of a crumbling Victorian house with a Primark bag in each hand. He looked around his huge lounge, with every top-of-the-range gadget and luxury furnishing, and then back at the scruffy house she called home. He tried to console himself with the idea she was a nasty bitch, who accused him of abusing her, who turned her back on him on a visit. She didn't want to know him. Well, good riddance; she would have been a pain in the arse anyway. Then he stopped at the photo of her walking a dog, smiling, and she looked like a child again.

He'd taken her from her real mother, just to shut his wife up. He didn't want people to think he was a jaffa; his mates had kids, and he didn't want to be the butt of their jokes — Eddie can fire bullets but they are blanks.

Kelly was a beautiful baby and she had loved him; her big green eyes lit up when he walked in the room. By the time she was four, they had what he thought was an unbreakable bond. But all that was history. He'd seen the look of hostility in her eyes that day on the visit to the prison. Not used to being rejected, he had certainly never expected it from his own daughter. Straightaway, he had a sickening feeling in the pit of his stomach, and it was a sensation new to him: it was guilt. He didn't like it at all and it made him angry. He threw the camera across the room and went to the drinks cabinet to pour a large brandy. "Fucking kid, who does she think she is!" he shouted out aloud. He knocked it back and cringed at the bitterness. As he walked back to pour another, he caught his reflection in the mirror. He stopped and had a closer look, smoothed back his hair, and then he smirked. In doing so it hit him — that look of satisfaction — he'd seen it before. In a blind panic, he returned to the photos displayed on his computer screen. He scrolled through and stopped at the photo of Kelly standing on a step with the Primark bags, large ones too. He zoomed in and looked at her expression. She was facing the camera and smirking; he recognised that look. Well he would, wouldn't he; it was his trademark expression. He shuddered at his daughter's smile — she was definitely mocking him.

He pulled the bill of sale from his pocket and looked at the date and then at the date of the photo. They were the same. That sarcastic 'up yours' grin, spread across Kelly's face, was meant for him. He scratched his head. It didn't make sense. He had the diamond and she was carrying two poxy Primark bags. But he felt his heart pounding and an eerie feeling crept over him, like he was staring at a ghost. Something wasn't right. She didn't seem the type to shop in Primark and those oversized bags looked odd. Finally, the penny dropped and from a great height. *Fuck!* He leapt like a caged animal from the seat, unlocked the safe, and pulled out the diamond. His hands were shaking and beads of sweat covered his brow. He walked over to the mirror and ran the edge of the diamond along the glass – nothing, not even a small scratch. Alarmed, he tried again. *Nada.* He held the diamond up against the light and frowned; it certainly shone like a rare gem, but it should have sliced straight through that glass. He dropped the stone onto the tiled floor and then stamped on it. He felt the stone break but registered it should have been unbreakable. As he slowly removed his foot, he glared down in horror at the shattered mess. It was no diamond: it was just a piece of cheap crystal, and he'd been had over, he, Eddie Raven. It would be funny, if it wasn't so outrageous.

Eaten up with anger, he smashed the computer off the table and looked for his car keys. He would have his hands round Kelly's throat for treating him as a mug. The only time he had ever felt insane anger was when he'd found out that Maureen had grassed him up, sending him down for twelve years. This latest piss-take though had all the hallmarks of a right royal cunt stunt.

He would teach his daughter how to show respect – she would be begging for forgiveness.

CHAPTER TWENTY

Friday morning, Betty had arrived early by taxi. The driver helped her with her suitcase up the steps. "Cor blimey, love, ya got another person in 'ere," he laughed. Inside, there was a buzz of excitement. Lippy had agreed to take the medication prescribed by the doctor because Rudy demanded she take it or there would be no holiday for her. It was doing her the world of good. She was more alert and had more energy. The boys laughed at her new hairdo: the purple was gone and in its place were strands of silver. She did look so much like the passport photo, it was uncanny. Kelly had helped her pack her suitcase, ensuring everything was washed and ironed. Then Rudy appeared with his luggage half the size of anyone else's. Kelly laughed, "Going for a weekend, Rude?"

Rudy squeezed her cheeks. "It's too hot for clothes out there, ya nah."

A large taxi minibus arrived. It was time. Phoenix, Solly, Ditto, and Reggie lined up in the street to say goodbye and wave them off. Betty was full of excitement; she had last used her passport years ago, and luckily, it was still valid. Kelly handed over a bulky envelope and hugged her. "Aunt Bet, listen, there's money in there. I want you to have a really good time and also please make sure Lippy has everything she needs, no matter what it costs."

Betty looked down at the brown packet. "Oh, Kel, are ya sure?"

Kelly nodded, walking with her to the front door. "You two enjoy, don't think about the money, please." Betty hugged her tightly and walked happily down the steps towards Ditto.

Wearing a summer floral dress and a hint of pink make-up, Lippy looked radiant. She stood in the hallway, and when everyone was in the car, she turned to face Kelly. "You have made an ol' girl very happy, Blue."

Kelly had seen that look before. Lippy was overwhelmed and the younger woman couldn't help but let the tears flow. She embraced Lippy for a while, holding back the grief. She knew it may well be a forever goodbye. "I love ya, Lippy, like as if you are me mum. You are how a mum is meant to be."

As Lippy held her away, she gazed into her eyes. "Bluey, you are the daughter I never had. You be strong and look after me boys and yaself. You a good chil' and I'm gonna miss me sweet pea." Huge tears trickled down Lippy's cheeks and she swallowed hard. "Goodbye, Bluey, me angel."

As soon as Kelly closed the door, she fell to her knees sobbing; saying goodbye had hurt like she could never have imagined. Clutching herself, she rocked; it would never be the same in the house again. Lippy was the matriarch, the woman who was the hub of it all: she was the linchpin of the household, who fed everyone, no matter what time of day or night; she would dazzle and charm everyone with her outrageous clothes and coloured hair; and she was a loving 'mum' to Kelly and the boys. In short, she was priceless.

Legend crept out of her bedroom and nudged her hand. She looked up and smiled, wiping her tear-stained cheeks. She could hear the boys opening the front door, and not wanting them to see her in this state, she went to the room to sit on the bed. The baby wipes were on the side, so carefully she removed one and cleaned away the make-up that had run and given her two black eyes.

Ditto was arranging some pickups from the beauticians; he felt he should be in charge while Rudy was away. This amused Kelly who smiled to herself. The boys were good friends and at least she had them to keep her entertained. She heard the door shut and then Phoenix, Solly, and Reggie were gone.

"Blue!" called Ditto.

She reappeared and entered the lounge. "All right, Ditz?"

He nodded but he too looked sad. "D'ya think Lippy will come back?"

Kelly had to bite her top lip, to stop herself from crying again. "I really don't know. I just hope she finds everything she wants over there."

Ditto checked out her genuinely sorrowful expression and hugged her. "You gave her something we couldn't. You got her that ticket home and the passport. The only thing she weren't too keen on was the grey hair. It made her look old," he giggled.

"I would have made her look like Elvis Presley, if it got her on the plane!"

Each found humour in a sad situation, like old times. In the midst of their banter, there was a sudden loud banging at the door. They both stared at each other. No one banged that hard unless it was the police. Ditto crept behind the curtain and peeked through a small gap.

He turned with a look of horror on his face. "It's Eddie Raven! What's he want?"

Kelly took a deep breath, flaring her nostrils. "Ditz, you go upstairs and I'll answer the door. I don't trust him."

"Nah, man, I'm staying with you."

Kelly wasn't having any of it. "Ditz, please go upstairs. If it gets ugly, then call someone, but leave him to me. He won't hurt me."

Ditto ignored her and headed straight for the door. Kelly shouted, "Stop!" but it was too late. He opened it and was faced with an enraged man: Eddie Cako Raven.

Before he had the chance to stop Eddie, he was pulled out of the house and thrown down the steps. Her father then stepped inside and shut the door, locking it from the inside.

Kelly, maintained her ground, with a scowl on her face.

"Ya got some fucking front, bullying your way in 'ere!" she spat.

Eddie's pulse was racing and a white foam gathered at the corners of his mouth. He wanted to punch her in the face, but he was looking at a mirror image, and it shocked him to the pit of his stomach.

"But, Eddie *fucking* Raven, you are a bully, ain't ya!" She inclined her head and stared in defiance.

He laughed with a bitterness that screwed his mind. He didn't know whether to lunge at her and stab her in the heart or hug her. "Where's the fucking dough, Kelly? No games, no riddles. I want me money. Now, you best get it or——"

"Or what, you'll shoot me? Stab me? Scoop me fucking eyeballs out?" She looked down at her feet and shook her head. "Or fucking what, Eddie?" she screamed like a woman possessed, causing Eddie to jump.

Eddie never expected her to be so bold and aggressive with her words. Little did he know though, she hated him more than the devil.

❧*❧

Outside, Ditto was shaking, aghast at what he could hear, but he was able to dial Keffa's number and prayed he would answer.

"Yo, Ditz, how's it hanging, man?"

"Keffa, it's Eddie Cako. He's here in the house, with Kelly. Please, Keffa, come over! I dunno what to do. He pulled me out and locked the fucking door."

A chill ran down Keffa's back at the thought of what that evil psychopath might do to Kelly. He rifled through his bottom draw, pulled out a gun, checked it was loaded, slipped it down the back of his jeans, and left. He'd had his throat cut by Eddie, and he wasn't going to let him hurt his girl.

♥*♥

As Eddie slowly stepped forward and waited for her to look scared or anxious, Kelly adopted the opposite approach – she just stared at him with contempt.

"Don't play big girls' games, 'cos big girls get hurt!" he said, in a low, menacing tone.

Kelly sneered. "See, there you go again with ya threats and bullying tactics. That's all you do in life, ain't it, ya take from the weak. Ya manipulate, coerce, and fucking intimidate, but *Mr Fucking Cako*, you don't scare me, because let me tell you a few facts, shall I?"

Her sarcastic tone stopped him in his tracks: he needed to hear this, as it might explain why she had no respect for him. He flicked his head for her to continue.

"There ain't nuffin you can do to me that could cause me more pain than what I have had to endure in my life." She stepped closer, glaring with fire in her eyes. "Ya see, me so-called muvver tied me to a cross. She stripped me bare and scarred me naked flesh and left me there hanging." She paused, taking a deep breath. "I was eight, fucking eight years old the first time, and it never stopped there. She continued torturing me in more ways than you, ya fucking hard-man gangster, would ever imagine. And it was all your fault. You turned Maureen into a monster. Ya fucking destroy people's lives, and you made sure you destroyed mine."

Eddie's shoulders were sinking like a deflating balloon.

"When I told the court you abused me, I weren't lying. You stole me from me real muvver and handed me to a God-fearing raving lunatic ..."

Eddie gasped. "You what?"

Kelly put her hands on her hips. Red-faced and angry, she leaned forward. "Oh, come on, Eddie, don't you play Mr Nice Guy now. I know the truth. So, as for playing big girls' games, I was never even a little girl. I didn't have that fucking privilege."

Eddie was lost for words; he had no idea she knew about Naomi, but then, he didn't know the extent of Maureen's cruelty either. He was there for one thing only – to get his money back. Motivated by his greedy need, he pushed the guilty feelings aside. She wasn't his daughter: his daughter was four years old, a sweet, wide-eyed, and doting child, who looked at him with adoration, not a grown woman, with hate engraved on her face.

❧*❧

Keffa swerved the traffic and skidded to a stop, a few doors up from the house. He saw Ditto in a panic. "Okay, mate, where is she?"

Ditto pointed to the house. "He looked so angry, Keffa. What if he hurts her?"

Keffa's face was tight with fury. "I won't let that bastard lay a fucking hand on her. Is the back door open?"

Ditto shook his head. "Nah, we keep it locked."

"Where's the nutty mutt?"

Ditto had to think. "He must be in Kelly's room, 'cos he's quiet, and he would have bitten Eddie's head off by now."

Keffa crept up the steps and leaned across to Kelly's window, sliding his long fingers under the frame and lifting it up. Then he turned to Ditto. "That beast is gonna bite me, ain't he?"

Ditto nodded. "I'll go in. He's all right with me. I'll open the front door. It's next to Kelly's bedroom."

362

Keffa stopped and listened. "I can hear her."

"What's she saying?" whispered Ditto.

"Giving him a mouthful, but I don't trust that cunt."

❧*❧

Unexpectedly, Eddie lunged forward and grabbed her hair, twisting it around until she was on her knees, surprised by the fact she didn't scream. "You are one stupid little girl. Ya think what I did was cruel, eh? Well, I fucking know what you did, Kelly Raven. I was there. Strange, 'cos ya saved me the job." He expected her to look shocked but instead she just sneered at him defiantly.

"Where's the fucking money, or, I swear, I'll slit ya throat?"

Kelly was bent at an odd angle, with Eddie's hands around her neck and her hair pulled back. He shook her, tightening his grip, but she said nothing and continued her act of defiance.

The tension between the two of them was like an elastic band, ready to snap: it was as if time stood still.

But the stillness of the moment was cut short. Legend barrelled his way towards Eddie, his huge mass descending on the man like a car trapped on a level crossing with an express train approaching. Eddie froze for a second – that was all it took for Keffa to get his gun up, fast and personal, in Eddie's face.

Ditto, like a ferret, ran between them, grabbing Kelly and pulling her away from immediate danger. He was shaking all over. Kelly took hold of Legend, as she watched the interaction between Keffa and her father.

Eddie recovered quickly, like the professional arsehole he really was, giving Keffa a smug look. "You should have learned your lesson the first time. Now, you know what happens when you fuck with me. Ya get hurt, don't ya!"

Kelly watched as Keffa smiled, this time unperturbed by Eddie. It was different now; he wasn't afraid for himself, he was afraid for Kelly. No one was going to hurt his girl, no one.

"Yeah, Eddie, I do know what happens. I still have the scar. But you ain't gonna hurt her. I won't let ya."

"So, pull the fucking trigger, Jackson, 'cos, if ya don't, ya know I'm coming back for ya, and next time, I will make sure I cut your head right off."

Kelly could see the sudden anguish on Keffa's face and then the realisation hit her. If Keffa killed Eddie, he would serve time. She looked at Legend, who was snarling and salivating, itching to get at his target, with his eyes transfixed on Eddie. "Seize, Legend, seize!" she screamed.

Instantly, the dog leapt and sank his teeth into Eddie's arm, pulling him down. Kelly could see Eddie trying to pull something from the back of his jeans, whilst being dragged about by Legend. At that moment, she feared for her dog: a knife versus Legend would not end well for her beloved friend. The man had no feelings.

"Legend, stop!" She screamed and rushed to his side, pulling him off before Eddie could get a grip of whatever was shoved down his back.

Meanwhile, Keffa grabbed Eddie and put him in a headlock. Tightening his grip, he marched him to the door and pushed him out. Eddie almost fell down the steps, but he regained his balance, and his pride, clutching his bloody arm and glaring back at the three of them standing there.

"You stupid woman, you know I'm coming back. I will promise you this, Kelly, you will wish you had never been fucking born, and you, Jackson, you're a dead man." He straightened his jacket, and leaving a trail of blood, he walked away, as if nothing had happened.

Still shaking, Ditto put his arm around Kelly and walked her back inside. Keffa followed, keeping his eye on the dog. Kelly saw how uncomfortable he was and took Legend to her room.

"Are you okay, Bluey?" asked Keffa, as he took a seat in Rudy's grandad chair.

She nodded. "Oh, I am so glad Lippy wasn't here. Imagine the fear on her face. Christ, she would never have got on the bloody plane."

Keffa and Ditto looked at each other in surprise. There was Kelly, having been attacked by her dad, watching her dog tear into him, and then there was Eddie making vile threats, and all she was worried about was Lippy. Keffa felt his heartbeat slowing down. Eddie had unnerved him, yet Kelly wasn't the least bit bothered by her father.

Eddie couldn't look at his arm. To see his own blood – and know the injury under his torn jacket was gruesome – was making him clammy and sick. As he gripped the steering wheel, he knew the dog had done some real damage because he felt the pain and his hand was weak. He had been in many a scrap in his time, but he had always come out on top – a few scars, here and there, but nothing compared to the injury under his clothes. It was triumphing that had always pushed his confidence. The fear in people's eyes, and the fact he had earned his reputation, drove him on. He thought he was invincible, but to be humiliated by his own daughter was hard to stomach.

He had to go to the hospital, the pain now unbearable. With every twinge, he imagined the damage being amplified. King's College Hospital was the closest, and as he pulled into the car park and waited for the barrier to open, he was still unable to look at his arm. Once he was parked, he shuffled out and nearly fainted when he realised he'd lost more blood than he'd thought. Gripping the top of his car, he waited for the feeling to pass, and then he walked in a trance-like state to the accident and emergency department. Luckily, the waiting room wasn't too packed. The receptionist at the desk took one look and asked him to sit down; she could see he was going a deathly grey colour. The tear in his jacket and the blood running down his arm, at a pace, galvanised her into taking prompt action.

"Wait there, sir, I will get a doctor to see to you right away." Eddie was now feeling very faint and had to lie across two chairs.

Moments later, he was aware of being helped into a wheelchair and a porter wheeling him into a cubicle. A doctor and nurse helped to remove his jacket. Eddie couldn't look, but even in his fuzzy state, he detected the nurse's eyes widen.

"Can you tell me your name?" she asked.

"Eddie Raven. Do you think it needs stitches?"

The doctor was trying to see if the flap of loose skin could be sewn back. It was obvious to him the muscle was visible and clearly torn. "We will need to operate right now. Was this a dog bite?"

Eddie was semiconscious now but managed to nod his head. Within minutes, he was prepped for surgery and wheeled away.

Once the operation was over and he was on the recovery ward, wide-awake, he demanded to be discharged. But the nurse was adamant he needed to stay for a few hours, just until the effects of the anaesthetic had worn off and the dressing reapplied. Eddie looked at his arm: the black bruising went from his shoulder down to his hands and was swollen like a tractor's inner tube. He was seething and the throbbing pain made matters only worse. Now he hated Kelly with a passion. He would hurt her in the worst way possible – no one messed with him and got away with it. Tied by blood or not, she was going to feel his wrath and pain.

Peter's patient had to have a peanut surgically removed, after his efforts to try to crush the nut and extract it had failed, because the toddler had screamed too much, causing them to panic. He'd had to anaesthetize her. It was all very quick, once she was asleep, and now she was in recovery as per procedure. Just as he headed back to collect his notes, he heard a voice call him. "Hey, Doc!"

Peter turned to see Eddie Raven, as large as life, propped up on the bed. He knew right away who the patient was, having seen him in the courtroom and of course Eddie had seen him too. When Tommy had told him that Kelly was seeing a doctor, he knew straight away who Peter was. Too cute and clever to leave any stone unturned, Eddie, probed into why he had been allowed down in the holding room before the actual trial. He was informed that the man was Kelly's doctor. When Tommy told him, Kelly was seeing a doctor, he put two and two together and bingo!

Pretending he didn't know who the patient was, Peter looked at him with a vacant expression. "Yes?"

"Well, hello, you're umm, oh, sorry, I've forgotten your name. You're my daughter Kelly's boyfriend."

Peter was stunned, not realising that Eddie was sussing him out. He was lost for words. Eddie then knew he needed to play a game, double or bust.

"She speaks very highly of you, very proud she is."

His face softened, as he approached the bed. "Oh, yes, she is a lovely person."

Eddie decided to try out his gamble on this doctor.

"You couldn't do me a favour could you? Err, sorry, what's your name? The tablets they gave me make me feel a bit spaced-out."

"It's Peter Thomas. Yes, they do make you feel like that, I'm afraid …" he paused, anxious to know how Kelly was doing. He missed her and couldn't get her off his mind.

"Well, Peter, I am stuck here, and I am supposed to be organising a do for her. The caterers will be at the house shortly and my guests will be arriving this evening. It's a surprise family get-together for Kelly. I didn't want to do it when she first came home, I wanted to let her settle in, but now I am here, recovering from a bloody dog bite. The neighbour's dog got out. It's one of those guard dogs. Anyway, I am in a bit of a quandary."

Peter nodded. "How can I help?"

"Well, now I have finally got to meet you, would you come along? I couldn't invite you before because I didn't have your number, and my Kelly will be made up if you were part of the surprise. I know how she feels about you. What d'ya say?"

Peter was unsure. He was under the impression that Kelly disliked her father, from conversations with Sophie, yet now it seemed as though they had reconciled their differences.

"Err, yes, well, I could, I suppose … Mr Raven, may I ask if Kelly is okay? Only, we haven't spoken since—"

"Since she left your house last Thursday!" interrupted Eddie, hoping that Peter would buy into his plan. He used his little nugget of information supplied by Tommy to gain Peter's trust.

"Oh, she told you, then?" Peter assumed that Eddie had built bridges with Kelly and now felt more at ease.

Eddie smiled. "Of course, she did. My Kelly tells me everything. I have to admit it was frosty at first, ya know, her not seeing me for years, but I guess she told ya about that?"

Peter was warming to him, naïvely sucked in by his puppy-dog eyes and the absence of his hard-man act. "Well, no, she didn't really say much about her family. So how can I help you, Mr Raven?"

Inside, Eddie was laughing; this was going to be a doddle. He could see what Kelly saw in Peter though; he was a good-looking man with class.

"No, please, call me Eddie, only Mr Raven makes me feel old. Anyway, the surgeon reckons I need to stay here until they can fix my dressing, and I should wait until the anaesthetic wears off. The problem is, I need to get home to sort out this party."

Peter never went over another surgeon's head, it wasn't professional, and yet if Kelly's father was organising a surprise for Kelly, and he was invited, he felt he must do something.

"Leave it with me, Eddie, I'll sort it out. How do you feel?"

"Like I've been bitten by a dog ... no, seriously, I feel okay. I am just taking up bed space."

After a brief look at Eddie's notes, Peter concluded that all seemed to be in order. He smiled at Eddie and left. The toddler with the peanut was sitting up in the cot, chatting for England, so Peter signed her discharge notes, and then he went to find Dr Mayo, Eddie's surgeon. He was scrubbing up, waiting for his next patient.

"Hello, Peter, how's your day going?" asked Dr Mayo.

"Yes, good thanks, Ralph. Now, your patient Eddie Raven ..."

Ralph Mayo's face turned serious and he frowned under his thick-rimmed glasses. "Yes, that was a feat and a half. Terrible mess that dog made of his arm. That reminds me. I need to take the details. That dog may have to be destroyed. I'm not sure if Mr Raven will have full use of his hands. Some of the nerves were severed. Sorry, Peter, what did you want to know?"

Peter knew Ralph well, having often shared a pint when they were juniors together.

"Any chance he can be discharged? Only I know the man, and he has a lot he needs to do at home."

Ralph looked Peter up and down. "I won't ask what, Peter, but if you feel it's more important than staying here, then I can discharge him. Give me a few minutes. I will organise his meds and get the nurse to redress that wound. Does he seem okay to you? Only, that wound is pretty bad."

Peter nodded. "To be honest, you would have thought he'd only had a tooth out."

"Must be one hard chappie, then," bellowed Ralph, in his haughty voice. Never had truer words been spoken.

Peter returned with the news, to the relief of Eddie. "So, he will be along in a moment to change the dressing and give you antibiotics. The only problem is you won't be able to drive for a few hours, so I suggest you take a taxi."

Eddie nodded, agreeing to all the terms. "Now, Peter, can you promise me you will not breathe a word to Kelly? It's a surprise." He tapped the side of his nose.

"Of course not, mum's the word. Oh, can you tell me the address? And what time do you want me to arrive? I get off at six tonight."

Eddie was elated, as he gave him his address; Peter was like putty in his hands.

"Seven thirty."

Peter was excited. He longed to see Kelly again.

CHAPTER TWENTY-ONE

Once Eddie reached home, he called the boys to come to his house. Cyril was the first to arrive, dressed in a smoking jacket and black slacks. As Eddie answered the door, he chuckled. "Cor, Cyril, this ain't the fucking gentlemen's club, mate!"

"You ain't wrong there, son. Fucking state of you! What's with the arm?"

"Come in, Cyril, we have a little job to do."

Cyril laughed. "Now, son, I am hanging up me tools. I'm retiring. I got meself a country manor. I'm toffing it up," he chuckled.

"Nah, nah, no bank jobs, nuffin like that. I need another arm. This one's fucked for the minute. Fucking dog bite."

"Oh, yeah, what's going on then, Eddie?" asked Cyril, with a worried expression.

Eddie led him into the lounge. "Take a seat, mate. Stiffener?"

Cyril nodded. "Scotch, two ice cubes, and a drop of water."

"I know, I know, Cyril, you've had the same drink as long as I can remember."

Peering around, Cyril spotted both the smashed computer and the camera. "So, what's all this about?" he asked, as he accepted the drink.

Eddie sat down and sighed. "I have been done over by a silly bit of a fucking kid and I want me money back, £1 million, no fucking less."

Cyril wiped his mouth and looked Eddie over. "I know you, Eddie, known ya since ya were a bleedin' little fifteen-year-old fucker. Never known ya though to fuck about when it comes to money, son. So, how's a kid managed to nick a fucking lump like that?"

Anxiously, Eddie jumped up. "Listen, never mind all that. I just want me money back, so here's the plan. I am up for a trade. At half past seven this evening, I will be in possession of something she wants, and I believe she will be only too happy to hand me back me fucking money."

Cyril didn't like the sound of it. He had known Eddie for years. Being twenty years his senior, he had acted like a father figure, always guiding Eddie on the right path of criminal activity. He had taught Eddie his version of the art of skulduggery, and he must have been a good teacher, as Eddie had sailed through the course. So much so, he could have gone on to teach his old mentor a thing or two. Cyril was old-school, his firm going back as far as the 1960s, but as he got older, he pulled away from it. He now had enough money to retire in luxury ten times over, and yet he still returned every so often, out of boredom. Eddie had run the manor before he was locked up. On his release, the old boys, Cyril, Blakey, and Frank were back on the scene, helping him to reclaim his businesses and take back his status. It was all done within a few months. They had always respected Eddie because he was a clever man, a no-nonsense and lairy villain, hugely admired, and respected for his ruthless side. Although the other men on the firm, the younger guys, were afraid of Eddie, and for good reason, Cyril could speak freely; there had always been an unspoken code between them. Eddie may have been the boss but without Cyril, Blakey, and Frank, Eddie would have only amounted to a two-bit car thief or cocaine dealer.

"So, Eddie, this exchange. I take it, it's a person?"

Eddie gave him his ugly satisfied sneer. "Yeah, you could say that, and he is gonna arrive of his own free will."

"So, what do you want me to do then, son?"

With a serious expression, Eddie pointed to the chair next to the computer table. "Tie him to that bleedin' seat. I would meself, but as you can see, I'm pretty fucked at the moment."

Just as Eddie stood up to pour another drink, there was a bang at the door. Blakey and Frank arrived together. Blakey was a huge man, in his late sixties, and still as hard as nails, with rippling muscles. No one could recall him ever smiling, and he always maintained his blank look. Frank was a stocky man too and fast with his fists. His nickname, 'the butcher', came about because he knew every tool from mechanics to abattoirs. Anything involving extreme pain, Frank was your man.

Blakey didn't say a word, as he sat heavily on the sofa and waited. Frank nodded at Cyril. "So, what's it all about, then?" he asked.

Cyril raised his eyebrow. "Eddie wants to reclaim his lost million from some kid," he laughed.

"Listen, I don't give a flying fuck that she is a kid. In fact, she ain't a kid, she's a woman. I ain't gonna laugh it off. The bitch has taken a fucking liberty, and I want me money back," spat Eddie, irritated that they saw fit to mock him.

Frank looked at Eddie's arm. "What ya gone an' done there, Cako?"

"Her fucking dog nearly took me arm off, so I am taking this theft personally, got it!" His voice rose a couple of octaves higher than perhaps was necessary, and it caused his friends' faces to turn sour. They knew then there would be no old-school banter. Eddie was serious and his tone harsh. They all knew how unpredictable he could be when his mind was set on something – no one would get in his way.

At the appointed time, Peter arrived dressed in a suit. Holding a bouquet of flowers, he knocked on the door. Blakey stood behind the door as Cyril opened it, and before Peter had even opened his mouth, Cyril had Peter's arm up his back whilst Blakey placed a black hessian bag over his head. The flowers were crumpled in the assault, leaving rose petals covering the hallway. They marched him into the lounge, with him shouting and wriggling, trying to get away.

The fear was like nothing Peter had felt before. He enjoyed watching horror films and old gangster movies, but now he was living one. He was pushed onto a seat and trussed up like a turkey for Christmas, except in this case, it was duct tape binding him to the chair. "What do you want from me?" he screamed.

Eddie could see he was shaking; his legs were bobbing up and down like a jackhammer.

"Shut the fuck up!" Eddie screamed back in his ear. "You will do as I say, and maybe you won't get hurt. Fuck up, and, well, you may not even live!"

Now totally petrified, he would agree to anything. His body felt limp, yet his knees were knocking of their own accord. He felt the plastic sheet under his shoes move against the marble floor, conjuring all kinds of horrific thoughts. He was well aware of the significance of the plastic sheet, but he couldn't fathom why Eddie had done him over.

"So, my mate, Frank 'the butcher', tell me what tools did you bring?" asked Eddie, in Peter's ear.

Frank laughed and unravelled his rolled-up collection of knives, wrenches, and tool grips. Peter felt faint when he heard the metal instruments clanging together.

"What do you want from me?" he cried again.

"That's my boy. Now, where's ya phone?" demanded Eddie.

Peter didn't even think to play a game; he had no intention of hiding anything, so gripped by terror. "In my pocket."

Eddie felt inside Peter's jacket pocket and pulled out the latest flash phone. He scrolled down, saw Kelly's number, and phoned her.

Keffa had insisted he stayed that night, and so he took her room whilst Kelly slept in Lippy's. They made plans the next day for all of them to move to Keffa's North London pad, as he hardly used it himself. Kelly was adamant she wanted to remain at home, and she would face Eddie again, if he returned. But with Reggie, Ditto, and Keffa all on her case, she finally gave in. She was packing up her bags and loading Ditto's car, when the phone rang. Seeing the name 'Peter' on her screen, she thought perhaps it was not a good time to answer. She let it ring and carried on sorting through her clothes but then it rang again. She sat on the bed and stared for a while. She had left Peter hanging over the last few days and thought it was unfair, and yet how could she bring him into her mad world? Apart from the timing, were they really compatible? And besides, she was having strong feelings for another man – Keffa. She left the phone on the bed and carried another box out to the car.

Ditto was a nervous wreck by now. "Blue, hurry up. If he comes back …"

Kelly rolled her eyes. "Where's Keffa?"

"He has popped home to fetch the keys. He said he will come back. You can travel with him. Me, Reggie, Phoenix, and Solly will follow behind. S'posed to be a right nice gaff."

Kelly laughed. "So, Ditz, it's gonna be a bit of a holiday, yeah?"

Ditto shook his head and looked at her with his innocent, sensitive eyes. "I will feel safe there, though."

She returned to the bedroom and noticed her phone flashing once more. Three more missed calls; that was odd, and not like him. Then, she almost jumped when it rang again. This time she answered and waited. Something wasn't right.

"Hello!" came the distinctive voice at the other end.

Kelly's nerves tingled, her throat tightened, and her heart raced.

"What do you want?" she replied, with an air of confidence.

She heard him laughing. "Oh, dear me, it's more like what do *you* want? Ya see, it's like this. I have your boyfriend and you have my money. Fair swap I'd say."

Hearing some men in the background laughing, angered her. She paused for a moment, trying to get her thoughts in order. She had no proof that Peter was there, only that Eddie was calling from his phone. She was livid that he was playing the bully boy again. The sound of his voice took her anger to another level. Would he really hurt an innocent man? And yet he was more than capable of harming Peter. Could she let that happen?

"You, Eddie, are a bare-faced fucking bastard!"

"Yep, I am, so this is what I want. You have an hour to bring me my money, or Peter, here, will lose a finger for every fucking minute you are late."

"I don't even know if you have him. All I know is you have his phone."

Eddie was raging. The cocky cow was playing games. "Frank, cut his fucking hand off!"

Kelly could hear the sound of metal and then Peter screaming, begging not to be hurt. In a panic, she shouted, "Stop!"

Eddie was still raging. "Stop, you say?"

"Don't you fucking hurt him, you nasty cunt!" she screamed.

"Well, little girl, fetch me my fucking money. You have one hour … I think I will take off his little finger anyway, a present for when you arrive."

Kelly knew he meant it. "If you touch him, Eddie, I will hunt you down ... you can 'ave your money. I don't want it anyway. But do not hurt him."

"Right, I will meet you at my house. Once I have the dosh, I will make a phone call, and your boyfriend will be released." He couldn't have Kelly calling the police and getting them all nicked. It was best to let her believe he had Peter locked up somewhere else.

With no time to argue, she pulled up the floorboards and stuffed the money inside a suitcase. She had remembered his address off by heart but had no idea where it was. Calling for a mini cab could take a while, and she didn't have that long. Her mouth was dry, and she knew she couldn't panic. She had to keep it together and concentrate on what she was doing.

Ditto, Phoenix, and Solly were standing at the bottom of the steps, with Legend on the lead, as they waited to load up the car. Reggie, though, was like an old woman, still neatly packing his suitcase. Like a bat out of hell, Kelly came running down the steps demanding the car keys. Ditto saw the look of panic on her face and the heavy suitcase in her hands.

"What's going on, Blue?"

"Nothing, Ditz, just please give me the keys. I ain't got time to explain. Please, Ditz, please," she cried.

Dumbfounded, Ditto handed them to her. Straightaway, with only one stall, his motor was down the street, at some lick too. Reggie came bounding down the stairs dragging his suitcase. "Where the fuck has she just gone?"

Ditto looked from Reggie to his new car; it was swerving haphazardly up to the junction.

"She ain't had enough lessons to drive that beast!" exclaimed Reggie.

"Fuck, Reg, I don't know what's going on. She begged for me keys and just shot off with a suitcase. Something ain't right."

Ditto tried to call Keffa but his phone went over to voicemail.

❦*❦

In the middle of trying to punch in the postcode on the sat nav, and trying to steer at the same time, she almost hit a lorry turning right at a mini-roundabout. At that point, the device sprang into action. "In two hundred metres, turn left."

Kelly took a deep breath; she had to concentrate on her driving, for she couldn't afford to be pulled over, not now. The sat nav read one hour to reach the final destination and she felt her face flush with anxiety.

❦*❦

Peter was sick with dread. He may have handled his brother's incarceration with support and confidence, but this was a whole new level. He had never even met a real gangster, and now he was tied to a chair blindfolded. If Kelly didn't turn up in time, they would remove a finger. There was no point in screaming and crying – all he could do was pray.

Smug with his plan, and cocky as fuck, Eddie knew he would get his money and his revenge. He would also give Kelly a good hiding for the trouble. He felt the sharp pains in his arm return and checked in his pocket for the painkillers. Hurriedly, he downed them with a brandy.

The men took their drinks into the kitchen, away from Peter.

"So, are you sure this girl won't call the filth and have them crawling all over this place?" asked Cyril.

Eddie shook his head. "Yeah, she thinks we got him someplace else. She don't know he's here."

378

"Eddie, I've known you to be ruthless, but you are normally tidy around things. I don't want to get involved in anything that's gonna risk me fucking liberty, not now I am retired, son," he said, as he placed his drink down and glared at Eddie.

"Fuck off, Cyril, don't be such a fucking tart!" growled Eddie.

"'Ere, Eddie, he has got a point. Who's this woman, anyway, and who's that slab of meat in there?" questioned Frank.

Usually, they would do as they were told, but there was unrest, and Eddie could sense it. He felt the pain in his arm again and looked from one to the other. He imagined he was the wounded wolf in the pack, and they were all looking to the alpha male to take his place. His attention turned to the timer of his new watch which had just pinged. The hour was up and Kelly was late.

✦*✦

Meanwhile, Kelly was stuck; a skip lorry was temporarily blocking the road. She grappled with her phone to call her father, but in doing so, the car jumped forward and stalled again. Panicking, she tried to restart the engine and ram it into first gear. Unfortunately, she only succeeded in finding third and stalled again. This time, the phone slipped out of her hand and under the seat. Luckily, though, the lorry pulled into a driveway to enable her to pass. There was no point in continuing to fish under the seat; the phone would have to wait. She was late.

✦*✦

Eddie looked at his watch, came to a decision, and glanced over at Frank. "Right, it seems to me that she's ignored my offer of a fair exchange, so, Frank, let's get to work!"

"Okay, boss," grinned Frank.

Cyril glared at Eddie. "I hope you know what you're doing, son." He could see Eddie was on edge and acting irrationally, as if this was personal. If so, they should not be a party to it.

Eddie shot him a sideways glance. "If you wanna turn ya back on me, then fuck off!"

Cyril didn't like the sound of that and thought better of rubbing Eddie up the wrong way. Frank was standing in the doorway, waiting for the nod.

The victim was still trembling. He had prayed for an hour and was feeling sick. He could hear everything but was effectively blinded by the black hooded bag. Frank retrieved the heavy-duty cutters from the tool bag. It always made for a cleaner cut.

He looked at Peter's well-kept hands and realised this man was no blue-collar worker. He swallowed hard, feeling uneasy; besides, he always knew the person he was cutting up. Without any warning, he pulled the hessian sack off Peter's head. Turning to Eddie, he grinned, "I never work unless me man can see."

But as soon as he turned back, to face his victim, he gasped and stepped away. Peter was grey-faced and wide-eyed, like a terrified child.

He knew that look. His little granddaughter had been run down in the street. Frank had been watching her, when, for no reason, she skipped into the road – aged just five years old – and a car, driving up fast behind them, swerved – but clipped her – sending her flying in the air. He could never get that image out of his mind, her eyes pleading with him to stop the pain. He called the ambulance and cradled her head. Racked with guilt and grief, he watched his most precious thing suffer. As soon as they reached the accident and emergency room, she was whisked away and into surgery. The doctor returned with good news; he had worked on her for hours and saved her life. The doctor had been so kind and gentle. He had even sat by her bed until she had woken up and then spent hours by her side, aiding her recovery, and

380

Frank knew that his potential victim was that doctor who saved her life. Now, he was staring at him, and he felt a wave of anguish. Without even looking at Eddie, he whipped out his Stanley knife from his back pocket and cut Peter free.

"What the fuck!"

Frank turned around with the blade in his hand. "You back off, Eddie, and let him go."

Peter felt a sudden surge of adrenaline; he launched himself from the chair and ran towards the hallway. Eddie was quick though and grabbed his arm. Simultaneously, there was a banging at the door followed by a woman's voice. "Open up, Eddie!" Kelly was so desperate to save Peter, she hadn't even bothered with a plan; she had the money, and Eddie could do what he wanted to her, just as long as no innocent person was hurt.

Eddie let go of Peter, using his good hand to open the door. That gave Peter the opportunity he needed. In a frantic panic, he didn't even acknowledge Kelly but ran past her, like a professional sprinter, down the drive and into his car. The skid was loud and left an impressive tyre mark on the drive. Eddie snatched Kelly by the hair and threw her inside, slamming the door shut.

He pushed her heavily into the lounge where the three men stood, awaiting their next move. She toppled over, the weight of the suitcase causing her to lose her balance. But she soon managed to compose herself and to stand up. As if her past had just slapped her in the face, she said, "Hello Uncle Cyril, Uncle Frank."

Cyril, open-mouthed, stared at her. He could see she was Eddie's daughter, no question. Finally, the penny dropped. Now he knew why Eddie was being so cagey: the firm would never have countenanced helping him, as it just went against the grain on every level.

Eddie grabbed her hair again and held her face to his, but Frank lunged forward and gripped Eddie's bad arm. "Leave off, Eddie, that's ya fucking daughter. Let her go, you arsehole."

Eddie had to bite down on his back teeth. The pain shot through him and he released his hold on her. Cyril then pulled her away, hugging her. "Now, Eddie, what the fuck is going on? 'Cos I, for one, don't like this one little bit, I gotta tell ya."

As the men backed away from him, fussing over Kelly, Eddie hated her even more.

It was Blakey who stepped forward.

"Who was that bloke you had tied up?" he asked, aggressively.

Frank answered before Eddie could speak. "I'll fucking tell you. He was my granddaughter's doctor. He saved my little Ellie from dying, and this cunt wanted me to cut his fucking fingers off ..."

Blakey pulled his fist back, as he looked at Eddie. "I should knock your fucking head off. Since when do we hurt people like that, eh?" He lowered his fist, flaring his nostrils. Eddie knew Blakey was one devious bastard but had never been afraid of him – until now. Blakey had a look that put the shit up him.

Kelly gave Cyril a thankful smile and stepped away. She placed the suitcase on the sofa and opened it. "There ya go, Eddie, and it's all there, all £1 million." With eager eyes, Eddie glared over at the case and nodded.

"Oh, and by the way, I didn't steal anything from you. That blue diamond was in my toy comforter. I thought it was a gift from you. I guess I was fucking wrong because you tossed me away and only thought of yaself. So there ya go, take ya money, and never cross my path again."

The men looked at each other and then at Eddie, who was visibly shrinking.

"Blue fucking diamond, eh, Eddie?" questioned Frank with a deep, threatening tone.

Cyril shook his head. "Well, Eddie Raven, I thought you was straight up. I really thought you was the mustard. Cor, you had me fooled, ya sly cunt."

His face flushed, Eddie was humiliated. He hadn't expected Kelly to go running her mouth off, and he had to think quickly. They had sussed him. He had killed Mickey and Jack over their double-cross scam, and he was patted on the back for it.

"No, Cyril, ya got it all wrong. Naomi gave me that diamond, when she found out her ol' man, Jack, had fucked me over." His explanation sounded lame, at the very least.

Frank was livid. He had liked Jack and Mickey, but he had to agree that deceiving Eddie on a job was below the belt. So, at the time, he had sided with Eddie. He knew Mickey and Naomi well. He wasn't best pleased that Eddie was fucking the kid, but he was well aware that Naomi loved her father and would never do him over, not even for Eddie.

At that moment, a set of lights glared through the window. A car had pulled up fast on the drive. Cyril turned to see who it was, thinking it might be the police. However, it was a Range Rover and a big black man was hammering on the door.

"Open the fucking door, Eddie, or I'll smash it down!" screamed Keffa.

Cyril laughed. "Who's this, then?"

Eddie now looked a shade sickly.

"If you fucking hurt her again, I swear to God you're a dead man!" came the voice from outside.

Frank cocked his head. "You no-good dirty swine, have you hurt Kelly before? I swear, boy, you have crossed the fucking line. You ain't playing with a full pack."

Blakey laughed. "I think our guest wants to come in, and I wanna hear what he's got to say." He didn't wait for a reply, as he opened the door to come face-to-face with a six-foot-three black man wielding a gun.

Blakey grinned. "It's Denzel Washington. Come in, mate. Eddie's in 'ere."

Baffled by the meathead's cool manner, Keffa nevertheless kept the gun pointed in front of him and followed Blakey into the lounge. As soon as he was in the room, his eyes surveyed the dynamics. Aware that Kelly was standing next to Cyril, he also saw Eddie in a very different light; he had certainly lost his arrogance.

Frank spoke up. "No need for the gun, mate. You wanna take Kelly out of here, take her."

Despite the invitation, Keffa wasn't taking any chances with this lot, and he continued to hold the gun, pointing it at Eddie. He swiftly sidestepped him and reached out for his daughter; she naturally put her arm around his waist. "It's all right, Keffa. I was just going to leave. Eddie has what he wants. Don't ya, Eddie fucking Cako?"

Eddie gave her a sideways glance and sneered. "I should have let you die at birth. You're no daughter of mine!"

"You're so right, Eddie, I am no daughter of yours or the daughter of the nutcase you left me with. Ya should have left me with Naomi. Maybe I would have grown up normal."

Cyril shot a look at Kelly. "What did you say, babe?"

Eddie was backing away; his arm was killing him, and he had just found himself in a hornets' nest with his daughter waving a stick.

"Oh, come on, Cyril, please don't tell me ya didn't know that me real mother was Naomi! This bastard took me from her; he gave me to his nutty wife and left me there to rot in hell."

Cyril's nerve in his face began to twitch. He had heard it all now: first the lie about the diamond and now this. He felt an anger rise from his feet and almost explode through his head. "That true, Eddie?"

Eddie laughed. "Don't be fucking stupid. This girl's full of shit. Look at her. She is one cocky bastard, determined to fuck me up, all 'cos I got locked up, and her mother was a bit strict …" Turning to face Kelly, he snarled, "But she obviously didn't teach you respect, did she?"

Cyril looked Kelly up and down; for a second he was buying Eddie's logic. She did look cocky and she was mouthy enough. Besides, that little yarn she was spinning seemed too far-fetched. He knew who Naomi was but still couldn't register that Kelly was her daughter. Naomi had gone missing years ago. Little did he know that she had done so at the same time Kelly was born.

Kelly saw the expression on Cyril's face and knew she had to convince him. The men in the room were all about reputation and honour among thieves. She'd heard it all in the nick; she knew what was acceptable and what wasn't. She moved away from Keffa. Standing in the doorway, she slowly turned, lifting her top. The men stared in disbelief, not assimilating at first what she was doing. Then Cyril gasped. Frank cried out, "Jesus Christ!" and Blakey rushed over to pull her top down.

She turned back to face them, "Now, Eddie, tell them. Me so-called mother wasn't just a bit strict … She was a torturous bitch, and she beat me to an inch of me life."

Keffa was livid and growled at them, "You all call yaselves men? Well, you all need to take a closer look at yaselves, 'cos, in my fucking book, Eddie has overstepped the mark, ain't ya, Eddie! And you, boys, ain't far behind him. Now, I expect you all to do the right thing." He nodded his head but maintained his cool front.

Just as she and Keffa left the house, Kelly heard Cyril say, "You're nothing, Eddie Raven, you're absolutely nothing now. You keep looking over your shoulder. Someone will come for ya. Just you wait, boy!"

Keffa opened his car door for her to step inside; she was still shaking with anger and fear. Keffa sat in the driver's side and pulled her close; he then made a call to a mate to return Ditto's car to him. "It's all right, Bluey, it's gonna be all right."

A vulnerable smile tugged at her cheeks. "You came for me, Keffa, that's all that matters."

He looked into her frightened eyes and smiled. "I told ya, I will always have your back."

He was true to his word; any trouble and he was by her side, like her shadow, except he was twice the size of her. She thought about Peter; he had shot past her with a look of abject terror on the way to his car. He didn't stay to help her or even stop her going inside that house. She didn't hate him for it though. She just knew he wasn't from her world; he was too clean. Keffa had risked his life twice for her now, and she knew he would do it again.

"You saw the scars, I, err ..."

Keffa smiled. "We all have scars, babe." The front door opened and out walked Cyril, followed by Frank and Blakey. She watched them walk down the drive. As Cyril approached the car, Kelly lowered the window. He leaned inside and gave her a sympathetic smile. "I am so sorry, Kelly. We had no idea. I would have taken you in meself to live with me."

He looked at Keffa. "You look after her, mate, she's a diamond."

Keffa nodded. "Always."

"Is he——" Kelly wanted to say dead. Nevertheless, she didn't have a chance to finish.

"Dead? Nah, babe, but he might as well be, by the time his little underhanded scams get out. His reputation has well and truly been flushed down the pan. A man like him needs his status upheld to survive. You wait, someone will come for him. But it's that satisfaction of knowing he will be sleeping with one eye open for the rest of his natural. It's like tenderising steak, if ya know what I mean." He kissed her cheek. "You are a good kid and a beauty, ya got that from ya mother, ya real mother. Now, she was a gem, a special kid, and beautiful. You look like her, Kelly."

Kelly felt the lump in her throat and her eyes began to fill up again. "Do you know where she is?"

Cyril shook his head, with a sorrowful expression. "I ain't seen her in over twenty years."

CHAPTER TWENTY-TWO

Toni pulled herself off the sofa and stood in front of the mirror, wondering whether to drown her sorrows or take the complete pot of tablets. She was having too many flashbacks, brought on by recent events; and since Kelly had entered her life, she was stirring all those demons from the past. Until now, Toni had successfully managed to push those harrowing events so far to the back of her brain that it was as if they had never happened, but now reality had kicked in and focused her mind. She thought again about her mother's sweet voice and her loving eyes, and then her father's face that was always black from carrying those coal sacks. They would have gone to their graves in peace, with no feelings of guilt or regrets. She looked at herself; her soulless green eyes could never have glowed with such sweetness as her mother's had. Just as her brother had malice in his blood, she had too.

Kelly's eyes had the same colour as hers, pools of emerald green, but those of her niece were round and innocent with a fresh kindness about them. She couldn't really understand why she despised Kelly; she had no reason to. In fact, she should have loved her and looked out for her, but who needed a kid running around?

She peered into her reflection again and was mortified when all she could see was Naomi's face, pleading with her, begging her. Then she saw her life fade away, as her eyes clouded over. It wasn't the butchery afterwards that affected her so much: it was the expression in her eyes, the windows to her soul.

What had it all been for, really? Had it been for her brother? She was weak, shallow, and pathetic. There was nothing strong about her; she acted on his orders all the time. Then she thought about him: he was feeble. He could kill a man with a bullet or slice someone's throat, but could he do the messing butchering? No. She had done the really grotesque acts. She, not Eddie, had cut out Mickey's and Jack's eyes. He couldn't stomach it. She wanted to seem hard and eagerly did the unthinkable. She loved the kudos and the respect. Yet, that was all it was, a massaging of her ego. Now, she was the one left with the guilt and the blood on her hands. She couldn't physically see the consequences of her actions, but in her mind, her eyes were fixed on Naomi and being met with an icy stare and a smirk. It scared her. Her body was now coated in a greasy sweat. She felt clammy, then sick, and had to lie down again. The sleeping tablets had been no help at all. They simply made her dreams turn into voids of hell where she was trying to kill Naomi once more. As she lay there, thinking about the bunny, she felt the urge to smash her head against the wall to stop the visions and the empty feeling in the pit of her stomach. She had to get up to be sick again. The room was closing in and her head was light. She tripped over the coffee table and fell on her face, puking at the same time. The cold sweat cloaked her, and she tried to move her head away from the stinking bile. Eventually, she got to her feet and pulled back the curtains to see darkness outside, but as to what time or which day it was, she had absolutely no idea.

Her car was parked at an odd angle in the street. She could drive to Eddie's, perhaps talk about the past. Maybe he could help her to get the hellish thoughts out of her head? It was too unbearable to live with the visions and the guilt. It was consuming her, sending her screwy. Yet he should share her pain; after all, he was responsible. He had made her do it and made her feel worthless without him.

Whilst Toni was in a state — not for her life but for her sanity — Eddie was worried for his life. He didn't know what to make of the men, as they silently left without a threat or a promise. It was strange and Eddie was not going to hang around to find out his fate. His arm was getting worse — the painkillers were absolute crap. However, he managed to fill a holdall with his money, diamonds, and deeds to his house. All he needed now was his passport, but he was in too much of a panic to think where he had left it.

He was on a life licence and not allowed to leave the country without permission from his probation officer for the next few years. His dream of living in Spain would therefore have to be carefully planned through the probation services and his pretty probation officer, who was sucked in by his charms. But he didn't have much time. He needed to get away tonight, if possible. On impulse, he thought about the pigs and convinced himself that Cyril was off to tell his mad brother, Howie, to starve the beasts ready for him. He shuddered and reached for the brandy. Those men's dying screams were still ringing in his ears; the crunching and snorting, as the pigs gored through their bones, made him break out in a sweat.

The loud bang on the door made him jump, so convinced was he that the firm had come back to get him. He peered behind the curtain to find Toni looking a wreck. He hurried to the door, pulled her in, and slammed it shut behind her.

"Fucking 'ell, Tone, ya look like ya just been dug up from a grave!"

She followed him into the lounge and glared around at all the luxuries, and then she looked at him dressed in his designer clothes. She didn't notice his bandaged arm, still distracted from her conscience haunting her.

"Make yaself useful and help me find me passport," he ordered. With his back to her, he desperately searched the drawers.

"I need to talk to ya, Eddie, about Naomi."

Eddie stopped what he was doing and faced her. "What the fuck is the matter with you? For Christ's sake, that was years ago. Why are ya going on about it now?"

"Eddie, it was wrong what we did!"

He rolled his eyes and turned to pull open another draw. "Yeah, well, Toni, so is taking your library books back late. Fucking get over it!"

"I can't get it out of me head. It's like she's haunting me."

He turned around again with his nostrils flared. "I'll fucking haunt you, if you don't shut your pathetic whingeing. Look, what ya got out of it, Toni, and now ya wanna moan!" He moved around the table, kicking the camera out of the way, and began searching the next set of drawers.

Toni was sitting on the sofa, agitated, her arms folded below her breasts. As she stared at Eddie, she realised he didn't care at all.

"Tell me, Eddie, what *did* I get out of it?"

The drawer was pulled completely from the cabinet and the contents emptied all over the floor. "I dunno, a car, a pad ... I dunno."

Toni's guilty thoughts were being magnified by the minute, and she was in a right state, as she looked at him in total desperation. Her lonely existence had just slapped her in the face. She had no family, only Eddie, and he was too interested in himself, even after all these years. If only she had stayed away from him and married her first love.

He was a northern lad from Leeds with an honest and fun-loving personality. Nothing gave him greater pleasure than when he was in Toni's company. He had offered to take her away to live on his father's farm, but Eddie hadn't approved and called him a poncing weasel. She had always wondered if Eddie had scared him off. Eddie wouldn't have been so cruel – surely, he loved her too much to hurt her like that? She stared at the mess Eddie was making of turning out his drawers. She wanted to laugh aloud because she knew where his passport was: he always kept it in his gun drawer. She smiled to herself; it would be out of date now, unless he had renewed it in the last couple of years. She got up from the sofa, walked over to the glass-fronted cabinet, and pulled open the drawer. Eddie was still swearing and shouting, frustrated that he couldn't remember where he had left it.

"I hate my life you know. I can't handle this sick feeling," she said, as she stared down at the opened drawer. The small grey gun was there, next to his passport. She knew it was loaded – it always was.

"I don't think I can go on. I wish I had gone up north with Max. I loved him, ya know."

Eddie was getting more frustrated by the minute and only had half an ear to his sister's chuntering. He wanted her to go and leave him in peace, to sort his shit out, but she was there, whining in the background. He finally pulled open the last drawer to find nothing but an old Rolex and a few bullets.

"What ever happened to Max, I wonder?" Her voice was dreamlike, as if she was in another world.

"Oh, for fuck's sake, will you shut up? That twat is six foot under. The wanker should have listened the first time. Now, help me look for the passport, or take ya droning someplace else."

There was silence, as it dawned on him the passport was in the cabinet with his gun. Slowly, he turned to face Toni, and his heart raced. She was holding the weapon in both hands.

"You should never have done that, Eddie. I loved that man and he loved me. You had no right. You let me believe he ran off with another woman … It's odd, 'cos in my heart, I knew you had something to do with it. But I never thought ya killed him, though."

Tense, Eddie watched his sister's strange behaviour. It was as if she was possessed by the devil. She even spoke differently. It was slow and meaningful. Her eyes were vacant as though she wasn't there. His throat suddenly became dry and he had difficulty in swallowing. It was a surreal moment, for sure, and a totally unprecedented moment in his life, as the shoe was on the other foot.

"We shouldn't have done the things we did – Naomi, Mickey, Jack, Maureen."

Finally, Eddie was able to process mentally the reality facing him. At last, he could see he was in trouble. "I never hurt Maureen. It wasn't me that killed her, it was Kelly. I saw her that night, and she was like a sick nutcase. I only went over there to find the fucking bunny, and I saw Maureen on the floor and Kelly over her, stroking her head. She is one evil bitch. So, Toni, honestly, it wasn't me. Please, sis, put the gun down."

But Toni's stare remained transfixed. "What about the others, though, Eddie? We killed them and we should never have. I can't live with it anymore and neither should you."

Then the unthinkable happened – fast. She fired the gun and watched as the bullet hit Eddie right in the middle of his forehead. Blood and brain matter went up the wall and covered the carpet. Then there was silence. She felt nothing: no grief, no pain, no guilt. So she turned the gun around, placed it in her mouth, and fired.

CHAPTER TWENTY-THREE

Two weeks later

It was Eddie's probation officer who discovered he was dead. As she lifted the flap of his letterbox to peer in, it was the smell that grabbed her. She called the police and they broke the door down. Lucy Kane was a young woman, working her way through the ranks, and had Eddie Raven assigned to her. He was a handful, she knew that much, but secretly she liked him, and he knew it. He had her wrapped around his little finger. She was happily married and so she held Eddie at arm's length. Her husband would have gone spare. He was a detective inspector, a bit of a workaholic, and she loved him, but at times he did piss her off with his whiter than white view on life.

She was worried when Eddie failed to show up for his appointment, and for a week he didn't answer his phone. The thought he had absconded was too much of a risk to her path up the career ladder, so she put the wheels in motion.

Cautiously, she followed the police inside and gasped when she saw the two dead bodies decomposing. The putrid smell made her gag so much, she had to rush outside into the fresh air. Maddox pulled into the drive and saw Lucy's predicament. "Stinks, don't it!"

She gave him a sideways glance. Smug bastard. Lucy knew only too well he was a bent copper. She found Eddie's files puzzling, because for every nicking he got off, Maddox was behind it. It was obvious why he had that satisfied grin on his face. Whatever Eddie had over Maddox, it would now go to the grave with him. Lucy then had a sudden thought. She would make sure that if there was anything in the house that could incriminate Maddox, in any way, she would see to it he left empty-handed. Her husband, DI Kane, had suspected Maddox for years of walking that dangerous line. But he turned a blind eye: after all, it wasn't in his remit. But then the chief inspector, with his built-in shit detector, had pulled him in not so long ago and asked him to keep a keen eye. Pillow talk had led to Lucy being informed of their suspicions.

She followed him inside and watched as Maddox sensed her eyes on him. He turned to her in his deep gruff voice. "You can leave now!"

Lucy gave him a relaxed smile. "No, I want to stay. I have a report of my own to write."

With contempt smeared over his face, Maddox was fearful to push her too far. He knew very well who her husband was and had half an idea he was being scrutinised, and so he needed to tread carefully. Hillary wanted him to retire and live the high life, jet-setting off to sun-filled places. He was smitten, and stupidly he had disclosed his fortune to her, although it was only courtesy of Eddie Cako and his firm. So the news that Eddie Raven was dead was like a dream come true. Eddie had enough on Maddox to send him down for a long time, but now he was dead, Maddox was a free man. He could retire and spend his money, living it up with Hillary. He would never have to watch his back again.

What was on his mind now was anything in the house that could link him to Eddie's corrupt dealings. He glanced at the phone, sitting on the table, and painstakingly stifled the urge to grab it. Realising that Lucy was eyeballing him, he was desperate to remove any taped conversations and certainly his number.

Eddie Raven had been a very crafty man and Maddox guessed he would have saved a few nuggets of info to blackmail him, if need be. For years, he had been supplying Eddie with tip-offs and losing evidence that could have locked Eddie up for a long time. The partnership they'd had stood both of them in good financial stead and he was not going to have it blown away through some do-gooder like Lucy Kane.

He kept one eye on the phone and one eye on her. Lucy could have cut the tension between them with a knife. She was cute and clocked his shifty eyes settle on the phone. Just then, forensics turned up and he was called outside. He glanced back at the phone and that idiotic move cemented her thoughts. As he left, she light-footedly stepped over to the table and slipped the mobile into her pocket. Then, pulling out her own phone, she photographed the holdall. With a nudge and a wink at one of the officers, she said, "I've taken a picture of that bag, just in case anyone decides to take it."

The police officer, PC Elliot Monk, smiled and nodded. "I'll hand it straight over to forensics, Mrs Kane."

"Thanks, Elliot, how are the kids?"

"Yeah, good, they will be starting school next September."

Lucy knew that Elliot was on the lookout. He had been given instructions by her husband and understood exactly how to play the game.

"Elliot, take this phone and make sure it's bagged up and sealed, prime evidence."

She slid the phone into Elliot's hand and left. With forensics now taking over, the lounge was a hive of activity. DI Maddox rushed back into the room and was frozen to the spot – the phone had gone.

❧ * ☙

Kelly was busily redecorating the lounge. She wanted the house to be fresh and inviting for when Lippy returned, if she was well enough to, of course. Ditto was pasting the wallpaper and Kelly was painting the skirting boards. She was amused at how Keffa and Ditto were so out of their comfort zone.

"Bluey, honestly, I can get decorators in and have this done in half the time. At least they'll know what they're doing. This is hard work," uttered Keffa, clearly not amused.

Kelly looked up to see him hanging the paper. He was right; he had no idea what he was doing: the wallpaper for the recesses, either side of the fireplace, had tropical birds, and yet they were now hanging upside down.

"They look stoned," laughed Ditto.

"Well, what a stupid design. Whose idea was it to have fucking birds?"

Kelly screwed her nose up. "Mine, actually, I thought it might brighten the place up." Then she laughed because it really did look stupid.

Keffa peeled off his new set of white overalls and folded away the ladder. "Right, stop!"

Ditto was still giggling. "He is right, Blue, let's just get the professionals in. I tell ya what. I've got some money saved up. We should go shopping and sort this place out. I mean, it's been this way for years."

Keffa looked around at the tired furniture, the cracked leather sofas, the threadbare carpet, and the 1950s pictures on the walls. He clapped his hands together. "OK, I am calling me mate in. He will have this room sorted in two days. It will be the bollocks."

"As long as the bollocks are hanging up the right way," she laughed.

Keffa adored her sense of humour and had the urge to pull her close and kiss her.

"Aw, for God's sake, Keffa, can't you leave her alone, or get a room." Ditto rolled his eyes and left to use the bathroom. Secretly, he was pleased to see Bluey with someone who could take care of her. He loved her himself but not in that way. She was more of a sister to him.

The incident with the doctor wasn't mentioned. Kelly had her reasons for doing what she had done, and Keffa wasn't going to delve too deeply. Really, he didn't want to hear that Kelly had previously had feelings for this Peter guy, and, for all he knew, may still have them. He wanted her for himself, and he would do everything in his power to make sure she was his. Little did he know that as far as Kelly was concerned, he wouldn't have to try too hard; she loved him anyway. When push came to shove, he was the one she ran to. In fact, she didn't have to run: he was always there ready to fight the world for her.

Just as they were about to go on a shopping spree, there was a loud bang on the door. Kelly didn't rush to open it; she had learned her lesson. Instead, she put her finger to her mouth, crept back into the lounge, and peeked through the curtains. It was two policemen.

"It's the Ol' Bill," she whispered.

Keffa shrugged his shoulders and looked at Ditto, who did likewise.

"I'll see what they want." With that, she opened the door.

"Miss Kelly Raven?" enquired the smaller of the two.

Kelly felt a *déjã vu* moment coming on, but she nodded.

"May we come in? Unfortunately, we have some bad news, I am afraid."

Kelly's thoughts were in turmoil; everyone she loved ran through her brain. All except Eddie and Toni, that is. She ushered the officers into the lounge, where Ditto and Keffa stood tall and watchful. PC Monk nodded in their direction.

Kelly offered the officers a seat but they were happy to remain standing.

"Miss Raven, we were called to your father's home today. I am afraid he was killed, maybe two weeks ago. Also, we found there your Aunt Toni, dead too."

Kelly was shocked, not upset, just surprised, and her face showed it.

"I am so sorry for your loss, Miss Raven ... Do you have any questions?" asked Monk. He was unsure how she would take the news.

"Who killed them?"

Monk looked at the other PC and then back at Kelly. "Well, from what we have seen, it appears that Toni shot your father and then turned the gun on herself. The thing is, we found a parcel at Toni's house and it's addressed to you." He handed her the oversized packet containing a bulky object.

"I know it's addressed to you, but because of the circumstances, we are required to watch you open it. Is that okay?"

Kelly was frowning but soon had the Jiffy bag open. She slid her hand inside and felt the soft velvet material of her toy bunny. As she held it in her hand, her first thought was what a sick bitch. But then she noticed a section had been carefully sewn again. The neat stitches were across the middle. She couldn't fathom why: then it hit her. Toni wouldn't have sent the bunny without a good reason. She was not in any way sentimental — mental, definitely.

"It's my toy I had as a kid. I guess she wanted to leave me something."

Monk didn't know what to expect, but whatever it was, it certainly wasn't a childhood toy. "We will leave you in peace, and again, I am sorry for your loss."

Keffa saw the two officers to the door and returned to the lounge. Kelly looked as though she had seen a ghost. "Are you all right, babe?" he asked, concerned by her deadpan face.

She looked up and half-smiled. "This was the cause of all the trouble. It's crazy because I loved this bunny. I couldn't bear to be separated from it and now it has so many meanings … I think there is something inside."

Keffa reached down and took the bunny, turning it over in his hands. "It's just an old stuffed toy."

"I wish it was, but it's more than that. It has held so many cruel secrets."

He handed it back and watched as she carefully unpicked the stitching. Ditto stood next to Keffa and they waited with bated breath. She pulled out the neatly folded note and slowly read the words that would cut her to the core.

Dear Kelly,

I guess if you are reading this now, then I am dead. I will probably be rotting in hell for what I have done. I know you will never forgive me and I don't expect you to. But I have to tell you the truth. It's the least I can do.

Your dear mother was Naomi McFarlane.

She is buried under the basement flat at 407 Hillingdon Court, Richmond.

Eddie and me, we killed her, and well, I don't know what else to tell you, except I am sorry.

Toni Raven

After rereading the words, Kelly just stood there, with the letter in her hands, and understandably, she looked an emotional wreck. So, unable to wait any longer, Keffa took the letter from her and read it himself. He knelt beside her and took her hands. "It's gonna be all right, Bluey. Tell us what you want us to do."

Kelly stared off into the distance. Somehow, she had to process the facts and in some way deal with them. She never knew her mother, so she shouldn't feel such heartache, but that wasn't the case. She swallowed hard and faced Keffa. "My God, they really were evil bastards. How could they? My poor mum, she never stood a chance." She broke down and cried. "Why! Why couldn't they have just left her alone? I could have been happy ... Loved, even!"

With his muscular arms, he pulled her into his chest and held her until her sobs subsided. Ditto was stunned; he paced the floor and then decided to make tea. They always had tea when there was bad news. He left Keffa consoling Kelly and headed for the kitchen.

"I can't even kill them with my bare hands. They didn't even leave me that pleasure. Jesus, Keffa, how terrible is that? My mum was a kid apparently and they killed her. I just hope that I have more of her in me than the scumbag Ravens."

"You must be the spit out of her mouth, 'cos you are nothing like them, babe."

Kelly smiled. "Well, I ain't done much to make her proud, but one thing's for sure, I am gonna make sure she is buried properly, a funeral and everything."

"Listen, Blue, we are gonna have to tell the police."

"Yeah, of course, you can call them now. Better sooner than later, just in case it's another fucking lie. I have had my fill of lies and secrets."

CHAPTER TWENTY-FOUR

Six weeks later

It was six weeks later when the police dug up the basement of Eddie's flat, and, as the note said, they discovered her mother. She found it hard to comprehend that her own flesh and blood could have been so cruel. The police had done their work, and the coroner had released the papers to certify how she died, so now the remains were ready for burial.

Kelly sat looking at the month's profits from the fake goods: they were on the up and business was going well. Legend was sulking because she hadn't taken him for a walk and she was feeling low herself. Legend touched her hand again and this time she sighed and got up. "Come on, then, let's go for a walk."

She slipped her jacket on and clipped Legend's new lead to his collar and stepped outside. Her mood was like the looming black clouds. As she slowly walked along the street, she observed a woman and two men sitting in a car parked across the road. She noticed the car because it was a bright red classy Jaguar. The woman, in her late sixties, was giving her a fixed stare. Kelly looked away, not really interested.

She continued walking in deep thought. That's how she was lately, down and thoughtful. The whole incident with the Ravens had shaken her. She wasn't so much angry as deeply sad. She thought that perhaps once she had buried her mother, she could then move on with her life.

The sound of high heels behind her snapped Kelly out of her hazy state. She turned to face the woman who had been sitting in the car.

"Are you Kelly Raven?"

Kelly looked her over, but she could not place this attractive middle-aged lady. Legend sat down and stared up at her. Kelly tried to suss out if she was friend or foe. She guessed right away she was a wealthy woman. From top to toe, she was dripping in designer clothes. The two men, standing either side, wearing expensive and fashionable suits and highly polished handmade shoes, looked as though they had stepped out of a tailor's store in Jermyn Street.

"Who wants to know?" she answered in a flat tone. She'd had her fill of aggravation and wasn't in the mood for more.

The stranger had a sadness about her and said, with a half-smile, "I am Sheila McFarlane, Jack McFarlane's widow."

Kelly knew the name 'Jack' but didn't twig right away.

"Naomi's mother."

A cold shiver ran through Kelly; she had never even considered Naomi's mother – her grandmother.

Still unsure if Sheila was looking at her with hate or compassion, Kelly avoided eye contact. "I am sorry, Sheila, I really am." With that, she turned to walk away, unable to bear any more conflict.

"Hey, please wait!" Sheila called after her.

Kelly stopped in her tracks. Hearing the softness in Sheila's voice, her shoulders sagged wearily. How could she face this person who must be torn in half with grief and all because of her? If she hadn't existed, then Naomi would still be alive. Any mother in her right mind would hate her, surely?

She heard the clip-clop of high-heeled shoes, and feeling a hand on her arm, she turned to face Sheila.

"You look like her, you know, you have her eyes."

Kelly couldn't hold back: she choked, and like a fountain, the tears ran down. Sheila held her close and stroked the back of her hair, whispering, "It's all right, I am here now, my sweetheart."

As Kelly pulled herself together, she studied them carefully. Whilst the two men and Sheila looked so alike in many ways, the familiar round green eyes she herself had were only evident on Sheila's face and those of her dead aunt and father.

"This here is Jack but we call him Junior, and this great hulk is Jordan, Naomi's brothers."

Kelly was disconcerted to see them so teary eyed. "I don't know what to say. I didn't know she had ..." her words trailed off, as she stared at the three of them.

"It's okay, darling," said Sheila, her arm around Kelly's shoulders. "I was grieved to think I had a granddaughter out there and I never got the chance to see you grow up. Look, can we go somewhere and talk?"

Kelly nodded. "I live there." She pointed to the house.

Once inside the lounge, Junior and Jordan kept staring at Kelly and smiling. Sheila sat amiably and stroked Legend, who nuzzled up against her legs. Kelly laughed. "He must know we are related because he is very choosy."

They sat drinking tea. It was awkward at first, until Kelly asked, "Did you know Maureen and Eddie well?"

Sheila nodded. "Yes, I did. Eddie was my husband's business partner. I have no need to tell you what that business was because I am sure you know by now. He was often over at our house. He was a lot younger than Jack and me. I didn't really mix with them, if I could help it. Then, when my daughter went missing and my Jack was found dead, I couldn't stand it. I moved to France. I was elated that Eddie was locked up for the murder and that his wife had grassed him. Yet, I still couldn't face her. I met you once when you were about a year old and it was strange because Eddie wouldn't let me hold you. You were beautiful, and I remember thinking at the time how much you looked like Naomi, but of course I had no idea you were Naomi's daughter, and so I just assumed I was imagining it only because I missed her so much."

Listening intently, Kelly had the sudden urge to know about her real mother. "Do you have a photo?"

Smiling, Sheila pulled from her large bag an album. "I thought if I met you, you may ask."

Kelly admired the woman; her voice was placid, very gentle, and her actions slow and graceful. She was nothing like Maureen. Her grandmother was a real sophisticated lady and she would certainly stand out in any crowd. She had wavy shoulder-length hair and a petite face which emphasised her big green eyes.

Sheila opened the middle of the album and there was the photo of Naomi. She was about seventeen and her face was beaming. Kelly was relieved she shared similar features to her mother, particularly her nose and eyes; however, her own skin was darker, and more like her father's.

"I do look like her."

Sheila chuckled. "You certainly have her voice. It's like listening to Naomi ... If only I had known." There was a sad despair in her tone.

Kelly could almost taste the bitterness. Sheila must have gone through hell and back. "I hate him, ya know, Eddie I mean, and Toni. I couldn't work out why they had wanted to be a part of my life."

She observed Jordan and Junior slyly glance at each other.

"But they didn't want me, they wanted ..." She stopped when she noticed Sheila on the edge of her seat, her eyes staring in anticipation.

Shelia nodded. "What were you going to say?"

Kelly shrugged her shoulders. "Oh, I dunno, I guess they were curious. Maybe they thought I could join their crazy family. Be a part of them, I s'pose." She tried to sound dispassionate.

Junior gave her an appraising look. "Kelly, come on, love, what did they really want from you?" His voice wasn't as sweet as his expression. Kelly's ability to read people's body language was off the scales at this point. She knew Junior was shit at hiding his real self.

She played it cool. "Like I said, maybe they felt I should be a part of them, and as I learned, Eddie was a man that got what he wanted."

Sheila's dainty posture and compassionate face changed completely. Now she appeared spiteful and her eyes narrowed. "Kelly, you are a part of our family now and we have no secrets. We can help you."

Kelly jumped up and stepped back. Legend did the same and was by her side, as if he sensed something wrong.

"Look, Sheila, no disrespect. I am sad for your loss, and me own, but I get the feeling you want more than a cosy cup of tea over a family reunion. I have had my fill with people wanting something from me. I don't need a family. I've got one."

Sheila stood up and stepped towards Kelly; her whole behaviour had changed, and now she wasn't a soft-hearted middle-aged lady ready to get out the knitting needles: she was a formidable woman with a confident streak.

Kelly looked at her and then at her sons, who were a foot behind her. This was no normal family; she was definitely the boss, but of what, though, Kelly was unsure. Still, she wasn't just their mother. Sheila emanated power and right now every inch of her radiated it.

Legend was getting agitated. Kelly knew what he must be thinking. His walk had been curtailed, one which regrettably was way overdue, and now here she was with people who were hostile. Then Jordan confirmed her thoughts. "Might be best to put that dangerous dog away. You don't want him hurt, do ya, love?"

Kelly's throat tightened. "What do you want from me?"

Junior laughed, a high-pitched laugh, which sent shivers down Kelly's spine.

"What do we want? Nothing, love, we just came to see ya and offer you a home with us." Jordan looked around the room with his nose in the air. "It's gotta be better than 'ere."

Kelly was angry and insulted but she kept her tone even. "Like I said, Jordan, I do have my own family and this ain't so bad. I am grateful but this is *my* home."

"And, my darling, what family are you talking about?" scoffed Sheila.

Kelly didn't like her snotty tone. "Rudy, Tulip, Ditto, Reggie, and Keffa, are *my* family."

Sheila sucked her lips inward and slowly nodded. "Mmm, Keffa, yeah?"

Kelly nodded. "Yes, Keffa, why?"

Sheila looked at both her boys and then back at Kelly. "Keffa is no more your family than the queen is."

How would they know Keffa? It was like before: more secrets and lies. She'd had enough of this other so-called 'family' of hers and their menacing looks.

"Right, out! The lot of ya. I am done with all this bullshit. You have no idea what I have been through, so you," she pointed to Sheila, "you take your two bulldog sons and sling ya hook. Leave me in peace."

"Oh, dear, dear me, Kelly. You really have no idea who I am, do you?" snapped Sheila.

"Yeah, I do, you're a trespassing pain in my arsehole right now. So, like I said, leave!"

Sheila gave her a scowling frown. "I think I was wrong about you. You don't sound like my sweet Naomi. She would never have been so rude."

With a fake over-the-top laugh, Kelly snarled, "Don't give me that bollocks. I don't know what game you are playing, but count me out. And, for the record, I don't care who you are, what you are, and who you know. If you had a real relationship with Naomi, then perhaps she would still be alive!" She had no sooner got the words out of her mouth when Sheila slapped her hard across the face.

Kelly wobbled and clutched her sore cheek, giving Shelia a defiant glare. Legend started growling, showing his teeth. Incredibly, Jordan pulled a gun from the back of his trousers and pointed it at Legend. "Get ya mutt out of 'ere or I'll …"

"You'll do what?" snapped Kelly, as she stood in front of Legend, ensuring he was out of sight of the weapon. "Go on then, fucking shoot me! A big man you are!"

To say Sheila was astonished was an understatement. She had assumed her granddaughter was a timid young thing who had just been caught up in the wrath of the Ravens. She had no idea that Kelly could be such a hard woman. The look in Kelly's eyes was that of her father's all right. At no time in her life had Sheila felt uneasy; but she did now. She was used to people agreeing with her. No one had ever had the guts to blast her like Kelly had done.

Angry now, Kelly remained unperturbed by the three of them.

Sheila flicked her head at the two men and marched past Kelly, heading for the front door. The older woman's gentle movements were now hard and quick. In some ways, she reminded Kelly of her own mother, that protruding jaw and foreboding in her eyes. Junior and Jordan followed their mother, like the two lap dogs they were. Junior stopped at the front door and turned slowly, looking Kelly over. "You have made a big mistake. We could have helped you, but you are on ya own and God help ya. Me mother don't like to be pissed off, and you have just gone and rubbed her up the fucking wrong way."

Kelly walked towards him silently, and when he had stepped outside, she slammed the door shut. That experience left her shaking with a mixed bag of emotions. There were so many unanswered questions, but she couldn't sit there playing happy families, when they had their own agenda.

She watched them out of the window, as they strode back to the car. Her eyes widened, when she saw Keffa pull up outside and Sheila turn on her heel and make her way towards him. Kelly stared intently, trying to read Keffa's body language, but he turned his back. Then she saw Jordan shake his hand and they left. Kelly's heart was racing; she felt a lump in her throat and her eyes filled with bitter tears.

The man she had grown to love, and trust, had secrets of his own, and they somehow included her. She watched him playing with his phone, as Sheila drove away. He then got into his car and vanished up the road. Her man, the one person she had given her heart to, had now betrayed her. She didn't know how or why but he was in on something. Her mind was running away with her; were Rudy, Ditto, Reggie, or even Lippy involved as well? And had Rudy just pretended he had found her roaming the streets all those years ago by accident? She took a deep breath; this situation was crazy, and she wasn't going to allow herself to be weakened by insane paranoia.

Her deeps thoughts were interrupted by Ditto, as he rushed into the lounge clutching a letter and sniggering to himself. She watched him; he was so like Rudy in the way his whole body shook when he laughed. He looked up from the envelope, with big boyish eyes. "Here, Blue, a present for you."

He handed her the envelope and urged her to open it. She tore away the sealed strip and pulled out the paperwork. The top of the page had her details and then a date for her driving test. She felt her anger and confusion subside: Ditto or anyone in her new family couldn't be anything but true to her. She dropped the letter and flung her arms around him. She held him tight, more relieved than anything.

"Cor, blimey, Blue, it's only a test," he laughed.

Kelly let him go and shook her head. "I know, Ditto, it's just ..." her words trailed off.

Ditto sat down and began untying his laces to his new, fresh trainers. "Tell me, Blue, what's wrong ... I mean, I know things have been shit for yous lately, but is there anything else?"

She sat beside him, running her hands through her hair. "Ditz, what do you really know about Keffa?"

Instantly, Ditto shot her an intense sideways glance. "Why, what's he done?"

Kelly took a deep breath and sighed. "I dunno, Ditz, there is something strange going on. Look, I have to go out for a bit. I think I need to talk to someone that may have the answers."

Ditto nodded. "Okay, but are you sure you are all right, Kel?"

Giving him a resigned smile, she left, heading for the makeshift office; once inside, she quickly logged on to the computer, googled a few details, and pinpointed the address. She kissed Ditto on the cheek and asked him to keep an eye on Legend, before she hopped into the awaiting mini cab. It seemed to her that Ditto was too kind and caring to be doing something behind her back. Yet Keffa, shaking hands with Jordan, was still taunting her mind. She had well and truly had enough of all the secrets.

The night was closing in and the only light was from the moon. It wasn't something she ever looked at, however. As the cab driver drove along the Kent country lanes, with the vast open fields, she got a sense of peace and took more notice of her surroundings, savouring the blue-lit fields. *One day*, she thought, *maybe I should live out here.*

As they turned off the main road, the driver stopped. "Well, we are here."

Kelly looked around but all she could see was what looked like another country lane.

"There's nothing here ... err, could you just drive a little further, please?"

Unexpectedly, what she thought was another narrow road was now lit up. It was a drive. As they continued, she noticed two enormous gates and was almost blinded by the security lights. She stepped out of the cab and then pressed the buzzer.

"Yes, can I help?" came the deep voice.

"Oh, hello, it's Kelly Raven to see Cyril."

She waited a few moments before the gates opened and then climbed back into the vehicle. The magnificent old mansion, standing proudly in all its grandeur, and the extensive gardens were completely illuminated. They approached the front entrance and Kelly paid the driver. The gravel drive crunched under her feet on the short walk up to the steps where a tall, stocky man was standing, dressed in a bespoke suit, and waiting for her. He nodded for her to go inside. She stopped for a second and thought about what she was doing. She was impulsive but then that was her all over. It might have been better, however, to have planned this before sticking her neck out. *Too late for that though.* Before she had a chance to change her mind, the squeak of bare feet could be heard, and then Cyril appeared.

"Kel, what are you doing here?" he asked, holding his arms out for a hug.

Kelly wanted to laugh at the extraordinary sight before her. There was Cyril, in his burgundy smoking jacket and Paisley cravat, smoking a cigar, with nothing on his feet, living in a mansion suitable for a duke.

"Come through, babe. D'ya fancy a tea, coffee, Scotch whisky?"

Kelly walked behind him into the drawing room. It was huge, and as she gazed around the stately residence, she smiled. "Cor, this is something else."

Cyril laughed. "Yep, I am fucking lording it up these days. I ain't taking me dosh to the grave, so I might as well live like a toff. Anyway, take a seat, babe. What can I do for ya?"

"I, well——" She didn't finish.

"Jeeves, in here, mate!" ordered Cyril.

Kelly wanted to laugh. "Is he really called Jeeves?"

Cyril winked. "Is he fuck. Nah, 'is real name's Ronnie Pratt. I can't 'ave a butler called fucking Ronnie. It would ruin me reputation. He don't mind being called Jeeves."

Ronnie appeared in the doorway. "Yes, sir?"

Cyril winked at Kelly again. "Jeeves, get me niece some refreshments."

Impassively, Ronnie turned to Kelly. "What would you like, madam?"

Kelly smiled convivially. "Tea will be fine, thank you."

As he left, Cyril laughed loudly. "Fuck me, it's like Downton Abbey, but it suits me. Now, babe, I don't think ya came all the way 'ere to talk about the price of eggs, so what's on ya mind? Need money?"

Kelly shook her head. "Cyril, I have been lied to, for so damned long now. All I want is the truth about everything. Me muvver, me real muvver, me farver, and now Sheila."

Cyril sat upright at that point. "Sheila?" his eyes narrowed and he rubbed his bristly chin. "Right, girl, it seems to me you have been born into a real complicated web of deceit. Jesus, if only I knew back then what I fucking know now." He took a deep breath. "Well, let's get something straight. You can trust me, babe, to tell the truth and spill the fucking beans, as it were. I mean, I ain't for all these underhanded shenanigans. It was different in my day. We never had women running businesses because their place was looking after the home and the kids. Not that I had any kids, well, none that I know of," he chuckled.

Kelly trusted Cyril; she had a vague memory of him, enough to remember his face, and how he was kind to her.

"Get yaself comfy, babe, it's gonna be a long night. Ya can stay 'ere if you like. I got fucking fourteen bedrooms, or maybe sixteen, I don't know. Anyway, you can take ya pick."

"Oh, I dunno, Cyril. I mean, I was a kid back then. I don't know ya really, do I?"

Cyril stood up and walked over to the huge drinks display cabinet. "I know, my babe, and that's a fucking shame. I should have stayed in contact with Maureen, ya know, just to keep an eye, really. Still, look at ya, a real stunner and with a good head on ya shoulders. Ya right not to trust me, well, anyone for that matter. You keep ya wits about ya, girl. But I won't hurt ya. I loved you when you was a nipper. You were always running around with a huge smile on your boat. Honestly, you would have melted anyone's heart. Ya sat on me knee and I would make up silly stories and you'd giggle."

Kelly smiled. "I remember there was a story about a tin man and his dog."

Cyril swung around. "Cor blimey, Kel, ya remember that, eh?"

Ronnie entered the room, carrying a tray of biscuits, a pot of tea, and a mug. Kelly wanted to laugh – he was hardly silver service. Cyril rolled his eyes. "Lucky I ain't paying you a full day's graft. You, me old mate, are still in training. A mug! It's supposed to be a teacup. Ya know, the ones with dainty flowers and shit."

Ronnie rolled his eyes. "Look, Cyril, I've been your minder for twenty years. I ain't any good with the butler thing."

"Now, me ol' son, times have changed. I have no need for a minder, but I do need a butler, so if ya wanna stay on the payroll, ya best get yaself off to butler school, and while you're at it, mate, do a chauffeur's course an' all."

Kelly was trying hard not to laugh, but the chuckle escaped and both Ronnie and Cyril were in fits. She felt herself relax, drawn in by Cyril's charisma.

"This is grand, though, Cyril. I mean this is like a lord's house. All ya need are a couple of Irish wolfhounds, a Barbour coat, and a shot gun."

Cyril laughed. "Well, I've got two Rotties, a Crombie, and a sawn-off shotgun. Ya see, I've gotta ease into me new status."

Kelly's memory of her so-called uncle was returning and she recalled how comical he was; her heart warmed at the thought of him.

"So, my babe ..." He had always called her that. She recalled him picking her up, spinning her around, and always plastering her face with kisses. "Are you sure you are ready for all the truth, and I do mean everything? I am assuming you want to know about ya ol' man?"

Kelly nodded. "Cyril, before I can get on with me life, I need to know where I came from and what my past was really all about."

Cyril got himself comfortable with a large whisky in his hand. Kelly poured the tea and nibbled on a biscuit.

"Eddie Raven was a kid when I first clapped my eyes on him, a real naughty rogue he was too. The cunt tried to nick me Bentley. That's how we met. Of course, I bashed the little shit into next week, but instead of running for the hills, the cheeky git asked for a job. I think he knew exactly who I was, and he hoped he could get away with nicking me prize possession, just to prove a point and get in with me firm."

Cyril smiled to himself, as he recalled Eddie in his younger days, a feisty, reckless teenager, having an egotistical personality. He knew it was a front, yet he was brazen, and it seemed to Cyril that having this young tearaway on his firm would either be a blessing or a nightmare. Luckily for Cyril, Eddie had the brains not to push Cyril too far and to take notice of his advice. Eddie was given small jobs to start with, picking up parcels, carrying out location recces, and all in all, playing the gofer. It was when Eddie got to twenty that the dynamics changed. He was casing joints and working out plans to take on big jobs – banks, the post offices, and travel agents. Cyril let him get on with it and only took a small amount of commission. Then, as Cyril got older and didn't need the aggro anymore, he let Eddie take over the firm. His men worked for Eddie, and to give him his due, he paid them well. Yet, that was all he was fair about; his greed for power and money grew at a rate of knots. Cyril gave him space to do things his way, but he still kept Eddie close enough to keep an eye on him.

The days of big robberies and the protection racket were all gone, as far as Cyril was concerned; he had his money, more than anyone else, and so he was happy to take a step back.

"So, I took your ol' man under me wing. I had a big firm an' all, including Jack McFarlane. Now, he was a good guy, older than Eddie, younger than me. He was shit-hot when it came to explosives and we had him on every job. Then, he got in with Eddie. Jack admired Eddie and they became good pals. They would drink together and share everything. I gotta say, Eddie was getting a bit big for his boots, though. He was becoming a cruel bastard, having men tortured for no real reason, other than to prove a point that ya don't fuck with Eddie Cako. Anyway, that was his business. Ya ol' man had his fingers in many pies, too many, and he was taking over manors which, quite frankly, he should have left alone – like Patrick Mahoney's. Now, he was an Irish geezer running North London. He came from money and used it to buy his men and run his rackets. That's where he should have stayed. But he didn't. Patrick came looking for Eddie because he had stepped on Patrick's toes. But Eddie, being Eddie, didn't give a flying fuck, and after a particularly awkward meeting, nothing was ever the same."

Cyril shook his head and swigged his whisky.

"It was Patrick Mahoney that I killed. I didn't mean to."

Cyril nodded. "I know, my babe, I know. Anyway, he would have hurt ya, to get his hands on that fucking diamond. Ya see, babe, I did some digging after you left that day. And I have to say, I had no fucking idea what was going on. That safe deposit box heist was the biggest one ever. Not only did Eddie and Jack know what was in there, but so did Patrick and Sheila."

Kelly frowned. "Who is this Sheila? I mean, I know she's Naomi's mother but …"

Cyril coughed. "Fuck me, Kelly, you really have no idea, do ya?"

Kelly shook her head. "No, Cyril, I really don't."

"Well, let me tell ya, that cosy little family set-up was brought together by marriage whose members were either evil, or greedy, or both. Right, Eddie's sister was hitched up with Patrick."

"Yeah, that was weird, Cyril, because I was inside with Toni. It was a couple of years, and, ya know, she never mentioned him or the fact that I killed her husband."

Cyril laughed. "She wouldn't, that was all for show, to strengthen the two families and pull the North London and South London manors together. Anyhow, Jack was Eddie's best mate, inseparable, so I guess he was like family. So, who better to marry Jack than Patrick Mahoney's sister, Sheila. She was a name back then."

Kelly gasped and threw her hands to her mouth. "You're kidding! So, I killed me grandmother's fucking brother?"

"Yep, ya sure did."

"And, my babe, she is one evil psycho. After she married Jack and had Naomi, she had already had, by the way, her two precious sons from a previous marriage, she fucked-off back to Ireland, running a racket of her own. She was much smarter than her brother. But now, this is the thing. She took her boys and left Jack to raise Naomi; she couldn't stand the child. She only wanted boys — girls didn't play a role in her life. So, anyway, that diamond heist was carefully planned — two blue diamonds, one worth fucking millions. They disappeared off the radar. No one knew who had them. Like fucking mugs, we all believed that Jack had them and had double-crossed Eddie. So, when Jack and Mickey were fished out of the river, no one looked bad at Eddie. He did what any decent villain would have done. Then, of course, you turned up and the truth came out. So, I think that's why that 'orrible bitch, Sheila, is on the scene."

Kelly looked at Cyril with some confusion on her face. "So, she is after the diamond … But I sold it and gave the money to Eddie. You saw me."

"Babe, that ain't the diamond they are after. Ya see, there were two, and it's the other one they want, the one that is worth a fucking mint. I guess Eddie put them in that toy because he knew Sheila would have his homes ransacked, so the safest place was with you."

Kelly stared out of the window in deep thought; it didn't make sense. That bunny only had the one diamond.

"Cyril, maybe Eddie really was double-crossed because I only had the one blue gem."

"One you say? Well, then, that is a bleedin' mystery. Listen, Kel, that cunt Sheila will be after you, I know her. She obviously thinks you know where the other one is as well. She will stop at nothing to get that diamond. I s'pose she thinks she has some claim to it ... I am sorry about ya real mother, Naomi. She was a lovely kid, and I knew Eddie had been sniffing around her, but then she disappeared. I had no idea she was pregnant with you. Jesus, that's fucked-up. I guess it's some consolation that those two scumbags Eddie and Toni are dead, eh?"

Kelly nodded but her mind wandered off; she thought about Keffa and what his role might be in all of this. Was he after the diamond too?

"D'ya know Keffa, that big black guy that turned up at Eddie's?"

Cyril scratched his stubble again. "Odd you should ask that because I didn't at the time. Then I got to thinking about him, and it dawned on me who he was."

Kelly put her mug down on the Queen Anne table and sat up straight. "Yeah, go on."

"He is an arms dealer, well he used to be, back in the day. As I recall, he had a good business in arms. He took the guns that were deactivated and reactivated them. Eddie slit his throat, ya know. Cor, that was a bad move. I honestly thought that Keffa wouldn't let the little incident go. I guess he must have thought better of it. He supplied Patrick an' all. Then, I never heard any more about him, until he showed up with you."

Their conversation was interrupted by a knock on the door. There stood a woman, dressed in a white pinny. "Err, Cyril, I'm off," she told him.

"Hang on a minute, Maggie, I ain't had me dinner … I would like a nice roast beef followed by apple pie and custard, and me guest would like the same."

The woman stood with her hands on her hips. "Now, I won't tell you again. My name is Mary, and you, Lord Fuckwit, can do one. My shift is over. And I always have Saturdays off. At least I did for Lord Chambers, gawd rest his soul."

Cyril got up from his grand chair and faced the irate woman. "What did he die of, then? No fucker told me."

She snivelled into her apron. "Yes, Cyril, he died, not long after you stole his stately home. He missed the old place, and to be honest with ya, I miss him. It's hard work slaving for you. Nothing is in a routine, and I can't live like this. I mean, who has a MacDonald's burger for breakfast? I am the housekeeper-come-cook. We have standards, ya know."

Cyril walked over and put his arm around her shoulder. "Now, now, ol' girl, I didn't steal this mansion. I won it fair and square at poker. And if I had lost, he would have had two fucking mansions, so don't go thinking me a thief … Okay, maybe I was, years ago, but not now. So, Saturdays you have off, eh? Well, do me a favour, cook me a nice roast, and you can have tomorrow and Sunday off."

Mary huffed and sighed. "Well, Cyril, things are going to have to change around here, especially if you want to be a lord. You can stop swearing for a start and have some bleedin' decorum. And stop walking around with ya bollocks on show. It's enough to give me the screaming abdabs."

Cyril conceded. "Yes, Maggie, I will, as long as you stop calling me Lord Fuckwit."

With that, she nodded, closed the double doors, and left. Kelly was amused by it all and then she glanced up at the huge oil painting of Cyril. He was sitting on a horse with a grin, beaming from ear to ear, dressed in a hunting jacket. It was all too surreal yet somehow homely. Cyril was as mad as a box of frogs, and yet other than his villainous reputation, he was as soft as shit.

He waddled back to his chair and tittered like a school kid. "I love that ol' girl really. She came with this place. I wind her up something rotten. Ya know, she loves me. She looked after me when I had a stomach bug. Cor, I was proper ill an' all."

Kelly laughed and jokingly replied, "She probably tried to poison ya. You ain't left the mansion to her in your will, 'ave ya?"

There was silence for a second. Cyril, with a twinkle in his eye, gave her a benevolent smile. "As a matter of fact, my babe, I *have* made a will. So, take a good butchers around ya, 'cos, Kelly, when I'm gone, this 'ere is all yours."

"What?" she murmured in a slow whisper.

"Well, my babe, I should 'ave been there for ya. I can't get over that you were taken from Naomi, the sweet child, and brought up, no dragged up, by that Maureen, tortured an' all. I would 'ave come for ya. You see, Kelly, I loved you when you was a little 'un. Like a child I never had, if ya know what I mean. Anyway, so yep, babe, this is all left to you."

As the evening went on, Kelly learned a lot about the people in her family: the evil tricks her father had got up to, the wicked grief Toni caused people, and Sheila, the woman behind Patrick and Jack. Then, when the conversation turned to her birth mother, she discovered how really delightful she was. Cyril only partly allayed Kelly's concerns about Keffa. He concluded that he had no ulterior motive other than Kelly had turned up in his life when he was maybe doing some kind of business with Sheila. After all, no way would Sheila let Keffa know about the blue diamond. It was dog eat dog, in their world.

Mary returned to the drawing room with the hostess trolley and wheeled it over to the table under the enormous windows that overlooked the stunning gardens. Cyril never used the dining room, being as it was too formal.

"This is me niece, Kelly."

Mary smiled her way and then glared back at Cyril. "Well, that does surprise me. I mean, I thought you were related to the Munsters." She turned to Kelly and winked.

"If you are staying tonight, love, there is the pink room, all fresh and aired."

Kelly smiled. "Thank you, Mary, I think I will."

Cyril rubbed his hands together, when he looked at the beautifully presented meal. "Cor, Mags, this looks lovely. Now, you ain't poisoned me food, 'ave ya?"

Out of the blue, Mary ruffled Cyril's hair and laughed. "I might have," she giggled, and then she left. Kelly realised that Mary did have a soft spot for Cyril but was probably missing her previous employer. After all, Cyril acting the lord was such a joke.

CHAPTER TWENTY-FIVE

The next morning, Kelly got up from her four-poster bed. She had spent the evening tasting Cyril's various ports and wines from the huge cellar. He enjoyed showing off his new-found mansion with all the trimmings. The pink bedroom was now renamed 'Kelly's room'. She left before breakfast, thanking Cyril for his hospitality and kissing him on the cheek. She noticed his eyes looked as though they were glistening.

"Now, babe, you listen to ya Uncle Cyril. Any hint of trouble, you just get ya arse over 'ere. No ifs or buts. Will ya promise me?"

Kelly nodded. "I will, I promise." She looked up at the stately home and smiled. "I can see me here as lady of the manor."

Cyril chuckled. "Yeah, Lady Fuckwit, eh?"

He was still waving, as she was driven down the long drive, and for a moment she realised that, in among all the madness, she did feel at home with Cyril. During the long drive back to the house, she thought once more about her conversations yesterday evening with him. She chuckled to herself; he was a right geezer, who clearly loved her, and she was glad she had him in her corner. And she loved Rudy and Lippy too, who were still in Jamaica, and who, by the sounds of things, would be there for another few weeks. Even her aunt Bet had agreed to stay a little longer. Yes, she knew she had people in her life now who loved her. But she was still weighed down with so much of the past, that her heart felt heavy, and her mind was whirling in circles, trying to fathom it all out.

The traffic, when they hit London, was heavy, even though it was a Saturday. As they turned the corner to her home, she saw Keffa's car parked outside. She felt a cold sensation and a deep sinking feeling. She was in love with him, but at this moment, she wasn't sure if she could really trust him. Everyone in her life seemed to let her down. Once the cab pulled up, she decided to have the whole 'Sheila thing' out with him. But before she even reached the door, Keffa was running down the steps, his face flushed, and snatching both her arms and shaking her.

"Where have you been? I have been worried sick that Sheila McFarlane has been sniffing around and you would suddenly go on the missing list."

Kelly could see the worry in his eyes; they told her he did care about her. Surely, he couldn't fake his feelings that well? She had ignored his texts and phone calls and should have phoned him, but her mind was all over the place, twenty-four hours ago.

"All right, Keffa, leave off. I only went to see me uncle."

He let her go and folded his arms. "Oh, yeah, what uncle?"

"Cyril, if ya must know." She waited to gauge his reaction and was surprised when he relaxed his shoulders and sighed, "Jesus, thank God for that. I thought Sheila's boys had taken you."

Kelly walked past him, hoping he would follow; she had questions that needed answering.

They both walked into the lounge and closed the door behind them. Ditto smiled at Kelly. "You okay, Kel?"

Kelly nodded. "Listen, Ditz, d'ya mind if I have a private word with Keffa?"

Ditz frowned, looking from Keffa and then back to Kelly. "Nah, 'course. I am off to collect me winnings from the betting shop." He rubbed his hands together.

Keffa was still flustered and looked uneasy. He didn't like the expression on her face and hoped he hadn't upset her. Growing to love her, he wanted nothing more than to see out his future with her.

"What's up, Blue?"

Kelly paced the floor. He admired her. In many ways, she had the full package: not only was she good-looking and smart but she had that indefinable quality about her which set herself off from almost everyone he had ever known. She was almost certainly impulsive but unquestionably she was a leader in his eyes. She stopped and her stare was laser-like. "Tell me, Keffa, what business do you have with Sheila?"

Keffa sighed and ran his hands over his head.

"If you must know, I used to supply arms. I'm not proud of it, and she was my customer, her and Patrick."

Kelly plonked herself down on the sofa and stared off into space.

"When you appeared on the news for killing Patrick and suddenly this kid turns up at Rudy's, well, I somehow guessed it was you. Then, of course, you came to my house and took me by surprise. There you were, just a bit of a kid, really, all mouth and trousers, but with a heart of gold. I probably fell in love with you then ..."

Kelly turned to face him. "Go on, Keffa, but cut out the crap."

Those words really stung. "Hey, listen, Blue, it's true, I'm not lying to you."

"Keffa, just tell me your dealings with Sheila!" she hissed.

"Anyway, once word got around, I was told to look out for you, if you showed your face in London. I never let on to her that you were here, though. Then I went to your trial. I saw Jordan, her son, hovering about, so I shot off. But he saw me, and the next thing is, I got a visit by her ladyship. She wanted to know everything."

Kelly nodded. "So, what did you tell her?"

"I told her to fuck off and leave you alone."

Kelly suddenly shot up from her chair and yelled, "You liar, Keffa, I trusted you. I saw you from the lounge window, shaking hands with Jordan, having your cosy little chat."

Keffa's face clouded over with disappointment. "No, Kelly, you got it wrong. I saw their car parked across the road and I waited. Then I saw them come out of the house. That's when I approached them. I warned them that if they should go near you again, I would kill 'em."

"I saw you, Keffa, shake Jordan's hand."

Keffa shook his head and smiled. "No, you never. You got that wrong. I was actually grabbing the gun that was in his hand to take it off him."

Kelly closed her eyes and tried to recall what she had seen. Maybe she was mistaken. "But you never knocked, you got in your car ..."

"Yeah, I followed them to make sure they didn't come back. Christ, why do you think I was so worried when you didn't come home? All those messages and calls I sent to you. Blue, I love you!"

"Do you know what they want from me?"

Keffa nodded. "You have something that belongs to them. I don't know what it is, but they want it back."

"They think I have a blue diamond, worth millions, but I don't have it. I sold the one I had and gave the money back to Eddie, but apparently, there is another one."

"Fuck me, Blue, that witch has killed people for less. Are you sure you have no idea?"

"Yes, I am sure. If I had it, she could choke on it."

"Right, we need to get you to a safe place, well away from here, 'cos, my sweetheart, trust me, she will be back."

Kelly knew then that he was being honest, and she felt sick with remorse for even thinking he would hurt her. "I am sorry, Keffa, really I am. I should never have doubted you."

He laughed. "Blue, you have gone through a living hell in your young life. I ain't surprised you don't trust me. But you will do one day, I promise."

Something interrupted her thoughts. She stepped back like a bolt of lightning, her eyes widening. "Take me to my house."

"What, your old house? I mean, where you grew up? What happened to it?"

Kelly pulled out her bunch of keys and smiled. "It was sorted out through probate. My solicitor made sure it was handed over to me. Not that I would ever go back there, but it's mine."

Keffa drove in silence, guessing this would be a difficult time for Kelly. She felt her mouth dry up, as they turned the corner. There was the bus stop, the one she had waited at every morning for the bus. It conjured up so many negative memories imaginable. It was here where she'd stood shivering because her mother had never allowed her to wear a coat, which was warm enough, or woollen tights to cover her freezing legs. It was this bus stop where the kids had mercilessly teased and laughed at her. Slowly, they pulled over outside the house of hell. It was midday and the sun shone brightly, but the house, which previously had been meticulously maintained, showed obvious signs of neglect: the lawn was now a jungle, the pruned rose bushes were strangled with bindweed, the glossy front door looked dirty and faded, and the nets inside seemed grey. She thought about Maureen somewhere in a grave; it was a place she had never even laid flowers, but why would she?

It was a while before she had the resolve to step out of the car.

"Blue, you don't have to go in there, you know."

Kelly gave him a wan smile, and it was as though she was that teenager again: a shy, self-conscious kid, with the fear of her mother's wrath on her mind. Keffa could see it in her eyes, and at that moment, he so wanted to reach out and hug her.

He followed closely behind and glanced up and down the road, as she slipped the key in the lock. She pushed the door open and held her breath — she almost expected her mother to come out of the kitchen screaming obscenities at her. It was silent; an eerie stillness prevailed which even Keffa was unnerved by. They stepped inside and closed the door. Everything was the same barring the dust. Gripped by a cold shiver, she stepped back and leaned into Keffa. He sensed her fear and put his hand on her shoulder as if to say, 'I am right here'.

The living room was as sparse as ever, with just the sofa, armchair, and the old television. Keffa noticed the only picture on the wall, the one of Jesus, and the odd wooden crosses dotted around. It gave him the creeps. It should have looked peaceful and calm, like a church, but somehow it seemed very unholy. At the end, by the patio doors, was a bare dining-room table. Kelly stared for a few seconds reliving sitting there, night after night in silence, drawing a picture or reading some religious book.

They climbed the stairs and stopped at the first room, her bedroom. It was as the police had said, ransacked. But not too much mess was actually evident — after all, Kelly had hardly had anything to call her own. As Keffa stood in the doorway, his heart sank. This room was like a prison cell, with nothing but the basics. Anyone could have lived here. There was no sign of Kelly's personality; it was all so weird and yet so sad. This was Kelly's past; a loveless home with nothing to even dream about. No wonder she spoke from the heart and was so grateful to Rudy and Lippy.

Kelly walked on and into her mother's room, where she looked very carefully around the walls, in thought. Hurrying back along the landing and down the stairs, with Keffa on her heels, she unbolted the back door and headed straight for the shed. More daunting than the house was that wooden shed. She stopped at the door, almost afraid to go inside. The very centre of her angst – the one place she feared more than anywhere – was before her; it was now covered in trailing weeds. She checked behind to make sure Keffa was still there. She knew the shed held nothing sinister, except those incredibly disturbing memories, but that fear, even at twenty-one, still gripped her around the throat.

Taking a deep breath, she pulled open the door. The smell was the same and the dark, foreboding place was smaller than she remembered, but even today, it still scared the shit out of her. Once the door was wide open, she could see more clearly. There were the slatted shelves with the ropes still attached. Even the sharply filed canes, which her mother had used to strip her back, were a visible reminder of those dark days so many years ago. She slowly ran her hands over the ropes and along the canes. She felt an overwhelming sense of pity for the eight-year-old child she once was. It was the height of the ropes that brought home to her how tiny she was when her mother had tied her up.

Keffa knew then that this was the place where his Bluey had been whipped. His stomach felt empty. It was like a horror scene. Kelly felt the pain clench her again and an unexpected tear rolled down her face. He squeezed her shoulder, just to let her know he was there. Then, unexpectedly, she sat on the floor and closed her eyes. He remained quiet but puzzled. She moved her hands across the surface until she found the floorboard she wanted. She then gripped this one and pulled it up. As she opened her eyes, there it was – the cross which had hung above her mother's bed. It was the same cross she had seen her mother carry out here, the night Patrick slept over, the night she was too scared to go to the bathroom. Years before, when her mother had locked her in the shed all night in the dark, she had sat there shivering. At some point, her hands had felt something loose and it was a floorboard. Then, she had very much hoped and prayed that tucked inside was a key to get her out, but there had been nothing, nothing except an empty box.

But this time, however, she hoped she would not be disappointed. There was no key to unlock doors or secrets, but there was something else: there was the cross. She held it in her hands and stared at the chunky ornate instrument, and slowly, she turned it over to reveal a secret hidden compartment. She opened it with her fingernail, and, there, like the heart of Christ himself, was the blue diamond. How ironic was that?

Keffa bent over and reached for her hand. "Come on, Bluey, let's get out of here."

She took it, and as he pulled her to her feet, she fell into his arms and hugged him, whispering, "All that carnage for the sake of a stone held hidden in a cross. My mother knew all the time that there was another diamond."

She handed it to him and walked back to the house. This would be the test. The diamond was worth more money than either of them could imagine, and she had placed that power firmly in his hands. Now she would see the truth.

He followed her through the house and out to the car. She watched him open her door and close it behind her. Then he hopped into the driver's side and gripped her hand. "Are you all right, Blue?" he asked, as he handed back the cross.

"Yeah, I am, Keffa. Come on, let's go home."

She looked back at the house one last time. For a second, she thought she saw her mother at the window, but it was probably just a ghost of a sick, distant memory.

"It must have been hard for you. It's been — what — six years since you have set foot back in that house?"

Kelly looked down at the cross. "I did go back, after I killed Patrick."

Keffa swallowed hard. Maureen's murderer was never found. He gave her a sideways glance and thought about the shed and those ropes.

430

The laws of his world consoled himself with the notion that Maureen deserved to be killed and Kelly would have had every right.

"I went back to say sorry to my mum. I hated her, but I'd committed the ultimate sin, and for some reason, I wanted to tell her, although I don't know why. When I got there and let myself in, the back door was open, and she was lying there on the floor, blood everywhere. I grabbed a knife, thinking the burglar, or whoever, was still around, and then I knelt by her side and stroked her head. But she was dead. It was strange really because I was petrified when I killed Patrick, seeing all that blood, but I wasn't scared when I saw me mum. I said my goodbyes, and I returned the knife to the kitchen drawer. I then headed back home to Rudy's. I never killed her, you know. I think it was Eddie. He killed her, looking for the blue diamond. He must have put one in my bunny and given one to her for safekeeping. The bastard must have known that Sheila or Patrick would come for him, and the last place they would look was at Maureen's. I dunno. It's all a mystery."

Keffa had no knowledge of any diamond until today. Now, he was more concerned that Sheila would do everything in her power to get her hands on it.

"Listen, Bluey, I don't want to frighten you, but I think it was Sheila who killed Maureen, and what concerns me is she won't stop until she has that diamond. I am not so sure about this. This just doesn't add up."

"What do you suggest I do?"

"Either give it to her, or sell it and buy yourself an army, 'cos we will need one."

"We?" she asked tentatively.

"Well, you don't think you are on ya own, do ya?"

CHAPTER TWENTY-SIX

Sheila was livid, after her visit to Kelly's; she had been unable to settle all night, so she did what she always did at times of stress – got up and made a pot of Earl Grey tea.

Patrick's house in North London was in her name, like most of what he had owned. She had always been the brains behind the outfit. Born with a silver spoon in her mouth, as her brother had, she was really the wild child, who dragged Patrick along with her. The North London protection businesses were funded by her and yet Patrick was the face behind it. That was until he got taken over by Eddie. Sheila was a good few years older than Eddie, and she secretly fancied the pants off him, despite marrying Jack.

As she sat there, up at the grand dining table, sipping her tea, she noticed the photo album open at a photo of Naomi – it was the one she'd shown to Kelly. The album was Patrick's, and if she was honest with herself, she wouldn't have recognised Naomi in the street. So, when she'd received the news that not only her daughter had been killed at the hands of the Ravens, but that Naomi's child had also been handed over to Maureen, it didn't move her an inch. The one burning passion was for the blue diamond.

It had been her idea from the start, when she'd first married Jack. She was the true genius behind the heist to steal the safe deposit boxes. She knew what was hidden in one of them and cleverly planted the seeds in Eddie's head. Of course, he boasted he was the schemer. Not that she cared, though, as long as she could get her hands on the most sought-after precious blue gem in the collection.

Her father was a very wealthy landowner back in Ireland. He had a long-term feud with Lord Charlton over money, due to an inheritance that rightfully should have gone to the Mahoneys and not the Charltons. The one item that they had really argued over was a blue diamond worth more than the two estates put together. After her father died, she made it her life's mission to get that diamond back, and for years she had Lord Charlton, her second cousin, followed. It was then she discovered he had visited a building specialising in rare and valuable diamonds in London, and she deduced that was where he kept the blue gem.

She sipped her tea and shuddered. Years of planning had gone into holding that special gem in her hand, but it seemed she was now faced with a woman who, somehow, made her uneasy. She could have held a gun to her face or even had her tortured to find out the gem's whereabouts, but something had stopped her. She was no stranger to the art of gaining information, or, for that matter, getting her hands bloodied. In fact, she had told Eddie that the only way into that specialist building was to use Mickey 'no thumbs' to interrogate a security manager working there to reveal the locations of keys, passwords, and outside patrols. She was spared some details, but she did read in the *London Evening Standard* that a man had been found in a skip with evidence of previous torture marks, and that he'd had his throat slashed, not far from those premises, and around the time she thought the heist had taken place. But now, at sixty, she left the violence to her sons and the others in her firm.

Her dear old brother lay dead in that grave, and he may as well have taken the fucking diamond with him, for all she knew. How had this all happened?

As the brains behind the heist, she was the only one who knew full well that of the two blue diamonds in the collection, the smaller one was worth in the region of £10 million and the larger gem was valued at around £1 million. Her plan was to play off Eddie against Jack and Jack against Eddie, with neither knowing all the details. She intended that Eddie would double-cross Jack and Mickey by stealing the larger diamond, duping him into believing he would be in possession of the more valuable gem. He never even questioned the possibility that the smaller diamond was only worth a few hundred grand and why would he? Naturally, Eddie's knowledge of diamonds was no greater than the average person, so he readily believed her, and assumed that the larger gem would therefore be the more valuable one, worth £1 million. But he was kept in ignorance of the 4Cs and that size is only one of the criteria for assessing the value of a precious stone.

At the same time, she had instructed Jack to cause a diversion long enough for him to steal the most valuable gem. Once Jack had handed her the 'real deal' for safekeeping, Sheila then planted seeds in Eddie's head about the double-cross, leading him to kill Jack and Mickey, which she knew he would.

So, all should have gone sweet until her brother became very greedy. He knew Eddie was in possession of a diamond worth a decent amount. It was not as valuable as the one they already had their hands on, but he still wanted it. Since Eddie was in prison, it was obvious he would have hidden it, and the most likely place was at Maureen's. Sheila found out that Patrick planned to visit Maureen en route to a dealer who was buying their most precious gem. Once at Maureen's, he intended on rooting around until he found the one Eddie had stolen, after which he would sell both gems to the dealer. But Patrick's murder changed things. Not only was Eddie's diamond still out there somewhere but Sheila and Patrick's one had also mysteriously disappeared from Patrick's possessions. Sheila had someone on the force who had taken a look at the inventory of everything logged by the police, but the only item of value was a gold Rolex watch. Now, both the diamonds were missing and from meeting her granddaughter and watching her closely, when she virtually clammed up and had the audacity to kick *her* out of the house, she had her suspicions she could be the only link to this saga.

All her idiot brother had to do was to take their gem to the dealer as planned and have the money deposited in her bank account. There had been no need to launder the substantial cash, as she'd had the fake certificates all made-up, another clever little stunt she'd planned. A maid, Kitty Buckle, had secured herself a job at Lord Charlton's stately home and was paid the minimum wage. Sheila knew the girl and offered her a fat sum to get her hands on the certificate. It was too easy, and by the end of the week, Kitty had the certificate in her bag and handed over to Sheila. A week later, she slyly returned the certificate, with Lord Charlton none the wiser. It had been a great money earner for the young woman and it continued to be. Sheila was laughing, now she had the certificate copied and changed in her name. As soon as Lord Charlton died, Kitty snatched the original certificate and burnt it in the fire. The gem was now legally Sheila's.

Biding her time, waiting for Lord Charlton to pop his clogs, had been a shrewd move because there would be no question as to the rightful owner of this gemstone. Bloody years she had waited for Lord Charlton to die, so much so, she'd almost wanted to finish him off herself. To add insult to injury, the old bastard had to go and die when Eddie was due out of prison. She clenched her fist; if only Patrick had gone and done what he was told. Why he hadn't just gone straight to the dealer was beyond her. The larger blue gem was worth peanuts in comparison, and yet she should have guessed that her little brother would go after it; he may have been a greedy sod, but perhaps he thought that in some way, by taking the other diamond from Eddie, it would be payback for always playing second fiddle to the man.

Sipping her tea, she allowed a sardonic grin. Eddie had been good company, that was for sure. Fucking everything in sight, he had even given her a good thrusting, every so often. She wasn't such a bad-looking woman in her day, always managing to look younger and keep herself tidier than many. Eddie liked sex and so did she, but she had standards. Jack was a useless fuck, and so she never batted an eyelid when she was riding Eddie in the other room.

Her thoughts drifted back to Patrick, her little brother; she had loved him, despite those negative thoughts about his greediness. Of all the times he could have died at the hands of another firm, he was killed by a fifteen-year-old child. Her suspicions that her brother liked younger girls, and boys, of course, were probably not far off the mark. She knew he fancied Eddie, but he married Eddie's bitch of a sister for status. It wasn't long before his sexual foibles were uncovered. She'd heard what went on at the trial and how Kelly had said Patrick had tried to rape her. She certainly wasn't surprised, but, then, did Kelly get her hands on her diamond and do a runner?

The night Sheila went to Maureen's house to find the diamond, Maureen looked so different. The once bubbly tart was a weak and pathetic woman, now on her knees praying for God to help her. Sheila was angry that Maureen didn't know where the diamond was and even more livid that she was praying like some nun for God's deliverance. Strange that: it almost made her question her own destiny. Would she, herself, go to heaven or hell? With six murders under her belt by her own hands and countless others by her orders, she knew, as Maureen prayed, that she was very unlikely to go to heaven in the express lane. Yes, hell was her destiny, for sure. The wailing and praying was more than she could take, and so to shut Maureen up, she snatched her hair, pulled her up off the floor, and like a knife through butter, slit her throat. More shocking for Sheila though was the fact that Maureen hadn't even struggled, as if she was ready to accept her fate.

The police inventory, the search through Patrick's belongings, including his suitcases left untouched there in the hallway, and her systematic fine-toothed comb inspection, revealed nothing. So, her conclusion was that Kelly had removed that gem from Patrick's luggage. One way or another, though, she would get it back.

❧*❦

Kelly was under orders to pack her bags and stay with Cyril for a while, at least until Keffa could put matters right. He would have to convince Sheila she was barking up the wrong tree.

"Keffa, I ain't scared of her. I will front her out, if she turns up again."

He shook his head. "No disrespect, Blue, but I have known you since you were a kid, and you don't know the way people like her operate. Trust me, she will have a gun up your fucking hooter and a knife in your back."

Kelly stood defiantly, with her hands on her hips. "Well, give me a gun, then."

Keffa turned around, clutching his head. "You ain't no Jesse fucking James. You ain't from this life. I swear to God, she and her boys are lunatics."

"I ain't from this life, eh? I ain't from a normal family, and I think I have more bottle than you give me credit for."

Keffa gave her a sombre glance and had to agree. "Babe, I know you have a lot of guts. I should know, 'cos you fronted me out. Listen, I don't want you in harm's way. It's only because I care."

Kelly agreed and sighed, so she made the call and it was all arranged. Ditto drove and griped all the way because Legend was in the back of the car, dribbling down his neck. Reggie was silent, too afraid to move too quickly, in case Legend bit him. As they drove up the lane, Ditto stopped moaning and started to laugh. "This is fucking mental. Look at the size of that house. Cor, your uncle must be a real rich geezer."

Kelly laughed. "Yeah, he is a lord now, ya know. Well, he thinks he is."

As soon as the gates opened and they approached the mansion, there was pandemonium. Frank and Stein, Cyril's two Rottweilers, had spotted Legend and were going nuts. Reggie was curled in a ball. The fifty kilos of mastiff was on his lap and was trying to get at the dogs. Cyril came running out in a long nightshirt and a shotgun, screaming at the dogs to stop. He fired the gun in the air and the dogs instantly backed away. Ronnie came out with two heavy chains and clipped them to the rabid-looking beasts before he dragged them away. Cyril was out of breath and laughing at the same time.

Kelly jumped out of the car, followed by Legend. But Ditto and Reggie were fixed to their seats. They were afraid of Legend, let alone two monster Rottweilers.

Cyril gave Kelly a hug. "I am glad you're here, my babe. I think it's safer. That mental midget, Sheila, is a ruthless bitch, and Keffa's right,

438

she will come for ya. You and Laurel and Hardy can stay as long as you want." He looked down at Legend. "Good boy! I s'pose you're the little fucker that bit Eddie." He stroked his head and laughed.

Ditto and Reggie warily stepped out of the car and looked about, still nervous about the two Rotties. They followed Kelly and Cyril into the grand house, nudging each other and giggling.

Cyril took them into the drawing room and excused himself to get dressed.

Kelly was laughing at the boys' shock of sitting in a stately home surrounded by pomp and antiques. She knew they felt out of place, by the way they sat so straight-backed and nervous. Yet, to her, not that she lived like a lady, it didn't feel so odd. Far from it; maybe it was Cyril who made her feel at home. Legend lay across her feet, totally untroubled.

Wearing his jeans and a plaid shirt, Cyril returned. "Right, then, let's get sorted," he said, rubbing his hands together. "It seems to me that we have a situation, and you, my girl, are gonna have to trust me on this." His head perched forward, waiting for an okay.

Kelly nodded.

"You two boys, I take it, aren't clowns, are ya?"

Ditto and Reggie shook their heads in unison. They weren't going to argue with Cyril; he had an old-school reputation and was obviously a gangster in the true sense of the word, unlike the youngsters running around causing mayhem selling a few grams of Charlie and pulling out a blade to show they meant business. There was a big divide between the real old-timers and the new kids on the block, and it had a lot to do with serious organised crime. The oldies gave more thought to planning their skulduggery; furthermore, they believed in a strict moral code, unlike their modern counterparts. One part if it was you don't hurt women or children.

Cyril walked and talked like a dangerous man, and even now, in his sixties, he still commanded attention. Kelly, on the other hand, saw him for what he meant to her: he was a soppy old git and she loved him dearly. Ditto and Reggie were not fooled by his extrovert ways. As far as they were concerned, he may be a bit nutty, but he was a player. They, of course, had heard all about the alleged nefarious activities in which Cyril had played an active role and simply knew him as a legend of his era.

"Now, boys, this is the closest I have to a daughter. She tells me that you two have looked after her for years now, and so I can trust you, can't I?"

Still afraid to talk, they nodded.

"Right, yes, good, good. 'Cos, that poisonous fucking dwarf is gonna find out soon enough that our Kelly is 'ere. She will send her boys, and by that I don't mean her two half-witted sons, I mean her fucking fanny-licking minders. So, it's like this. I will not be pulling any punches or taking any fucking prisoners. So, boys, what you may witness, you are gonna have to take a blind eye to. Got me?"

Ditto smiled. "Honestly, Mr Reardon, you can trust us. We always have Bluey's back."

Cyril nodded, now satisfied. "Right, come with me, then. Let's get sorted."

They all followed him down to the cellar and watched as he pulled back a rug to reveal the door to a secret underfloor room. They realised how strong he was, when he lifted the heavy trap door with one hand.

The wooden staircase led to a massive basement. It looked much like an army storage unit, with shotguns, rifles, handguns, knives, rounds of ammunitions, and cans of toxic substances.

Kelly gasped, "Christ, Cyril, what's all this for?"

Cyril laughed, "Oh, my girl, you have a lot to learn. I hardly worked in a fucking office, now did I? Anyway, boys, grab yourselves a gun and make sure you have ammunition."

Ditto and Reggie were placid in the grand scheme of things, not having handled a baseball bat never mind a gun before. It showed too: they looked a bundle of nerves.

"Oh, don't fucking tell me, ya ain't fired a gun? Well, boys, man up, 'cos this might get a bit messy. 'Ere, I tell ya what, Frank 'the butcher' and Blakey are coming over. They can take you out the back and give you a few lessons. Think of it as a day out clay pigeon shooting."

Kelly felt uneasy. Judging by Cyril's preparations, it looked as though Sheila was one hard-faced bitch. "Cyril, is this all necessary? I mean, I could just give her what she wants. I don't want anyone to get hurt."

"Now, babe, you listen to me. I know it ain't your fault that you were born into this world, but the fact of the matter is you were. Like it or lump it, you need protection right now, and it's my job to give it. If it ain't Sheila trying to take from you, it's only gonna be some other greedy cunt."

Kelly frowned in puzzlement. She had no idea what he was on about, but whatever it was, she wasn't happy about it.

"Kel, don't you get it, babe? You are a very wealthy woman. Fuck me, everything Eddie owned will go to you, and I know the filth can't touch it. All his money was carefully put through the washing machine."

Now Kelly was even more confused than ever. "Washing machine?"

"Oh, dear, dear me, let's go back upstairs ... boys, you get yaselves sorted and try not to shoot each other." He pushed her back up the staircase and into the drawing room. "Look, babe, I don't need to tell you how our firm got our money. The thing is, ya can't just rob a bank or a G4S van, and buy houses and cars, 'cos you have to explain where the money comes from. So, we make sure it goes through the bank account legally. Christ, I have all sorts of businesses that do that. Anyway, so did ya ol' man, so all his millions are not touchable. It all goes to you. Now, being that you are Eddie Raven's daughter, and the owner of a few haunts, like a nightclub and a pub, some cunt will want their share. Ya father had enough enemies."

Kelly swallowed hard and suddenly felt her world crumbling; she wasn't ready to take on the gangster underworld, and she had no idea how she would do this on her own. She didn't want loads of money either; all she wanted was a quiet life, whatever that was.

Cyril could see the look of despair on her face and felt compassion for the girl. "It's all right, my babe, you have your own firm, me, Frank, Blakey, and the boys, and I don't mean fucking Bill and Ben down there."

She laughed and then nodded. "Has it all come to this? I suppose this is what my life is all about now."

"Well, it's up to you. But it's all yours for the taking. The money's good and the pubs and club take in a decent earn. The protection racket, that's pretty much sewn up, but I guess it will always be challenged, and of course there's the diamond. Once you sell that little nugget, you can live like a queen."

Kelly had a lot to think about. He was right, she would be a very rich woman, but all that money had come from crime, and if she was to spend a penny of it, then she would be like them. But, if she turned her back on the money, then she would forever be thinking *what if*. She hated bullies more than anyone and right now the biggest bully was Sheila. She may not have had the chance to sort out her father and Toni, but she was determined to bring down Sheila, with or without help from Cyril.

The rest of the day was filled with Cyril's guided tour and the boys making the most of the facilities. They were like kids on holiday. The east side of the house was mainly the entertaining area with a games room, in which Ditto thought all his birthdays had come at once. For, not only was there a snooker table, a bar, and a huge curved TV and gaming centre, there was also an indoor heated swimming pool, sauna, and Jacuzzi. Which silly sod said crime doesn't pay? This was heaven! But Ditto and Reggie were astute enough to realise that with this lifestyle came exceptionally high risks, and so, as they gazed in wonder at all this luxury on tap, they were not planning on following in Cyril's footsteps any time soon.

Whilst the boys skipped from bedroom to bedroom choosing theirs, just delighted to enjoy the facilities, Kelly was unpacking her small case in what was now her own room, and in doing so, she was deliberating on what she wanted in her own life. The truth was, she had left school with nothing, served time for manslaughter, and only knew how to sell fake goods and maintain the books. Was one side of her genes naturally aligned to the criminal fraternity? She knew one side wasn't! What could she really turn her hand to, and who would employ her anyway?

Cyril was downstairs with Frank, Blakey, and Beano. Beano was another man in their firm and their ear to the ground. Like a Native American tracker, he could sniff out anyone. A trusted man, with a highly trained skill, he really should have worked for MI6, but he earned more money getting involved in covert operations for those who employed him, mainly Eddie's firm. He had never liked the man though.

"So, Beano, what did ya find out?" asked Cyril.

Beano, a small man with a cheeky grin, replied, "Since Patrick's death, his manor is now run by the Carters. They took over the protection, literally overnight. The Jolly Roger has been claimed back, the cocaine is drying up because the Colombians only dealt with Patrick, and so there is trouble, and Shelia is in the middle of it all. By all accounts, she took her little firm over there, throwing her weight about, and she managed to get out before Johnnie Carter blew her head off, not literally though. The Colombians won't deal with a woman, so right now, boys, she is desperate to get her hands on that diamond because before long she won't have a business left. She might have been the brains behind it all and so dangerous in that respect, at one time, but it's different now the Carters are a big firm and they see her as an old woman. She's lost three of her men — dead — already, and two others have also quit."

Kelly was listening outside, taking it all in. As soon as she appeared in the doorway, the men all greeted her like she was a child, hugging her and kissing her, and calling her the baby.

"So, the poisonous dwarf is weak and has probably taken a good bashing to her reputation. I think it's time I had a word with my grandmother because, like all tormentors, she needs to be taught a lesson."

The men were startled, and it was at that point they saw a woman, not a cute, lovable niece. Observing her face critically now, they saw she had a glint in her eyes, like Eddie's, and a cool yet sharp countenance, which they admired. She could be an asset to their firm.

"Kel, this ain't a game, babe. She is still a fucker and handy with a tool."

"I know, Cyril, I ain't naïve. I might not have grown up in the life, and the truth is I can't even load a gun, let alone hold up a bank, but I ain't scared either. I ain't scared of anyone, to tell ya the truth, so maybe that's my problem, but I have made my decision. I am going to wipe out that bitch, so she can't harm another living soul."

Frank, in his gruff voice, laughed. "I gotta hand it to ya, babe, you do have guts. I watched you rip into Eddie. A fearless fucker you are."

"I have got a plan. She can have the diamond back ..."

"What!" screeched Blakey. "No fucking way, that's yours! Don't give it to her, it's worth millions!"

Kelly laughed and looked at Beano. "Can one of you go to any jewellers and just buy a big blue crystal about two inches long and an inch wide? Sheila won't know the difference, unless she has a picture."

The men chuckled and Beano wasted no time. "Right, no worries. I'll be back later. I don't need to know the plan. I just hope that you know what you are doing."

Kelly nodded and waited for him to leave. All eyes and ears were on her. "So, tell me about these places I own. Do they serve food?"

Frank nodded. "Yeah, top notch as well, why?"

"I might not be able to use a gun, and I don't think I could stomach slitting her throat, but I sure as hell can poison the bitch over a nice roast beef and a cosy family reunion."

"So why the fake diamond?" asked Frank.

Kelly smiled. "My back up. I can't guarantee she will dine with me, but I can make sure she never gets her hands on the gem."

The three men looked at each other, grinning.

"And what about Bill and Ben?" asked Cyril.

Kelly laughed. "They are on holiday. I don't want them hurt. You see, daft as they are, they kept me safe for years and looked after me well. I love them like me own brothers, so I want them out of the way."

"And Keffa?" asked Cyril.

"Oh, yeah, I need him out of the picture, too. He was going to have a word with Sheila, to tell her to back off. I'd better call him."

The phone rang but there was no answer. Kelly felt her heart racing. *Please pick up.*

Ten minutes went by and there was still no answer. She began to pace the floor, panicking. If they had got to him, she wouldn't bother with the poison; she would use one of Cyril's hand grenades and blow them to Timbuktu.

She returned to the men and instantly they could tell something was gravely wrong. "He's not answering. He always answers to me." A lump lodged in her throat and the blood drained from her face. Cyril put his arm around her and pulled her close. The tears trickled and the men saw Kelly as a child again. They were all eager to comfort her.

"Listen, babe, he may be in the shower," suggested Frank awkwardly.

Kelly looked at her phone; it suddenly lit up, blasting out a tune. It was Keffa's number. Her shoulders relaxed then and she smiled at the men. "It's him."

She answered the call and froze; her eyes flashed with anger, and every muscle in her face tightened, as she listened to the demands made by Sheila. Christ, another one of her dear friends was being held hostage by a devious bastard. The men deduced then that Sheila had him.

"If you hurt him, I swear to God, I will slice you in half. 'Ave ya diamond, but touch Keffa, and you are a dead woman walking. Do you hear me!" she screamed down the phone.

Now in a rage, she pushed past Cyril and headed for the cellar, with the men following her, trying to calm her down. With little effort, she hauled back the trap door and jumped down the stairs. Her eyes flitted from one gun to another before focusing on a handgun. Trembling, she snatched the weapon and looked at the ammunition. "Cyril, load this for me."

446

"Hold on a minute, Kelly, what's going on? You can't go in with all guns blazing!" declared Frank.

"Oh, no? I most certainly can! I am gonna shoot the woman. She has Keffa. I don't even know if he is alive. She laughed at me down the phone. The bitch laughed at me, calling me a silly little girl. Well, girl I'm not, and I'll show her silly, when she has a bullet through her nut."

Frank grabbed her arms and tried to calm her down. "Don't be reckless. It won't do any good. You have to be sensible and plan."

Kelly slowed down her breathing, yet her eyes remained wild. What was she doing? Of course, she couldn't go shooting anyone. Not only had she never loaded a gun, she had never fired one. All the anger, fear, and desperation had momentarily left her uncontrolled and looking totally foolish. This wasn't her; she was better than that. "Sorry, Frank, I don't know what I was thinking."

The phone rang again, and yes, it was Sheila. "Now I have your attention, Kelly, listen to me very carefully. I am not playing schoolgirl games, so if you want your boyfriend back in one piece, you will do as I say. Any funny business, and let's just say, there will be no black cock for you tomorrow."

Kelly had the phone on loudspeaker, so the others could hear. Cyril grabbed a pen and paper from off the side table. He scribbled, *stay cool, listen to her terms.* She nodded.

"So, what do you want, Sheila?" Inside, she was seething but knew she had to concentrate: she had to play the game.

"Good girl. Now I want to meet you, alone. Bring the diamond, and Kelly, I mean alone. Don't go bringing your two idiotic sidekicks, 'cos they will get hurt."

Cyril nodded to Frank and whispered. "Sheila has no idea Kelly is with us."

"Where?" was all Kelly said, fighting back the urge to verbally tear into her.

"Your home, of course," replied Sheila, sarcastically.

Kelly was nonplussed by the front of the woman. "What do you mean, my home?"

Sheila laughed again down the phone which got Kelly's back up. "Maureen's, the house in which you murdered my brother. It seems only fitting, really. You bring the parcel and Keffa gets released. It's that simple. So, I will see you here in, let's say, an hour."

Yet another déjà vu experience, she thought, just like Eddie kidnapping Peter. But this time, she wasn't going to act recklessly. She was going to listen to the men. After all, this was what they did; they were the poker specialists, when it came down to someone's life on the line.

"Sheila, I will be there, and you can have the poxy stone, but I can't make it in an hour, it's impossible. I am down in Hastings."

Cyril was smiling and nodding, letting Kelly know she was saying all the right things.

"An hour or else," demanded Sheila.

Kelly was shaking and Frank put his hand on her shoulder to ease her nerves.

"Listen to me, Granny. I ain't superwoman, I can't defy time, so if you want the diamond, then you will have to give me two hours, and if you hurt Keffa, then you can kiss your arse goodbye!"

There was silence for a few seconds. The men looked at each other with half-smiles. The young woman was doing just fine. Then Sheila spoke. "All right, Kelly, two hours at Maureen's, you on your own, with the diamond, and Keffa will live."

"Put him on the phone or there's no deal," ordered Kelly, in a calm tone.

"He ain't here. Anyway, you don't call the shots, I do. So, if you want him alive, then do as you are told. I ain't playing games, Kelly. If you want to test me, then you will have a dead boyfriend on your hands, and believe me, madam, it will be messy."

Blakey moved away into another room to make a few phone calls, while Cyril and Frank stayed with Kelly. Cyril nodded for her to agree.

"Okay, but if you hurt him, you are right, it *will* get very messy."

Sheila laughed again down the phone. "Kelly, you have no idea what messy looks like, so stop acting the hard prat and just do as I tell you, and then you can go back to your shitty life with your pathetic so-called family ... Two hours!" she yelled and then slammed the phone down.

Blakey returned. "Right, Kelly, does Keffa still live at Latchmere?"

Kelly nodded and listened as Blakey was talking to someone on the phone. Once he had finished, he smiled. "Well, Kelly, Keffa is at his flat we think because his car's parked outside along with her boy Junior's little two-seater red Porsche, the flash prick. So, it's my guess no more than two men have him. All the other cars parked outside there are accounted for."

The plan was put in place. She felt relieved she had Cyril and the others on her side. They were like the A team. She wanted to laugh at the madness of it all. Yet they seemed to know exactly what they were doing. It was just like a military exercise she had seen on the television.

Cyril explained that Sheila had taken too much for granted and hadn't done her homework properly and fucked up big time by assuming that Kelly was alone in this world. She had mistakenly thought that by taking Keffa as a hostage and using him as a bargaining chip, she had removed Kelly's only ally. Sheila was so determined to

449

get her hands on the diamond, that she had too many fatal flaws in her plan. "This, my girl, will be a walk in the park."

Kelly drew the layout of the house, so once they were in, there would be no surprises.

Frank and Cyril piled into one car; they were picking up two of their men on the way. Beano was good at his job and had returned with a blue crystal. She laughed when he'd handed it to her. "Cor, I know who to go to when I do my Christmas shopping." He inclined his head and shyly smiled. He found himself in awe of her looks and admired her mature approach to it all. Blakey and Beano jumped into another car; they were off to Keffa's flat with Kelly's set of keys to get in. Keffa had given her them, a few months ago, to use if ever the need arose.

Kelly left Ditto and Reggie alone in the house, oblivious to what was going on. They were in a world of their own, enjoying all the amenities. Ronnie stayed behind. He would keep the property safe from intruders. Before she left, she poured some poison into a perfume bottle from a container she had found down in Cyril's war room. The men left fifteen minutes before her, and for old geezers, they had just become very dangerous tooled-up gangsters. It took Kelly by surprise how they changed from doting 'uncles' to significant hard-faced killers, and she was relieved they were on her side.

The drive back to her home gave her time to think. She was worried about Keffa but felt confident in the belief her men knew what they were doing. It was strange she was about to embark on a mission to take out Sheila, her own grandmother. Yet, she pushed the idea to one side that the woman was family because she had learned a long time ago that blood is not thicker than water, not her blood at any rate. The last time she'd done this, trade for a man's life, she was in a state, tearing through the streets, sweating, shaking, and acting rashly. Not this time though. She was on a mission and her focus was not on releasing Keffa because she knew Blakey and Beano would see to that. This time, she was intent on ridding the world of more members of her evil family. Reality had slapped her in the face. Her life was so far removed from religious brainwashing that now she was thinking like a criminal. Even driving without a licence was a risk but one that sat her at the back of the queue after murder.

By the time she reached the house, Cyril and Frank had secured Sheila and Jordan at gunpoint.

Their plan was simple and executed to perfection. After dropping Cyril and Frank off in a cul-de-sac behind Maureen's house, for them to make their way towards the back of the property, two men on Cyril's payroll created a distraction. They pulled up outside the house, with the music blaring, and then jumped out of the car and pretended they were having a massive argument. Conscious that the fracas the men were causing would have the Ol' Bill on the scene, Sheila and Jordan rushed outside to break up what was now a full-on fight and send them on their way. This provided the opportunity for Cyril and Frank to slip inside undetected through the back door, as they waited to catch Sheila and Jordan off guard at gunpoint.

Sheila was more angry than scared, but that was her all over. Like Eddie, she thought she was invincible. But Jordan was shitting himself, and unlike his usual bolshie self, he remained quiet and still.

Sheila glared at Cyril. "I thought you had retired from the game."

She was sitting at the dining-room table, quite composed for a woman with a gun at her head.

"Yeah, you can't keep a good man down can you, and anyway, I came out for the guv'nor."

Sheila tilted her head. "But Eddie's dead."

Frank laughed and his deep gruff tone unnerved Sheila; suddenly fear consumed her.

"He is dead, isn't he?"

Cyril nodded. "Yep, proper brown fucking bread."

"So, who are you on about?" she asked, searching their faces for answers.

Kelly pulled up outside as planned and was greeted by two men who looked to be in their forties. The taller guy, with a nasty scar down his cheek, smiled and showed his false gnashes. "You can go in, Kelly, Cyril's inside."

The other man opened the front door for her. She took a deep breath, composed herself, and waltzed in to find both Jordan and Sheila at the dining table. Frank and Cyril had big cheesy grins.

"That's the guv'nor!" retorted Cyril.

Sheila frowned as she gazed at her granddaughter who wasn't a lost youngster with no savvy but evidently a resourceful and determined woman. Kelly stood tall and still, focused on her adversary, her eyes cold and unblinking, and her body language comparable to that of a boxer who was just about to knock out her opponent with one punch. Sheila had to admire her. She was young and beautiful and yet her eyes looked daunting and devious. The sneer on her face was all Eddie's — she was her father's daughter all right. That look would put the shit up most men and have them quaking in their boots. She realised that Kelly meant business; if she didn't think of an exit strategy quickly, she would be toast, like her brother.

"Kelly, you think you have the backing of this motley crew. Well, let me tell you, sweetheart, they are only after your diamond, your money, and probably a fuck at the end of it."

Cyril was livid she could say such a sick thing and pulled his hand back to smash her in the face, but Kelly shouted, "No, Cyril, don't lower yourself. You don't hit women."

Cyril complied and Sheila could see the power Kelly had. It angered her. Kelly was a kid in comparison; she shouldn't have this much clout. She tried a different tack.

"Kelly, can't you see what they are up to? They only want what you have. They are scumbags. They ain't family but I am. I wanted to get you here to talk, and believe me, I wasn't going to hurt Keffa. I just wanted your attention, and it was the only way I knew how to get it." By now, she sounded pathetic, almost grovelling.

Kelly was holding the small bottle concealed in her hand. "Ya know what, Granny, I think we need to sit down and talk over a nice brandy. I am sure we all need a drink. Let's clear the air and get some facts straight."

Sheila noticed the change in Kelly's voice and stupidly relaxed her shoulders. Perhaps she had built up false concerns about this girl's attributes. She sensed a weakness and would aim to exploit it. She was a hard case herself, she had proved it, but had Kelly? For all she knew, her brother's death may have been an accident. But she hated this woman for it, nonetheless.

Kelly went to the kitchen, where she knew her mother kept a bottle of brandy under the sink, and sure enough, it was still there. She retrieved five glasses and poured the brandies and put them on a tray with the bottle that only had enough for one or two more glasses. Assuming plan A was successful, she laced the remainder of the brandy with the poison. She fervently hoped this would work; otherwise, her fallback position would be plan B, the fake gem.

After placing them on the table, she nodded for them to take a glass. Sheila snatched hers first, from the opposite side of the tray, just in case it was poisoned. Cyril took one, followed by Frank.

Sheila watched to see if the men drank theirs and was relieved to see them down it in one and slam the glasses back on the tray.

"Go on, Sheila, I think we all need a drink, and you, Jordan," smiled Kelly, in a reassuring tone, as if they were best buddies. Cyril watched his 'niece' with pride, pleased with the way she was handling things. Sheila was dry-mouthed but swallowed the brandy, along with Jordan, who was still shitting himself.

Kelly took a seat opposite her grandmother and her niece.

"So, Sheila, it seems to me, and correct me if I'm wrong, you have overstepped the mark, and I for one don't take too kindly to people that mess with me family."

Sheila felt sick, listening to Kelly, talking exactly like Eddie. 'Correct me if I'm wrong' was his saying.

"So, dear ol' Granny, get on the phone and call your men. If they don't let Keffa go, then Frank 'ere will start using his tool kit, won't ya, Frank?"

Frank and Cyril were amused by Kelly's role at playing the hard woman but went along with it anyway. "Yep, I think some of me tools 'ave gone rusty."

There was no secret regarding Frank's nickname, 'the butcher', and Sheila felt her stomach contents rise to the back of her throat.

Almost immediately, Cyril's phone rang; it was Blakey. "Mate, we 'ave a problem. Junior and his sidekick have given Keffa a right messy hiding. We are gonna have to call an ambulance, but that means the Ol' Bill sniffing around and two dead fuckers in Keffa's flat."

"Get him in your car. King's College Hospital is just down the road. The ambulance will take too long. Get Beano to take out the rubbish, down to me brother Howie's place. The pigs need fattening anyway."

Kelly kept her eyes firmly on Sheila and Jordan, while she spoke to Cyril. "What did they do to Keffa?" Her voice, like a robot, was too calm and controlled for the situation.

"Sorry, Kel, he got beaten pretty badly, but Blakey's taking him to the hospital now."

Sheila suddenly blurted out, "And my boy?"

454

Cyril shook his head. "Your boy and his mate are now fattening up me brother's pigs."

Sheila swallowed hard; she loved Junior, but Jordan was her favourite.

Kelly smiled at Sheila. "It appears that you are a clever liar, so here's the thing ..." She stopped and poured the last of the brandy into Sheila's and Jordan's glasses. There were still a few dregs in her own glass. "Firstly, you should never 'ave lied, and secondly, you should never 'ave hurt Keffa."

Sheila felt her nerves take over, as the blood drained from her head, and her stomach churned over. She had a weak bladder anyway and the warm liquid was pouring away and dripping on the floor. Her legs shook and her throat tightened. She glanced at the brandy, and to calm her nerves, she downed it in one. Jordan had never seen so much fear in his mother's eyes; he followed suit, knocking back the drink.

Kelly stood up and smirked. "It seems to me, you wicked old bitch, this game is over. I ain't a silly little kid. Sadly, I have inherited the sins of my father."

It wasn't long before Sheila knew this for herself. The muscles in her throat constricted, she felt some burning in her stomach, and her racing pulse was enough to realise she had just succumbed to poison. Jordan died first, followed by his mother.

Kelly turned to Frank and Cyril. "Well, at least they didn't make a mess." She pulled from her pocket the fake gem and held it up to the light. "I didn't need this, then." Kelly drove to the hospital in record time; all she could think about was Keffa, praying that he would live. She left Frank and Cyril to clean up. It was at that moment she realised she had reached a tipping point: her old life had now morphed into a new one. Oppressed, tormented, and imprisoned mentally for much of her younger years by her mother, who was to blame for her own lack of confidence, the subsequent prison sentence for the manslaughter of Patrick had actually had the opposite effect, in that it had acted as a catalyst for releasing all those powerful traits in her personality which determined who she really was.

She liked the term 'guv'nor': it had a certain cachet to it.

Also, secretly, she wasn't averse to enjoying her new-found authority.

CHAPTER TWENTY-SEVEN

Six weeks later

The rain was a gentle fine spray and wasn't enough to ruin the arrangements. The cars pulled up outside the house in Peckham. The mourners gathered to pay their last respects, waiting on the pavement for Kelly to appear. She stepped out of the house, wearing a neatly fitted black dress and a beautiful large hat. Dressed in such a sophisticated style, the men could not help but notice how stunning she looked.

Lippy and Betty followed, both still horrified by recent events in their absence. Rudy held on to Lippy's arm to help her down the steps. She was still a little weak, but her trip to Jamaica had improved her health, and the new medication was working.

ক্ষ*ঞ

In fact, considering Kelly's ordeal, Lippy was unusually calm and in good spirits. A stretch limousine had picked them up from the airport, for her comfort more than anything else. Kelly, along with Keffa and the boys, waited eagerly for the limo to arrive.

They had, as Keffa suggested, brought the decorators in and overhauled the whole house. The new furniture in the lounge was grand and yet comfortable. The only piece untouched was Rudy's grandad chair. The new soft carpets and subtle colours on the freshly plastered walls gave a homely and warm feel. The windows were replaced with triple-glazing, to keep out the draughts and the noise from the street, and then dressed with luxury heavy curtains. Kelly organised Lippy's bedroom, replacing all the mismatched wardrobes and drawers with top quality built-in furniture, so that all her posh frocks could be hung up behind closed doors and not be seen dangling haphazardly off anything with a ridge. She had also bought the softest high-quality bedding. Kelly did, however, keep some things that were of obvious sentimental value. The kitchen she'd had refitted with solid wood units and granite worktops but kept the layout the same. The ill-assorted cups and Lippy's huge cooking pot remained, but the gadgets were all replaced with ones that worked properly. Kelly knew that no matter how poorly Lippy was, she still liked to spend time in the kitchen, and so she made sure everything was easy to use. It was, all in all, a very satisfactory outcome: the house looked like a millionaire's pad.

Lippy and Rudy had no idea they would be walking into a newly decorated home and the surprise was met with overwhelming tears. Lippy flooded Kelly's face with kisses and wiped the tears of joy with the back of her hand. "Oh, I missed you, Bluey, and look what you have done! I can't believe it. I feel like a queen," she cried.

"You are, Lippy, you are the queen of your castle."

Rudy was gobsmacked, and instead of his usual animated self, he wandered from room to room, taking it all in. He ran his hands across the new fabrics and couldn't help but marvel at all the top-class design features that had been installed with no expense spared.

"Do you like it, Rudy? I mean, it was probably cheeky, but I just thought ..."

He flung his arms around her. "It's perfect, Bluey, just like you."

Betty was surprised by the change in Kelly; not only was she so grown-up, she also had gained a real air of confidence. She was so proud with how her niece had adjusted to all the traumatic events. Most people would have probably ended up in a nuthouse.

Cyril and Frank were waiting by the cars with each member of the firm. They nodded in Kelly's direction, as a mark of respect. With help from Lippy and her aunt Bet, she arranged for the cars to be covered in roses and did the same in the church. It was more like a wedding than a funeral though. With no expense spared, she paid for a huge marble angel to stand over the grave. But like Kelly said, "It's the least I can do."

The service was short but sweet and the church was filled with mourners: men from the past, friends, and acquaintances, they all came to pay their respects. Some, of course, were there to be nosy; after all, it was a shocking state of affairs and left many with sadness in their hearts. Kelly, however, greeted everyone with her head held high. In turn, they responded with compassion and admiration. Kelly soon realised that with the public display of loyalty given to her by the firm, others followed suit.

As they left the church and gathered around the graveyard, Kelly looked down at the empty hole and a tear left her eye. Keffa sensed her emotion and slid his hand around her waist. "She will be at peace now, Bluey," he whispered. She looked at the gravestone to the left and read the inscription: JACK MCFARLANE, LOVING FATHER.

The coffin was lowered and Kelly threw a pink peace rose on the top. She swallowed back the lump lodged in her throat and regained her composure. Her dear, sweet mother, the only innocent person in all this mess, was finally laid to rest without ever living long enough to watch her baby grow up into a fine young woman: her daughter. At least her real mum would be side by side with her father, Jack.

As the service came to an end and Kelly walked towards the cars, she spotted a familiar figure standing by some trees, away from the crowd. A thin red-haired woman, holding a small posy of flowers, lifted her hand to hesitantly wave. Kelly hastened her pace to greet her, and as soon as they were a foot apart, Kelly threw her arms around her. "Ruth, what are you doing here?"

Ruth looked down. "I read about it in the newspaper and I just had to come and … well, I don't know, really, I just wanted to see if you were okay."

Kelly hugged her again. "I've missed you, Ruth. How are you doing? How are the kiddies?"

Ruth gave her her best fake smile. "Yeah, we are good, you know, plodding on, like."

Then she shyly turned her head and that's when Kelly saw the bruise. This wasn't the time or place to discuss how her Ruth had received that black mark, but as soon as the funeral was over, she was going to do something about it.

"Ahh, bless you, Ruth, for coming. You can put the flowers on the grave, if you like."

Ruth looked down at her cheap bunch of a few straggly carnations. "Well, it's not much."

Kelly sensed her embarrassment. "Ya know what, Ruth, it don't matter about flowers, it's what's in your heart that counts. Are ya coming back to me pub? We are holding the wake there?"

Ruth shook her head. "I would really love to, but the ol' man don't know I'm here, so I best be off."

"Where are you living, Ruth?"

The fear was written all over Ruth's face, and Kelly knew then she was controlled by her husband. The thin shell of a woman was imprisoned in a loveless marriage, abused and used by a vicious man.

"Oh, a flat in Lewisham, at the back of the hospital, in Main Street, number 15. But I can't have visitors. He don't like it."

Keffa walked over to Kelly. "Babe, they are waiting for you." He nodded respectfully at Ruth.

"Okay, Ruth, well thank you for coming. It means such a lot to me." She hugged her and then linked arms with Keffa. In the distance, she could see a few reporters and the men trying to move them on. She was told this would happen and was advised not to let them get a mug shot of her, or her face would be all over the news again. The story had been a sensation.

The headline had read **Gangster Eddie Raven and his sister in suicide pact: girlfriend dug up from basement**.

It had taken a week or so for the stories and news reports to die down. Kelly decided to leave the burial for six weeks, hoping it could be a quiet family affair without the reporters sensationalising it. Yet, they were there again, trying to capture a few images just to dig up the story once more. It infuriated Kelly that she had to cover her face before stepping into the blacked-out car.

Lippy and Betty sat opposite and Keffa was by her side.

"You all right, Kel?" asked Bet.

Kelly nodded. "The dirty bastards, they couldn't even let us say goodbye in peace. All I can say is, God help 'em, if they even try to step foot in me pub, 'cos it's off limits to the public."

Bet saw the fierce look in her eyes and knew then that her once sweet and naïve little niece was now a force to be reckoned with. She had the hardest of men by her side, there for the duration.

As they approached the pub, Kelly took a deep breath and held her head up like Cyril had told her to. Frank opened her door, and as she stepped out, he kissed her cheek and whispered, "Keep that chin up, babe. You are the guv'nor, remember."

The pub was filled to the rafters, and it was Kelly's job to welcome the mourners and stay in control. Cyril and Frank had coached her over the last six weeks. It was as though they wanted her to fill Eddie's boots. She had the businesses and the clout to keep them running, with guidance from her firm and Keffa by her side, of course.

After an hour or so, the door opened, and in walked Johnnie Carter with two of his men, as bold as brass. Cyril and Blakey spotted him and nodded to Frank, but by the time they weaved their way through the crowd, Johnnie was face-to-face with Kelly. A few mourners stepped aside, knowing full well who the uninvited guest was. Kelly had never met the man but sensed the tension in the air.

"What do you want, Carter?" demanded Keffa, having never left Kelly's side.

Waving her hand for Keffa to be quiet, she carefully placed her drink on the bar and glared at the menacing-looking but smartly dressed man, wearing a black Crombie. By that time, Frank, Cyril, and Blakey were there. Johnnie sneered when he realised she had very dangerous men watching her back.

"I came to pay my respects!" His voice was deep and harsh, a result of too many fags and booze. Much like Eddie, he had the air of a cocky and arrogant individual, which irritated Kelly even more.

The new guv'nor of South London looked down at Carter's shoes for a couple of seconds, which made him feel uncomfortable, and then she looked up. The atmosphere in the room suddenly dropped several degrees, as everyone waited to hear Kelly's response. But by merely raising an eyebrow, and in her clearest voice, she replied, "To me or to my mother, Mr Carter?"

Johnnie had heard that Eddie's daughter had taken over the manor, and at the time, he had laughed out loud; this would be easy pickings, and he could get his hands on South London as well. With the cocaine drying up, he wanted to run his scams further afield. Yet, looking at this young woman, it soon dawned on him that Kelly was another Eddie, just by the sneer she gave him and the sarcastic tone in her voice. She was composed and daring but he was unnerved.

"Well ... err, both, I suppose. I worked with your father, you see, and since you——"

He had no sooner got the words out of his mouth when Kelly jumped in.

"Actually, Mr Carter, you didn't work with my father, and correct me if I am wrong, but I do believe you tried to *take* from my father. So, let me make something very clear. You have North London now and it will stay that way. I, on the other hand, have my businesses south of the Thames, and that, my friend, is how it will remain." She grinned and picked up her drink, taking a swig of the brandy.

Johnnie looked from Kelly to all the intense eyes surrounding her. He was escorted out of the pub along with his two footmen. Cyril nearly wet himself laughing. "We taught you well, you little fucking rogue."

Kelly clinked glasses with him and winked. "Well, Uncle Cyril, I am being taught by the best."

∼*∾

The days following the wake, cemented Kelly's confidence. She knew, in her heart, she could run the firm, with the help from the men. Putting aside her firm's commitments for the time being, there was one issue she had to deal with first. Ruth was on her mind, and although she knew it was probably none of her business, she couldn't rest until she knew for sure she was all right.

She had passed her driving test and was now the proud owner of a Range Rover, much like Keffa's, who jokingly accused her of copying him. But she had set her heart on one since the day she had sat in his as a kid and had admired the plush interior.

All her new-found wealth was hard to comprehend at first; she owned pubs, a club, and was in receipt of weekly money and lots of it. Eddie's three homes were up for sale, as she couldn't bring herself to move into any of them. His money was transferred to her bank. Cyril had employed the best lawyer, his very own man, to secure all of Eddie's assets into Kelly's name. Of course, fake paperwork was carefully compiled, but that was all part of the life she was now living in, and it was a world that for some reason she easily slid into.

The only issue she had was where she should live. The small box room at Rudy's was her safe haven, and having her family around her was what she wanted; and yet, there was Keffa, who had followed her everywhere, making sure she was safe. Their relationship hadn't even started properly, as it had all been too hectic. In between the madness were the odd stolen kisses and loving words. Nevertheless, Keffa was happy as long as one day she would be his wife. He could wait — after all, he had done so since she was fifteen.

Kelly sat outside the run-down flat and watched. It was bitterly cold outside, and she had her car's heating turned up to full blast. Keffa was by her side, reading the newspaper.

"'Ere, Blue, you will never guess what? That DI Maddox has been nicked and it mentions Eddie Raven. Fuck me, the old cunt was working for him. No wonder he was hell-bent on having you locked up. Well, now he has his just desserts." He chuckled. "Imagine him inside with all those men he arrested along the way. I wouldn't want to be in his shoes."

Kelly smiled. "Good. That's one more degenerate out of the picture. Now for another."

The door opened and out stepped Ruth, wearing a thin jacket and ushering three little girls down the path. Kelly's heart sank; she looked even thinner than before, and none of them could have eaten a solid meal in weeks. Then the husband appeared; he was a big man with a beer in his hand. They didn't look like a couple at all. Whereas his wife and kids were wearing tatty clothes, all far too small, as though they were clothed third-hand, he had on a fur-lined flight jacket and designer boots. Kelly swallowed hard, feeling her temper rising.

"Look at that asshole and her in fucking rags!"

"What have I told you about swearing? It ain't ladylike. But I see what ya mean."

Kelly watched as Ruth's husband grabbed Ruth by the shoulder. Immediately, her face became screwed up in pain. The three little girls bunched together, holding each other's hand. They looked deathly white, and it was at this point, Kelly didn't care if she was poking her nose in. She couldn't bear to see that man browbeat her friend.

"And make sure you stay out of the house all day. I don't want them screaming brats running around, when I am conducting business. Got it!" he growled.

The sky was dark and it was going to rain or snow. She saw Ruth nod and keep her eyes down, terrified of the overbearing lump of a man – her self-styled husband.

Ruth hurried the children on and her husband went off in the opposite direction.

Kelly, wasting no time, followed, stopping directly by Ruth.

"Quick, get in."

Ruth's eyes darted up and down the street, and then she looked down at her three tiny thin children who were frozen. Their pale freckled faces looked blue, and their huge round eyes appeared frightened. What did she have to lose? She wasn't allowed home until night time, and it was too cold to stay outside. She only had a few pence to sit in the café. Feeling that there was no time to waste, she urged her kids to get in the back, which they were excited to do, having never been inside a big flash car before. She followed them in, and within seconds, Kelly was away and up the street.

Ruth was still a bundle of nerves. "Where are we going, Kelly?" she asked nervously, looking at Keffa.

"Ruth, I am going to take you somewhere and show you something, and if you decide to return back here, then that's up to you. I will go away and leave you in peace."

Ruth trusted Kelly and sat back without another word. At least her girls were enjoying the ride and were warm for the time being.

Kelly drew up outside her old house, and this time she didn't shudder; the front looked the same, but inside, it had been given a complete overhaul and brought into the modern world. She'd had the shed taken down and the back garden tidied up.

"Come inside, Ruth, I want you to see something." Ruth frowned but followed Kelly in. The three children skipped along the path, giggling. The heating inside had been left on and the warmth embraced them.

Wiping her feet on the mat, she asked, "Is this your home, Kelly? It's beautiful."

Kelly shook her head. "No, it used to be. I own it, but I can't live in it. It holds too many bad flashbacks for me, yet it is a decent size for a family to make a proper life for themselves."

Ruth nodded. "Yeah, I agree, it's lovely, Kel. But why bring me here? What did you want to show me?"

The children skipped past their mother into the living room; they stood by the patio doors and stared in fascination out into the garden. "Mummy, look, there are swings and a slide. Can we go out there?" asked the eldest child.

Ruth frowned and then the penny dropped.

Kelly put an arm around her shoulders. "Do you love him, Ruth?"

"Love him, nah. If the truth be known, I hate him, Kel. But what can I do? I ain't got money and that stinking flat is his. If I tried to leave,

466

he would bash me up, not that he needs any excuse, and me girls, well, they can't move without him on at 'em."

"'Ere, Ruth, take these keys and make some good memories for yourselves. Bring this house back to life, how it should be."

Ruth placed her hands over her face and almost choked, crying; it was so much to take in. Kelly knew only too well what a life of subjugation could do to the soul. Ruth had been dragged down, stripped of her character. It had left her totally despondent and powerless and too shit-scared to move without her husband telling her to.

This house offered her freedom, and her children could live the life they should be entitled to, to laugh and talk, play on the swings, and be happy. Then reality hit her. "But he will come and find me."

"Oh, no, he won't. I promise you that."

Ruth saw that look on her friend's face and didn't need to ask questions. She had seen the men at the funeral and how they treated her with such high regard. Her husband was a nobody, in comparison.

"But I can't repay you, Kelly. I don't have a penny to my name."

"Oh, about that," replied Kelly. "You can earn your weekly wages by making sure your girls are happy. Ruth, I have more money than I know what to do with. I can't go through life and merrily indulge myself, knowing me mate is struggling. I hate bullies, Ruth, and you, my friend, have been bullied for too long. Please, just take the keys and the weekly money and give the girls a good life."

Little Rosie, the cheeky six-year-old, had snuck upstairs and with a squeal she came bolting back down. "Mummy, where's the little girl that lives here? She has so many toys up there to play with." Her delightful face looked up at Kelly. "Have you got a girl? Can we play in her room? She's got a dolls' house and My Little Pony toys and ..."

Kelly bent down and touched the child's cheeks. "I don't have a little girl. I guess I have just inherited three little nieces. Those toys upstairs are for you and your sisters, so go on and have fun."

Ruth and Kelly followed the children upstairs, just to see the look on each of their faces. Keffa went up too. He was choked up; the last time he had seen Kelly's old bedroom had been a heart-wrenching moment. Now, here he was, gazing at a paradise for kids with funky furniture, colourful bedding, and hand-painted murals on the walls. The toys were everywhere, in every nook and cranny. The children were shrieking with excitement and Ruth was numb with shock.

As Kelly said her goodbyes, she took one last look at the house, and there at the window, she saw three shiny faces with huge smiles and not the ghost of an evil mother.

Keffa was at a loss for words; he would never have even thought of doing such a kindness. Underneath the hardness that Kelly had taken on was still a soft woman. As she was about to start up the engine, he put his hand on her knee. She slowly turned to see his face, the man she loved so much. In his hand was an envelope.

"Open it, Blue."

Inside were two tickets to the Caribbean.

"Me and you, babe, two weeks, just us, no business, no running around saving the world, just time out, please."

Kelly laughed. "Well, first there is a final piece of work I need to do."

Keffa rolled his eyes. "Now what?"

"Pack my bags and move in with you, of course, if you want me to."

He didn't say a word; he just pulled her close and kissed her.

CHAPTER TWENTY-EIGHT

A year on

Kelly's club, recently renamed Naomi's, was becoming popular with the stockbrokers and city slickers. She had, for the most part, changed the décor; it operated as a wine bar during the week, and at weekends it was a nightclub, staying open until the early hours. However, there was one part of the club she had left largely untouched – the old pub bar, after Cyril's mates had twisted her arm. She had her own men running the businesses, overseen by Cyril, Blakey, and Frank. All of them swore they were retired, though.

Cyril met with the men every Thursday for a business lunch, so he said, but really it was just an excuse to have a good old-fashioned pub lunch and a few beers. She liked the place and its atmosphere, but most of all, she relished the feeling of being someone and of having the respect the punters gave her. She had earned herself a reputation although what that was exactly would become clear in time, but she had the right kind of support behind her and was looking forward now – now her past was just that, her past.

"Hello, me ol' son," greeted Cyril, as Frank took his seat.

Blakey nodded and looked at the menu. "Pie and chips all round, boys?"

Frank laughed. "As always, mate. I don't think ya need a menu. We have the same dinner every fucking week."

"So, Cyril, what's on the agenda today?" asked Frank in his gruff voice.

"Our, Kelly, the little rogue, 'as only gone and secured a fucking deal with the Colombians. I swear that kid is clever. Who would Adam and Eve it, eh? There was us old-timers, running around protecting her, pretending she was like Eddie Cako, a woman with clout, and blow me, she goes and completely 'as the manor running in her name. Now the Colombians are in her back pocket."

Blakey lifted his pint. "I'll drink to that."

"Yeah, it's outlandish how that happened. S'pose people believed all along she meant to kill Patrick and assumed she was so dangerous from the age of fifteen." He laughed. "Then showing up Johnnie Carter, the way she did."

"Oh, and not forgetting shit-legs Sheila and her boys ..." added Frank.

"Come to think of it ..." mused Cyril, as he paused and looked at the two men, "perhaps it wasn't a game. Maybe Kelly is a dangerous woman that should be feared. After all, boys, she has got resolve. Have you seen that fucking look in her eyes when she's pissed off? That's Eddie, all right."

Frank nodded. "I for one couldn't give a flying fuck. She can fuck over whoever she likes and will have my backing. Ya know she has paid for a flat in Oxford for my Ellie to go to university? She may be Eddie's daughter all right but she ain't all Raven. I see her sweet mother in her, when she's not conducting business, that is."

The doors opened and all eyes looked to see who had arrived. Each punter nodded and smiled as Kelly, dressed in her Barbour jacket, khaki jeans, and her hair plaited to one side, strolled in. She kissed each of her men on the cheek and graciously took her seat.

"So, I got me first shipment of Charlie arriving at midnight. Are you three still in, or, Uncle Cyril, 'ave you retired again?" she laughed.

"'Ave I fuck. Right my girl, what's the plan ...?"

Kelly smiled, and for a second she was her father, sitting there in his chair and wearing his cocky grin.

As she reflected briefly on her life up to this point, she realised she was her father's daughter but only in a good way. Crime was in her blood, but she recognised her heart was in the right place. She didn't know what the future would hold for her, but she knew one thing: she wanted to do good for her mother, Naomi. She was Eddie's daughter, and she carried his sins, but not through want, only through blood.

The sequel to Cruel Secrets

Wicked Lies

Available Early 2018

Also by Kerry Barnes

The Vincent Trilogy

Ruthless

ISBN 978-84897-497-5

Ruby's Palace

ISBN 978-84897-801-0

Raw Justice

ISBN 978-19997262-01-1